LUCERO

MAYA MOTAYNE

BALZER + BRAY

An Imprint of HarperCollins*Publishers*

Also available by Maya Motayne

Nocturna

Oculta

Balzer + Bray is an imprint of HarperCollins Publishers.

Lucero

Library of Congress Control Number: 2023933502
ISBN 978-0-06-284279-4
23 24 25 26 27 LBC 5 4 3 2 1

First Edition

To Annabell (Bananabell) and Luís
Manuel (Luís Mac 'n' Cheese)

MUNDO

The Lost Ocean

The Jade Sea

Bei Hua

WEILAI

Cape Abuja

The Pinch

The Bash

The Brim

The Bow

The Crown

The City of
SAN CRISTÓBAL

THE DARK

Dezmin remembered the moment he slipped into the dark.

He'd been standing with Alfie as a strange girl burst into the Blue Room, her eyes wild with fear and purpose. He'd seen the dead guardsmen behind her, their bodies leaking red onto the tiled floor. He should have been terrified of her, but she'd looked so afraid— like Alfie did when he woke from a nightmare.

He'd once carved Alfie a dragon figurine as a token of bravery to keep him from making that same heartbreaking face.

Dezmin had opened his mouth to calm the girl—maybe he could stop whatever she was planning. But before he could say a word she thrust her hand forward, splaying her fingers wide. The floor beneath him opened and down he fell, catching only a glimpse of Alfie's panicked expression before the hole closed around him, leaving him in a sea of inky black.

No, not a sea—the sea had a soul. It had currents that pushed and pulled, and waves that frothed and roared. This was not a sea; it was nothing.

He felt nothing and nothing felt him.

He could not tell if he had been here for hours or years. A lifetime or a moment. Space and time held its breath as Dezmin suffocated in the darkness, paralyzed and lost. But that hardly mattered, because the one thing Dezmin was certain of was that this quiet purgatory was eternal. No matter how much time had passed, he still had infinity to go.

Until one day there was a sound. The first he'd heard since Alfie had shouted his name as he fell into the dark.

Hello, my child.

To hear himself referred to as a child, as something beloved—as anything at all after such endless silence—it made Dezmin want to laugh, to weep. But he could do none of those things. He could only stare.

The voice was deep, hypnotic. Dezmin had expected to see a man standing before him, but instead he saw a dragon figurine floating there in the dark—the very one he'd given to Alfie to ward off his nightmares. Was he hallucinating? Why would the figurine appear before him here?

To see something from his life before felt like fate, destiny, salvation. In truth, it was none of those things.

It was simply bad luck.

HOMECOMING

Alfie couldn't breathe.

With his father's body at his feet and Dezmin standing before him, he felt as if his lungs had been plucked from his chest.

But the being standing here wasn't Dezmin. It was wearing Dezmin's body, true, but inside was Sombra—like rancid wine poured into a beautiful bottle.

Alfie's brother looked the same but different—he looked *wrong*. His features were sharpened, and he even looked taller, as if the god were stretching him from inside the same way you broke in a pair of shoes or flexed your fingers in a new pair of gloves. Was Dezmin in pain from this physical contortion? It made Alfie feel sick to his stomach.

How could this be happening?

Only six months before, he and Finn had battled the god of darkness and, with the help of a prisoner named Xiomara, they'd banished Sombra to the same dark void that Dezmin had been lost to. Afterward they'd returned the god's stone arms safely to the vault and moved forward with their lives. Yet now here Sombra stood, on the very dais where Alfie and Princess Vesper had just taken their betrothal vows. A layer of flower petals still dusted the floor. Lit candles floated in the air, bathing the vast ballroom in soft light.

Sombra looked as if he'd just arrived to his own surprise party.

Alfie felt utterly alone as he faced this worst possible incarnation of his brother, his best friend. Luka was out of reach, still in the grip of the Englassen guardsmen who'd restrained him as the king had been murdered. Finn was behind him, pinned to the ground by another set of guards after she had burst into the ceremony.

"No applause? Are you not pleased by the homecoming of your long-lost prince?" Sombra gestured at Dezmin's body with a grin.

Dezmin was nothing but a garment to Sombra. The unfairness of it all struck Alfie like a slap. He'd spent endless nights desperately wishing for his brother to be found, only to have him return controlled by a monster.

"Leave my brother's body," Alfie rasped, finding his voice. "*Get out!*"

"Ah, but why would I?" Sombra asked. "I quite like it here."

"This is ridiculous!" cried the petulant voice of Prince Marsden.

Alfie started. Sombra's appearance had been so shocking, he'd nearly forgotten that moments ago the Englassen royal family had tried to magically enslave all of Castallan. They hadn't succeeded, because the spellwork required the blood of every living member of the royal family, and they hadn't had Dezmin's.

"Guards!" Marsden roared, spittle flying from his thin lips. He pointed at Sombra. "We will repeat the ritual with Prince Dezmin's blood. Restrain him at onc—"

In the blink of an eye, Sombra materialized in front of the flustered Englassen prince. It happened so fast that Alfie never saw him move, but he *felt* the air whip past him as if he'd stuck his head out of a speeding carriage.

Standing so close to Marsden that their noses could have brushed, Sombra looked at him like a child contemplating squishing a bug. "You make far too much noise."

Marsden opened his mouth to protest, but Sombra snatched him by the tongue. Alfie heard the sound of muscle and sinew snapping as the god wrenched it from Marsden's mouth.

Bile rose in Alfie's throat.

"*Marsden!*" Queen Elinore screamed as her son fell to his knees, blood pouring from his lips. She, Princess Vesper, and King Alistair all rushed forward, crying out for help.

Still holding the prince's detached tongue between two fingers, Sombra waved his free hand, as if shooing away a fly. With a loud *crack*, the Englassen royals' necks snapped sharply to the left and they fell, dead before they could even reach Marsden. The Englassen prince himself had gone silent, blood still seeping from his lips as his eyes grew glassy and still.

The Englassen royal family had been wiped from existence in mere moments.

"Now that I have returned"—Sombra dropped the severed tongue, moving on with ease—"my reign over this world can begin. It will be short, but no doubt memorable." He met Alfie's gaze, a glint of excitement in his eyes. "Of that you can be certain."

Alfie was still reeling as Sombra made an elegant sweeping motion with his hands. A shudder bloomed on Alfie's skin. From the corner of his eye, he saw something dark slithering. For a moment he thought shadows were crawling on the floor-to-ceiling windows, but he was wrong. It was much worse. A wave of black crept across the sun-dappled sky, as if a pot of ink had spilled onto the heavens. It didn't look like a regular night sky where there were pinpricks of stars and different shades of dark. It was matte black, as if the sky itself had been painted in one even coat.

A few paces to his left, a Castallano woman's shadow clawed its way forward, pulling itself up from the ground. The woman it belonged to shouted in fear, recoiling from the sight of the monstrous thing coming to life at her feet. The shadow had no face, no mouth, but somehow Alfie knew it was hungry.

"Alfie." Luka's voice shook. Alfie followed his cousin's gaze. Every shadow, even his mother's, began to darken and arch off the ground. They were no longer a cast of the light; they were touchable, fluid, thickening like black ink as they hunched their way into life.

He'd never seen anything so ghastly. They did not move the way *propio* shadows moved—reflecting the emotions of the person they were attached to. They moved like ravenous beasts, breaking free from whatever had once kept them tethered to the floor. Even Alfie's own shadow rippled at his feet. He could feel it fighting against Sombra's pull. The hairs on Alfie's neck stood on end as an overwhelming energy, cold and dark, swept over the chamber.

"Mijo," his mother said, fear lacing her voice tight as her own shadow slithered forward. She reached out a hand, but she was too far away to touch him. Alfie's shadow stretched toward her to close the distance between them.

Time slowed to a crawl.

Then came a terrible sound—a cacophony of *snap*s. With a twist of their shapeless forms, the shadows broke free of the feet they'd once belonged to and hovered in the air. His mother stood still with shock.

"*Mother!*" Alfie shouted, panic burning through his veins.

Before he could move, the shadows rushed forward, forcing themselves down the throats of their masters. His mother choked, gripping at her throat to stop it, but it was no use.

Amada went limp, her head hanging down, obscuring her face from his vision. The room was full of shadows pouring themselves into the bodies of their victims, leaving them in a loose-limbed stance, as if they'd fallen asleep standing up. Then, without a word, they began to raise their heads. Each one's eyes were completely black, not a dot of white in them. Just like those who had become shadowless when Alfie and Finn had accidentally released Sombra the first time.

"What have you done?" Alfie asked. Focusing, he felt for the sacred connection between himself and his moving shadow, and engaged his *propio*. He looked around the room. He should have seen an array of colors, each person's magic its own shade, but instead everyone's magic was the same pitch black. He frowned. What would this mean for his own abilities? Could he still match and work with the magic of others if everyone's magic had turned black under Sombra's command? Would he still be able to travel through the strands of magic? How could he combat this horror if he did not have his *propio*?

"I have begun my reign." Sombra's eyes were alight. "I am here to finish what I once started."

Finn groaned and hobbled up to Alfie, blood seeping from a wound in her stomach. The guardsmen who'd been holding her down when she'd crashed the betrothal ceremony had let her go— now that they were shadowless, they were no longer interested in subduing her. Like everyone else in the room, they stood at attention, eyes on Sombra. Alfie still didn't know why Finn had burst in at the last minute the way she had.

"I tried . . ." She winced as she pressed her hand against her wound, her eyes trained on Sombra. "I tried to get to you before the ceremony happened. . . ."

Alfie blinked at her, the truth dawning on him. Somehow she'd known what the Englassens were up to, but hadn't been able to get to the ceremony fast enough. There was a strange tenderness in knowing that even after she'd walked out of his life because of his impending marriage to Vesper, she'd still been the one to put the pieces together first. The one to find a way to save him at any cost. He pulled her to his side gently, afraid of worsening her injury.

"I know," he said. "I know."

By the look on Finn's face, it was clear she'd had no clue that Sombra would be returning too. No one could have predicted this.

Alfie pressed his hand to Finn's wound, his eyes still on Sombra. "*Sanar*," he murmured, but the cut kept bleeding beneath his touch. "*Sanar*." Still nothing. Not only did the magic not work when he called upon it, but something felt *wrong* now. Magic had always flowed through his body like warm water, but now it crawled over the skin like flies on a corpse, skittering away from Alfie's touch when he reached for it.

Finn watched him, a question in her eyes, but Alfie didn't know how to explain.

Was this Sombra's doing too? Had his return changed the very fabric of magic?

Luka dashed over and, trembling, came to a stop in front of them, his face wet with tears. They'd wished so often for Dezmin's return, but not like this.

Never like this.

"And you two again," Sombra laughed, amused at the sight of Luka and Finn. "The four of us reunited in the very room where you once managed to best me. How ironic."

"Ironic," Finn said with a pained grimace. "Or annoying. Depends on who you ask."

Alfie's mind was a flurry of panic, his gaze snapping between his now black-eyed mother, Luka, Finn, the sea of shadowless, and the deranged god. In the midst of it all, Alfie spotted James on the far side of the room, surrounded by the Englassen guards who had been, at Prince Marsden's command, holding him back; now they stood blankly by his side.

James too still had his shadow. So aside from Luka, it seemed the only people who had been spared were those with *propios*. But why was Luka not affected? Was it because Sombra's magic had saved Luka before and given him inhuman strength—or was it just luck?

Castallanos were taught that *propios* were a blessing—a sign of a greater connection to the balance of light and dark that had created magic and their world—but Alfie had never imagined it would spare those who possessed them from becoming slaves to Sombra.

James looked terrified. Alfie knew he himself would feel the same if he were in a situation like this, alone, without friends or even allies. But after the boy had helped Prince Marsden—though he'd been forced to do so—with his plan to enslave Castallan, Alfie couldn't bring himself to beckon James over to stand with them.

"Let Dezmin go," Alfie demanded again. He'd wanted to sound strong, but he could barely manage to keep his voice from shaking.

"You speak as if I stole my way into his body. But I was warmly invited," Sombra said.

"You're lying." Luka's voice was rough. "Dezmin would *never*."

"I cannot inhabit a body I am not invited into, boy," Sombra said to Luka. "And watch your tone. You are in the presence of the same god who once saved your pathetic life."

"How?" Alfie demanded, his gaze on his mother. She looked serene. Her husband's corpse was mere feet away, yet she only had eyes for Sombra. "How is this possible?"

When Finn's cruel adoptive father, Ignacio, had wielded Sombra's powers all those months ago, Alfie had watched as the people who he turned black-eyed then infected each other one by one. But this time, at Sombra's command, they had all become shadowless in the space of a breath. It was as if he'd been plunged into a nightmare where you could not run no matter how fast you pumped your legs.

"With the help of your dear brother, of course," Sombra said. "In my name, he destroyed the light. Now humans are finally free to embrace their true natures as creatures of chaos."

Alfie felt ill. It made no sense. How could Dezmin have helped Sombra? How could they have destroyed the balance of light and dark while they'd been trapped in Xiomara's void?

"*Why?*" Alfie shouted, his voice breaking around the single syllable. "What do you get out of this?"

Sombra met his gaze with a cruel smile. "I get *everything.*"

"We stopped you once," Luka said, his chest heaving—from trying to restrain his anger or his terror, Alfie couldn't tell. "We'll do it again."

"Ah, yes, we've played this game before. But the rules have changed. This time there will be nowhere for you to run. No toy dragon to trap me in." He leveled Alfie with a glare. "No way to stop me from taking what you stole."

A dizzying panic surged through Alfie. The stone arms. Sombra was going to take them again. When he and Finn had released Sombra last time, the god had taken over Ignacio's body. He'd been a force to be reckoned with then, but he'd become even more powerful once he'd procured his stone arms. After they had banished Sombra to the void, the arms had been secured in the vault once more, the magical protections tripled and reinforced. But would that be enough to stop him now?

"Guards!" Alfie shouted, but none responded. They weren't his to command anymore—they were Sombra's. Only a wounded Finn and a trembling Luka stood between the god and the stone arms that were locked in the palace vault.

"You want the arms?" Finn raised her fists, one bloody from putting pressure on her wound. Alfie could see sweat gathering on her upper lip. "Then you'll have to fight for them."

"I would venture to say there are simpler ways." Sombra thrust his hand downward as if reaching for something, his fingers flexing.

With a *crack*, the ballroom floor broke open. Alfie pushed Finn behind him, shielding her as gravel and sharp shards of rock shot up from the ground, a gray cloud of dust following close behind. When Alfie blinked the debris from his eyes, he saw Sombra's arms had burst free of the rubble and were now racing across the floor to their owner. Sombra had broken through the protections without even approaching the vault.

"I will return to my immortal form." The stone pieces skittered up Sombra's legs and onto his arms, encasing them. "And you will not stop me."

"Mierda," Finn cursed, and Alfie knew what she was thinking. Sombra was already so powerful that he could make everyone shadowless in the blink of an eye. How much more powerful would he be now that he was in possession of part of his immortal body again?

"Hear me now!" Sombra shouted. "Today is the beginning of the end. I was locked away by your little prince, but my destiny never wavered. In the very cage that imprisoned me, I found a new path. I destroyed the balance of magic in favor of the dark and have brought Nocturna to this pathetic world. Soon it will crumble in on itself like a dying star, and your gods will finally pay the price of banishing me."

Alfie's mind raced. Nocturna was the consequence of Sombra casting the world into darkness—the end of all things good, the unraveling of mankind.

The end of the world.

Nocturna was what he and Finn had fought to prevent last time they'd released Sombra. He'd thought they were safe from that fate. He couldn't understand how this could be happening now. The balance of magic was hidden in the heart of the world, a sacred place that no man had ever found. The void where Sombra had been imprisoned was barren of life, virtually inescapable. How had he managed to leave the void *and* find such a place of legend? Every hour Alfie had ever spent reading and researching magical theory seemed wasted in this moment of not knowing.

"You're delusional," Finn said, brandishing a dagger. "But I can fix that."

Alfie wished he had even half her confidence. Sombra was exponentially more powerful than he had been the last time they faced him—and since he was using Dezmin as a vessel, Alfie could not bring himself to hurt him.

How could they possibly win?

Luka gripped Alfie's shoulder, and as their gazes met, he knew Luka was worrying about the same things.

"Is that so?" Sombra asked Finn, spreading his arms wide. "Then why don't you try."

Finn didn't need to be told twice. Dezmin wasn't her brother— she only saw an enemy. Her wound long forgotten, she dashed forward, too fast for anyone to stop her.

"Finn!" Alfie shouted, running after her. His mind raced, trying to come up with what spell to use, but what could he do to stop this? Hurt Dezmin to hurt Sombra, or hurt Finn to stop her from hurting his brother? Would Dezmin die if they killed Sombra?

"*Paralizar!*" he shouted at Sombra, hoping that his magic would at least stop the god from harming Finn, but nothing happened. Why was the magic not responding?

Sombra didn't even seem to notice. His eyes, alight with amusement, only followed Finn.

Alfie should have been terrified that he was about to watch Finn run directly to her death, but at that moment he saw something on Sombra's face that shocked him—and gave him hope.

Blood was trickling from the god's nose—from *Dezmin's* nose.

"Is he *bleeding*?" Luka asked, his eyes wide.

Still smiling, the blood from his nose splashing his teeth red, Sombra raised his hand, letting Finn's dagger pierce his palm. It sank straight through. She twisted the blade deeper, her eyes wide at the sight of the blood flowing down his arm.

If Sombra could be injured, then maybe he could be killed. Hope caught in Alfie's chest, quickly tempered by pain—it was also Dezmin's body that Finn had stabbed.

"Finn!" Alfie shouted again.

His voice seemed to rouse Sombra. With a quick hand, he gripped Finn by the neck and tossed her. The thief slammed against Alfie, sending them both rolling across the tiled floor.

When they came to a stop, Alfie raised his head and watched Sombra touch the trickle of blood coming from his nose. The wound in his palm was still oozing red. He wasn't healing instantly the way he had the last time.

The prince and the god locked gazes, and for a moment so fleeting that Alfie wondered if he imagined it—

Alfie saw uncertainty in Sombra's eyes.

"I'll let your loving subjects do the honor of ending you." Sombra raised his bloody hand and squeezed it into a fist.

At his command, the ballroom sprang to life as shadowless Englassens and Castallanos lunged at one another viciously with the vigor of old enemies. Alfie watched a woman ransack the body of the man she'd stabbed, stuffing his jewels into her pockets. Hair was torn from scalps, thumbs dug mercilessly into eye sockets, screams of pain stifled by slit throats.

"Stop!" Luka shouted. Pandemonium surrounded them like a whirlwind until the three of them stood back-to-back. Luka gripped two fighting men and pried them apart. "Stop it!"

The men turned on him, their fists raised. Using his enhanced strength, Luka threw them, sending them skidding on their backs to opposite sides of the ballroom. Without skipping a beat, they launched into fights with new opponents. It didn't matter who they fought so long as blood was shed and life was lost.

All Alfie wanted was to find his mother, save his brother, bury his father, and stop this wave of violence—but there wasn't time for any of that. He couldn't even ask the guards for protection because they were shadowless as well, jumping into the fray with horrifying grins.

"We've got to stop Sombra!" Alfie cried to Luka and Finn. "We can't let him escape!"

The god had bled and not healed, which meant that he was somehow vulnerable. They needed to take advantage of that. But would doing so mean hurting Dezmin? The pain of that thought was too much to bear. Alfie hid from it, pushing it aside for later.

"He disappeared into the rush of people!" Luka said. "I can force my way through and look for him!"

Alfie stepped closer to Luka. "We'll be right behind you." Alfie turned to Finn and held out his hand. Luka could run through without a problem, but he and Finn might get separated.

She laced their fingers together. "Ready."

"All right, here goes!" Luka began to run.

Alfie gripped Finn's hand and made to follow, but skidded to a halt as a figure moved past him, a blur of red silk and fury.

"*You!*" Queen Amada shouted.

Alfie watched in horror as his mother leaped at Finn, shoving her away from Alfie with both hands. Alfie's hold on Finn's hand broke as Amada pushed him behind her, protective as a tigress with her cubs. "You have brought my son nothing but violence and danger."

"*Qué?*" Finn caught herself from stumbling backward into a fight between two Castallano guardsmen.

"Stay behind me, Mijo," Amada said to him.

Alfie stared at his mother in surprise. The last time they'd faced Sombra, the shadowless had had no memory of who they were—they'd simply been thoughtless monsters. But the queen recognized him. She was still some version of herself. Maybe she could be reasoned with.

"Mother," Alfie said. "Mother, listen to me. Finn is—"

"Alfehr was sheltered and protected before he met *you*," Amada hissed at her. "He stayed out of trouble. The day he fell into your hands, I lost my baby. That ends today."

"I'll have you know that I've saved your very tall baby many times, thank you very much!" Finn sank into a defensive stance, daggers in each hand. "Prince, you better control your mamá before I do it for you."

Alfie gripped Amada's shoulders, but she shook him off and threw her hand forward as if gripping the air. "*Sofocar!*"

Finn gave a choking gasp, the daggers falling from her hands as she clawed at her neck, trying to free herself from the magic that stole the breath from her lungs. Alfie stared in shock. Why did the magic work for his mother and not for him? Finn's strained cries shook him from his reverie.

"Mother, stop!" Alfie grabbed her by the arm. "Stop it!"

But Amada's gaze was glued to Finn. The thief dropped to her knees, her eyes growing bloodshot.

Not seeing any other choice, Alfie tackled his mother, forcing her to lose focus and take her eyes off Finn. As they rolled to the ground, Finn fell onto her backside and heaved a desperate, ragged breath.

"Let me go!" Amada shouted. She shoved him away and crawled forward, snatching one of the daggers Finn had dropped. Still on all fours, she tried to stab Finn's feet as the thief crawled backward like a panicked crab.

"Stop!" Alfie stood and lunged forward, grabbing her around the waist as she tried to leap at Finn. She bucked against him, wild with rage. "*Paralizar!*" he shouted at Amada, but her body still would not stop moving. He reached for the magic with his mind, as he always did, but it crept away from his touch. "*Paralizar!*" Nothing was working; nothing made any sense.

"Prince." Finn grabbed the remaining dagger and stumbled to her feet. Through gritted teeth she took in hungry gulps of air. "I know you love her, but I am not getting murdered because you're a mamá's boy!" She pulled a second dagger from her sleeve, this one with brass knuckles on the hilt to slip her fingers into.

"I'm trying—" Alfie began before Amada elbowed him in the stomach, wriggling away when his grip loosened. She launched herself at Finn, dagger raised high.

It was as if time slowed just so he could marvel at this moment: his mother, shadowless and savage, poised to kill the girl he loved. Finn looked at Amada as she approached, still and calm. It was the look of someone who had been charged many times and come out alive. Bloodied, but alive.

"*Don't hurt her!*" Alfie shouted.

Finn tossed him a look as Amada slashed at her. "What do you want me to do, hug her?"

"No stabbing," Alfie sputtered. He grabbed Amada by the shoulders and tried to subdue her again. "Please, anything else—but no stabbing!"

"Fine!"

With a grunt, Finn headbutted Amada, sending her stumbling back against Alfie's chest. Before Alfie could speak, Finn followed up with a brass-knuckled punch to the queen's temple. Alfie caught his mother as she went limp.

"Finn!" he shouted at the sight of blood oozing from his mother's head.

"What?" Finn said, rubbing her forehead with a wince. "You said no stabbing!"

THE ENEMY OF MY ENEMY IS MY FRIEND (SORT OF)

Luka barreled through the crowd, his heart thumping in his chest as he scanned the sweeping room for Sombra.

Faces blurred as he ran past. Strangers—Castallano and Englassen alike—tried to grab him and pull him into skirmishes, but Luka just shook them off. People he'd known for years barely looked at him, too engrossed in their own violence to take notice.

The world had truly gone mad, and Sombra was nowhere to be found in the chaos.

"I don't think he's here anymore!" Luka shouted over his shoulder, but Alfie and Finn were no longer behind him. He spun in a circle, panic surging through his veins. Alfie and Finn were all he had left, the only ones who could look him in the eye with the gaze of a friend instead of a monster. How could he have lost them so quickly?

A fist smashed into Luka's cheek. A normal man would have been sent stumbling sideways by the force of that punch, but Luka's strength kept him rooted in place.

"Your people will return to their masters!" the shadowless Englassen man shouted. "We will finish what Prince Marsden started."

Annoyance bubbled in Luka's stomach. Englass's bigotry and delusions of colonial glory were the last things he would be tolerating today. Still, it was interesting to see that the shadowless retained their own consciousnesses this time—including their prejudices. This Englassen had become a monster, yet he still had the presence of mind to be racist.

How fun.

"Englass will rule this heathen land again," the stranger went on. "We will—"

With a frustrated growl, Luka gripped the man's collar with both hands and tossed him as if he were playing a very ambitious game of catch.

The man flew clean across the ballroom and out the window, disappearing in a spray of colored glass.

Luka winced. Alfie wouldn't have approved of that move, but what he didn't know wouldn't hurt him.

"There! That boy is one of the Castallano royals!" another man shouted. "*Kill him!*"

A group of Englassens closed in on him from all sides, and Luka took a steadying breath. They would all take a trip out the windows if that's what it would take for him to find Alfie and Finn and get out of here in one piece.

"Luka!" a voice called. James barreled through the ring of shadowless, colliding with him.

"Don't touch me!" Luka shouted, shoving him away. No matter

how small a role he'd played, James was at least partially to blame for King Bolivar lying cold and dead on the ballroom floor. Prince Marsden had said as much before Sombra tore his tongue out.

James took a step back, holding his hands up in surrender. "I know," he admitted.

Luka blinked. He'd expected the boy to at least try to explain his way out of it. It was infuriating to hear him just admit to it.

It was only then that Luka noticed the Englassens weren't attacking him anymore. He looked around him. The shadowless surrounded them, but every time they got within five feet or so, they screamed and winced, moving away in fear.

"Illusion magic," James said. "We're safe."

After a moment Luka remembered what Prince Marsden had said—the Englassen royals had used ungodly spellwork to force James's body to possess multiple *propios*. Illusion was one of them.

Luka was thankful to have a moment of calm, but he refused to let James know that. "I suppose illusion magic was very useful when you were killing Castallanos under Marsden's command."

Marsden had fostered a climate of political hostility in the city by creating a fake Castallano nationalist group that objected to the summit with Englass and forcing James to murder the participating delegados in its name. That political tension was what had pressured Alfie to agree to marry Vesper—if not for that, Castallan would still have a king and Alfie would still have a father.

James didn't speak; he just looked at Luka with a guilt so earnest that it made Luka want to punch him in the face.

Curiosity forced Luka's tongue. "What did you create an illusion of?" It was one thing to make them invisible, but the boy had somehow ensured that the shadowless didn't set foot near them.

"A raging fire burning through the room. When they get close they'll feel the heat of it. It'll keep them away."

Luka cocked his head. Smart. Luka was a flame caster himself but had always been wary of using it in the ballroom full of rich tapestries and cloth banners, lest he set the entire room ablaze. But the *illusion* of flames was perfect—all the threat without the actual damage.

"If you stay close to me, I can maintain the illusion around us and we can get to the prince and the girl," James said. "I can only keep up the illusion within a certain radius. . . ."

Luka scowled at the boy before forcing himself to step closer. As someone who had kept his shadow and his sanity, James was an enemy to Sombra too. The enemy of his enemy was his friend, even if he was also a conniving, lying jerk. Luka rubbed his temples. Life was annoyingly confusing right now.

"Fine," Luka relented. "Follow me."

Luka and James moved through the room, the shadowless parting before them thanks to James's illusion. It wasn't long before he spotted Alfie and Finn.

Luka's blood ran cold.

Finn stood protectively, fighting off the shadowless with her daggers and fists, while Alfie crouched over the queen's still body.

Forgetting James's perimeter, Luka ran forward, James trailing close behind.

"Please, please," Luka begged as he knelt beside his aunt. She couldn't be dead. They couldn't lose her too.

"She's all right," Alfie said, startling at Luka's sudden appearance. Alfie's gaze found James, his voice dropping low with quiet fury. "Why is he here?"

"Why is no one trying to fight me anymore?" Finn asked, turning around when her opponents suddenly stepped back with fear. "Oh, hey, Bathtub Boy." She cocked her head. "And Englassen boy whose name escapes me."

"I created an illusion," James said, taking a step away from Alfie. "No one will come near you so long as you stay close to me."

"And why would I do that?" Alfie stood, anger rolling off him like an electric current. "I've already paid dearly enough for your existence."

Luka couldn't remember ever seeing Alfie this angry, especially with someone who was clearly afraid of him. He shook his head free of that thought. Who cared if James looked scared and contrite? He deserved every ounce of anger Alfie had to give.

"Because we need him," Finn sighed, wiping her bloodied fists on her pants. "I can't fight these fools forever. If he can get us out of this room, I'm with him." Alfie shot her a look. "For now," she added quickly.

Alfie's searing gaze found James again. A tense silence brewed between them. Amid the ballroom's chaos, Luka felt as if he were standing in the eye of the storm.

"Fine," Alfie finally said through gritted teeth. With careful hands he picked up Queen Amada, carrying her in his arms the way she had carried them as children when they'd fallen asleep in their playroom. "We need to get somewhere safe."

Luka reached out to wipe the blood oozing from Amada's temple.

"Somewhere safe," Finn repeated, a broken laugh parting her lips. "Still so optimistic."

"Well, at the very least we can get out of this death trap of a ballroom," Luka said, looking at James expectantly. "Lead the way, traitor."

James blanched as they moved tentatively through the length of the ballroom. When they reached the double doors to the hallways, he asked, "Where are we going?"

Luka glowered at him. "You don't have the right to ask questions."

"Come on now." Finn rolled her eyes. "He needs to know where to lead us."

"To the left," Luka said, his voice strained. "If we go down the hall and make a left and then a right, there's a way to get into the secret passages in the walls. We should be safe there." Luka glanced behind him to where the chaos in the ballroom raged on. "Or as safe as we can be, considering."

The palace halls weren't as packed full of shadowless as the ballroom was, but there were still enemies to be avoided. Small groups of Castallano and Englassen guards fought, staining the tiled floor with rivulets of blood. Machetes flew through stomachs and kneecaps. Hands were chopped free of arms. The people in the ballroom were mostly nobles, so they didn't know how to really fight. But these guards had been trained for chaos, and Sombra had wiped all the honor from them.

"Englass had their guards stationed outside the ballroom, ready to attack." Alfie shifted Queen Amada in his arms as Luka watched the carnage unfold. "All this time, they were preparing to take over and we had no clue."

James stiffened, and Luka hoped he knew better than to speak right now.

"Yeah, they were good and ready to take over," Finn said as she pulled a bloody machete from the chest of an Englassen corpse. She surveyed the blade carefully before tossing it aside. "But they didn't."

"Not because of us," Alfie said, shame lacing his words. "Sombra is the one who put an end to it. If he hadn't showed up and dragged Dezmin into this, they might've killed the rest of us and taken Castallan by force."

Luka's eyes stung at the mention of Dezmin, of Sombra's voice coming out of his mouth. "It wasn't him," he told himself in a desperate murmur. "It wasn't Dez." But Luka wasn't sure if he believed his own words. Sombra had seemed particularly gleeful about Dezmin being a willing vessel. Was he telling the truth? Had Dezmin *changed* after he'd been lost to the void?

As they moved through the hall, the shadowless guards shouted in alarm and moved out of the way, seeing a fire rather than three tired friends, an Englassen enemy, and a comatose queen. With quick steps, the group made it around the first corner. They just needed to get to the end of this hall to find the passageway. Once they made it there, Luka could sob in earnest.

Alfie shifted Queen Amada in his arms, cradling her close. He held her like a talisman, like his last hope.

Like a boy who was terrified of becoming an orphan.

Luka knew that life all too well and couldn't blame Alfie for his fear. Amada's face looked peaceful in her sleep, and he finally understood why parents watched their children doze. When they were asleep, they were safe, accounted for.

"Prince . . . ," Finn began, and even in the wreckage of this moment, Luka marveled at how her face softened when she looked at Alfie. Luka turned back to Amada.

Her black eyes were wide open.

Before Luka could say a word, she jerked out of Alfie's hold and gripped Finn by the hair. "I told you to stay away from my son!"

"Mamá!" Alfie tried to grab her, but the queen was too quick. She launched herself at Finn.

"They need to stay close to me or—" James shouted as Amada tackled Finn to the ground, sending the pair rolling ahead of the rest of the group.

They came to a halt with Amada straddling Finn, squeezing the thief's throat tight between her delicate hands.

"What is it with you and choking people?!" Finn croaked.

"Wait!" James shouted, but it was too late. Finn and Amada had disrupted the illusion of the fire. They were all visible now.

The shadowless turned.

"The queen of Castallan!" a black-eyed Englassen shouted, catching the attention of his comrades. "Kill her! For the crown!"

"*Shit, shit, shit*," Luka shouted as he and Alfie sprang into action, leaving a bewildered James behind. Luka didn't even spare him a glance. If the boy wanted to hang back and be a coward like the rest of his people, then so be it.

While Alfie tried to haul his mother off Finn, an Englassen guard raced forward and swung her sword downward. Luka couldn't tell if she was trying to kill Amada or Alfie, but he'd make sure she was unsuccessful either way.

Dashing forward, he caught her by the wrist and slammed her hand against the wall over and over again until she dropped her sword. Then, with a kick to the belly, he sent her flying. But just as quickly as she was knocked away, others ran to take her place.

"*Fuerza!*" Alfie was shouting to repel them, but they kept coming. Luka stared at him in confusion. Why wasn't his magic working?

Luka deflected another guard, this time with no weapon, just his fists. Two more men leaped forward, their black eyes wild and soulless, each with a sword in hand.

They were too quick for him to catch. Luka didn't see what happened next so much as he felt it—a shadowless woman ducked past him while he was distracted by the other two.

"*No!*" he shouted. He wouldn't let this happen again. He couldn't watch someone else he loved taken from him, not today, not ever. He wouldn't survive it.

Luka caught one sword in his hand, letting it tear through the flesh of his palm. But it was too late—a scream of pain rang out behind him. Which of his loved ones would he have to mourn now? He whirled around to see.

It was James.

The Englassen boy had thrown himself in front of Alfie and the queen. Luka blinked, wondering if this too was some sort of illusion.

The shadowless woman dug her blade deeper into James's shoulder. "Get out of the way, fool!"

Luka gripped her by the upper arm and tossed her in the

direction of the ballroom as Alfie finally wrestled his mother off Finn. Throwing people was becoming startlingly common.

"Are you all right?" Luka asked James.

"I'm fine." The Englassen pressed his hand against the wound, his eyes scanning the carnage in the hallway. "We've got to get out of here."

Luka didn't know what to say to the boy. He'd written him off as a coward and a betrayer, but James had put his body on the line to stop Alfie and Queen Amada from being hurt. He could have used his illusion magic to protect himself and run away, but he'd stayed.

And now Luka didn't know if he could hate him quite as much as he wanted to.

"They're here!" a familiar voice shouted, jolting Luka from his warring thoughts.

After years of skipping class and turning in his homework abominably late, Luka had never been so happy to see Paloma and the legion of dueños that trailed behind her.

But wait—what if they were shadowless too? Was this just one more enemy to fear?

In a panic, Luka searched their eyes. They still had whites to them; their bodies still had their shadows. He didn't know how they had not been affected by Sombra's return, but he was too relieved to question it.

"Contain the shadowless and protect the royal family!" Paloma shouted. Some of her brethren spread out through the hall as others raced past to get to the ballroom.

Luka watched numbly as the dueños began trapping shadowless in circles of magic, one by one. They moved in pairs, one dueño drawing the written magic quickly with chalk while the other worked to hold the shadowless in place. Upon seeing their comrades trapped, the others ran, disappearing down the halls like mice scurrying back to their holes. Once again, Luka wondered why the magic was working for the dueños when it hadn't for Alfie. What was going on?

"Paloma," Luka said, his voice thick with emotion. Everything was going to be all right. Paloma always knew what to do, and today would be no different. It couldn't be different. Luka wasn't sure he'd survive if it was different.

The dueña squeezed his shoulder as she passed him to get to Queen Amada. Sweat dripped down her face, and Luka wondered what she'd faced on her way here.

"The queen must be contained." Finn was still gasping for breath on the floor when Paloma approached, reaching for Amada.

"Don't take her!" Alfie pleaded, still holding Amada against him, his arms locked over her chest in an X. "Please, she's still my mother!"

"Alfie—" Paloma said.

"*She is all I have left!*" Alfie shouted, his eyes shining. "Please!"

Paloma held his gaze, unrelenting. "Let go of her."

"Release me! You don't command me!" Amada shouted at her, spittle flying from her lips. "I am the queen—you will obey me or you will hang!"

Luka blinked at how ferocious she looked. At how she threatened Paloma like an insect beneath her foot instead of a trusted friend and confidante. This was not the queen they knew. Not the mother they knew.

Alfie seemed to see it too. His throat working, he looked down at Amada where she squirmed against him. After a long moment, he let the dueños pin the queen on the ground.

When the written magic had been put in place around her, Amada stood and threw herself against the invisible wall keeping her caged.

"*Release me!*" she demanded. Her eyes were trained on Alfie, desperate and mad. "You won't survive without me! You're not ready!"

Alfie brought a shaking hand to his lips as Amada pounded her fists on the barrier.

The dueños raced about, imprisoning more shadowless in rings of magic, but Luka felt just as trapped in this horrifying moment.

King Bolivar was dead.

Dezmin was back, and so was Sombra.

Queen Amada had become a monster.

"Listen to me, Alfie. You need me," Amada shouted. "*You're not ready!*"

As Alfie bent forward, sobbing, his hands on his knees, Luka couldn't help but agree with her.

Whatever was to come, they weren't ready.

THE BALANCE

Finn had no idea how her life had reached this point.

She'd lived every moment of it, but still—how she'd come to be standing in a meeting chamber waiting to discuss the end of the world with a group of dueños, a prince (now king), and Bathtub Boy was beyond her.

The room was vast but austere, with a long table that Finn could imagine the king, queen, and their advisors sitting around, making decisions that would affect everyone but themselves. Back when the king was alive, anyway. Aside from that, the room was unfurnished except for the floor-to-ceiling curtains covering the windows on the eastern wall.

When a dueño moved too close to where Alfie sat, silent and dead-eyed, Luka blocked him. "Give him a moment."

Finn shot the dueño a warning look. With Alfie's father dead and his mother locked away in the dungeons with the other shadowless, he had suddenly become king. The dueños were anxious to speak to him, but a few more minutes wouldn't make the world end any faster.

Feeling the need to fill the silence, Finn turned to Paloma. "Where's the Englassen kid?"

Luka crossed his arms, huffing. Well, that had clearly been the wrong question to ask. But the boy had jumped in front of Alfie and taken a blade to the shoulder when he could've left them high and dry; the least Finn could do was ask if he was still breathing.

"He's being healed and monitored by our brethren," an elder dueño called Bruno said. His mouth was fully obscured by an impressive white mustache and beard.

Finn cocked her head. Now that the adrenaline had died down, she remembered that Alfie had tried to heal her before but couldn't. Yet after they'd been taken to safety, one of the dueños had done so. The dueño had looked oddly strained when doing it, but he'd still healed her. Why couldn't Alfie? Her eyes strayed to where he sat, unmoving. She supposed that watching your father die might make it hard to perform magic, even if you were a desk magic nerd.

"Where is the diviner?" Paloma asked Dueño Bruno.

Alfie stiffened in his chair.

Finn sucked her teeth. "What does she have to do with this?" The diviner was the last person she wanted to see. Just days ago, during the peace summit, the woman had shown Finn a vision of Alfie being stabbed only for Finn later to find out, mid-stab, that it was actually she herself who would be attacked while disguised as him. It felt so embarrassingly obvious now.

"She can use her gift to help us decide our next steps," Paloma explained.

Finn frowned, recalling the diviner's words.

Your destinies are so intertwined that I could not see his future until I found you.

"We don't need her—we already know what to do next," Finn pressed on. "We need to gather Sombra's relics before he can get them himself."

It was the only logical path. They'd already learned the hard way that if Sombra obtained the stone relics of his body, it would only make him more powerful.

"She's right," Alfie said, rising from his chair. "He already took the arms. Obviously he'll be going after the other relics next."

"And can't you dueños just do what you did to the shadowless in the hallway?" Finn asked, thinking of how they'd caught them in circles of magic. "Go trap them all?"

Bruno shook his head. "You don't understand, child. For one, how do you hope to find Sombra's relics? Do you or Prince Alfehr have some means of traveling from kingdom to kingdom faster than a god to procure them? Especially with the shadowless running about? And what will you do with the relics afterward?"

Finn had no answer to that. Alfie cleared his throat, his eyes darting to his shoes.

Bruno continued. "And Sombra has *destroyed the balance of magic*. It is not just Castallan—the entire world has been affected. We have warded the palace grounds to keep any more shadowless from entering, but their numbers are great. You saw how we struggled in the hall; how do you think we would fare trying to trap thousands—millions—of them one by one?"

Finn's stomach dropped. The whole world had changed? Last

time, Sombra's release had only affected San Cristóbal. "You don't know that the whole world—"

"Yes, we do." Paloma walked to the far side of the room. With a wave of her hand the curtains parted, revealing a row of floor-to-ceiling windows and a view of the palace grounds.

Finn had expected to see the horrifyingly dark sky that Sombra had conjured, but was stunned into silence instead.

"Is that—" Alfie began, his voice low with panic. "Is that *the moon*?"

The ebony sky was spattered with strange shards of light, as if a globe of snow had broken, scattering its pieces through the heavens. Moonlight descended over the earth unevenly, a mere suggestion of its usual luminosity. Alfie and Luka stood on either side of Finn, staring.

Finn's eyes widened. "No, it couldn't be." But she couldn't see the moon anywhere.

"Sombra's return shattered the moon like a piñata?" Luka said, his eyebrows shooting up into his hairline. The image should've been funny, but Finn couldn't bring herself to laugh.

"The natural order of the world has been disrupted to the point that the moon itself is no longer whole." The finality in Paloma's voice made Finn's stomach drop. "Dueños from other kingdoms have contacted us with the news that their people have also become shadowless."

If the moon was in pieces, did that mean its light would go out, pitching the world into endless darkness? Was the sun gone too? Finn chewed the inside of her cheek, the weight of saving the entire world falling on her like an avalanche of stone.

"Know this," Paloma said. "Sombra failed last time, but now he's done it." She gestured to the view of the moon through the windows. "This is Nocturna."

Finn swallowed. She was living in a myth—and not one of the fun ones. The legend spoke of how Sombra and Luz, goddess of light, had fought when deciding whether mankind should carry darkness or light within their hearts. Sombra would not accept the compromise of the balance. He wanted to cast the world in shadow and bring about Nocturna—an unraveling of all things good. In punishment, he was cast out of the heavens.

"The world cannot survive this imbalance for long," Bruno said.

Finn turned away from the window. "What do you mean by that?"

"The balance of light and dark is what creates magic as we know it; it keeps our world healthy and livable. When Sombra destroyed that balance, he infected it with his own intentions, desires—for humankind to transform into the worst version of itself and self-destruct," Paloma explained. "The shadowless were merely the beginning. Soon our world will begin destroying itself from the inside out. The very elements that keep life sustainable, such as the moon, are falling apart. And they will continue to do so until this world ends."

"What even *is* the balance of light and dark?" Finn asked. Every Castallano knew the myth—the union of a woman of pure light and a man of pure dark created magic as they knew it. But she had no clue what it *really* meant.

"The legends are true. When a man of dark knelt before a woman of light, they created the sacred balance. It is located at the very heart of this world." When Finn only stared at her, the dueña went on. "It's a sacred place hidden deep in the metaphysical realm of magic where no human can find it. It is the seed from which everything we know comes. To tamper with it is to tamper with the fabric of reality, magic—even the very foundations of the world."

Finn blinked. She hadn't thought of the heart of the world as a physical place so much as an idea or a children's tale. "So it's like this world has a soul . . ." Finn rubbed the back of her neck, trying to wrap her head around it. "And Sombra's corrupted it, made it like him?"

Paloma nodded, somber.

"And since the balance of light and dark creates magic, now magic is ruined too," Luka said, his voice hushed with fear.

Alfie looked at Luka, eyes wide, and Finn knew he was thinking of how his magic hadn't worked when Sombra arrived in the ballroom.

"So Sombra wasn't just being dramatic," Alfie said, his voice hushed.

"What do you mean?" Paloma stared at him. "What did he say?"

Luka cleared his throat. "He said that he destroyed the balance in favor of the dark, and that the world can't survive that way—that it would fall apart like a dying star."

"And that our gods would pay for banishing him." Alfie's eyes were closed, as if he was willing the words not to be true, not to have been spoken.

"But what does that even mean?" Finn asked Paloma. "It can't be *literal*."

From the way the dueños exchanged knowing glances, it seemed that it could be.

"Let me explain," Paloma said, walking to the dark wood mantel where a gold scale sat. Finn had seen one when she'd robbed a judge's office once. The scale was a symbol of justice, balance. Though the system that led to Finn being thrown into prison was hardly fair.

Paloma set the scale on the table. Bruno flexed his fingers, pulling several stone pebbles of similar size from the palace walls. "Before Sombra was released, light and dark were perfectly balanced, hidden in the heart of the world where no one could disturb them." Paloma placed an equal number of pebbles on each side of the scale. "When Sombra was released the first time, he attempted to upend the balance in favor of the dark by infecting humans one by one." Paloma dropped more pebbles onto one side of the scale until it began to tip. "Every human he infected brought more darkness to the world. But you two stopped him before he could do much damage—after all, he would have had to infect the majority of humans in the world to truly destroy its balance." Paloma took the extra pebbles off, returning the scale to equilibrium. "But this time he has somehow managed to infiltrate the very heart of our world and destroy the light entirely." She knocked all the pebbles off one side. One plate of the scale shot upward, while the other dropped to the table with a clatter. "That is where we are now. The light has been destroyed, so there is nothing to counter the dark. Nothing to counter his power."

Finn stared at the losing side of the scale, her skin feeling too tight for her bones.

"Is that why my magic won't work?" Alfie asked. "Is it gone forever? Can only the shadowless use magic now?"

It made sense. After all, Queen Amada had easily used a suffocation spell on Finn while Alfie couldn't even do simple healing magic.

"No, that can't be," Finn insisted. "The dueños still used theirs to heal me and trap all the shadowless in the ballroom."

Alfie looked to Paloma, endless questions burning in his eyes.

"Magic is still usable, but its rules are different." She spoke in the tentative tone of a parent about to tell a child that their beloved imaginary friend was not real.

"Different how?" Alfie asked.

Finn could see him unraveling. The prince had spent his life studying the rules of magic, understanding its languages, its limits. Without that framework, he was at sea.

"As Luka pointed out, the balance of light and dark is what creates magic. At least, the system of magic that we know. But Sombra has infected that, and now it follows his rules. Sombra's goal was to strip humankind down to its worst qualities, to creatures of greed, anger, and shame. So the magic will only respond to the calls of those who embrace those qualities."

"Like the shadowless," Finn said.

Luka's brow furrowed as if he were attempting a very complicated math problem. "Then how are *you* all using magic?" He gestured at the dueños.

"We dueños have been studying the balance of magic for years. Connecting with it is an essential part of our training," Paloma said. "When Sombra slaughtered the light, we felt his intentions infiltrate what was once pure. We knew this meant that in order to call upon magic, we would need to focus on our negative emotions—our fear, our shame, our anger. We had to focus on such things as we saved you all and trapped the shadowless. And even then, we will never be able to lean into our worst selves the way the shadowless can. So even if you *can* access it, your magic will be substantially weakened."

"That's why it didn't work when you tried to heal me," Finn said to Alfie.

The prince looked both relieved and terrified to know the answer to that mystery. "So that's what we'll have to do to use magic?"

"Yes," Paloma said. "Unfortunately."

"Well." Finn crossed her arms. "I'm really good with anger. At least there's that."

Paloma shook her head. "Understand that some anger is cathartic, necessary even. But that is not the type of anger that Sombra's magic will call for. He'll call for the kind of anger that destroys. Likewise, he won't demand the type of shame that leads to self-reflection and growth. He'll demand the type that drowns you."

Finn crossed her arms. She hated feeling *anything*. Now she'd have to do it to use any of her magic. This day couldn't get any worse.

"Wait, wait, wait." Luka rubbed his temples. "Why aren't we all shadowless right now? How are we still ourselves?"

"That is a complicated question," Paloma admitted. "We are all still ourselves for different reasons. For the dueños, it is because part of our training is rigorous meditation, and only through that practice can we maintain our own balance, with great difficulty," she added.

Finn looked the dueños up and down. "Is that why you all look like shit right now?"

Bruno huffed, his mustache flopping indignantly.

"Yes." Paloma glared at Finn. "Diviner Lucila has maintained her balance because of the similar studies required to become a diviner. In the case of Prince Alfehr, Finn, and the Englassen boy, it is because they have *propio*, and *propios* represent—"

"—a deeper connection to the balance of light and dark, we know." Finn rolled her eyes.

"That is a very simplified way of seeing it," a dueño called Eduardo said, his voice dripping with condescension. "It is the way we teach civilians and children, not how it truly is."

"Still, I don't understand. If we have a stronger connection to the balance of light and dark, wouldn't we be the most affected when Sombra corrupted it?" Alfie asked.

"Those who are blessed with *propios* do have a stronger connection to the balance of light and dark, but that's not all there is to it. Think about how your *propios* function." Paloma turned to Finn. "Whenever you use any magic, you pull from its very source. And pulling from that source has rules. For spoken spells, you must verbalize in the language of magic. For elemental magic, you need to move with intention to control your element as you see fit. With written magic, you must write the language of magic. But your *propios* defy these rules. Finn changes her face without speaking a word, without writing, without performing an instinctual movement needed for elemental magic. She changes her appearance without following any of the necessary practices. Why is that?"

Finn looked to Alfie, her brow furrowed, but the prince was

staring at Paloma, something dawning on his face.

"Because we don't," Alfie said, his voice hushed. "We don't call from the source when we use our *propio* magic."

"Then where do we get it from?" Finn asked, annoyed and confused.

"There's a reason why it feels so different when you call upon your *propio* than when you call upon other forms of magic," Paloma said, her eyes on Alfie, watching him piece the answer together.

"We don't have to pull from the source of magic for our *propios* because we call upon ourselves." He looked at Finn, eyes wide. "We are our own source of magic."

Finn looked back and forth between them. "*What?*"

"Those with *propios* are born with their own source of magic inside them, separate from the original well that everyone else draws from," Paloma explained. "You are your own conduit, as exemplified by those special talents that belong to you alone and need not follow the rules."

"So that's why when Sombra corrupted the balance, it didn't affect us." Finn cocked her head. "We aren't a part of it the way everyone else is."

Paloma nodded. "You draw upon the source when you use regular magic, and you will continue to do so now that Sombra has corrupted it—but you are also your own, individual source. That's where your *propio* comes from. That is why Sombra must ask permission to possess your soul. You don't have to fight to maintain your balance like we dueños do. It is intrinsic to you."

"Why'd you keep this from us? From everyone?" Finn asked. What was the point?

"Because if people understood that those with *propios* are their own well of magic," Eduardo explained, "they might realize that, with the right spellwork, those people can be used as a source of magic, of power, even of life. We're lucky Englass didn't get that far in their studies."

Alfie put his hand on his mouth, shocked.

"So we could be used as sacrifices to power strong spells?" Finn grimaced.

"Indeed." Eduardo nodded. "Among other things."

Silence swept the room as the reality settled in Finn's mind. She met Alfie's eyes, but the prince said nothing.

"Okay, we've cleared that up, but what about me?" Luka asked, arms open in question.

"To be quite honest," Paloma admitted, "we have no idea. We can only think that since you possess some of Sombra's strength, you can resist his pull."

"I mean," Finn said, musing, "I guess in a way Sombra sort of gave you a *propio*. Usually it would require magic to make you as strong as you are, but you just *are* superstrong."

Luka stared at her for a long moment before finally shrugging. "Fine, I guess."

"Now that we are all on the same page," Paloma said. "Without the light to counter the dark, the world will collapse. Sombra has replaced balance with his own influence, and, as is his will, the world will begin to destroy itself from the inside out."

"Destroy itself?" Luka asked, his brow furrowed.

Paloma nodded. "We can't know exactly how—but yes, just as he said, it will fall apart."

"But how?" Finn asked. "How did he even find a way to get to the heart of the world and destroy the balance? We put him in a void! How could he have done it from there?"

Paloma looked annoyed at herself for not having the answer. "We don't know."

"How much time do we have?" Alfie asked, and Finn knew things were bad because the prince sounded eerily calm.

"We cannot be sure," Paloma said. "We are hoping the diviner has some insight."

Finn knew Alfie would always be uncomfortable around the woman who had told him he had no future, and for a moment, she thought he might object to seeing her, but then he nodded stiffly. At a time like this, they needed all the help they could get.

"When Sombra was first cast out of the heavens, the dueños dealt with him," Alfie said. Everyone knew the legend of Sombra being banished from the realm of the gods and how the world's first dueños had trapped him. Finn herself had heard the tale many times from her parents while they were still alive—though she'd never thought she'd live to see the day that he returned, let alone be a character in the tale herself.

"So if the dueños took care of it last time, do you know what we need to do to stop him now?" Luka looked at Paloma and her comrades hopefully.

"It would have been nice to be asked that the last time you released him," Dueño Eduardo sniped from the back.

"It would be nice if you shut your mouth," Finn quipped back.

Alfie raised a silencing hand. "Enough." He shot Finn a guilty look. "They're not wrong. If we'd come to them the last time, maybe we wouldn't be here now. Maybe . . ."

The prince's voice petered out, and Finn already knew what he meant to say. Maybe they would've found a better solution than placing Sombra in Xiomara's void. Maybe then, Sombra wouldn't have returned in possession of Dezmin's body.

"Millennia have passed since Sombra was first imprisoned," Paloma said. "Ever since he wreaked havoc on San Cristóbal six months ago, we have been searching our sacred texts for exactly how the dueños separated Sombra from his body and trapped him in stone, but we have not yet found the answer."

Luka stared at her. "How can that be? That's the most important detail to pass down!"

Paloma could only shake her head. "Perhaps they didn't want the information easily found lest someone use it to release him."

Before Alfie could speak, Dueño Eduardo interrupted. "I should think the dueños of the past didn't expect Sombra to be released again after they'd worked so diligently to trap him, and then released once more a mere six months after *that*." He sniffed. "Perhaps they didn't think we would need the instruction."

"You're very sassy for someone who doesn't have any maldito answers," Finn said, her fingers twitching for a dagger. She was tired of watching the prince's face fall as the dueños not so subtly blamed him for all that had happened.

"And you are quite loud for a common girl with no business in the palace in the first place," a dueño shouted from the back.

"Which one of you said that?" Finn stepped forward, pounding her fist on her chest. Alfie gripped her by the shoulders to hold her back. "Look me in the eye when you—"

Luka rolled his eyes, raising his voice over Finn's. "What about the *other* gods? Can we not ask them how to defeat Sombra?"

Finn quirked a brow. Maybe Bathtub Boy was onto something. If they wanted to know how to kill a god, maybe they needed to ask some.

"The gods turned away from humankind after Sombra was captured," Dueño Bruno said. "As is written in the legend."

"But perhaps they will give us an audience, considering the situation," came a quiet voice from behind them. They turned to see the diviner standing in the doorway, her faraway gaze on Alfie and Finn. "You and I are on the same page, Master Luka."

Luka looked far from enthused to hear it.

"Now that the missing piece is here," the diviner said, turning to Finn, "I can unveil your shared destiny—the power of which is so great that it may show us the path to stopping Sombra." Her eyes returned to Alfie. "Your future was obscured from me because she was missing, but it was always clear that whatever destiny lay in wait for you was vast—world-changing."

Alfie blinked at her. "It would've been nice to hear that a decade ago when I thought I simply had no destiny to speak of."

The diviner tilted her head. "It didn't seem prudent to say at the time."

Luka pinched the bridge of his nose while Finn groaned. "I'm going to scream."

The diviner continued, unbothered. "Though, as legend says, the gods turned their backs on humanity after Sombra was first imprisoned, I believe the weight of your destiny will grant us an audience with them."

"Why would they care now?" Finn asked. "They didn't last time."

"Your destiny is intertwined with the fate of this world, a world that the gods love very much. I don't think they will sit silent when it is in this much peril. Perhaps they will give us the insight we need to put an end to Sombra."

From the looks on the dueños' faces, it was clear they hadn't thought this was an option.

"The world no longer obeys the rules of logic," the diviner said. "Anything is possible."

"If you think divining us together will grant you truths from the mouths of the gods themselves," Alfie said, and Finn could hear the tinge of doubt in his voice, "then please do it."

Finn swallowed thickly. She didn't want to face whatever the diviner had to say, but if Alfie was willing to endure it even after the pain of his last divination, then so was she.

"Let's get this over with." Finn crossed her arms. "How does this mierda even work?"

"In order to move forward," the diviner said, "I need a conduit."

"Name it and you shall have it," Alfie said, and Paloma nodded in agreement.

"If we wish for the help of the gods, I will need a slab of larimar."

"Where are we going to get a whole slab of larimar?" Luka asked.

"What's larimar?" Finn asked.

"A rare blue gemstone found only in the mountains of Castallan," Alfie said. "There are myths that say the gods are made not of flesh and bone but of larimar. Others say that wherever the gods stepped, the ground turned to larimar. It's considered quite sacred."

"It was aggressively mined during the Englassen occupation," Luka added. "Hard to find."

"My mother has some jewels inlaid with larimar," Alfie offered. "Would that work?"

The diviner shook her head. "I would need a slab of pure larimar for this purpose. It is a conduit and an offering that the gods would recognize and respond to. Small pieces won't work."

"Who would have access to so much of something so rare?" Luka mused.

"I think I know a guy," Finn said. Every pair of eyes in the room fixed their gaze on her.

Luka smirked. "Of course you do."

THE CASTLE IN THE SKY

In the center of the city, on the roof of the tower that held the two-faced clock, Sombra paced, his mind a tangle of anger and confusion.

At least Dezmin wasn't the only one confused anymore. He thought back to all that had happened before this to try to figure out how he'd gotten here, how he'd made this horrid mistake.

He had always been the perfect son. Being the firstborn of a king required it, and Dezmin always did what was required. He was never late to a history lecture or a meeting with his parents' advisors. He attended countless trips abroad in his family's stead to strengthen old alliances and broker new ones. He molded his personality into one that teetered on the knife's edge of friendly yet not to be trifled with—the human equivalent of a firm handshake and a carefully crafted smile. He courted the young ladies his parents asked him to court, regardless of how he felt on the matter. He studied the way of the sword to sharpen his body, politics to sharpen his mind, and poetry to soften his heart.

And when the pressure threatened to break him from the inside out, he beat it into submission. He smiled and waved. He kissed hands. He blessed babies.

As he built himself into a lifeless statue of perfection, he watched his parents' pride blossom while the space between him and his brother grew wider and wider.

But he could not move to close the distance.

To be the perfect heir was a complicated dance with an endless array of partners, a game of smoke and mirrors where only glimpses of the truth were revealed for the shortest of moments. To close the distance between him and Alfie would be to stop the dance mid-song and admit the truth—that he was only twenty-five years old and already tired.

He enjoyed the pomp and circumstance of his position and the power that came with it, yet a larger piece of him wished he could step aside. If he did, though, it would be Alfie who would be saddled with the responsibility, the weight of a kingdom on his back.

Kind and anxious Alfie, who Dezmin had held in his arms the night he was born. Even back then his brow had been furrowed, as if he was too nervous to cry. Seeing his baby brother's soft, golden eyes open for the first time had made Dezmin's *propio*—his ability to bring life to any inanimate object—bloom.

No, Dezmin would carry the responsibility. And he did so, for as long as time allowed him.

Dezmin had been the perfect son until he wasn't. Until he destroyed his world for a way out of his own pain.

This was what he deserved for his selfishness. He'd played the part of a fair ruler-in-training, and the gods had seen fit to test just how much he was willing to sacrifice. He'd failed and now the world would fail with him.

Sombra kept pacing, moving Dezmin's body without his permission, like a game piece on a board. Dezmin felt ill with the sheer violation of it, but the god didn't seem to care or notice. It was as if he had come into Dezmin's home, locked him in the attic, and carried on, ignoring the cries echoing from above.

There was nothing Dezmin could do but watch Sombra's thoughts whip through his mind in an angry fervor. The crushing weight of the god's strength threatened to break Dezmin into pieces, the pain of it so sharp that he longed for the dark days in the void. Sombra's spirit had such a tremendous pull—Dezmin was swimming upstream, Sombra's current threatening to pull him under, to dissolve him into the god's immense power. Every moment was spent fighting to keep himself separate. The god's thoughts were so loud, so all-encompassing, that Dezmin could barely hear himself, could barely feel himself as an individual.

He wondered how long it would take before he couldn't distinguish himself from Sombra at all.

Sombra had come to the two-faced clock with the intention of relishing in the chaos he'd birthed from high above the city. Below him, San Cristóbal had exploded into pandemonium, fights and other fits of passion breaking out on every street.

Sombra had expected to feel euphoric at this moment, but Dezmin saw that all he felt was anger. It was strange to feel this partition within his own body, a hard line between Sombra's thoughts and his own.

"Why am I weaker now?" Sombra demanded, staring at his bloody hand. "*Why?*"

The wound in his palm was healing slowly, but it was still bleeding. Dezmin felt it smart and sting. He marveled at the unfairness of it all. He could not control his own body anymore, but he could still feel the pain of its wounds.

Dezmin watched as Sombra remembered his last visit to the human realm, when a mere wisp of his power had inhabited the body of a man named Ignacio. Back then Sombra had healed quickly, and the god couldn't figure out why he was now vulnerable in a way he hadn't been then.

Dezmin watched Sombra's confusion unfurl, the past informing the present. Now that he'd returned, procured his stone arms, and disrupted the world's balance, shouldn't he be even more powerful than he was before? Shouldn't he be untouchable?

"Is it you who has done this?" Sombra asked the black sky. And Dezmin watched his thoughts turn to the gods who had banished him from his heavenly throne, as if they'd set some sort of trick to hobble him.

As Sombra stood on the precarious tip of the clock tower, Dezmin saw panic in the god's mind, the desire to remain protected and safe until he could figure out why he was vulnerable.

With a delicate wave of his unwounded arm, the clouds began to shift and take the shape of a castle in the night sky. With every ounce of magic the god used, pain tore through Dezmin's body, a tree branch struck by Sombra's lightning.

"Finally," Sombra said when the work was finished. Thunder rumbled through the cloud palace, floating over the rings of the city like a dragon from a children's tale, ready to open its mouth and burn all beneath it to a crisp. "I *will* heal, and when I am ready, I will bring this world to its knees in prayer.

"I can procure my relics whenever I wish," Sombra told himself, and Dezmin hated how confident he sounded. The god was smoothing out the fissures of doubt inside him, the fear. "Only a god can best a god. There is no one to oppose me."

Blood poured from Sombra's wounded hand, the strain of building his new fortress manifesting itself in splashes of red dripping from his fingertips. Dezmin willed the blood to flow, willed his body to deteriorate.

He'd rather have no body at all than one that could be used to hurt those he loved.

THE MISSION

Luka watched Finn twist a dagger in her fingers, annoyance drawing her face tight.

"What do you mean I can't go?" Finn sniped at Paloma. "I'm the one who knows where the lumbar is!"

"Larimar," Luka corrected her, trying hard to look away from the ivory pieces in the sky that had once been the moon.

Paloma had made it clear that Alfie and Finn would not be going to retrieve the stone conduit that the diviner needed, and the thief was not taking it well.

"Whatever!"

The argument was a great distraction from James, who had just been brought into the meeting chamber. He sat at the far side of the room, surrounded by a group of dueños. They poked and prodded at him, quietly asking him questions. Believing that they were the only ones worthy of possessing *propios*, the Englassen royal family had forcibly experimented on James to see if *propio* abilities could be moved from one body to another. While they had succeeded, it had also made James ill from the strain of having multiple *propios* within his body. The dueños were examining him to figure out how such a thing was possible.

Luka couldn't believe that he'd trusted James at first. If he'd been more careful, would King Bolivar still be alive? How could Luka not have sensed what was going on?

But then again, James had also been stabbed in the shoulder while protecting Alfie. He could have left them in the hallway to fend for themselves, but he'd stayed. Luka couldn't reconcile those two sides of James—the helpful, kind boy who'd walked puppies with him, and the traitorous Englassen murderer.

Luka didn't realize he was staring until James's eyes met his own. He looked away.

"You and Prince Alfehr are essential to stopping Sombra. I won't have you getting killed in the Brim," Paloma argued, shooting Finn a stern look. "Someone else will fetch the larimar."

"She's right," Alfie said. "If even one of us dies, the diviner won't be able to see our futures and figure out what must be done to stop Sombra."

Finn threw up her hands but said nothing more.

"I can do it," Luka said. The idea of going out into a city full of shadowless under a broken moon was terrifying, but he had a feeling that Alfie and Finn were going to be up to their eyeballs in danger soon. He wanted to do his part when and where he could.

"No," Alfie said.

"Why not? I still have my strength. And I'm no stranger to the Brim. If Finn gives me directions, I'll be there and back in no time." Luka also wouldn't mind stepping out for a while, even if it meant facing some danger. The palace was full of so many memories of Dezmin and King Bolivar. Every room made him want to sprint away in an effort to outrun his grief, but he knew that, at some point, he would run out of steam.

"It's not safe," Alfie said. "We don't know what it's like in the city now that Nocturna is here. And it'll be harder for you to use magic when you need it."

"I could go with him," James said, his voice so quiet Luka scarcely heard it.

Finn had to grip Alfie by the shoulder to stop him from crossing the room to get to James. "Haven't you done enough already?" Alfie spat.

"Prince, calm down," Finn said, her tone measured. "We might need him."

"For what?" Luka asked. "To betray us again? He should be locked in the dungeons!"

Paloma cut her eyes at Luka and Alfie. "I'm shocked to see that a thief has more sense than the two of you."

"You're welcome," Finn said.

"Our resources are limited. We do not have an endless supply of allies to help us," Paloma continued. "You would both do well to keep your emotions in control. This world is now ruled by chaos; we cannot follow suit." She shot them a disappointed look. "Grow up."

Her words cracked like a whip, and they had no choice but to obey. After learning that James had been the one killing delegados at the peace summit, Luka didn't like the idea of keeping him close, but there were very few people who hadn't become shadowless monsters. It didn't make sense to squander him if he could be useful.

"I have many skills," James said quietly. "Thanks to Englass's experiments, I have multiple *propios*. I want to use them to help." He met their gazes, afraid but determined. "I want to make up for what I've done by helping return the world to what it was before." He turned to Luka, his gaze full of shame. "Please, let me help."

Luka's jaw clenched. If Luka's feelings toward him weren't so tinged with distrust, he might feel sorry for him. But Luka had volunteered for this excursion to get away from complicated feelings, not to immerse himself in them. Adding James to the mix would ruin it.

James coughed to break the silence. "After all, it certainly doesn't matter if I die, which makes me an ideal candidate for this."

"True." Finn cocked her head. "With all his *propios*, he and Bathtub Boy would make a good team."

Luka glowered at her.

"Look," Finn pressed on. "He betrayed us and all that. We know. But it was by force, he just proved himself semi-trustworthy when he took a hit for Alfie, and we don't have a lot of choices here. Sometimes you've got to play in the mud to get things done."

Luka didn't want her to be right, but she was. Still, maybe he could get out of this. "Having multiple *propios* might be useful, but it makes you ill." Only days ago, the boy had been so woozy that he'd fainted in Luka's arms, sick with fever. "You'll only slow me down."

"That was true," James said. "But ever since the return of the prince's brother, my illness has gone. I feel fine, strong."

Luka wanted to scream. It was just like an Englassen to benefit from the world falling apart.

"He speaks the truth," one of the dueños surrounding James chimed in. "Magic has changed entirely since Sombra's return. Now his body is able to house multiple *propios* without any ill effects. The imbalance has allowed it. It's fascinating."

"I would like to help," James said, ignoring the dueño. "Please."

"Your help is not being requested," Paloma said tersely. "You have no choice in the matter, and you will stand trial for your crimes once the world is righted, is that clear?"

James nodded.

"Very well," Paloma said. "The two of you will obtain the larimar."

THE ARTS DISTRICT

When Luka and James walked out the palace doors, the first thing Luka noticed was the silence.

Castallan was a land of brightly colored birds that sang as they flew and gentle breezes that rustled the leaves, but now there was only the sound of their own feet as they walked the stone path that led through the palace grounds.

The dueños had drawn a perimeter around the grounds to keep the shadowless out, making it safe to exit the front doors without fear. But this silence was eerie enough to make gooseflesh blossom on his arms.

Luka toed the yellowing grass on the ground. He could've sworn that the grass had been a lush green earlier this morning before the betrothal ceremony, but maybe he was remembering that wrong. . . .

"I thought we might use my speed *propio* to get to the city," James said to Luka, pulling him out of his thoughts. "Paloma said the horses have fled the stables, so there isn't much other choice. I won't be able to move quite as fast with you on my back, but I'll still be much faster than a regular man. We should be able to get to the Brim and find Miss Finn's gem dealer in no time."

Felix Arroyo, Finn's black market connection, was their best shot at finding a slab of pure larimar large enough for the diviner to use to summon the gods.

"Fine." Luka climbed onto James's back carefully, making it clear that he took no pleasure in their closeness. While he and James had flirted a bit before Luka had learned of his part in Prince Marsden's plans, he wanted the boy to know that any chance for romance was now off the table, down the stairs, and locked in the basement.

"You'll want to hold on tighter than that," James suggested gently.

"I'm fine," Luka said. "Just go."

He could feel James's back muscles tense at his tone. "Very well."

Luka yelped as James took off. It felt as if he were riding a two-legged horse—he had no choice but to grip the boy tight, crossing his ankles around James's waist and leaning forward so that his cheek was pressed against his back.

There was a wide expanse of land between the palace and the rest of the city. Luka worried that they would bump into the shadowless once they crossed the dueños' perimeter, but they were moving too quickly for any shadowless to take notice. They were too focused on fighting.

The boys sped past a woman who used her flame casting to light a man on horseback on fire. She knocked his torched body off the steed and then took the beast as her own. Luka could smell the horse's burning hair as they passed. He could only imagine what awaited them in the city.

When the stone walls of the Bow were in sight, Luka tapped James's shoulder and shouted, "Stop here!"

James skidded to a halt, his heels digging into the dirt, leaving a pair of deep tracks like those of a braking carriage. Luka dismounted and stretched his legs. James hadn't been lying; his speed far exceeded that of any man Luka had ever known.

"Impressed?" James asked a bit awkwardly. Luka could tell he was trying to break the tension.

"Finishing fast isn't always a good thing," Luka quipped, annoyed with himself for participating. Before James could drag him into further conversation, Luka strode past him, calling over his shoulder, "Let's get this over with."

The wooden gates to the Bow had been ripped off their hinges. On the other side, Luka could hear laughter and the sound of bottles being smashed. He swallowed. James had used his illusion *propio* to make them appear as if they had black eyes and no shadows, but what if the shadowless could sense that they were different? If they did sense it, would they even care? From what Luka had seen, the shadowless focused on little else but creating chaos, so perhaps the illusion wasn't even necessary. But better to be safe than sorry.

"If something happens, I'll put you on my back and run," James said, seeming to know what he was thinking, which annoyed Luka even more.

"Fine," Luka said. "But only if it's an emergency. We don't know if your speed will draw attention to us. With me weighing you down, we won't be able to get away completely unseen, and we don't want a horde of shadowless chasing us back to the palace."

"I hadn't thought of that," James said sheepishly. "Very well;

then I will carry you back only if we must."

"Great."

Rather than listen to James be awkward any longer, Luka summoned whatever courage he could muster and hurried toward the gates.

"Please stay close," James said as he caught up. "I can only create illusions within a certain radius."

Luka gritted his teeth. "Fine."

Together, they stepped through the gates, alert and tense. Once a quiet ring full of haughty nobles, the Bow was now in shambles. Luka could count on one hand how many of the stately haciendas' stained glass windows were still intact. Stones had been thrown through them—for fun or for robbery, Luka couldn't be sure. As they walked deeper into the city, things only seemed to get more absurd, like peeling back layer after layer of a chaos onion. At least no one seemed to take notice of them.

Ahead, a statue in a beautiful public fountain had been destroyed and a group of aristocrats had stripped off their expensive clothing to swim naked.

The sound of shouting drew Luka's gaze down to where a noble was trying to stop a thief from stealing from him—the thief headbutted the man before pressing his fingers into his eyes, and the noble screamed, blood pouring down his face.

"He's going to kill him!" James moved to stop them, but Luka shot out a hand, holding him in place.

"We're supposed to be shadowless too, remember?" Luka said. "We can't stop any of this or we'll give ourselves away."

Over James's shoulder, Luka could see two of the nude swimmers staring at them suspiciously, so Luka did the first thing he thought of to keep their cover.

He punched James in the face.

James hit the ground, a look of shock on his face. Then he caught on. He grabbed an empty bottle of rum and smashed it against the ground.

"Well, come on then," Luka shouted. "I hear Englassens fight dirty."

James flinched briefly before playing along. He barreled into Luka, driving him back and around a corner, out of sight of the swimmers. They were alone in an alley with no eyes on them, but Luka kept shoving at him angrily. He couldn't stop himself. And why should he have to after all that James had done?

"We're safe now," James said as he dodged Luka's fist. "You can stop!"

But Luka wouldn't stop. All the frustration rushed out of him, boiling over and searing everything it touched. "What if I don't want to?"

As the images of Bolivar's corpse and Marsden's snide face flashed in his mind, all Luka wanted to do was punch things.

"Stop!" James was a blur of movement, dodging swing after swing with his speed. He never even raised a fist to hit back, which only angered Luka even more. "Why are you doing this?"

"Because if you'd found a way to tell us what was going on, then maybe he wouldn't be dead!" Luka shouted.

Flustered and gasping from all the dodging, James caught Luka's fist in his hand. Luka's jaw tightened at the realization that, with his speed, James could've stopped him anytime he liked. "I did what I had to do to protect my family! You of all people should understand."

Luka froze, humiliated that he'd been foolish enough to open up to James about the death of his own family. He wrenched his hand free. "Don't bring them into this."

He didn't want to sympathize with James; he wanted to stay angry.

But what would Luka have done if his own family had been in danger?

Luka punched the wall, his fist cracking the stone of the alleyway. James had the good sense to not say a word.

"Can you just answer one thing for me?" Luka asked.

The Englassen nodded, his pale face flushed.

"Was it hard for you?" When James only looked at him quizzically, Luka went on. "Was it hard for you to lie to me? To all of us?"

He understood why James had done as Marsden commanded. After all, the lives of his loved ones were on the line. But how James felt while he'd done it was another topic entirely. Had James been laughing at him the whole time while he pretended to care? Had he found it simple to lie to gain Luka's trust?

"Yes," James said, his voice rough with guilt. "Yes, it was hard to lie. Nearly impossible when it came to you."

For a long moment, there was only the sound of their ragged breaths as Luka felt the anger coil back inside him. It wasn't completely gone, but it had cooled. Luka pulled his fist out of the alley wall, embarrassed that he'd lost himself so fully. "I'm sorry."

James shook his head. "So am I."

Luka shook the gravel off his fist, too emotionally wrung out to look James in the eye. "Let's just go."

They left the alley, silence reigning as they walked farther from the palace and deeper into the violent depths of the city. Neither spoke a word, and Luka wondered whether it was because of how awkward their relationship had become or because they were too focused on keeping an eye out for any shadowless who might decide to start a fight.

"I'm sorry if this is a silly question," James began, shattering the quiet. He pointed ahead. "But that wasn't there before, was it?"

Luka looked up and his jaw went slack. He stopped in his tracks to take in the mass floating over the ocean beyond the rings of the city—a palace made of thick gray clouds. Thunder and lightning rumbled through its wispy walls. It stood out against the dark of the sky, stunning in its sheer impossibility.

"Sombra," Luka breathed. Who else but a god could create such a thing? It loomed tall and foreboding, airy yet solid at the same time.

"He made himself a castle in the sky?" James asked.

"Yes," Luka said, a smile curling his lips. "He did."

"And this is a good thing?" James asked as Luka walked on, picking up his pace.

Luka grabbed James by the shoulder and pulled him out of the way of yet another shadowless brawl. For a former cold-blooded murderer, the boy was easily distracted.

"People don't build fortresses for fun. They build them because they're afraid," Luka said, his eyes on the castle. "So afraid that he needs to hide high above the city, out of reach."

Their world was falling apart, but at least Sombra was scared. That had to mean something, didn't it?

James cocked his head. "I was just going to say perhaps he's a bit dramatic, but I like your interpretation much better."

Luka snorted, and as the chaos of Nocturna unfolded around them, the two shared a small smile.

Finn had told them that her black market connection was in the arts district. The walk to the city's center ring was longer than Luka wanted, but at least the tension was gone. He was no longer a coil of anger waiting to spring on James.

As they walked, Luka found himself surprised by what Sombra's influence brought out in people. He'd thought that the destruction of the light would make everyone evil, cruel. But the results were more varied. As they'd seen in the Bow, there were nobles who simply wanted to swim naked without a care for the decorum that had kept their lives as structured as a corset. There were those who robbed and fought. There were couples of every type who, to James's red-faced dismay, chose to have sex in any public location. And there were those who seemed to turn to cowardice and shame, clinging to the shadows and whispering pitiful, heartbreaking things like, "Don't look at me, please don't look at me."

Darkness was not simply one shade. It was as unique as each soul in the city.

The closer they got to the arts district, the quieter the Brim became. Did the shadowless have a bedtime to adhere to or was this just some strange coincidence? It wasn't as if there was anyone to ask, so they just continued to the center of the market, where the stalls and shops were empty and unattended. Sombra's cloud palace loomed in the distance, a watchful eye that seemed to track their every movement.

"We're getting off lucky, it seems," James said, to break the heavy silence. "No shadowless to get in the way here."

But Luka wasn't so sure. Of all the times to be lucky, now, in the middle of the end of the world, did not seem likely.

As they carried on, James stepped in a puddle. With a grimace, he shook his foot, leaving pink and orange splatters in his wake.

Luka tilted his head. "Did you just step in paint?"

"Seems so." James shrugged.

"Odd," Luka said as they went on. He didn't know why the paint made a hard stone of dread form in his belly; after all, with the moon in tatters, a puddle of paint should hardly feel suspicious.

Still, it felt off, like a sign of something worse to come.

"Master Luka," James gasped, and Luka stopped in his tracks at the sight of the something worse that had indeed come.

A dismembered hand lay in the dirt, splattered with green paint. A few paces beyond it was a leg. And finally a bloodied torso. All were covered in bright paint.

"What could've done this?" James asked, his hand over his mouth.

The limbs didn't look as if they'd been chopped off with a blade. They looked as if they'd been torn off. *Mauled.* The lanes of stalls were strewn with bodies.

Before he could speak, he heard a low, feral growl.

Luka turned slowly, afraid to make any quick movements. Behind them was a tiger, but it wasn't orange with stripes of black as it should be. It was a splash of different colors—greens and blues and purples. Two other tigers appeared and began closing in from either side of them.

Luka knew of only one man who could create beasts like this, and he'd been lucky enough to miss their first meeting.

"These shops belong to me," a voice called. "And I'm afraid you're trespassing."

Luka didn't need to turn to know that behind him stood Ernesto Puente—the Tattooed King.

THE ARMORY

Finn's fingers danced over the selection of blades, sabers, machetes, and daggers.

After Luka and James left to retrieve the larimar, half the dueños had swarmed Alfie, asking him magical theory questions that Finn couldn't hope (and didn't want) to grasp. So, with some free time on her hands, she'd found herself in the royal armory. It was beyond anything she'd ever seen. Each blade shined as if freshly polished. Finn wondered if there was a servant whose whole job was to wait for a single fleck of dust to fall on a blade only to furiously polish it again. Then she wondered if that servant was shadowless now, wreaking havoc on the city.

Finn buried that thought under her excitement about sharp things.

She weighed a dagger in her palm—perfectly balanced. Finn was accustomed to using whatever weapon she could find and letting her stone carving magic make up for how poorly her throwing knives were made. After all, metal was stone's shinier cousin, and

Finn was cordial with the whole family. But these daggers would fly to their target without any help from her.

Paloma had said that elemental magic wouldn't work the same way as before. That Finn would need to lean into her darkest emotions to reach it. But Finn hadn't tested the theory herself. Usually, it only took some focus and physical movement to manipulate metal.

Finn fixed her gaze on the daggers, raised her hand, and made a beckoning motion. The daggers stayed put. The familiar feeling of the magic flowing through her did not come. She was utterly disconnected from it.

Feeling naked, she took a breath and steeled herself. On whatever journey she and Alfie went on, she would need her magic, so she should practice accessing the emotions that would let her use it.

Finn thought back to one of the first times she'd stolen as a child, and the guilt she'd felt pilfering from the stall of a man who'd always been kind to her parents when they were alive. She closed her eyes, sinking into that feeling, and then tried to beckon the dagger again. It barely twitched. The feeling of magic tingled over her skin but did not flow through her as it had before.

"Coño," she mumbled. Clearly that memory hadn't been enough. She chewed the inside of her cheek. She knew the exact type of memory that *would* be; she just didn't want to think about it.

But there wasn't much of a choice, was there?

Finn rolled her neck from side to side, willing the tenseness to leave her shoulders, and thought of one of the many times she'd run away from Ignacio. She had been a child, maybe thirteen. She'd made it to the pub at the edge of town, a place to steal some food before a longer journey, and there he was. Leaning against the wall of the pub, arms crossed, his face frighteningly blank.

It wasn't Ignacio that made the memory so shameful, so awful. It was what she'd felt in that moment when their eyes had met—she'd felt relieved to have been found and dragged back home, where she deserved to be.

Finn could feel the magic now—it skittered through her, the feeling of a centipede crawling over your skin and under your clothes, too quick for you to catch.

When Finn beckoned again, the magic oozed through her, thick and slimy. The dagger surged off the wall so fast that she lost control. She just barely ducked as it sailed over her head, taking one of her curls with her.

Finn turned to see the dagger notched into the stone wall, pinning the lock of hair to the spot just beside the doorway where Paloma stood. The dueña looked far from amused.

"These weapons are yours to take." Paloma tugged the dagger free. "No need to kill anyone who catches you here."

"Old habits die hard." When Paloma only stared at her, Finn quirked a brow. "Do you need something?"

"I wanted to speak with you before you and Prince Alfehr are divined." Paloma spoke calmly, but Finn couldn't help but feel a sense of foreboding. As if there was an underlying threat waiting to emerge beneath the dueña's placid words.

Finn crossed her arms. "Then spit it out."

Paloma looked distastefully at the weapon-lined walls. "I'm sure you're aware of how much the prince cares for you."

Finn nearly dropped the blade she was inspecting. "I don't know what you're—"

Paloma raised a silencing hand. "Please. We are facing the end of the world as we know it. There is no time for pretending."

Finn swallowed, looking away from Paloma's face. "Yeah, I'm aware. What does any of that have to do with the mission at hand?"

Paloma shook her head. "Everything, unfortunately. And if you don't already know that, then perhaps you're not as clever as I'd thought."

Finn scowled, wanting desperately to move away from this topic. "I'm clever enough to know that looking for the right weapon is more important than talking about . . ." She waved her hand with annoyance. "*Feelings.*"

"You know just as well as I do that the prince is a six-foot-four stack of feelings," Paloma said. "And if he is emotionally compromised, it could make things difficult."

"What do you want me to do about it?" Finn asked, discomfort wriggling under her skin.

Paloma closed the distance between them, her dark eyes assessing. "I know the prince's intentions are pure, but yours? I'm not so sure."

"I've never pretended to be pure, and I've never asked you to think so," Finn said, raising her chin. The dueña was very tall, and Finn felt her shadow flaring out behind her to create the illusion of size and strength.

"The prince loves you." Paloma said it as if it were an obvious fact.

Fire is hot.
Ice is cold.
Alfie loves Finn.

A tense silence splattered the room, and Finn's shadow wilted. It wasn't as if she didn't know—after all, Alfie was easier to read than the books he liked so much—but the words had never been said to her face.

She stepped back, her mind cramping as she tried to come up with something to say.

Finn had gone to Alfie's rooms last night because she'd thought they would never see each other again. She'd thought that by this time today he'd be officially betrothed to the traitorous tomato-headed Englassen princess. And the night they'd spent together had been perfect because it was too short for her to ruin. Too short for him to truly understand what a mess she was and walk away. It was perfect because it had ended as soon as it started.

But things hadn't gone to plan and now there was more time—time to talk about what had happened and how they felt. Time for her to hurt him and herself. The thought of it was enough to send her shadow scurrying away like a mouse.

"Did you hear me?" Paloma asked, her voice strained with irritation.

"Yes," Finn spat. "I heard you." How could she not have heard what the dueña had said? It was bouncing around the inside of her head, a relentless echo.

"Well," Paloma said, her hawk eyes still on her. "What do you have to say?"

What *could* she say? That she knew exactly how he felt and that she felt the same? That she'd spent months tiptoeing around that feeling, praying that if she were quiet enough it would stay asleep, but now that they'd spent the night together it was wide awake? That the prospect of having more time together was exciting, but devastating? Wondrous but terrible?

"That sounds like a personal problem," Finn finally said, picking at her nails in practiced nonchalance. "How the prince feels is none of my business."

Paloma sighed heavily, as if Finn had said exactly what she thought she would. And there was an odd comfort in that—in disappointing people in the exact way that they expected. After all, if you filled the role that was given to you, acted just as bad as someone assumed you would, you never had to do the scary work of finding out if you could be more. If you could be different.

"For the sake of the world, keep that flippant thought to yourself. If you intend to hurt him, wait until the mission is complete. Your journey will be perilous. He will need his wits and any confidence he can scrounge to get through it." She shot Finn a sharp look. "And he's been hurt enough today."

With that, the dueña walked out of the armory.

Finn hated to admit that she agreed with Paloma. The prince had been hurt more than enough without her adding to it. And if there was anything she was good at, it was hurting people.

She didn't need Ignacio's voice in her head to tell her that.

For the first time in months she felt the desperate, overwhelming urge to change her face, be someone else for a moment. Someone who was normal, not broken. Someone who would love the prince, not hurt him. At least Sombra's return hadn't affected her *propio*.

Finn gave in and reached for her face. If she changed it just for a moment or two, she'd feel better after. It was something she'd done as a child when Ignacio hurt her or when she hated herself too much to look in the mirror.

Her shaking fingers stroked her nose, willing it to grow longer, but her nose would not move. Would not grow or shrink. The same for her lips and cheeks, her hair and ears.

"What?" she whispered, pulling at her face to no avail. The last time this had happened, it was because the mobster Kol had blocked Finn's *propio*. But Kol—and her *propio*-blocking ability—was dead and gone now.

Finn's ability to change her face was gone. Paloma had said that *propios* weren't affected by Sombra, so why was hers not working?

Finn caught a slice of her reflection in the shining metal of a blade, and the fear in her eyes was sharper than any weapon in the room.

THE DEATH OF AN ARTIST

"Now," the Tattooed King said, his voice light and conversational as he gestured at the nest of stalls surrounding them. "What brings you to my humble abode?"

"Mierda," Luka cursed. The tigers made of paint circled them hungrily.

James turned to the Tattooed King, bewildered. He had no clue what they had just stepped into.

"The stalls in this district contain items of great beauty," Ernesto said, and the trio of tigers came ever closer. They had no eyes, only swaths of color. "Paintings, sculptures, gems. They are works of art and need to be nurtured and protected by an artist."

The man was just as Alfie had described. His eyes were milky and sightless. His white hair was a sharp contrast to his body—a patchwork of brightly colored, moving tattoos.

"We're only here for one thing," Luka said, choosing his words carefully. "We'll leave as soon as we've retrieved it." He knew the

Tattooed King wouldn't believe him, but Luka needed time to think, to figure out a plan.

"You wish to steal from my collection?" Ernesto spat, and the tigers' painted hackles rose, frothing at their tips like angry waves.

"I don't think this man is going to be amenable to a negotiation," James whispered. "Do you want me to finish this?"

Luka flinched. Was that the term that Prince Marsden had used when he'd ordered James to kill Castallan's delegados? He shook his head. There was no time to think about that.

"Use your speed to get to him. I'll keep him talking," Luka said. "When he's distracted by the sound of his own voice, go after him." Luka had dated enough artists to know that they all loved to hear themselves wax poetic about their work. A murderous artist wouldn't be any different. "I can take care of myself."

Luka had no idea if he'd be able to handle the circling tigers, but he needed James to move confidently and end this before it started.

"Very well," James said.

"Everything here belongs to me!" the Tattooed King shouted petulantly, insulted that Luka wasn't granting him his full attention.

"Why aren't you in your creepy little room made of skin?" Luka asked. Alfie had told him about it in detail—it had sounded as if the man needed to be in that wretched flesh-walled room to create the paint beasts. But now it seemed he could do it out in the open.

"Ah, you know of my work," he said, looking charmed. The tigers' hackles flattened, looking less hostile as Ernesto's mood lightened. "Thanks to Sombra, my artistry needn't be sequestered in that little room any longer—"

Luka didn't see James move so much as he felt the air shift. He expected the Tattooed King to fall, but instead there was only a crisp *snap*, like the sound of biting into a plantain chip. Then came James's screams of pain.

A tiger had leaped and snatched James out of the air by the leg, snapping the bone in its jaws. James hung from the animal's mouth, his leg caught at an unnatural angle between its teeth.

"James!" Luka shouted. Alfie had said the tigers couldn't exert much force since they were made of paint—the beasts could restrain you but not much else. But things were different now. They had become carnivorous, living beings in their own right.

"Hush," Ernesto said, and at his command the tiger swung to the left, slamming James's head into a wooden stall. James fell still as the tiger deposited him on the ground.

"You seem smart," the Tattooed King said, not even sparing James a second glance. "But not smart enough to realize that I see and hear through my creatures. I heard you telling him to 'use his speed.' My pets were ready for him." He patted the tiger's head fondly, the paint shifting under his touch. As he turned, Luka caught a glimpse of the man's back and recoiled with a gasp.

Swaths of skin were missing, as if it'd been flayed. Luka's stomach turned. The Tattooed King didn't need his skin walls anymore because his *propio* had somehow evolved. He could use his own skin to bring life to his art. But hadn't Paloma said that their *propios* wouldn't be affected by Sombra's return? Was she wrong?

And if she was wrong, what other monsters had been made stronger by Sombra's influence?

"Art needs feeding," the Tattooed King said. "Creativity is a gluttonous beast, constantly hungering for more. After I finish with you, my pets will feast on you and your quick friend." The tigers crept closer still. "Your flesh will fuel my next work. I can't think of a more honorable way to die."

He clapped his hands and the trio of tigers leaped at Luka. One gripped him by the arm, digging its teeth in, but thanks to his strength, Luka was able to pull himself free. The tiger's jaw exploded in a splatter of paint. Luka's arm stung from the puncture wounds, but at least now he knew that, with enough force, he could make the beasts splatter.

He took each beast head-on and punched, watching their limbs puddle into paint only to slowly re-form. He was bleeding from too many places to count. The tigers may have been made of paint, but their teeth drew blood as if they were made of flesh and bone. Luka didn't know how much longer he could hold out.

When the tigers closed in on him again, he was too tired to raise his fists. But then an idea flickered to light in his mind.

When he was a child, Luka had boiled the pots of paint in art class until the contents became a gummy, steaming mess, sending his and Alfie's art teacher into a fit of fury.

He could use his flame casting! He'd been nervous to use it in the ballroom full of cloth tapestries and people (shadowless, but people still), but here it was just him and the Tattooed King. He wouldn't harm anyone by accident.

A smirk tugged at Luka's lips as he threw his hand out, willing a barrage of flame to turn the creatures into colorful steam.

But no fire came. Luka shook his hand and flexed his fingers. Nothing.

"What the f—" A tiger leaped forward and headbutted Luka,

sending him flying backward into a stall.

"Too slow!" the Tattooed King laughed, like a child watching a puppet show. "Perhaps if you had the speed of your little friend, you would've landed a blow in time."

Crawling out of the splintered wood, Luka groaned in pain. His head ached where it had thwacked against the back wall. Why was his flame casting gone?

"Coño," he mumbled. He'd forgotten that magic had changed. He needed to lean into the worst parts of himself to access magic, something the shadowless did naturally.

The Tattooed King's endless laugh drew Luka's gaze forward. The man looked delighted as he watched the tigers creep closer to their prey. He seemed content to keep their approach slow, clearly wanting the beasts to play with their food a bit before digging in. Luka's stomach dropped at the thought of being gnashed between their teeth and swallowed down a painted throat.

"Shame, shame, shame," Luka repeated to himself. "Think shame."

A tiger lunged at him, and Luka thought of the time he'd given his very worst ex-lover a second chance. He shot his fist forward, waiting for the fire to bloom from his knuckles, but nothing happened. He didn't feel the flow of magic; instead he felt it running away from him, slipping between his fingers like slime.

"Shit!" he shouted as the tiger brought its gargantuan claw down. Luka tried to roll out of the way, but the creature's nails dug into his shoulder.

With his hand pressed against the bleeding wound, Luka ran to a kiosk of lanterns that he and James had walked past a few stalls down. The colorful, stained glass lanterns were lit from within with thick, many-wicked candles.

"There's nowhere to hide, boy," the Tattooed King called. "Face me with honor!"

"Hard to face you with your little pets around!" Luka shouted back. Why hadn't that memory worked? Giving Gabriel another shot was probably the most shameful thing he'd ever done. At the very least it was in the top ten.

A memory prickled at the back of Luka's mind, begging for attention, but Luka swatted it away. He didn't need to think of that. He would figure something else out.

Two paint tigers advanced on the stall, pawing at the wood wall and counter. Luka yelped as one of them tore a chunk of counter away with its scarlet teeth. When a candle fell against the tiger's jaw, the paint sizzled and popped, but the creature barely noticed.

Candles were a good start, but he could hardly do any damage with their tiny wicks. If he couldn't use his flame casting, then he'd need something to make them grow.

Luka scoured the stall until his foot tapped something with a quiet *ping*. There were bottles of rum hidden in the back of the kiosk along with a ledger.

"Thank the gods," he said. Just what he needed to fan the flames—and also what he needed to stay sane. Carefully taking a swig, he lined the stall's counter with the thick candles and then stood behind it.

"Why are your tigers so weak?" Luka asked, the bottle of rum held firmly in his hand. "Is it because they're poorly crafted? Perhaps the artist who made them was a bit . . ." Luka thought of the word his artist ex-boyfriend detested hearing in critiques. "Sloppy?"

The Tattooed King glowered before shouting, "Kill him!"

The tigers rose on their haunches, their bellies exposed. Luka prayed to any god who was listening to make this work, and then he blew a stream of rum against the row of candles. The flames roared to life and shot forward, colliding with the monsters with a loud sizzle. The creatures' mouths stretched open in strange, garbled screams that reminded Luka of when he and Alfie would take baths together and shriek underwater. Before Luka's eyes, their coats boiled and burst into clouds of colored steam.

He met the Tattooed King's gaze with a smirk. Maybe he could actually win this.

"Ah, don't look so pleased with yourself. There's always room for more!" Ernesto said, as if he were offering Luka a second helping of dinner. "It's lovely to have a fresh set of eyes to admire my work."

Ernesto clutched at his forearm, and Luka watched in horror as the tattooed flesh peeled from his bones and into his waiting hand. At his command, tendrils of paint rose from the paint cans around him, twisting around the patch of flesh until it became another paint tiger.

"Art and pain are often one and the same, aren't they?" he said as he pulled at the flesh of his chin. This time a hulking quilbear materialized. "With every work of art you create, a piece of you goes along with it. It is the ultimate suffering." Ernesto stumbled where he stood, unsteady on his feet. He was getting tired. The more he took from himself the more he would bleed.

If Luka exhausted the man enough, maybe he would die. There wasn't much rum left. Luka needed to figure out how to access his flame casting or the tigers would be well fed.

The memory prickled again, and again Luka begged it to retreat. He couldn't think of that, not after everything else that had happened today.

"Is that all you have to show me? Just tigers and a single quil-bear?" He tore pages out of the ledger and shoved them into the necks of the few remaining bottles of rum.

"Watch your tongue, boy. I fight for my art," Ernesto said as he took the flesh from his elbow and made a scaly caiman. "And it fights for me."

As the quilbear launched itself at Luka, he lit the parchment, then thrust the bottle down its wet throat. He wrenched his hand out, and the bear's teeth scraped at his forearm, but it was worth it to hear the bottle explode within the beast. The bear's skin boiled before it erupted, soaking Luka in blue paint.

Sweat poured into his eyes as he fought the beasts over and over again. He created bombs with the bottles and parchment, and even lit a nearby kiosk on fire. He lured the beasts to him before jumping out of the way, letting them barrel into the flames behind him, disap-pearing into splatters of paint and smoke. The Tattooed King tore more and more flesh from himself until Luka could see more muscle and sinew than skin. The man was faltering, and Luka need only push him a little closer to the edge.

If he could survive long enough to get him there.

When the swing of a bear's paw sent Luka flying down the lane of stalls, the Tattooed King gave a laugh. "Are you ready to die now?"

Luka stood slowly, his body aching. He was out of rum, out of options. A slash above his eyebrow brought a gush of blood, making it hard to see.

That memory, that horrible shame, was all that was left in his arsenal.

"Well, if I'm going to die," Luka said, gripping his arm where the bear had slashed him with its claw, "I'd like to see your full collection." Luka gestured at the paint animals that circled him. "Surely this isn't all you've got."

"And who says you deserve to see all I have to offer?" Ernesto spat. Too many patches of flesh from his face had been sacrificed, and the muscle and sinew visibly tensed and moved as he spoke.

"Who else has lasted this long in a fight against you?" Luka crowed, gesturing at the severed limbs littering the ground. He mustered every ounce of feigned respect that he could before he spoke again. "If I'm to die by your hand, I would like to see your greatest work before I perish."

The Tattooed King looked at him with respect, and Luka had to bite the inside of his cheek to stop himself from breaking character.

"You may not be an artist, but you have the heart of one," Ernesto said. "I will surround you with beauty until you draw your last breath."

As a new barrage of beasts approached, Luka fell into the memory of his family's bodies, hot with fever and wet with sick, the shame he'd felt at having survived when they had not. The memory of sitting in that house with the corpses for days before he called for help, begging to join them and being denied that relief. The echo of shame when Alfie hurt so many just to save Luka—and when, once again, hundreds died, Luka survived, like a cockroach.

The magic poured through him now. It didn't feel the way it usually did; rather than flowing like water, it was viscous and clotted, crawling through him like a snail leaving a trail of ooze in its wake. He wanted to turn away from it but couldn't. He needed to find the larimar so that Finn and Alfie could be divined. He would think about the very worst of his memories for the rest of his days if he had to.

With a shout, Luka threw his hands forward and a wave of fire burst free, overtaking the beasts and leaving nothing but scorched paint in its wake. To create more beasts, the Tattooed King kept plucking at his own flesh like a scavenger picking a corpse clean, and Luka kept burning his art to nothing. Whether his eyes were stinging from the horrible smell or from the strength of the memory, Luka couldn't tell.

The man was dying, and his monsters were dying with him.

The paint creatures began to falter, their attacks lacking the force they'd once had. The closer Ernesto got to death, the weaker his creations became.

Luka sidestepped a limping tiger and made his way to where the Tattooed King stood at the center of the chaos, surrounded by burnt paint and the limbs of past foes. The man had removed his clothing to more easily pull the flesh from his body. He looked like something that existed only in nightmares, a skinless man with a satisfied grin on his face. Luka raised his fist. If he had to deal the final blow, he would. For Alfie and Finn and the world that needed larimar to set things right, he would kill a man. But still he hesitated, his fist shaking.

"To die for one's craft," the Tattooed King said as he dropped to his knees, the burning stalls illuminating his bloodied face. "There is no better way to leave this world."

With a final shaky breath he fell onto his bloodied side. The last of his beasts began to whimper, an odd keening like a teakettle whistling, and Luka watched with a strange sadness as the creatures began to melt. Some dragged themselves forward to be close to their fallen master, but none reached Ernesto. They dripped slowly like candle wax until all that was left were puddles of thickened paint.

Luka let his arm drop limply, numbness sweeping his body. If this was only the beginning of Sombra's effect on the world, what else lay in wait? Not wanting to look at the corpse any longer, he turned and walked over to where James lay, not bothering to dodge the puddles and shattered glass. The boy was still knocked out, but his breath and heartbeat were steady. Luka would let him sleep a little longer.

He walked down the lane of shops, many of which were now on fire. He calmed the flames with his magic and kept moving. Luka found the shop of the rare gem dealer that Finn had told them about. The paint-splattered corpse of a man who Luka could only guess was Felix Arroyo lay sprawled at the entrance, as if he'd tried to run but had been no match for the painted beasts.

With careful steps, Luka walked the length of the shop, scanning the endless shelves of gems secured in glass boxes. He passed displays of imported amethyst, emerald, and sapphire, but there was no larimar to be found.

"Coño," Luka cursed under his breath. How long did he have until other shadowless noticed that the Tattooed King was dead and it was safe to ransack the arts district? He needed to find the larimar, grab James, and get away before he had another fight on his hands.

The adrenaline from his fight with Ernesto had faded. His head and bones ached; his wounds bled. Luka wanted nothing more than to sit and fall asleep, but that would have to wait. He rubbed his eyes and forced himself to focus.

"I'm better at losing things than looking for them," he sighed, and began searching every shelf of the shop. He kicked open the locked door in the back corner and found an office. Pulling out desk drawers and turning them over, Luka found nothing but ledgers. He even found a safe and used his strength to pull it open but there were only pesos inside.

Luka paced the front room of the shop, the same spot on the floor creaking each time he passed over it. "There has to be larimar here somewhere," he told himself. The diviner had given no alternatives for a conduit. They *needed* this. The wooden floor creaked for what felt like the millionth time. "*Shut up!*" he shouted, his frustration getting the best of him.

Like a toddler throwing a tantrum, Luka stomped on the spot. His foot sailed straight through the wood into a hollow beneath the floorboards.

"Gods damn it," he groaned, and tugged his foot free, sending chunks of wood flying every which way. And there, hidden beneath the floorboards, winked something shiny and light blue.

"*Ha!*" Luka knelt down and pulled the larimar from its hidden spot. "I knew my emotional immaturity would pay off one day." The slab was the length of Luka's forearm, sky blue and veined with white.

With the larimar in hand, he rushed back to James. No

shadowless had approached yet, but it was only a matter of time. The only thing scarier than a villain like the Tattooed King was the power vacuum he left behind and the vile people who would try to fill it.

Luka carefully lifted James onto his back, thankful that he didn't wake him in the process. The boy's leg was bent at an odd angle, and if he woke up the pain would be so severe that he wouldn't be able to keep quiet. Luka adjusted him gently until his chin tucked over Luka's shoulder. "Just sleep tight for now."

They'd used James's speed to get here, but they'd be using Luka's strength to get home. The pace would be much slower, but they'd get there. With James on his back and the larimar in his rucksack, Luka began the long trek to the palace.

As children, Luka and Alfie had been taught art history together. Alfie loved it, of course, while Luka had been painfully bored. He didn't remember much of what he'd learned aside from one thing—the legacy of an artist lies not in his success in life, but in the influence of his work after death.

Luka vowed that when this was all over and the world returned to normal, he'd never speak of Ernesto or this battle again.

The Tattooed King's legacy would die with him tonight.

AN AUDIENCE WITH THE GODS

Alfie had always been the studious sort.

From a young age, he had found that when his mind filled with swirling tendrils of anxiety, the best solution was to fill it instead with facts and theories. He plugged the holes that leaked uncertainty with pages torn from tomes of magic, history, and arithmetic.

Watching Luka walk out of the palace with no protection aside from an Englassen traitor had thrown Alfie's mind into the dark, gaping maw of his worst thoughts.

Just as he had as a child, Alfie plumbed the depths of knowledge instead.

After shaking off the dueños, he had gone straight to the library, seeking answers to the endless questions that had been blooming in his mind since Sombra's return. Paloma and the other dueños were off refreshing the warding magic and making sure the spellwork keeping the shadowless in the dungeons was holding. These were not normal prisoners, and a single layer of magic was not enough to keep them at bay.

Finn had made herself scarce, stealing away to the armory to prepare for whatever was to come after Luka returned with the larimar.

If, the anxious voice chimed in his head. *If Luka returns at all.*

Luka had left nearly four hours ago, and with each minute, Alfie's fears seemed to loom larger, changing from wispy shadows to something solid, something very much alive. Alfie slammed a book open, smothering that voice with every turn of the page.

"Prince Alfehr," a voice called, startling him.

Paloma stood right beside him holding a tray of food. He'd been so engrossed in his book that he hadn't even heard her footsteps.

"Has he returned yet?" Alfie asked, his heart racing.

"Not yet." Paloma shook her head. "But be patient. It's quite a trek."

And who knows what monsters they'll run into, his mind whispered.

She glanced at the tome that lay open on the desk. "What answers are you seeking?"

"Whatever answer we need to end this," Alfie admitted.

Paloma placed the tray on the far side of the desk and took the book from his hands. "I fear that books won't be of much use this time. No scholar could have theorized this situation."

Alfie stared at her. In all his years learning from her, Paloma had never told Alfie to stop seeking answers in books. "This is the most extensive library in the kingdom. The answer *has* to be here." If it wasn't here, then the answer didn't exist, and Alfie couldn't handle the finality of that.

Last time Sombra had escaped, Luka had been here in the library when he'd discovered that Sombra's relics were made of stone, not bone; Alfie and Finn had also found important information about Sombra in one of Paloma's books. There had to be an answer. How could any of them be expected to survive in a world with millions of shadowless? How would Luka survive, wherever he was now?

"I have always taught you to come here for answers." Paloma settled into the leather armchair beside his, a somber look on his face. "But this time the answers are not here; they're out there." She gestured to the row of vast windows. "We cannot research this; we can only fight against it. Even if the diviner has some information to give, we still will not know everything.

"When we venture out to put a stop to Sombra, we will do so unprepared. We will learn by doing. Trial and error. Guesses and mistakes." She held his gaze for a long moment. "People will die. Many already have. And sitting in this library will not yield the answers to how we can put a stop to that. You'd best accept that now, while we're still safe behind these walls."

Alfie's throat ran dry. One of his most potent memories of Paloma had been after a rough session of horseback riding when he was a boy. He and Luka had gorged themselves on sweets before their afternoon riding lesson and they both had puked flan and pineapple cake all over themselves and their ponies.

Planning is key. You knew your riding lesson was coming, yet you scheduled your meal poorly. Paloma had tutted as she handed them both a glass of water and guided them to the baths. *When you don't prepare, you prepare to fail.*

That mantra had shaped how Alfie saw the world. How he chose to approach life. And now she was telling him to pluck it from his mind, as if it wasn't so ingrained that to remove it would remove a piece of himself too.

"So what, then?" Alfie asked, panic lacing his words. "We just proceed blindly?"

"No," Paloma said gently, and he was surprised by how much patience she had for him. "We take the little we do know, and we move forward."

Alfie cradled his head in his hands, his temples pounding.

"And Prince Alfehr?"

Alfie looked up at her uneasily. What more could she have to tell him? "Yes?"

"The fate of the world rests in our hands," Paloma said, and though Alfie already knew this, hearing it from her lips made it even more terrifying. "The pressure is enormous; the amount of loss will be staggering. At some point, it will become unbearable. You will want to give up, to let Sombra win. But we are now responsible for the countless souls living in this world, and we don't get to give up and decide their fate because we're too tired, too sad, too sick, too lost. We do not make that choice for anyone. We are not Sombra." She gripped his shoulder so hard Alfie could feel it to the bone. "When the time comes, when there is nothing left for you to give, I need you to stand up and fight regardless. Do you understand?"

Alfie flinched at the reality she'd painted, and he could do nothing but nod and hope that, when the time came, he would be equal to the task.

"Eat," Paloma said, pushing the tray of food toward him. "The best thing you can do is get some strength. I've insisted upon it for the dueños too."

His stomach growled, the scent of pollo guisado wafting about his desk. It must've been from the banquet that had been prepared to celebrate Alfie's betrothal to Vesper. He chewed the inside of his cheek. He hadn't mourned Vesper or any of the Englassen royals. He felt a pang of guilt before shoving that thought away. They had not mourned the death of Alfie's father; he needn't mourn them.

Alfie inhaled the food, bringing the rice, chicken, and wedges of avocado into his mouth in quick scoops. Paloma let him forget his manners in peace.

"Finn is probably hungry too," Alfie said, wondering where she was now.

"Don't worry about her," Paloma said, her voice a little sharp. "I passed by the armory to make sure she was still there before having a colleague deliver some food to her too."

"Thank you," Alfie said.

Paloma was opening her mouth to speak when a dueño walked into the library, Finn following close behind. Alfie stood from his desk so quickly he nearly knocked over the glass of water Paloma had brought him.

"Prince Alfehr," the dueño said as he walked quickly up to the desk. "Master Luka and the Englassen boy have returned."

Finn closed the distance between them, and Alfie's stomach knotted when he saw her worried expression. "Where are they?" Alfie asked.

"The infirmary," Finn said to him. "The dueños took them there and then sent for us."

She had barely finished the sentence when Alfie started running, Finn and Paloma keeping pace with him.

The first thing he noticed was that both boys were splattered in paint, but that was hardly important compared to their many injuries. James wasn't even conscious as a pair of dueños worked on his leg. Luka sat upright, his face drawn as another dueño healed a bloody wound on his shoulder. He smelled of smoke and scorched paint.

"I'm fine," Luka said as Alfie rushed to his bedside. "Really, I'm fine."

Alfie knew that his cousin was both resourceful and unnaturally strong, but the world was different now and he hadn't been sure Luka would make it home. He'd done nothing but pace as they waited, every possible scenario playing out in his mind. But Luka was here now. He was safe.

"You don't look fine," Alfie said, his eyes burning. The only thing that stopped him from embracing Luka was the fact that he was covered in wounds and bruises.

Finn crossed her arms. "You look like you got carried away finger painting. You two have a little too much fun in the arts district?"

"I'm back in one piece, isn't that all that matters?" Luka said, trying to make light of it, but Alfie could tell he was holding back something about what he'd faced in the city.

"Well done," Paloma said, inspecting the larimar. Alfie hadn't even heard her come in.

"See, Paloma," Luka said. "I'm only a disappointment in the classroom."

"I never called you a disappointment," Paloma said, a rare gentleness in her tone. "I said you were wasting your potential."

"Same difference," Luka joked before turning to Finn. "Seems you were right. Felix Arroyo had plenty of larimar in his shop."

"Did he give it to you willingly?" Finn asked in a way that told Alfie the man didn't part with his jewels easily.

Luka shook his head. "He was dead before we got there." He fell silent. "Things are different out there. Every ring is absolute chaos."

"I presume everyone is resorting to violence," Paloma said, a grave look on her face.

"Not necessarily," Luka said. "It runs the gamut. There are those who fight, steal, and kill. Likewise, there are some who just want to run about naked—relatable," Luka added. "But some— I'm hoping only a select few—have become truly monstrous." He looked at Alfie. "We ran into an acquaintance of yours—the Tattooed King."

Alfie's stomach dropped. "*What?*"

Alfie had met the Tattooed King when he was investigating Los Toros, the fake nationalist group the Englassen royals had created to sow unrest in San Cristóbal—and he'd almost lost his life in the process. He'd thought they'd never meet again. After all, just days ago Finn and Luka had gone to find him again in a desperate attempt to learn the identities of the members of Los Toros and save the peace summit, only to find his shop abandoned. Alfie had hoped the man had fled the city.

"He took over the entire arts district of the Brim," Luka said. "He put up a fight when we came to take the larimar."

"He wasn't in his horrible flesh room, though," Alfie said, relieved. "So surely he couldn't do anything as bad as before." It had been clear that the man's power was limited to that room, as he needed his flesh canvas to summon his paint creatures.

Luka shook his head. "He did worse. He said that since Sombra returned, his *propio* is even more powerful. He no longer needs his room." He swallowed thickly. "He uses his own skin now."

Alfie's stomach turned as Luka explained how the Tattooed King had flayed himself to make more and more beasts until he died. Alfie felt ill.

"But I thought you said that *propios* would be unaffected by Sombra upending the balance?" Finn said to Paloma.

"They shouldn't." The dueña looked perplexed. "It doesn't make sense."

Alfie rubbed the back of his neck. If *propios* were somehow affected, were there other people like Ernesto who had been empowered and strengthened by Sombra's return? And had Alfie's own *propio* changed as well? He'd used it to see the colors of everyone's magic in the ballroom and it had seemed the same. . . .

"Oh, and Sombra has also built himself a palace in the sky," Luka added.

"*Qué?*" Finn and Alfie said in unison.

"Imagine the kind of night I've been having that I almost forgot that," Luka said with a half-hearted laugh. "But, yes, I saw it hovering over the Suave."

"For what?" Finn asked.

"For protection," Alfie reasoned, and Luka nodded in agreement. "If you could stab him and draw blood, then he must be in some sort of weakened state. He's putting space between us to keep himself safe."

"Then we've got a shot," Finn said, a grin curling her lips. "We've just got to figure out how to end him."

"The best chance we have at coming up with a plan is to return to the diviner with the larimar," Paloma said, still looking astounded by Luka's revelation. "We will figure out how *propios* are being altered, but first we need to get you two divined." She carefully took the slab. "Thank you for your service, Master Luka, and for your information on the city. We will take what you've learned to move forward." She spoke with genuine gratitude. "For now, you may rest here."

Alfie didn't want to leave him while they did the divining, but Paloma was right. It needed to be done as soon as possible.

"It's all right, sourpuss," Luka said. "I'll be fine." His gaze turned to the neighboring cot where James slept, his eyes softening. "Someone should be here when he wakes up anyway."

Alfie felt a hot stab of anger. Had Luka forgiven the boy so easily? Was Alfie being childish for holding on to his anger even though James had had no choice but to bow to Prince Marsden's demands?

Alfie silenced that thought. He'd deal with his feelings about James after the world was saved.

Luka read his mind instantly. "I'll come find you once they're done healing my wounds. Shouldn't be long."

"Yeah, yeah, we'll tell you all the good parts. Let's go," Finn said, gripping Alfie by the elbow. "Sleep it off, Bathtub Boy!"

"You don't have to tell me twice," Luka called, reclining into his pillows as they hurried out the door.

When Alfie, Finn, and Paloma presented the larimar to the diviner in the meeting chamber, she looked pleased. "This will do nicely."

"Yes, it's a very nice rock," Finn said, impatient. "What now?"

"Now," the diviner said, "we ask for an audience with the gods."

A small table from the diviner's parlor had been brought into the chamber along with three chairs. This way, they could place the slab of larimar in the center of the table and hold hands around it, using it as a conduit.

The diviner held out her hands, looking at Alfie and Finn expectantly.

Sweat gathered at Alfie's temples. What if the divining told them that they had no hope of defeating Sombra? Or what if the diviner was wrong and having Finn here didn't make a difference? What if he still had no future?

"Hey," Finn said. "Why so nervous?"

Alfie knew that she must be anxious too, though she wasn't one to show it.

She held out her hand, a smirk on her lips. "Have you never held a girl's hand before?"

Alfie twined their fingers, her callused palm anchoring him. He held her gaze, wanting to speak but knowing better. The room was full of dueños, all waiting to hear the reading. There was no privacy whatsoever, but he hoped she understood what holding her hand meant to him. What last night had meant to him.

Paloma moved to stand behind Alfie, her hand on his shoulder. Finn's gaze darted away, her eyes trained on the larimar.

"Prince Alfehr," the diviner said, wiggling her fingers. Finn had already taken her other hand. "If you please?"

"Sorry," Alfie said awkwardly. His hand had looked so small in hers when she'd divined him as a child. Now his overtook hers, eclipsing it.

The diviner took a breath before she spoke. "Today I will divine the shared destiny of Prince Alfehr and Finn Voy. The weight of this destiny is vast, for it is intertwined with the fate of this world. I ask the gods to deliver this prophecy to me with the guidance we need to save the world from Sombra's grasp."

The diviner guided their hands to the larimar, and Alfie shivered as his palm touched the cool, smooth surface of the rock.

The diviner breathed deeply, sitting completely still with her eyes closed. Alfie kept expecting the quiet to end, but minutes went by. Finn shot him a look, but Alfie could only shrug. His childhood divining hadn't taken this long, but then again his divining hadn't been as important back then. Alfie's face went hot under the gaze of everyone in the room waiting to hear a great prophecy only to hear silence.

"Are we supposed to do something?" Finn whispered at him.

"I don't know." Alfie glanced at Paloma for an answer, but she had none. "She didn't say—"

The diviner gasped, her head falling back so that Alfie was staring at the underside of her chin instead of her face. His spine straightened as a surge of heat ran through the stone and through his fingers.

Finn was struggling in her seat, trying to jerk away from the table, but Alfie couldn't pull their hands apart if he tried. It was as if their skin was magnetic.

"What's happening?" Finn asked. She leaned her chair back and pressed her feet against the edge of the table, pushing away with all her might, but the table did not budge. "Why can't we let go?"

"Don't fight it," Paloma said as the larimar began to glow.

Finn shot her a look. "Easy for you to say!"

The diviner's head snapped forward, her eyes glowing blue to match the larimar. When she opened her mouth, the voice that emerged was not her own.

> A boy of many colors and a girl of many faces,
> born to release Sombra and end his reign.
> Together they will journey under dragon's wing
> to seek him out from head to foot,
> with shadows nourished to aid the fight.
> Before the shared day that each claims as their own,
> must they face that which is most feared
> and restore balance through sacrifice,
> lest Sombra's darkness devour all.

The diviner's head flopped forward, her chin against her chest.

The glow died out, the slab of larimar lying lifeless on the table once again.

Alfie, Finn, and the dueños were left in a stunned silence as the clock struck midnight.

The diviner gave a yawn, raised her head, and opened her eyes. "Well." She surveyed the shocked expressions around her. "That was quite a lot of information, wasn't it?"

A STREAM OF STARLIGHT

Dezmin knew what he'd done.

He had only wanted to go home. But instead he'd slaughtered the light and thrown the world into chaos.

And what more fitting punishment than to be trapped within his own body, forced to watch his home collapse, taking all he loved with it.

He had been so lost that the promise of seeing his family again had blinded him, made him ignore every instinct inside him to bask in the light, not snuff it out.

No, that wasn't right. He knew that killing the light was wrong, but in that moment he had cared more about being set free.

Did that make him evil or simply human?

He didn't know the answer, but it hardly mattered. He was still trapped inside his own body, watching as Sombra sat on the throne of his empty palace, weak and weary.

The current of the god's power surged inside Dezmin's body, and he felt the pain of it in countless stings, like the snap of a whip against his flesh. It tugged at him, trying to change his course, to make him part of it. But Dezmin refused. He fought to keep his mind clear, his thoughts separate from Sombra's, distinct. It was as if he were drawing boundaries in sand and Sombra was a wave, washing it away each time, leaving Dezmin to carve out another, then another. Dezmin leaned into the pain of it, the punishment that he'd earned for himself when he snuffed out the light in exchange for his own freedom.

"You know," Sombra said, and it took a moment for Dezmin to realize that the god was actually addressing him. Sombra hadn't spoken to him since they'd left the void. "Your existence does not have to be one of suffering and mediocrity. You are fighting the natural way of things—the dominant force absorbing the submissive. Let go. Let yourself become a part of me. You will live an endless life of glory instead of struggling to preserve your own pathetic existence."

Dezmin wanted to insist that he would never give in, but the promise of disappearing into nothing, of leaving this guilt behind, was tempting. Was that the appropriate punishment for what he'd done? To give up and dissolve into nothing until he became one with the enemy?

"Your whimpering is becoming repetitive." Blood leaked from the corners of Sombra's mouth, and the wound in his palm still wept. He hadn't recovered from the strain of building this palace, and Dezmin could feel the god's frustration bubbling up. "I have more important matters to attend to than your melancholy. Suffer if you wish, but do so silently."

Thanks to his newly built fortress high above the city, Sombra was safe from any who might wish him harm. But he was furious.

He was a god; hurting him shouldn't even be *possible*.

The ceiling of the palace was transparent. Sombra had wanted the gods who abandoned him to have a good view of his success, his destruction of the world that they held so dear. But now they would only see his failure.

Dezmin felt Sombra's thoughts race. Were they laughing at him from their celestial thrones? Did they know why he was suddenly weak?

Crack.

Sombra's grip on the arms of the throne grew so tight that they cracked under his fingers—though they re-formed in the blink of an eye. Just that ounce of magic brought a blood-spattering cough rumbling from his chest. Before Sombra could continue his tirade, a shudder rolled up his spine. The sensation was overwhelming, gripping both Sombra and Dezmin in its fist, familiar and terrifying all at once.

"The gods," Sombra breathed.

There was no human equivalent; none of the senses could describe it. Sombra simply *felt* it, so Dezmin felt it too. Its presence drew Sombra's gaze upward.

Sharing the same eyes, Dezmin and Sombra watched a flash of blue streak across the sky—a blue the shade of larimar.

He watched the light fall in a perfect arc to the palace.

"They asked the gods for an audience," Sombra whispered. "And the gods acquiesced."

Sombra's mind was alight. His old comrades were telling his enemies how to defeat him. They were all working against him, whispering behind their hands as he struggled.

He might be too weak to storm the palace and demand answers, but he needed to know. Any advantage, any bit of knowledge that they had garnered, he needed to have as well.

"I will pluck the secrets from that boy's body and discard the rest," Sombra said. Scenario after scenario unfurled—Sombra stripping the flesh from Alfie's bones until he spoke, Sombra plucking his brother's golden eyes from his skull . . .

No! Stop! Please don't hurt him. Do what you want with me but don't hurt him, Dezmin begged, finally finding his voice after his own guilt had silenced him for so long. But even to Dezmin himself it was scarcely a whisper, the equivalent of a fly buzzing beside a lion's ear.

"Hush," Sombra said, his voice sharp. "A mere human cannot demand anything from a god. A human can only pray to one. And I will bring this world, your brother included, to its knees in prayer."

Dezmin felt Sombra push him back, farther and farther into the recesses of his own body. It was as if the house had expanded upward and the attic where Dezmin was shackled had risen even farther from the ground, from the door, from escape.

HOPE

"I trust that you have the answers you need," the diviner said, calm and unbothered, as if the gods hadn't just seized her voice as their own and delivered a prophecy.

"*Qué?*" Finn wanted to hurl the slab of larimar out the window. "What do you mean?" As far as she was concerned, the diviner had spouted some pretty words, but nothing more.

"The gods would not offer a prophecy that you could not decipher," the diviner said.

"No real information on how to take out Sombra. Nothing of value," Finn complained.

"That's not true," Alfie said. "It said that a boy of many colors and a girl of many faces must stop Sombra. So we know it's our destiny."

"That was already obvious," Finn said.

"It also stated that you two must 'seek him out from head to foot.' Further confirmation that you must go after Sombra's relics, and the order in which you must find them."

"Do the dueños at least know which kingdom hid which piece?" Alfie asked Paloma. He tried to keep his voice calm, but Finn could see the panic in his eyes. "I don't want to waste any time when we go find them."

Paloma nodded, looking relieved to know something. "We do. Sombra's head is in Uppskala, his torso in Englass, his arms were here, his legs in Weilai, and his feet in Ygosi."

"I believe the gods also revealed why *propios* have been altered," Dueño Bruno said, a pensive look on his bearded face.

"Then speak up," Finn said. Paloma had said Sombra destroying the balance wouldn't affect *propios*, but clearly she'd been wrong. Her own *propio* wasn't even working, but apparently everyone else's was enhanced.

"The fifth line of the prophecy—shadows nourished to aid the fight."

"Our shadows." Alfie blinked. "As in our moving shadows."

Paloma cocked her head, considering. "The gods must have built this fail-safe in case Sombra ever fully returned. The only people who can naturally defy his will and oppose him are those with *propios*. They have altered your gifts to give you the best chance of winning."

Finn crossed her arms, not wanting to admit that her own abilities were weakened. "But they strengthened a bunch of pendejos too. Like the Tattooed King."

"It's not the gods' way to favor a few individuals over all," Eduardo, the snooty dueño, said. "So they granted it to all who have *propios*. It works in your favor and against it—balance. Be thankful that they did this at all."

"He's right," Paloma said before Finn could insult the dueño's long nostril hairs. "This is the balanced way to do it. Such is their way."

Alfie caught her gaze. "It's better than nothing."

Finn couldn't help but wonder how his *propio* had changed. And why wasn't hers working?

"Fine, but the prophecy didn't mention anything about facing Sombra head-on," Finn said. "What are we supposed to do when we have the relics? Recite the pretty prophecy at him?"

Alfie's brow furrowed. "That's true. We still don't know much about what to do with him. We don't know why he bled in the ballroom or why he's holed up in his palace in the sky."

The air in the chamber stilled.

"You saw Sombra bleed?" Dueño Bruno asked. All eyes swiveled to Alfie and Finn.

It was an easy thing to forget with everything else that had happened today.

"Yeah," Finn said. "I saw it up close and personal when I stabbed him through the hand."

"Explain everything that happened," Paloma demanded.

"Well, first he arrived and killed the Englassen royal family. Then he unleashed the dark, blackened the sky, and turned shadowless. After that he taunted us for a bit before summoning his relics from the vault." Alfie rubbed the back of his neck. "Then he started to bleed. First from his nose, without any of us touching him. And again when Finn stabbed him."

The dueños were already conferring among themselves, and Finn wished the old fools would speak up.

"So it happened just after he put the arms on?" Paloma asked.

"Yeah," Finn said, tracking their train of thought. "But how would putting on his own arms hurt him? Last time, once he had possession of his arms, he grew more powerful." Finn grimaced. That was when Ignacio had become a dragon, an unimaginable feat of magic.

"But things are different now," Paloma said, understanding seeming to dawn on her. She walked back to the scales. "When Sombra was last here, the world's balance was still intact."

"Yeah, yeah, yeah. We know," Finn sighed. "How does that explain him being weakened? Wouldn't the balance being destroyed in favor of the dark only make him stronger?"

"Not necessarily," the diviner chimed in. "The darkness will lend strength to his stone relics . . . but perhaps now they carry too much power for a mortal body to hold."

Alfie stiffened in his chair. "You mean it's hurting Dezmin?"

Paloma looked at him solemnly. "It makes sense. The only difference between then and now is that the balance of light and dark has been disrupted. The pieces are too powerful now to be worn by a human body. Sombra needs to don all of them at once to transform Dezmin's body into his immortal form, but until then he's forcing a mortal to carry pieces of a god, pieces that are much more powerful than those Ignacio carried months ago."

"It's killing him," Alfie said, his voice shaking. "The weight of it is killing Dezmin. That's why he bled."

Finn rose and reached for his shoulder, unsure of what to say. She could feel him shaking under her fingers. "Then what do we do to stop this?"

"We take advantage of the fact that in his weakened state, Sombra can't retrieve the rest of his relics on his own. We follow the rest of the prophecy to the best of our knowledge." Paloma looked at Alfie. "The only way to end Sombra's reign and save Dezmin is to follow the words of the gods."

Alfie leaned into Finn's grip and recited the prophecy to himself once more, his brow furrowing as he tried to uncover the meaning behind the words.

"What about the dragon part?" Finn asked. "Journey under dragon's wing or something."

The room was silent.

"Maybe it'll be clearer to us later," Alfie offered.

Finn quirked a brow. The prince was not one to just hope they'd figure things out along the way. He always insisted on a plan before acting.

"What other choice do we have?" Alfie said, reading her mind. He and Paloma met eyes, and Finn had the feeling they'd spoken about this earlier. "We can't waste time trying to figure it all out now while Dezmin suffers—while the world suffers."

"All right," Finn conceded, not wanting to worry him any more than he already was.

"There's still the final line," Paloma said. "The prophecy states that you have until 'the shared day that each claims as their own' to save this world?"

That sounded like a deadline—if so, they would do well to find out when it was.

"I'm not sure . . . ," Alfie said, cocking his head in thought.

Finn chewed the inside of her cheek. "Maybe the day we met?

But who remembers that?"

Without hesitation, Alfie said the date.

Finn stared at him.

"I have a good memory," he said a bit too quickly.

"Regardless," Paloma said. "That would mean we have months to stop this. Sombra would never move so slowly."

"What does it even mean? There's no day that anyone can own. Not even you royals are rich enough to buy one." Finn squinted at him. "Wait, *can* you buy a day?"

"Hold on," Alfie said, his brow furrowing. He turned to Finn. "When is your birthday?"

Finn named the day with a shrug. When everyone turned and looked at her, she crossed her arms, face growing hot under everyone's stare. "What?"

"That's *my* birthday," Alfie said.

Finn blinked at him.

She'd been aware that when she was little the clocks in her pueblo would always chime on her birthday. Her father had always told her that it was for her. But, of course, as she grew older she learned it was because she shared a birthday with a prince. She hadn't thought of it in years. Ignacio didn't like it when she celebrated her actual birthday. He told her that her true birthday was the day she met him. Even after Ignacio was dead, it didn't feel right to reclaim that day. After all, she wasn't the girl she was before Ignacio had sunk his claws into her. It didn't make sense to go back to it. She took to considering herself birthdayless rather than choose another day.

"I wouldn't be surprised if you two were born at the very same time," Lucila said knowingly. "Down to the minute."

Alfie looked at Finn, a question brewing in his eyes. "I'm told I was born just after—"

"Midnight," Finn said, knowing what he was going to say. Her parents had told her that she'd clearly wanted an early start to the day. She'd arrived just after the stroke of midnight.

"Your birthday is only six days from today," Paloma said gravely.

"Six days," Finn murmured. She could taste the impossibility of it on her tongue.

Six days was hardly long enough to plan a heist, let alone save the world. The shattered moon gleamed weakly in the sky. Finn forced herself to look away.

"While you two retrieve the relics"—Paloma looked over her shoulder at the dueños behind her—"my colleagues and I have a plan that we hope will tell us how to defeat Sombra once the relics are in our possession."

"How?" Alfie asked, looking grateful for the help.

"While you were indisposed," Paloma said to him, "we decided to seek answers from our brethren. As you know, after the gods cast Sombra from the heavens, it was the world's first dueños who trapped him in the rings of magic."

Finn nodded. It was a story every Castallano child knew. "Yeah, but they're all dead and gone. How could they help us?"

"Wait," Alfie said, his eyes widening. "Do you have a way to speak to them?"

"Possibly, yes." Dueño Bruno stepped forward to stand beside Paloma. "It's part of every dueño's journey to make a pilgrimage to a sacred oasis, one connected to the dueños of the past."

"It's usually only done on certain holy days, but there's no time to wait for that," Paloma said. "And now that the world's balance has been upended, perhaps the veil between us and the dueños of the past has become thinner."

"Every dueño gets to talk to dueño ghosts from centuries ago?" Finn asked. She'd always thought of them as boring, bookish people, but that actually sounded exciting.

"Not quite," Paloma said. "We can often feel their presence at the sacred spring or, in very rare cases, feel their guidance. But, again, the world does not follow the rules of logic anymore. Perhaps we can use that to our advantage and speak to them directly, just as we spoke to the gods tonight."

"The dueños will know how to defeat Sombra and free Dezmin." Alfie leaned forward in his seat, his eyes bright with hope. She could see him clinging to it by the very tips of his fingers—hope for the world, hope for Dezmin. "I know it."

Finn looked away from the prince. Her life had taught her to know better than to hope so unabashedly. Alfie was different, and she liked that about him, but if there was no way to save his brother she'd have to watch his faith come crashing down. She wasn't sure if she could bear that. She glanced at Paloma. From the look on the dueña's face, Finn knew she was thinking the very same thing.

They still didn't even know *how* Sombra had destroyed the balance from the void. As far as Finn was concerned, they were going in blind and unarmed.

"While you and Finn search for the pieces of Sombra's body, we will take our pilgrimage to the sacred spring to commune with the ancient dueños," Paloma said. "Gods willing, you will return with his relics, and we will return knowing how to use them to defeat him."

Finn rolled her eyes. The gods had already made it clear that they weren't going to be of much help from here on out. They'd have to handle this themselves, and Finn preferred it that way. She didn't like the idea of fate and destiny, of lives written out before you were even born. It reeked of Ignacio and his puppet strings. She'd rather her life stay in her own hands, hers to save and hers to destroy.

But then again, according to the gods, fate had brought her to Alfie and him to her. So maybe it wasn't so bad. As the dueños talked among themselves, she stole a glance at him.

Dueño Bruno whispered something in Paloma's ear and she nodded in agreement. "Give us a moment to let our colleagues in the other kingdoms know what is to come. We'll regroup after and get ready for our respective journeys." She looked at Finn and Alfie. "You two look as if you could use a moment to rest."

Only after Paloma said that did Finn realize she was bone tired.

"You'd be surprised how exhausting an audience with the gods can be," the diviner said. Finn wondered if that was why the woman still hadn't risen from the table. Maybe she was too tired to move. "You must be relieved, Prince Alfehr."

Finn snorted. What on earth was there to be relieved about?

Alfie tilted his head. "What do you mean?"

The diviner looked at them both curiously, as if confused by how they couldn't see it. She repeated the first lines of the prophecy:

> *A boy of many colors and a girl of many faces,*
> *born to release Sombra and end his reign.*

When they said nothing, she shook her head in disbelief. "You don't see what this means?"

"It means we've got a lot of work to do," Finn said. "And very little help getting it done."

"Well, yes," the diviner reasoned. "But there's more. You two were born to defeat Sombra. And the only way to defeat him was to first *release* him." She looked at Alfie, her gray eyes softening. "I know you carry terrible guilt for releasing Sombra from his cage, but you were born to do it so that you could free the world from his evil for good. It was not simply an accident—it was your fate."

Alfie's eyes widened. "You're sure?" he asked, his voice shaking.

"I was the vessel through which the prophecy was spoken; I felt its meaning. Free yourself from the weight of that guilt, Prince Alfehr. You must travel light to save this world."

The diviner stood and walked out the door, leaving them to digest her words.

Finn had carried her fair share of guilt in her life, so a bit more these past few months hadn't done much to slow her, but for Alfie it was different. She could see life returning to his face, hope blooming in place of despair.

She smiled. Hope looked good on him.

"I thought this all happened because I was foolish and selfish, a future king who would only hurt his people," Alfie said. "But now, knowing everything that came before has led us to this . . . we'll never be able to make up for those we lost, but if we can complete this destiny, we can at least begin to balance the scales." Alfie took her hand. "All we lost won't be for nothing. We'll make the world a safer place for generations to come."

Finn's heart raced. She'd watched the prince die far too many times. She'd watched him die when he'd learned that the effort he'd gone through for the peace summit had been in vain, had been a lie. He'd died again with his father. And again when his mother was dragged away into a dungeon. But now he was returning—resurrecting. And he looked so wonderfully alive.

Finn squeezed his hand. It seemed that hope was contagious, and as much as she wanted to resist, she let it sweep over her, flowing from the prince's fingers to hers. "Then we'll do it."

He met her gaze, and a slow warmth kindled in Finn's belly. They were the only two in the room now, and in the silence, the memory of the night before emerged—flickers of taste and sound and touch, shared breath, the soft juncture of his neck and shoulder where she'd bit him, so overwhelmed by pleasure that she needed to temper it by causing just a little bit of pain.

His eyes drifted down to her lips and Finn found herself leaning forward. Their noses brushed, the feeling somehow both familiar and forbidden.

Queen Amada's voice rang in her head:

You have brought my son nothing but violence and danger.

Finn pulled back, and Alfie flinched, startled by the sudden movement. Finn was overwhelmed by the desire to change her face, as if her body wasn't right anymore, as if her skin was itching from the inside out. But her *propio* was gone, and there was nowhere to hide.

"Finn," Alfie began, reaching for her hand. "Maybe we should talk about what hap—"

Luka burst through the doors, grinning. "All healed up and good to go!"

"And the Englassen boy?" Finn asked, hoping Alfie would forget if she rerouted the conversation quick enough. He was going to ask her to talk about their night together, but she wasn't ready.

She never would be.

"He's awake, but still resting. It's apparently very tiring to have your leg broken in three places by a paint tiger." Luka pulled up a chair beside them. "Now tell me all about your date with the gods."

THE PREPARATION

"So the Tattooed King almost murdered me thanks to the gods powering up everyone's *propio* to give you a better chance at stopping Sombra?" Luka asked.

Finn nodded. "Yup."

"And to reverse Nocturna and stop the world from ending, we have to go fetch Sombra's limbs while Paloma and the others ask the ancient dueños about how we stop him for good?" Luka asked. "And we still have no clue *how* Sombra was able to do what he did from Xiomara's void?"

"Yes and yes, but it has to be just me and Finn who retrieve the relics," Alfie said gently. "It's part of the prophecy—the two of us have to do that part alone."

"Oh," Luka said, his face falling. "I see."

"It's not by choice, Bathtub Boy," Finn reassured him, a smirk curving her lips. "If it *was* by choice I still wouldn't let you join us, but I'm just saying it's not by choice."

Luka snorted. "Thank you, Finn."

"You're welcome," she said diplomatically.

Alfie would be lying if he didn't admit he was a little relieved that Luka wouldn't be in harm's way. He had a feeling his journey with Finn would be perilous, and he didn't want Luka to get caught in Sombra's crossfire again. Even in Sombra's weakened state, Alfie doubted Luka would be lucky enough to come out unscathed a second time.

"Rest assured that you will have your own role to play, Master Luka," Paloma said as she walked through the doors, closely followed by Bruno and Eduardo. They seemed to be the most senior of the dueños. "We will need all the help we can get on our own journey."

"Of course," Luka said, trying to hide his disappointment. "I'm just a bit tired of watching you walk into danger without me." He shrugged and sighed. "But I know better than to defy a prophecy from the gods."

Alfie wanted to say the right thing to make Luka feel better, but the dueños were looking at him expectantly, as if they had information to impart. "Did you connect with the dueños from the other kingdoms?"

Paloma shook her head. "We've lost all contact. My Uppskalan colleague has not responded since Sombra's return." Alfie could tell she was anxious about Svana, who Finn called Paloma's girlfriend. "We have always kept in good contact regarding the state of magical affairs in this world, but now there is only silence. I fear they are in no condition to contact us at the moment."

Castallan had the advantage of having experienced Sombra's return once before, but the other kingdoms were likely less prepared.

Were any of the international dueños even still alive? Alfie felt Finn's eyes on him before he turned to look at her. She knew he was nervous. But then, everyone probably knew. He didn't hide it very well.

"So what's our next step?" Finn said, pushing the conversation forward. "How are we getting to Uppskala, or anywhere else for that matter?"

Bruno stepped forward. "We think Prince Alfehr's *propio* may be the key to your travel. As we learned from the prophecy and Master Luka's encounter with the Tattooed King, the gods have enhanced *propios* to aid you on your journey. It stands to reason that yours has evolved as well."

Alfie nodded. It wasn't an outlandish assumption to make. He couldn't imagine his *propio* being able to take him and Finn across oceans, but then again, he'd never imagined having an audience with the gods either.

"Unfortunately, the knowledge in this room is all we have." Paloma met Alfie's eyes, then Finn's. "You two will have to take the lead here. We cannot offer much help when it comes to your journey."

Silence swept the room. When he and Finn had last faced Sombra, Alfie had kept it from Paloma, but he'd always thought that maybe the dueños could've helped him if he'd been brave enough to tell them what he'd done. This time he'd turned to them for help instead of hiding, but there was nothing they could do.

Everything rested on his and Finn's shoulders.

Finn stood. "Then we'll figure it out." She eyed the dueños. "Don't you have your own journey to prepare for? Quit staring at us and get ready!"

"She's right," Paloma said, before Dueño Eduardo could object to Finn's tone. "Let us prepare and leave them to do their part."

The dueños shuffled out of the room grumbling, but Paloma stayed behind, her eyes on Alfie. "Remember to stay alert, and be mindful with your magic. Striking first is not always the best method."

Warmth bloomed in Alfie's chest. Paloma was so worried for him that she was parroting all the lessons she'd taught him as a child.

"I'll stay level-headed," Alfie assured her.

"I hope you will," she said, eyeing Finn.

The thief shifted uncomfortably.

"And remember that we have no idea what effect Sombra's relics have on their surroundings now that the balance has been destroyed. Be careful." She handed both Alfie and Finn satchels made of simple, sturdy fabric. "We've used the strongest magic we can muster to make these. They will stretch to hold anything you put in here, and when you place the relics themselves inside, they will be transported back here for safekeeping. Remember, *propios* are changing, magic is changing, the world is changing—and so anything is possible."

"Got it," Finn said with a nod when Alfie couldn't find it within himself to speak.

"And take this pocket watch to keep track of time until your birthday," Paloma said, handing Alfie a clock on a silver chain. She looked at Finn before correcting herself. "Birthdays. You'll need to stay aware of how much time you have left. The dueños and I have one as well."

Alfie looked at the watch's silver case before opening it. It looked normal on the outside, but within it was more than a normal clock. Of course it had the regular hands counting seconds, minutes, and hours, but above that was the month and date. He swallowed thickly. Six days was not very long at all.

Paloma looked as if she was coming up with any excuse to stay just a bit longer. "I wish you both luck." She paused, and Alfie could see regret in her gaze. "I wish I could be of more help to you."

Alfie's eyes burned. "You've been of service to me since the day I was born. Now it's my turn to serve. Leave this to us."

Paloma held his gaze for a long moment before nodding and shutting the doors behind her.

"So . . . ," Luka began. "Your best bet is that Alfie's *propio* has become powerful enough to take you all the way to another kingdom?"

Alfie kneaded his temples. "It seems impossible."

"That word doesn't even exist anymore," Finn said. "Not fully. Everything that's happened in the last few hours is 'impossible' by normal standards. Why not this too?"

Alfie cocked his head. She wasn't wrong.

"What do you plan to do once you get to Uppskala?" Luka asked. "How will you find Sombra's head?"

"Well, assuming the dueños are right and I can somehow use my *propio* to get us there, we'll use Sombra's blood to track it down— some got on Finn's shirt when she stabbed him."

Finn nodded, proudly displaying the bloodstained shirt she'd tucked into her satchel. She'd thought of that herself.

"In the meantime, we need to prepare," Alfie said. "Gather everything we need before we start trying to travel." When Finn looked confused, he added, "We'll need to pack weapons, food, and medicinal tonics. And we're going to Uppskala first—the last thing we need is to land in the frozen kingdom with no coats or boots to protect us."

"I've already got all the weapons from the armory that we could possibly need," Finn said, and Alfie believed her.

"Then I'll get healing draughts, any books I might need, the cloak, and anything else that might come to mind," Alfie said. He and Finn had used the vanishing cloak—a garment that rendered those who wore it invisible—to sneak about when they'd first released Sombra months ago. It could come in handy.

"And I've got something for you to take," Luka said. He handed Alfie a roll of parchment. "For us to keep in touch on our journeys. One for me and one for you."

Alfie smiled. Luka had magicked two pieces of parchment so that they could relay messages to each other. They'd done the same thing six months ago when Alfie and Finn had gone to free Xiomara from prison and Luka had stayed behind to masquerade as Alfie so no one would know the prince had skipped the Equinox Ball. And here they were again, at the beginning of another deadly journey to stop Sombra.

"Thank you," Alfie said.

Luka's eyes were shining when he looked away from Alfie. "I'll help you gather whatever you need for the trip."

"And I'll sleep," Finn added with a yawn as she made her way out the meeting chamber. She called over her shoulder. "Wake me when it's time to go."

Alfie just nodded. It was nearly three in the morning, and who knew when they would get a good night's sleep again.

As Alfie walked with Luka to the palace apothecary in silence, a painful twinge of nostalgia seized him. These halls were full of too many memories to count. Memories of the days when he, Dezmin, and Luka used to run about with wooden swords. Back when Paloma held all the answers and Alfie was certain he'd learn everything so long as he stuck by her side. How things had changed.

By the time they reached the apothecary, a small circular room that held shelves of draughts, salves, and medicinal powders, an untamable wave of emotion had welled up inside him, threatening to spill over. Alfie fought to keep it at bay.

"These will surely come in handy," Alfie said to break the silence as Luka watched him fumble with the bottles. Maybe if he just kept talking, he could ignore the thorny fear blooming inside him. He wouldn't have to think about his father lying dead in the burial chamber, or Dezmin left to suffer in a void only to be captured by a dark god, his body falling apart from the strain. If he kept talking, maybe Luka wouldn't feel the tension in the air, the fear of being in this room full of memories and the fear of leaving it and never seeing it again. "This one is great for burns, and this one is—"

"Alfie," Luka said quietly, catching his gaze. "It's all right."

Alfie met his cousin's gaze, and the pain in Luka's eyes sent him down the well of his own. He gripped the edges of the table and took in a shuddering breath. Luka didn't make him talk about it. He simply stood with Alfie and let him grieve what had happened and what was yet to come.

Alfie forced himself to stand upright, blinking to keep from weeping. He couldn't fall apart now.

When he'd collected everything he needed from the apothecary, and he could speak without his voice breaking, he turned to Luka. "There's something I need to do before I leave," Alfie said, his eyes burning. "I have to see her. Will you walk with me?"

Luka gripped him by the shoulders. "Of course."

Together they walked down a maze of tiled halls until they reached a quieter, less frequented part of the palace. The pair of dueños guarding the door stepped aside without question. The door opened to a flight of stairs that descended into the dark.

Alfie held tight to him, not ready to let go and make the walk to the dungeons.

"I can come with you," Luka said after a long moment. "You don't have to go alone."

Alfie forced himself to withdraw from the hug. "This is something I have to do on my own. I'll meet you in my rooms after."

Alfie couldn't walk down those stairs knowing that Luka was waiting for him. He wanted to do this his way, on his own time.

Luka opened his mouth, looking as if he wanted to argue, but instead he relented. "All right. I'll see you after, then."

With one last look from his cousin, Alfie stepped through the door and shut it behind him. Gooseflesh erupted over Alfie's skin as he walked down. The air in the dungeons was always so damp and clammy. But he supposed that was the point of a dungeon—to be uncomfortable. Unbearable, even.

His throat burned at the thought of his mother there, cold and alone.

He walked down a long aisle of iron-barred cells packed with Englassen and Castallano prisoners alike. Some shouted expletives at Alfie, threatening to finish the job that Prince Marsden had started. Others begged for help, pleading their innocence. Alfie hurried forward. Paloma had told him that his mother was being held in her own cell to keep her safe, a small comfort.

Tucked into the back of the dungeon was the final cell, and there, on the wet, dirty ground, sat his mother. Alfie's heart ached at the sight. Her red gown was in tatters. He could see a purple bruise forming on her forehead from Finn's headbutt. Her black hair was coated in dust and dirt, and Alfie couldn't help remembering when he was a boy, watching her comb through her wet, thick hair before scrunching it, encouraging the curls, the very same ones he carried.

Amada looked up, her black eyes meeting his gold.

"Alfie!" She ran to the bars, gripping them tight. "Have you come to release me, Mijo?"

It was that last, tender word that broke him. Hot tears slipped down his cheeks and nose. "I'm so sorry, Mamá." He choked back a sob.

She stared at him, unshed tears glistening as she waited for him to step forward and unlock the cell. When he didn't move, her face fell.

"Why would you do this to me?" Amada asked, gripping the bars, and Alfie fought the urge to demand she be released. He couldn't bear to see her cry. She was black-eyed and shadowless, but she was still his mother.

Alfie willed himself to speak. "I'm only doing this to protect you until we can make everything right again. I'm going to leave, and when I come back I'll fix everything."

"Leave? You won't survive!" She shook with panic. "You need

to stay here with your mamá, Alfie. Don't go, don't leave me here! I can't lose you, I'll have no one left."

"I have to." His words were quiet, hushed with pain. "I have no choice."

Her chest rose and fell rapidly, and Alfie watched the sorrow in her eyes morph into something darker. When she finally spoke, her voice was low and sharp. "It's always you who survives."

Alfie's spine stiffened. "What?"

"First Dezmin, then your father." She shook her head. "You've always been the weakest of us all, yet it's you who survives. It should've been you who died first."

Alfie's mouth went dry. "Mamá, please—"

"If you go out there, you'll die," she seethed.

"If I don't stop Sombra, the world will end," Alfie protested. "What do you expect me to do?"

"Stay here and die with me," Amada said, her gaze softening. "Stay here so I won't lose anyone else. We'll watch the world end together."

Alfie stared at her, shocked by her words. Stay here and let the world end? Let millions upon millions of people die? How could she ask that of him?

When Alfie didn't speak, Amada's face turned stony.

"You're not ready," she said as if it was a fact she regretted. "But you won't listen to your mother. You're going to go out there and get yourself killed. If it was your father or Dezmin who was left, then maybe there would be a chance, but not you, Mijo. Not you. I am *done* grieving my family. I am *tired*." She turned away from him. "If you walk out of this dungeon without me, you're no longer my son, no longer mine. And when you pass, I won't have to mourn the death of a stranger."

Alfie knew she was not in her right mind, but it was still *her* mind. This time, the shadowless had retained part of their old selves. So did part of her really believe these things? Did she wish he had disappeared instead of Dez? Did she think him so feeble and weak that he shouldn't even try to stop Sombra?

"Please don't say that," Alfie begged, his shadow stretching toward her.

Amada stepped back. "Get out."

"Mamá, please look at me," Alfie sobbed. "Please."

Amada walked to the back of her cell and faced the wall.

FROM KILLER TO KILLER

Finn's nose wrinkled as she walked into the infirmary.

She should be napping, but first she needed to do something. She wouldn't be able to sleep until she did. The infirmary stank of medicinal plants, balms, and salves. It made her think of every wound she'd ever had to treat while leaning against a piss-stained alley wall. She hadn't had the remedies in the glass-paned shelves of this room. All she'd had were her wits.

"Would've been nice," she mumbled as she passed a dark wood table where a dirty pestle and mortar lay. A dueño must've been here, grinding up something to heal the Englassen boy after he and Luka returned with the larimar.

Rows of beds with crisp white sheets filled the vast room. All empty, save for one.

At the sound of her footsteps James sat up, his leg wrapped and elevated. He looked around fearfully, raising himself onto his elbows. Finn wanted to laugh. The boy had murdered a handful of Castallano delegados and was chock-full of *propios*, but he was scared of her.

"Settle down," Finn said as she pulled up a chair to his bedside. Its legs scraped the floor with a grating screech. "I'm not here to kill you."

James looked at her skeptically before reclining onto the bed. "Then why are you here?"

"To talk."

"Forgive me." James cocked his head. "But you don't seem like the talking type."

"Usually I'm not, but I'm making an exception."

James didn't say anything. He fisted his hands in the white sheets and waited. In that moment Finn saw something in the boy that she hated—herself.

She saw the guilt squirming under his skin, burrowing into his bones. Ignacio had forced her to do many things that still haunted her to this day. Though she hadn't chosen to do them, it was still her hands that had poured the poison or held the blade, her clothes that were splattered with innocent blood.

What she'd done would stay with her forever.

The voice of Emeraude, an elderly thief lord who had mentored Finn until she was murdered by her fellow thief lords, bloomed in her mind, low and raspy with age.

We are all haunted houses, full of the ghosts of our pasts.

How she wished that that annoying dessert-obsessed vieja was still alive, but she could honor Emeraude's memory by helping James just as the abuela had helped her.

"Listen," Finn said. "From killer to killer, there's a life for you beyond this." James looked at her, a tentative hope in his eyes. "It doesn't seem like it now, but there is. Really."

"How?" he asked.

Finn shrugged. "You just need to find the right people."

"What people?" he asked as if this was a math problem with a specific, indisputable answer, but that was never the case when it came to the questions that mattered most.

Finn thought for a long moment. "The people who see you for what you could be instead of what you've done."

Silence settled between them. James's hands unfisted from the sheets.

"Do you think Prince Alfehr will ever forgive me?" he asked quietly, as if scared of the answer.

"He's soft," Finn said, and she hated how her voice became hushed when she spoke about him. As if she were whispering a secret behind her hand. "He needs time, but he'll forgive you eventually. He's forgiven worse people."

"Miss Finn—" he blundered. "Sorry, Señorita Finn."

"Just Finn," she corrected him, cringing at the formality in his voice.

"Finn." He held her gaze, and Finn could feel the gratitude rolling off him in waves. "Thank you."

"Uh-huh." Finn stood and stretched her arms over her head. "And Alfie will be more inclined to forgive if you keep his cousin safe. So I'll tell you what Luka has told me every time Alfie and I leave to do something life-threatening." Finn leaned over him, so close that their noses nearly brushed. "Bring him back in one piece or there'll be trouble."

The Englassen looked to be fighting the urge to burrow into the mattress. "Master Luka hardly needs me to protect him, but I'll be there to do it regardless," James said, a determined set to his jaw.

"Good," Finn said, satisfied. "Then I'll see you later, if I don't die."

With that, she turned on her heel and strode to the doors.

"Where are you going?" James called after her.

Finn didn't bother to turn back around. "To take a nap before we have to save the world. Again."

THE WISP

Dezmin had wallowed for long enough.

He'd let his sadness make him complacent. But now Sombra wanted to find out what Alfie had learned from his audience with the gods, and Dezmin had seen what Sombra was willing to do to his brother to get those answers.

He couldn't sit and stew in his own melancholy any longer.

He had to do something. He had to try.

He couldn't free himself from this prison, but what if there was a way to stop Sombra from inside his own body?

Dezmin focused, willing his body not to move when Sombra called upon it to, but it didn't even slow the god as he paced the throne room, muttering. Dezmin couldn't stop a single finger from moving. And Sombra didn't even seem to notice his attempt.

"If the gods are offering mere mortals an audience," Sombra seethed, "they will grant me one too, whether they like it or not."

Sombra flexed his fingers and Dezmin felt the power within him whip into a frenzy, battering him from the inside out. He felt the horrible pull of Sombra's power again as it tried to absorb him, swallow him whole. He was a fish trying to escape the gaping maw of a whale.

"They will bear witness to my greatness," Sombra said, and Dezmin could see that he was summoning every piece of larimar in the city to him. Shards of the stone were pulled out of the walls where they were inlaid, like teeth pulled from an unwilling mouth. Hidden pieces burst free of secret vaults in black market shops in the Pinch and the Brim. Necklaces and earrings flew out of jewelry boxes in the posh haciendas of the Crown.

Dezmin closed his eyes against the storm of power rushing around him, bleeding him dry of any energy he hoped to cling to. How much longer could he survive this? How could he help Alfie if he couldn't even slow Sombra down?

As the god's power whipped against him, rattling his bones, a thought struck him.

If Sombra's power could touch Dezmin, then could Dezmin touch it? Could he somehow use it as his own?

If he could capture a wisp of Sombra's power, perhaps he could somehow use it to tell Alfie that Sombra knew of their audience with the gods and that he was coming for them. He needed to warn them—and beyond all else, he needed to apologize for what he'd done.

Maybe this was his chance.

He sat shackled inside his own body, the flames of Sombra's power closing in on him from every angle—but he would rather burn himself reaching into the flames than simply wait for them to singe him.

Dezmin reached out with his mind and gripped a hot wisp of Sombra's power, stifling a scream of pain as it seared him. Sombra had stolen control over his physical body, but Dezmin could still move within the cage that Sombra had locked him in. The thread of power fought his grip, wriggling free before he could even hope to use it.

For a moment, Dezmin was afraid that Sombra heard his scream, but the god was so distracted that he didn't seem to notice.

Tentatively, Dezmin tried again but, just like before, the power burned his palm. He bit back a shout before letting it go. It bucked him off like a horse mounted by a stranger.

Sombra's magic did not see Dezmin as its master. It wouldn't let him take hold of it.

The god's words struck Dezmin, a bell of clarity ringing in his mind.

Your existence does not have to be one of suffering and mediocrity. You are fighting the natural way of things—the dominant force absorbing the submissive. Let go. Let yourself become a part of me. You will live an endless life of glory.

If he let himself begin to meld with Sombra, perhaps then the god's power might see him as its master. And, so long as Sombra himself didn't notice, he could use it to find a way to help Alfie.

Every fiber of Dezmin's being told him to fight the current of Sombra's power, to swim and not drown. But now he'd need to fight against his will to survive. He needed to feed parts of himself to Sombra.

He needed to let pieces of himself die.

Dezmin let the current pull him under. He held his breath,

choking in the whirlwind of Sombra's power. Strips of himself were being torn away, disappearing into the shadow of Sombra's might.

When he couldn't bear it for a moment longer, Dezmin swam back to the surface, breaking out of the undertow with a gasping breath. He gagged on the air, coughing painfully. He felt horribly light, a sliver of who he'd once been. So much of him had been lost.

Please let it be enough.

Dezmin tried again to reach for a wisp of Sombra's power. He closed his fist around it and this time it was no longer scorching hot, but warm. The wisp of power resisted only for a moment before calming in his grip. If Dezmin could have controlled his body, he would be sobbing.

"Go home," Dezmin whispered to the strand of power. "Please, go home."

As Sombra continued summoning the larimar, Dezmin willed the wisp to travel down from the palace in the sky and through the rings of the city. He guided it carefully, afraid that the thing would collapse, or worse, return to Sombra if he pushed too hard. All of Dezmin's senses were wrapped up in the wisp. He could feel the tendrils of wind graze it.

Beneath the shattered moon, it passed two boys in the Pinch who had been the best of friends but now fought until they bled, their minds addled by the jealousy and anger Sombra had unleashed. They fought until only one was left standing, and by the time it was over the survivor hardly remembered why they'd been fighting in the first place.

It passed through the Brim, where the Tattooed King's body lay still and skinless.

It passed through the Crown, where nobles had forgotten the delicate rules of high society, and were thieving and murdering instead.

Finally, the wisp found the yellowing greenery of the palace grounds. Dezmin saw through the wisp's eyes as it tapped against the magical barrier the dueños had placed around the palace.

"This is not Sombra," Dezmin murmured through the wisp, praying that the god wouldn't hear him. Now that he'd given some of himself to the god, he was magic itself, and he spoke to the protective spellwork around the palace like a friend. "It's Prince Dezmin. Please let me come home."

After a moment's hesitation, the barrier relented, and Dezmin slipped through the shattered windows of the ballroom, where the carnage of Sombra's arrival still covered the ground. Dezmin could feel the wisp fighting his guidance, yearning to return to Sombra like a dog resisting the pull of its leash. He needed to house it somewhere, in something he could control. He needed to combine the reach of Sombra's power with his own *propio*—bring an inanimate object to life and use it as a vessel for the magic. He tried to imbue a bloodied blade with the wisp, but it was too large, too unwieldy. Then there was a forgotten ring on the ground, but once Dezmin had settled the wisp into it, it was hard to get it to move. He'd nearly given up hope when there, among the corpses on the tiled floor of the ballroom, lay the very toy dragon Dezmin had made for Alfie to guard him from his nightmares.

It was simply good luck.

Dezmin guided the wisp into the dragon. At first it resisted, ricocheting around the inside, but as Dezmin soothed it the wisp calmed, settling into the toy. The dragon gave a long stretch, as if waking from a deep sleep. Dezmin wanted to marvel and sob at the feeling of even a small piece of himself coming home to the palace where he'd been raised, but there was no time. He had to focus. He needed to find Alfie. Needed to tell his family that Sombra knew of their audience with the gods and was coming for them with everything he had.

Under his command, the dragon moved slowly, its tiny feet making little headway in the gargantuan hall. It was too far away now—he was losing connection to the toy. Dezmin could feel the wisp of Sombra's power fading. He must not have taken enough. The toy fell still.

Dezmin wanted to keep trying, but Sombra was finishing summoning the larimar. He had to let go of the toy or, now that Sombra was no longer distracted, he might see what he'd been up to. He'd failed.

"What's this?"

The dragon had not reached Alfie, but it had reached someone. Luka bent over and picked up the figurine.

The last thing Dezmin saw through the dragon's eyes before the connection faded to nothing was his beloved cousin's face. How he wished he could embrace him and tousle his hair.

How he wished he could embrace anyone at all.

Dezmin's mind returned to Sombra's palace. The cloud walls of the throne room were inlaid with every piece of larimar in Castallan, a shimmer of blue nestled into the billowing walls. It would be beautiful if it hadn't been made by the hands of someone so awful.

"The gods will see me just as clearly as they saw those mortals,"

Sombra said. "Whether they like it or not."

His breath ragged, Sombra dragged his weary body to the throne and slumped in the black chair, releasing a cough that sent blood splattering onto his lap. Expending the magic to summon the larimar had left Dezmin's body in shambles.

"I am meant to wield power and magic," Sombra said. "Why is it hurting me?"

Dezmin hoped Sombra would never learn why using his magic was having this effect on him. Hoped that the god would just keep using it until Dezmin's bones collapsed into dust.

He hoped that using a wisp of Sombra's power to try to find Alfie had contributed even one drop to the blood that passed his lips with that painful cough.

Dezmin smiled. The god did not know it, but Dezmin was fighting.

And he was drawing blood.

THE HYPOTHETICAL

As Finn left the infirmary, she couldn't get Paloma's voice out of her head.

If you intend to hurt him, wait until the mission is complete.

The dueña had said "if," but Finn knew that it was more of a "when." Everyone, Queen Amada included, seemed to believe that she had no business being anywhere near the prince, and part of her agreed, had always agreed. That was why she'd packed her things and left in the first place. And now she'd been prophesied to help him save the entire world.

If the gods had really handpicked her and Alfie for this, they'd only been half right, and if it went poorly, she knew whose fault it would be.

Finn clenched her jaw. How she wished she could change her face and hide from how she felt for just a moment. She'd intended to go take a nap after talking to the Englassen boy, but her feet kept carrying her in listless circles, her shadow darting about in frustrated arcs.

"Señorita!" a gravelly voice called.

Finn rolled her eyes and looked over her shoulder. Dueño Bruno was trailing her from the end of the hall, his beard bouncing as he moved. In his arms was a mound of something red.

"Paloma asked that you have armor for your journey."

Finn frowned at the sight. This was the armor that the red capes, the Castallano guards, wore. There was something blasphemous about wearing their uniform, but then again, there was also something blasphemous about Sombra returning and the moon cracking like an egg.

"Fine," she groused, snatching it from him.

"Very well," Bruno said hurriedly. He gave a nod of deference and turned to leave.

"Wait!" Finn said. "I have a question. Hypothetically speaking . . . can *propios* stop working?"

He shook his head. "No; as Paloma said, they are sacred and exist outside the balance of magic. Not even Sombra's return could take them away." The man cocked his head. "However, perhaps if someone else's *propio* was the ability to stifle other people's *propios*—"

"Yeah, yeah, I know," Finn said. She didn't need to be reminded of how the gangster Kol had once blocked her *propio*. "That's not the kind of situation I'm talking about. I'm talking about if, hypothetically, someone's *propio* just stopped working. Not because of anyone else's magic. It just stopped working on its own. Hypothetically."

Bruno stared at her, his eyes flickering down to her shadow.

"Are you saying—"

"I am *saying*." Finn raised her voice over his. "That I am curious about this particular hypothetical."

"Right, of course." He cleared his throat. "*Propios* are intrinsic to one's specific personality, their soul. It's tied to emotion, to memory. There have been instances in which an internal blockage may lead to one's *propio* not working."

An internal blockage? Finn sighed through her nose. What did that even mean?

"Okay, well, hypothetically, would you have any potions to fix that blockage thing?"

"You misunderstand me," Bruno said carefully, and Finn remembered that he was the nice one. Dueño Eduardo with the nostril hair had been the rude one. "I mean an emotional blockage, and such things can only be fixed through introspection and—"

Finn was done listening. "Great," she huffed, walking around the dueño, the red armor in her arms. She had to feel her maldito feelings to use magic and now she had to feel them to get her *propio* to come back too? She bit the inside of her cheek to stop herself from screaming.

"Have I said something to offend you?" the dueño called after her.

"Yes!" Finn shouted back, leaving him bewildered in the hallway.

THE PLAN

Before seeing his mother, Alfie had been full to the brim with so many emotions—fear, anxiety, disappointment.

Now he felt nothing.

After leaving the dungeons, he'd found Luka in his rooms and wept until his throat grew raw and his head pounded, trying to exorcise the shame that had burrowed so deeply inside him. Luka could do nothing but rub his back and murmur words of comfort.

Eventually he stopped crying, falling into a somber silence. He had thought he'd need to collect himself before he met Finn to leave on their journey, but he found that there was nothing left to collect. His mother's words had wrung every emotion out of him, leaving him hollow. He thought of how the human body went into shock during extreme pain, to protect itself from feeling anymore. Could that happen to your heart too?

Alfie changed into his father's flexible leather armor, black and trimmed with gold. King Bolivar had always said war was something to mourn, and mourning colors would never be more fitting than they were today.

Alfie had never worn armor before, never thought he'd need it for anything other than ceremonial purposes, but here he was.

When he and Luka returned to the meeting chamber, they found Finn asleep on the chaise, lying with one arm over her head and her palm flat on her stomach. She was wearing similar armor, too well made to be hers. Alfie wondered who had given it to her.

He reached out and touched a soft, dark curl. He didn't want to wake her. Not when reality had become such a harsh place.

"Hey." Alfie squatted next to the chair. "Levántate."

Finn jerked awake so quickly she nearly headbutted him.

At the sight of Alfie, her shadow calmed. "Sorry about that. I always wake up ready for a fight. Old habits die hard."

"It's all right."

Finn looked at him and then at Luka, her gaze sharp and assessing. "You went to see your mother."

His throat burning, Alfie nodded. He felt Luka squeeze his shoulder from behind.

"She said terrible things to him," Luka said.

Finn was silent, her fingers tugging at loose threads in the chaise. "I know what it's like to hear someone who's supposed to love you tell you that they wish you were dead."

Alfie watched her, his heart heavy as his shadow stretched toward her. Of course she'd experienced it. Ignacio likely had said such things to her daily.

"But those weren't your mother's words. That wasn't your

mother," Finn said. "It was someone else. Someone manipulated by Sombra's magic."

"But what if the dark magic made her speak her true feelings?" Alfie said, his voice breaking. "What if that's how she's felt all along, and Sombra's influence only brought it to the surface?"

"You don't know that," Finn insisted. "No one can say what thoughts have ever crossed anyone else's mind. And even if she did think it, every thought we have isn't actually how we always feel. It's just a thought. It doesn't have to mean everything. Or anything at all."

Alfie looked away from her. She was right; there was no way to know if his mother's words came from her heart or from Sombra's corruption. Still, he couldn't forget the sound of her echoing all his worst insecurities back to him.

"Prince, you are letting one day eclipse a whole lifetime," Finn said. "Before today, before all of this, did your mother spend her life loving you?"

Alfie didn't hesitate. "Yes."

"Then she loves you." She said it with a certainty that Alfie envied.

Relief poured through him, and Alfie couldn't stop himself from pulling her into a tight embrace, lifting her off her feet as he buried his face in her neck.

In the blink of an eye the world had become such a fearful place. Magic had changed for the worse and a dark god was threatening to cast the world in his shadow, yet what had taken the most from him was the loss of his mother's love, sending him adrift in an already turbulent sea. Finn's words had found him and brought him home, if only for a moment.

"Thank you," he murmured.

"You still say that too much." Finn ran her fingernails over his back in smooth circles, something she'd learned that he liked during their night together—even when she comforted him, she always did it with a slight edge. "You've got me defending a woman who tried to murder me this morning. What a time to be alive."

Alfie barked a laugh. It shouldn't have been funny, but somehow it was.

He squeezed her tighter. "I don't say 'thank you' too much. You still haven't heard it enough, and I'm working to remedy that."

As he held Finn, her words still ringing in his ears, Alfie couldn't help but wonder what she felt for him. He wondered if last night had confirmed something for her the way it had for him. No, not confirmed—that made it seem as if Alfie had been questioning his feelings before. Part of him had already known, but last night had let sunlight illuminate his feelings. Revealing them, not confirming.

Did she feel the same?

"So," Luka said, crossing his arms and tapping his foot. "Is this a lovers-only hug or a friendship hug?"

Alfie choked on his spit.

"Cállate," Finn grumbled before stepping away from Alfie, gripping Luka by the collar, and pulling him into the embrace.

The dueños and the diviner had left the meeting chamber, but the slab of larimar still lay on the table. It looked so strikingly normal now. As if it had never channeled the voices of the gods.

When they finally broke away from the hug, silence swaddled the room.

One would think there would be great ceremony to the departure of two people prophesied to either save the world or die trying. But that kind of thing was for children's storybooks. Most of the dueños were busy renewing the warding magic that kept the shadowless away. There was no time for hand-holding. Only three people in a room, waiting for the most perilous journey of their lives to begin.

Alfie and Finn slipped boots and sealskin cloaks over their armor to keep them warm in the Uppskalan cold.

"How will you begin?" Luka asked, his eyes darting between Alfie and Finn.

"Last night, we learned that Finn could travel through the magic with me so long as we match shades," Alfie explained.

"Last night, eh?" Luka winked, and Alfie felt his face grow hot. "What else did you learn?"

"Don't be jealous, Bathtub Boy," Finn chided.

Luka gagged.

"Both of you hush," Alfie said, embarrassed. "When I match the colors of our magic, it tricks the magic into seeing Finn as an extension of me," he explained. "Once we enter, we'll see if things have changed . . . if my abilities have changed."

It sounded ridiculous as he said it, but they'd learned from the prophecy that their *propios* had been strengthened to help them in their battle against Sombra. It would only make sense that his ability to travel would be stronger now—but would it come with a price, like the Tattooed King sacrificing his own flesh for his art?

"Makes sense," Luka said weakly, clearly unsure of what else to say.

More silence. Finn picked at her nails, her eyes lowered.

Alfie realized that no one wanted to say goodbye.

His throat burned.

"You'll be careful?" he asked Luka.

"Absolutely not." Luka shook his head. "But I'll make it back in one piece." He gripped Alfie's shoulder and pulled him into a fierce hug. "You have to be careful, though. So careful."

"I will," Alfie said, his voice rough with emotion. "I will."

"As usual, I'm depending on you to bring him back," Luka said to Finn over Alfie's shoulder.

"This is our third go-round," Finn sighed. "Doesn't my track record speak for itself?"

Luka stepped back, and Alfie could tell from his roughness that it had taken effort to let go. The ultimate struggle was watching the ones you loved walk away to a place where you could not follow. It was why Alfie hated goodbyes. Why he preferred to steal away into the night.

"I should go, then," Luka said, stepping toward the door.

Every step he took pierced Alfie's chest more deeply.

"Wait." Luka strode over to Alfie, holding something the prince had never thought he'd see again. When he carefully placed it on Alfie's palm, it was as if a ghost had been dropped back into the world of the living.

The toy dragon on its chain.

"I thought you should have it," Luka said. "I found it just outside the ballroom. It must've been left behind when . . ." Luka didn't finish, his face grave.

Alfie swallowed thickly. It made sense that the dragon would have returned to their world when Sombra did. After all, it was in that very vessel that he and Finn had trapped the dark god. Sombra had hatched from his egg and left the shell.

The toy had brought Alfie hope and courage long ago when Dezmin had told him to wear it to ward off nightmares. And it had given him the bravery to trap Sombra once before. Maybe, just maybe, it would give him the bravery he needed again.

"I'll leave you both to it," Luka said, but before he could step away again, Alfie pulled him into another hug.

"I love you," Alfie said. "I'll be back."

"Te amo," Luka said. "And you'd better be."

Finn gave him a nod. "See you soon, Bathtub Boy."

Luka shot her a wan smile. "Don't be late."

Luka strode out of the room, rubbing his eyes with the back of his hand as he closed the doors behind him.

Alfie let the tears slip down his nose for he didn't know how long, until he saw Finn's shadow reaching out toward him on the floor like an outstretched hand. Then her fingers were entwined in his.

"The sooner we go," she said, squeezing his palm, "the sooner we get back."

"You're right," Alfie said, wiping his face. "I just don't know what we'll find when we walk into the realm of magic this time."

The prospect of what he might find there was terrifying. Like opening the door to your own home to find nothing as it was. After all, Sombra's return had caused the colors of non-*propio* magic to blacken and match his own. The realm of magic couldn't be the same as it once was.

"Prince, this whole travel-through-the-magic thing was already weird to begin with," Finn said. "How much stranger could it get?"

Alfie gave a bark of a laugh. It sounded unfamiliar, the laugh of someone who had thought he'd lost everything but kept finding there was more still to lose. "A lot stranger. Exponentially stranger."

Magic had once been a door that Alfie knocked on to take him from here to there. A familiar face was always waiting on the other side. There were rules and expectations; there was etiquette. But thanks to Sombra, things had changed. Now it was more like a door you kicked down, not knowing if friend or foe was on the other side.

Would the magic even let him in this time, let alone allow him to bring Finn? Before, he'd only had to match their colors so that the realm of magic would recognize her as an extension of himself. Would that still work?

He could already see it in his head. Instead of the colorful connective threads of magic that stitched the world together so seamlessly, there would be black, knotted tangles. And instead of the peaceful energy he knew, a current that connected all people, places, and things, it would be cold and dead, stagnant with Sombra's evil energy.

"Whatever you're thinking is probably much worse than what we'll actually find," Finn said, her eyes scanning his face. "Let's go. Do you have the doorknob?"

Alfie pulled the knob out of his pocket and let it fall onto the tiled ground. It sank into the floor, settling in. As a boy, having a *propio* that let him transport magically from one place to another had been overwhelming. The only way he could make it feel doable was to use the knob to imagine creating a door from one place to another. Now, in this time of fear and uncertainty, Alfie was grateful to have something that made things feel a little smaller, less complicated.

He and Finn crouched over the knob. Their fingers still interlaced, Alfie let his magic flow into her and felt hers sweep over him, an exchange of energy that painted them both a vibrant shade of purple. He stared at her.

"Your magic," he said. "It's changed."

It shouldn't have been so easy to get her magic to match his, but unlike the constantly shifting reds her magic had once been, this time it was one color—a single shade of garnet.

Finn chewed the inside of her cheek before finally speaking. "My, um, *propio* is kind of on the fritz. I can't change my appearance anymore."

Alfie blinked at her. "What? Since when?"

"Since I tried to use it today," she said, her eyes darting away from him.

It wasn't right. Finn's magic was like champagne, bubbling and fluctuating, too lovely to be contained by a single color. Now it had gone flat.

When he opened his mouth to speak again, Finn cut him off. "I'm handling it. We don't have time to dwell."

Alfie frowned. Finn was always first in line when it came to burying her difficulties and handling them on her own. He wanted to discuss it further, but she was right, they had no time to waste.

"All right," he relented, and she looked relieved to hear him move on. "Are you ready to go?"

Finn squeezed his hand and nodded.

Alfie checked his pocket watch. Half past six in the morning. On a normal day the servants would be waking to prepare breakfast now. The stable boys would be feeding the horses and mucking out the stalls. Alfie would be reading in bed, too tired to rise, but too awake to fall back asleep. The palace would be rousing from its sleep. But today was not a normal day.

The prince turned the doorknob. The floor opened and swallowed them whole.

LA GUITARRA

Where the realm of magic had once surrounded him with a gentle guiding energy, like a soft current pushing a child's paper boat, now Finn and Alfie landed on cold, hard ground, with only darkness as far as the eye could see.

"Mierda," Finn cursed, rubbing her knee. "That was rude."

But Alfie was too distracted to respond.

It was exactly as he'd feared.

The strings of magic that had once been all the colors of the rainbow were drenched in black. He saw pinpricks of color buried in the dark—the magic of the few who could resist Sombra's pull—but the otherwise endless gloom was overwhelming. Before, the threads had been alive, thrumming with life, currents that could carry him where he wished to go. But these were lifeless.

"I don't even know how to use these," Alfie said. How could the magic take him farther than he had ever traveled before if he didn't understand how magic worked anymore?

"Bueno." Finn grimaced as she plucked one of the blackened strings. "This isn't ideal."

Alfie couldn't decide whether to laugh or cry or scream. "Everything is knotted and dead." He turned in a frantic circle but saw only more darkness. "How can I possibly—"

"Wait, stop," Finn said.

Alfie frowned at her. "I know you don't like it when I ramble, but I don't know what else to—"

"I'm not telling you to shut up for my sake!" Finn said. "The more you stress, the more knots are made in the strings."

Alfie blinked. "Qué?"

"Look around you," she said, gesturing at the endless void they stood in.

Alfie waited. "Nothing's happening."

"Because you're waiting, not stressing," Finn said, tucking a stray curl behind her ear. "For a moment, give in to your most anxious, stressed self—and see what happens." She clapped her hands. "Go."

Alfie took a breath and let the terrifying nature of the situation overwhelm him. The stakes were so high, and their chances were so low and—

"Oh." Alfie watched knots and tangles of darkness growing every which way.

"This place is responding to what you're thinking," Finn said. "How you're feeling."

Before even stepping into the magic, he'd imagined tangled masses of black strings, and that was what he'd found—a manifestation of his own anxiety.

Alfie blinked. "That's new."

"Maybe this is how your *propio* has expanded," Finn said. "You can affect how the realm of magic presents itself. If you can do that, maybe you can change how far we can go!"

Alfie blinked. "Fascinating."

"Why don't you take a breath and let me try," she said.

Alfie stared at her. "If it's my *propio*, how will you do it?"

"We're the same color magic now, right? So this place sees me as an extension of you." She shrugged. "Which means it should change based on how I see things too, right?"

Alfie tilted his head. "Good point."

"You're not the calm, cool, and collected type, but I am. Maybe I can make it present itself in a more . . ." She looked around at the tangles of black. "Manageable way."

"Like what?" Alfie asked. His mind was running through theories about how magic manifested itself—

"You're doing it again!" Finn gestured around them. The strings were tightening and knotting further. "You're stressing. Let's try something simple."

"Sorry," Alfie said, sheepish. He took a breath and tried to calm the anxiety, tried to let his mind go gloriously blank.

Nothing changed.

He sighed in frustration. "Is making your mind go blank easy for you?"

"Honestly, it's one of my favorite pastimes."

Alfie closed his eyes and breathed. "Let me try one more time." With each exhale he imagined his worries slipping from his mind.

When he opened them again, the strings had disappeared, and

they were standing in an empty space, as if the magic was waiting for them to tell it how to present itself.

"Good," Finn said. "Stay blank, let me take a crack at it." She looked around her. "I'm imagining the world—"

Alfie nearly screamed as the actual planet bloomed above their heads in its full, gargantuan size, so huge that they could see only a small bit of the very bottom.

"Never mind, never mind, too overwhelming!" Finn yelped, and the globe blinked out of existence.

Alfie wiped the sweat off his forehead. It was good to know that he wasn't the only one capable of doing this incorrectly.

"Strings, strings," Finn mumbled to herself, and as she spoke strings sprouted around her aimlessly.

"You don't have to use what you've seen of the magic before to define what you imagine now," Alfie said, watching in wonder as more and more strings formed around her.

"I don't have to," Finn agreed. "But it makes it easier. It's like lying. The best lies carry a bit of the truth in them. The best reimagining of the magic should carry a little of the truth in it too. A little of what it was before."

"Very well," Alfie said, letting her think. If their *propios* were meant to help them defeat Sombra, then maybe this was her part of the equation. Maybe Alfie was supposed to bring them into the realm of magic, and she was supposed to shape it based on her own idea of how it should function.

"What has strings?" she mumbled. Then her eyes brightened.

She held out her hands and a guitar materialized within them, but it didn't look like any guitar Alfie had ever seen. The wood was a patchwork of color, like the world of magic he remembered. And instead of the usual six, there were countless strings. Most were obsidian, but there were flecks of light here and there.

Finn weighed it in her hands. "I imagined a guitar with all the world's strings of magic." She held it out to him. "For you to play."

"Me?" Alfie said, his fingers touching the colorful wood. "Why me?"

"You can touch and feel magic, Prince," Finn said. "Play the strings and feel. Find whichever one will take us to Sombra's relics."

Alfie carefully took the guitar. "You'd think it would be heavier."

The sudden weight of it slammed him onto his backside.

"I imagine that it's light!" Finn shouted. "*We* imagine it light!"

Alfie cleared his mind and imagined an airy, light instrument, and the guitar followed suit.

"Sorry," he said.

She eyed him warily. "You'd do well to reflect on the power of thought." She grimaced. "I'm never saying anything like that again. I sound like a dueño." She snapped her fingers at him. "Start strumming."

Alfie held the guitar in his hands. What would it feel like to strum the strings of the world? Each string would be a living, breathing person, a soul, and the connections that tied each person to another. Connections that crisscrossed over their kingdom like a grid. And as his fingers ran over the strings, he would have to feel the heart of each one until he could find a piece of Sombra. Alfie began to pluck the strings individually.

It was like playing guitarra, but each note brought him into someone else's mind. Each string he touched was a person, a connection. He pulled his hand back.

"You all right?" Finn asked as he took in deep breaths.

"Just overwhelming," he said. "I usually don't have this ability to skim my fingers and feel the presence of every person there."

"Should we try something else?" Finn asked.

"No, no, I can do it," he said. "Let me just narrow the scope to Uppskala."

He needed to calm himself, to stop getting lost in the overwhelming task before him. He needed to make it smaller, more manageable, like how he used the doorknob to access his *propio*.

Alfie began humming a slow, sad Uppskalan ballad. It was a song he had heard Paloma hum so often that, even now, it made him feel safe. He wondered if it was Svana who'd taught her the tune. As Alfie hummed, he felt the guitar lighten, responding to the music, and he knew without questioning that now there were only Uppskalan strings left.

He skimmed and scanned, his mind flooding with the identities of everyone he must save from Sombra's fate. Their thoughts were darkened, their identities twisted, but they were still human. He would make it right for them. As he plucked the strings of people he did not search for, they disappeared only to be replaced by others to play and search through.

When Alfie looked up, Finn was unknowingly swaying to the rhythm.

He paused his playing, his lips quirking upward. "Do you know the Uppskalan waltz?"

Finn gave a sharp sigh through her nose. "What do you think?"

It was a silly idea, but didn't they deserve a moment of distraction? In the face of having to comb through every soul in need of saving, it was lovely to see her move to the beat, to find joy in it. "Dance with me while I play."

"What?" Finn blurted far too loudly. "It'll distract you from finding the string to Sombra's head."

"So now you care about staying on task?" Alfie laughed.

"Since when do you go *off* task?" she quipped back.

When she didn't budge, Alfie went on. "It'll help me, I promise. This task is draining and difficult; it'll help to have some fun to keep my head above water."

Finn rolled her eyes. "Fine. What do I do?"

Alfie marveled at how hard she was trying to not look embarrassed, which only made her look that much more embarrassed. It struck him that she wouldn't do this for just anyone.

Still holding the guitar, Alfie stepped closer to her until they were five paces apart.

"The Uppskalans keep things very boring, then," she said. She wasn't wrong; compared to a Castallano bachata where, with the right partner, you'd stand so close that you could feel each other breathe, this dance was a pantomime of celibacy.

"Follow me," Alfie said. He took a breath and began playing again, each string bringing forth a new soul. He flinched as their pain flooded him, threatened to drown him, but when his eyes found Finn, he felt himself resurfacing, gulping fresh air.

"Two steps back," he said, and Finn mirrored him. "Two steps forward." She followed his instructions and Alfie plucked through more and more Uppskalan people. "Now clap twice."

"How will you clap if you're playing?" she snorted.

"You'll do it for me."

Finn smirked, then raised her hands high just beside her cheek and clapped.

"Now we step around each other in a circle," Alfie said, still playing. They circled each other, sneaking glances at one another over their shoulders, back-to-back for a brief moment before facing each other once again. "Then we repeat, but we get closer each time."

They held eye contact as they moved, until Finn burst out laughing from the sudden seriousness of it all.

"Stay on beat," Alfie chided.

"I'm trying!"

Looking through the strings was certainly more difficult this way (multitasking wasn't his favorite), but it was more bearable. Keeping pace with Finn and watching her dance anchored him here. Without it, he feared he'd be lost in the magnitude that the strings represented. As they drew nearer and nearer to each other, Alfie's mind strayed to their night together, to the rhythm they'd found in each other.

Alfie wasn't sure how long they danced in the dark emptiness of the realm of magic, but at some point they'd stopped moving. Alfie still held the guitar, plucking the strings, but he wished he was holding her instead.

Finn leaned forward, careful not to graze the guitar, and Alfie dipped his head to meet her—

Twang.

Alfie startled as he plucked a string that overwhelmed him with the need to run. Gooseflesh covered his body. The other strings had names and faces attached to them—this one only had power.

Power and hunger.

It had to be a piece of Sombra's body. Alfie gripped the string carefully between his fingers as sweat dripped down his nose.

"I found it," he said, his eyes screwed closed in concentration.

"This one?" Finn asked, grabbing the string as well.

Alfie did not have time to speak another word. As soon as Finn touched the string, they were pulled forward into the dark toward their destination.

Perhaps if Alfie hadn't been so focused on what was to come, he would've felt the toy dragon twitch where it lay against his chest, but he was lost to the pull of the string and what lay ahead.

The magic parted before them, like a curtain plucked to the side, and they were flung back into the world that was Sombra's to destroy and theirs to save.

THE POND

Alfie and Finn slammed against the ice-encased snow of the Uppska-lan tundra with a painful *thwack*, their quiet dance long forgotten.

The cold sank directly into Finn's bones, wriggling under her skin like an icy hand slipping into a glove.

"Mierda!" she cursed, her teeth chattering. Even with her coat and boots on, her face was still exposed, and the chill was so intense that it burned the flesh. There wasn't any time to marvel at how Alfie's magic had pulled them across oceans when her face was about to break off. Finn pulled the hood more closely around her face, leaning into the warmth. "Thank the dioses for magic."

They were stranded in the white wilderness, surrounded by snowcapped mountains reaching for the sky. Aside from the frozen lake before them, there was nothing to interrupt the endless ivory as far as the eye could see. Finn spotted a family of pale-furred deer in the distance. How on earth could anything survive here?

"How do Uppskalans live in this weather?" Finn asked. She

glanced up at the shattered moon. The snow gleamed under its dim light.

"Uppskalan cities are enchanted to trap heat," Alfie said. "But we're in the wilderness. There's no need for that kind of magic here, so the weather is as it naturally is—deadly."

"So we're all alone here?" Finn asked, her mind turning back to the last time they were truly alone. In his rooms, her heels digging into his back.

Paloma's disapproving look flashed through her mind.

If you intend to hurt him, wait until the mission is complete. Your journey will be perilous. He will need his wits and any confidence he can scrounge to get through it.

Once again, Finn wished she could change her face, hide from the judgment that followed her—the judgment that she deserved.

She needed to stop thinking about that night. For Alfie's own good it couldn't happen again. She would only hurt him. Everyone knew that but him.

"Being here alone is probably for the best," Alfie said, not noticing her internal struggle. "If we were in a more densely populated place we'd be surrounded by shadowless."

Finn nodded. They were lucky that the Uppskalans had hidden their relic here instead of in a busy city. The threat of an icy death was more than enough to worry about.

Finn watched as Alfie pulled out his pocket watch. He started.

"What?" Finn took a look. The hands were zooming around the clock at hyperspeed. "I guess being in the realm of magic put it on the fritz."

Alfie cocked his head as the hands finally settled into a regular rhythm. "Perhaps time works differently there. It's past noon." He pocketed it. "It took us six hours to get here."

She nodded. "Not bad considering the distance."

Next he took out the enchanted parchment he shared with Luka and scribbled a note to say that they'd arrived safely in Uppskala, then tucked it back under his armor for safekeeping, his focus returning to the freezing terrain. Alfie shivered. "Do you feel that?"

"What do you—" Finn began, but then she felt it too. Something heavy in the air—not a scent, but a feeling. It was chilling, but not in the way of snow and ice; in the way of spirit. It was . . . soulless, darkness incarnate—Sombra. "I feel it."

"It's the same sensation I felt when I plucked the string," Alfie said.

Finn had a feeling that others wouldn't be able to sniff out the presence of Sombra's relics quite as easily. She and Alfie truly were born for this. When their eyes met, she knew he was thinking the same.

"I guess we don't need to use his blood to track him after all. Let's follow the feeling," Finn said, eyeing the mountains warily. "And hope he's not too hard to find."

They advanced into the snowy oblivion, their steps guided by the invisible pull of Sombra's dark aura. It was like playing a game of "hot and cold" with much higher stakes.

In the silence, Finn couldn't help but think of her stymied *propio*. So far, Alfie was doing all the work by transporting them with his. Guilt and a sense of uselessness gnawed at her from the inside. Would she be able to play her role in the prophecy without her *propio*?

Or would she be the reason the world ended, squeezed to dust in Sombra's fist? All because of a stupid emotional blockage.

The dueño's voice sounded in her head.

There have been instances in which an internal blockage may lead to one's propio *not working . . . such things can only be fixed through introspection.*

What ridiculous emotional nonsense could be tripping her up?

Finn glanced at Alfie, at the delicate sweep of his profile. He met her eyes, granting her a small smile, and for a moment Finn was overwhelmed with grief over something she hadn't yet lost and had never deserved.

Finn looked away, stuffing those loud thoughts down. They were irrelevant, they didn't matter in the face of saving the world.

She'd figure it out and do her part. She'd find a way to get it done.

"You've got to be kidding me," Finn sighed when the pull of Sombra's magic led them to the base of a tall mountain.

"You can't have expected it to be simple," Alfie said.

"No, but I still hoped." Finn grimaced. "How are we going to do this?"

Alfie thought for a long moment. "I've got an idea," he said. "Have you ever been sledding?"

Finn squinted at him. "Do I look like I enjoy cold, snowy activities?"

"First time for everything." Alfie whipped his hands about, but the snow didn't move.

"Magic doesn't work the same way," Finn reminded him. "Remember?"

Alfie blinked at her for a moment before it dawned on him—they had to focus on their negative emotions to access magic now. "Right."

"Have you tried it yet?" she asked, thinking of how she'd attempted it for the first time in the armory, just before she realized she'd lost the ability to change her face.

He nodded. "Yes, in my rooms." From the way he said it, Finn knew it hadn't been a great experience. Alfie took a deep breath and closed his eyes. She watched his jaw clench as he moved his hands again. The snow slowly formed itself into a large sled with space for two. It moved gracelessly, without the usual fluidity that came when Alfie charmed water, but Paloma herself had said their magic would be less effective now; after all, they couldn't lean into darkness as completely as the shadowless could.

Finally, Alfie squeezed his hands into fists and the sled clenched inward, solidifying. As he opened his eyes, Finn could swear that they were shining with a veneer of unshed tears. She wondered what he'd had to think about in order to call upon the magic, but she knew better than to ask. After all, she wouldn't want him to ask her, and she was thankful that he wasn't pushing her about why her *propio* wasn't working. At least for now.

"Well." Alfie cleared his throat, his voice sounding thick with emotion. Finn pretended not to notice. "Sleds usually take you *down* hills, but we'll use this one to go up." When she didn't move, Alfie climbed on first. "Come on."

Finn begrudgingly got on, cursing under her breath when her backside hit the cold snow seat.

"Ready?" Alfie asked her. The snow whipped around them, nearly obscuring his words.

Finn stared up at the mountain and swallowed. "Let's get it over with."

Alfie took a breath and thrust his arms forward. The sled began to slide up the mountain. Finn gripped her hood close around her face to stop it blowing back from the force of the wind.

For a long moment they let the sled glide on in silence. They could hardly see in the snowy wind, so Alfie didn't go too fast. If it were Finn in control they'd be zooming to the top.

"Mierda!" Alfie shouted.

Too late, Finn looked ahead of them just as they crashed into something, the sound of shattering glass filling her ears. Whatever it was had thwacked her in the forehead and then fallen into her lap. The sled careened to the left as Alfie skidded to a halt.

Her heart hammered in her chest. "What was that?"

"I'm not sure," Alfie said, his eyes wide. "I think . . . it might've been a person."

"Qué?" Finn asked. Who in their right mind would be here? She looked down and picked up a frozen piece of a man's jaw from her lap. "Looks like you're right."

"Are you all right?" Alfie asked her, breathless.

Finn nodded, tossing the jawbone over her shoulder and out of the sled. "I'm fine. You?"

Alfie nodded, his gaze darting to where the body had once stood.

"Prince, I know you have a soft heart, but the man was already dead." She stared at the scattered pieces of the corpse under the wan moonlight. "Honestly, he's probably thankful to change position after so long." She hopped out of the sled.

"Don't say that." Alfie snorted, holding back his laughter. "Where are you going?"

"To see if he had anything of value on him!" Finn said, as if it were the most obvious thing in the world. She rummaged through pockets, but all she found were a few dull blades. A couple of thick-furred snow rabbits hopped away as she kicked at the snow in annoyance.

"Do you really think that's necessary?" Alfie called.

Ignoring him, Finn walked a few feet ahead. At the sight of another corpse by the side of the trail, she burst out laughing. He stood tall, pointing forward as if he were leading an expedition of one, but that wasn't the funny part. The man wasn't wearing a shirt, revealing an obnoxious bird tattoo on his chest. He'd truly thought his body was strong enough to outrun the snow.

Men really were something.

"Do you see this?" Finn shouted at Alfie. "No shirt!"

"Finn," Alfie said. "Don't make fun of him. Come on!"

"But look—" Finn turned back and gasped. The man was no longer pointing a single finger forward. Now it was an outstretched fist. And she could swear that he'd turned his head a little, just enough to cut his frozen eyes at her.

"Finn, let's go!"

The thief rubbed her eyes. She must have imagined it. "Yeah, yeah, yeah, I'm coming!"

Finn mounted the sled in silence, embarrassed at being spooked by a dead, shirtless pendejo.

"Oh," Alfie said, his gold eyes widening. "I think I know where we are."

"Spit it out, then."

Alfie grimaced. "Dead Men's Mountain."

"What?"

"Hundreds of years ago, Uppskalans would challenge themselves to reach the top of these mountains on their own with no magical assistance."

"No coat?" Finn asked, balking.

Alfie shook his head. "They take pride in the unforgiving landscape of their kingdom. They believed a true Uppskalan could scale a mountain with no help. That it would bring great honor to their family."

Finn rolled her eyes. "And instead they found death."

Alfie nodded. "I remember the Uppskalan princess once telling me that some foolish men used to come here wearing as little as possible to prove that they could survive the worst of Uppskalan weather."

Finn stared at him. "Were they drunk?"

"Extremely." Alfie's eyes darted to the shirtless corpse. "It's how they tried to keep warm for as long as they could. Quite the example of masculinity gone awry—"

"Let's keep going," Finn interrupted. She was happy to be kind to the prince to stop him from stressing, but not kind enough for a lecture.

"We'll have to move at a slower pace," Alfie said with a frown. "I have a feeling that's not the only corpse we'll encounter on the path up."

"Fine," Finn said. If it were up to her, she'd just plow right through them.

Alfie moved as fast as he could while dodging the bodies. By the time they finally reached the top, Finn had lost count of how many they'd passed.

As Alfie stopped the sled on the flattened mountaintop, Finn felt the overwhelming pull of Sombra once more—a strange shiver up her spine, an instinct to turn and run in the opposite direction. It felt wrong to move *toward* something that felt so overwhelmingly evil.

"We've got to be close," Alfie said, shivering where he stood. "Sombra's presence is strong here."

Finn nodded and dismounted the sled, feeling woozy. She'd never realized that air could have weight to it, but this high up, each breath felt like it was half-stolen before it reached her lungs.

"It's up ahead," Finn said, scanning the ground. She could ignore the dizzy spell. They had work to do. "I can feel it."

As she stepped up to the edge of a frozen pond, Sombra's presence overwhelmed her. Before, it was as if they'd been tiptoeing on the surface of Sombra's spirit, but now they'd broken through and fallen into its depths. Unlike the lake they'd traversed below, the pond was small, its diameter scarcely wider than she was tall. Finn had expected to see a crystalline surface. After all, what could disturb a pond at the top of a very tall mountain in such a cold place? But instead there was a coating of feathers and frozen blood on the ice. Finn stared. Why was this iced-over pond covered in dead birds? It looked as if they'd all flown straight down to slam against it.

"The relic has got to be in the pond," Finn said, grimacing.

"Why would so many arctic starlings end up here?" Alfie asked as Finn squatted near the edge. "They are well adjusted to flying in this weather. It doesn't make sense."

Finn rolled her eyes. Of course he was also an expert on birds. What *didn't* this boy know?

"I don't know, maybe the birds had a rough night." Finn made to step onto the pond's surface. "Let's just get to—"

"Wait!" Alfie grabbed her, pulling her clear off her feet.

"Prince!" she shouted as he placed her back down. "What—"

"Just wait a moment," Alfie said. He bent over and scooped some snow into his gloved hands. He packed it tightly into a snowball.

"Now doesn't seem like the right time for a snowball fight," she said, but he ignored her.

He threw the snowball straight up, high over the pond.

"Well," Finn said, crossing her arms as the ball shot up overhead. "We've established that you're good at throwing snowballs—"

Before she could finish her joke, the snowball rocketed downward, slamming into the ice as if it had been hurled down by the gods themselves. It landed so hard it exploded, spraying them both with powdery snow.

Suddenly it clicked in Finn's mind. "So the birds . . ."

Alfie swallowed thickly. "The birds didn't fly into the ice. They were compelled, pulled down."

Finn stared at the pond, taking a large step backward. "Why?"

Alfie chewed his lip. "We know that Sombra's influence has infiltrated and altered the very soul of his world. His intentions have warped the way we use magic. Maybe his return has warped all spellwork too? What if whatever enchantment was originally placed on this pond has evolved?"

Finn cocked her head. "You think they enchanted the pond to protect Sombra's head, and now that the world's unbalanced, that spellwork morphed into . . ." She gestured at the bird massacre. "This?"

Alfie nodded. "My best guess is that they magicked the relic to stay at the very bottom of the pond and never float up even during the warmer seasons, but the spellwork morphed to pull *everything* in and above the pond downward. This couldn't have been the original intention of the magic," Alfie went on. "All the dead birds just draw attention to an otherwise unremarkable pond."

So if they tried to get to the stone relic, the pond's magic would pull them under and drown them. How could they possibly retrieve it now?

Finn turned to the prince. "I don't suppose you have any bright ideas?"

Alfie shook his head. "I'm a water charmer, so part of me hopes I'll be able to use the water to propel us out . . . but I have a feeling the water itself might not work in the ways it usually does."

"Give it a shot," Finn said. She didn't want to make Alfie think of difficult things just so he could charm the water, but his water-charming abilities were their best chance of not drowning.

Alfie let out a breath and Finn looked away from him to avoid seeing his face crumple as he thought of whatever awful thing would grant him access to the magic. He raised his arms and made a pulling gesture. Nothing happened. He dug his heels into the snow and tried again. The ice cracked, but no water rose from beneath it.

As the prince grunted with effort, small tendrils of water rose from the ice, only to snap back into the pond like a frog's long tongue returning to the back of its throat.

Alfie sputtered, breathing heavily. "The water is bewitched to pull downward as well. I've never been fought by my own element like that."

"Coño," Finn cursed. "Stupid pond."

"I don't understand how we can even begin to get there." Alfie looked at her warily. "I don't think my water charming will be of much help up here."

"That's it!" With those words, an idea sparked to life in Finn's head. "Up here is the wrong way to go about it."

"What?"

"If everything above the pond gets pulled in and drowned, then we can't go above it or through it. So we have to go *under* it."

"We tunnel under the pond and take the stone pieces from the pond floor." The prince's eyes widened in understanding. "You're brilliant." He winced. "That'll be a lot of work on your part."

Finn bit her lip. She'd felt useless without her *propio*, but now she was the only one who could do this. She'd have to do some heavy-duty stone carving, and, thanks to Sombra's return, that would mean thinking of things she desperately did not want to think about.

She forced herself to shrug. "No use wasting time saying things that everyone already knows." She spread her feet into a wide stance and took a deep breath. The ground beneath them was cold and tight, unlike the loose, sun-kissed earth of San Cristóbal. This would be a challenge.

"Let me help," Alfie said before she moved. With a grimace,

the prince used his water charming to clear the snow and ice from a large circle of earth beside the pond, just large enough for them both to move through together.

Finn flexed her fingers and cracked her neck. "Let's get to it."

For what felt like hours, Finn dug into every difficult memory of her life with Ignacio that she could summon. From the day they'd met, to every escape attempt, every killing; and as she broke deeper into the frozen earth, she felt herself crumbling too. She felt herself shrinking into the little girl she'd once been—Ignacio's daughter. The little girl who went to sleep every night wishing she wouldn't wake. She gritted her teeth as the magic crawled over her skin like the itchy silk of a spider's web. But she refused to complain, or to take a break. She knew the moment she stopped the prince would look at her with those large, sympathetic eyes, which would only make her feel worse. She didn't want to be seen or pitied; she wanted to be numb. So she kept her head down and kept going. Alfie did his best to help by melting ice and wetting the earth so that it was easier to move. He even tried using spoken spellwork.

"*Romper!*" he said, his focus on the frozen earth. But the rock was so cold and tightly packed that it barely fractured. When he did manage to break through, the pieces simply shifted to become yet another wall. Desk magic didn't seem to be of much use in the face of this challenge, so the brunt of the work fell on Finn's very tired shoulders. Alfie hovered behind her, his anxiety at not being able to help as charming as it was annoying.

When they finally were almost ten feet belowground, Finn took a break. She hunched over, hands on her knees, and breathed in the shallow air as deeply as she could. Alfie had conjured a ball of light to illuminate the way.

"Well, at least it's a little warmer now that we're underground," Alfie offered.

Finn glared at him.

"Sorry," he murmured. "Just trying to stay positive."

She wanted to snap back that he needed to stay *negative* to get the magic to work, but that wouldn't do any good. "How much farther?"

Alfie pressed his hand into the eastern wall of dirt, sensing his element on the other side. He moved his arm down the wall, squatting to feel for the end of the pond. "The end is level with our feet. Dig just a bit deeper, then to the left, and we'll be beneath it."

Finn wiped the sweat from her brow. To think she was working so hard that she was sweating even in this cold. She wasn't just physically tired, but mentally drained from dwelling on things she'd spent years pretending hadn't happened. It was as if Sombra was punishing all who could resist him by forcing them into the darkest corridors of their own minds. She rubbed her temples, her head pounding beneath her fingers.

"Are you all right?" Alfie asked, his voice hushed.

She nodded. "I'm fine, let's just get this over with."

The prince looked like he wanted to say something more, but he swallowed it down and let her get back to work.

Finally they were in position, squatting under the icy pond. She could see clearly through the ice all the way up to the starling-splattered surface above.

"I see it," Alfie said, crab-walking beneath the ice until he was under the center of the pond. "It's his head."

Finn crawled over to him and looked. The closer she got to it the more uneasy she felt. The hairs on the back of her neck stood up.

"Yeah." She shuddered. "That's got to be it."

Alfie rubbed the ice with his hand to clear the condensation from their warm breaths.

"Is he guapo?"

Alfie stared at her. "What?"

"I mean, is he good-looking?" Finn asked with a shrug. "I don't know, I've never seen the face of a god. I figure he's got to be pretty impressive, right?"

"Yes, well . . ." Alfie looked up at the head uncomfortably, bringing the light closer to the pond. "He has a very defined jawline."

"Good to know." Finn plopped onto the ground, laughing at his awkwardness. "This part's all yours. Do your agua thing."

Alfie nodded nervously. Neither of them knew if this part of the plan would work. Thanks to the mutated magic, the pond sucked everything downward, but now that they were beneath it, they had to hope that if Alfie melted the bottom layer of the ice, they'd be able to pull the stone piece out, like a loose tooth.

Alfie pressed his hands against the ice. It took longer than usual, but Finn watched as he finally willed a wide oval around the stone piece to melt—but the stone head didn't wait to be pulled. It shot out of the pond, nearly landing on Alfie's feet. A gush of icy water followed.

"Shit!" Finn shouted as the prince hurried to freeze the water.

How had they not realized it before? The mutated magic created a pressure that sucked everything downward, so opening a hole in the bottom was a release of that pressure, shooting out at the same speed those starlings had hit the ice.

"Freeze it!" she yelled.

"I'm trying! The pressure of the water is breaking through the ice I'm trying to make!" Alfie shouted back.

Finn moved to summon dirt from the ground to plug up the hole but was stopped cold in her tracks when something else shot through the oval hole in the ice—an outstretched arm, then another, and then a slack, emotionless face.

"*Prince, move!*" Finn cried.

But it was too late. The man surged through the hole, landing in a twist of wet limbs. Had someone been following them on their trek up the mountain? How had he survived in the cold without a shirt—

Finn gasped, spotting the bird tattoo on his chest. It was the frozen corpse they'd seen on the mountain.

The shirtless fool was *alive*.

THE HUNT

Dezmin had almost reached Alfie.

He could feel the warmth of his brother's skin beneath the toy dragon, hear his heartbeat, but as quickly as the connection came, it was lost.

He'd waited until Sombra was using his magic to find more larimar, then he reached for another wisp of the god's power and sent it out into the world in search of Alfie.

It was strange to wield Sombra's power and feel the extent of his strength. Unlike last time, the wisp of magic hadn't floated toward the palace to find Alfie, but instead had burrowed into the fabric of reality itself, spiriting itself away into the realm of magic.

This was a place that Dezmin himself had never been. With his *propio*, Alfie had always been the one with a talent for meditation and complex magic, but Dezmin's life was so grounded in the physical world and responsibility to the throne that he had never had the patience to learn. He looked around until he saw Alfie and a girl standing amid endless black strings. Even in his rush to reach Alfie,

Dezmin froze in awe at this place he had never seen but had always been a part of.

Just as the wisp had settled into the dragon that Alfie wore as a necklace, just as Dezmin heard his brother's voice, Alfie and the girl had grabbed a string and disappeared, and the connection had broken. He had no time to try again without Sombra noticing, so he was left with no choice but to return to the palace in the sky. He would have to wait for Sombra to become distracted once more.

Before, Dezmin had fought against the pull to lose himself and fuse fully with Sombra, but in order to use Sombra's magic, he'd had to feed pieces of himself to the god, further intermingling the two of them. He couldn't regret it, though. Not when it let him get a glimpse of Alfie and Luka. But he felt smaller, less substantial. He was a small, soft bouillon cube in the stew of Sombra.

How much time did he have before he disappeared entirely?

He watched as Sombra paced in his throne room. He could see the undulations of the god's thoughts, feel his emotions—anger, paranoia, an undercurrent of fear.

Now that Dezmin had given parts of himself to Sombra, the god's thoughts had gotten so loud that Dezmin almost confused them with his own.

"I would gladly retrieve my relics myself and kill those fools for standing in my way." Sombra looked down at himself in disgust. "But this body is *weak*."

The skin of his palm had barely healed, a thin membrane of flesh keeping it from bleeding, and the iron taste of blood still lacquered his throat.

Dezmin watched as the memory of being wounded in the palace

played in Sombra's mind. He was a god, but he'd bled like a regular man. Dezmin had felt the attack when the girl stabbed Sombra through the hand. After all, it was Dez's own palm that had been struck. Pain aside, he was grateful to know that Sombra was not indestructible.

At least not yet.

"I must know what the gods told them," Sombra said, his voice rough with anger. He'd spotted a stream of blue starlight flowing to the palace—a signal that the gods had been summoned for an audience. "They would not return to the realm of man for no reason. They know *something*."

Dezmin hoped Sombra would never find out. If he couldn't leave his palace in the sky, he'd need someone to find out for him. And who in their right mind would be willing to help a monster like Sombra?

The god stopped mid-step. In his anger, Dezmin had let his thoughts move from a whisper to a shout.

"You have a point, boy," he said. "Lucky for me, no one is in their right mind at the moment, are they? They might not think twice about helping a monster, as you so eloquently put it."

Now Sombra was happy, excited. Dezmin could feel it.

What had he done? Could Sombra hear him more easily now that he'd sacrificed pieces of himself to the god?

Dezmin could only watch as Sombra threw open the glass doors to his great balcony. Castallan unfurled beneath them, pricks of lantern light punctuating the city rings.

"Good people of Castallan and the world," Sombra shouted, his voice magnified by magic.

Dezmin felt Sombra pouring a hypnotic command into his

voice, one that would reach the ears of every shadowless in the city and beyond.

"I speak to you as your king, as your god. I ask one favor of you!"

Dezmin could sense the eyes of the people turning up toward the balcony. They were waiting with bated breath.

Sombra grinned, speaking only for Dezmin to hear. "I will make sure your brother has no help. Not from dueños or strangers. He will have *no one*. All thanks to you."

Please don't, Dezmin begged, but the god carried on with his speech.

"Those who still possess shadows and whites in their eyes have refused my rule! They want the world to return to the way it was before. Rules, order, law!" Sombra spat with disgust. "Is that what you want?"

Shouts of anger roared through the city.

"These cretins must be extinguished. Find them and bring them to me and I shall reward you with the riches and glory that only a god could give! And those who bring me dueños, you will be doubly rewarded!" The city beneath them rocked with cheers.

Dezmin's mind raced with panic. The dueños would certainly know the details of Alfie's audience with the gods. After all, Alfie would have relied heavily on Paloma and her colleagues to help. If any of them were caught, Sombra would learn whatever information he needed to become strong again.

"Enlisting the help of others is not in my nature," Sombra murmured to Dezmin. The god's nose was bleeding again from the strain of using magic to connect with the shadowless below, but he was too pleased with himself to notice. "But for you, I'll make an exception."

The crowds shouted his name as the hope that had begun sprouting in Dezmin's chest faded to nothing. How many people would be killed because of one loud, stray thought. Dezmin forced his mind to quiet.

"Ah, so silent now," Sombra teased, but Dezmin could tell that the god had no interest in prying deeper into his thoughts. He only wanted to hurt him. "You don't even know the best part. Whoever they bring me will give me more than just information."

Dezmin could see what Sombra had planned for any dueños or *propio* users brought to him. Fear and disgust curdled in his stomach. It was not death; it was something much worse.

"When a human's pathetic body is ill, it needs sustenance to heal, does it not?" Sombra said. "I don't know what knowledge the gods have about why I am so weak, but until I find out, I need to gather my strength. I think it's time we feed."

THE WORRY

Luka had always dreamed of a life of adventure.

He would commission a fabulous ship to explore the world in the lap of luxury. He'd eat fine meals and have fine lovers on every continent. He wouldn't return until he knew the rest of the world as well as he knew his own bedroom. Only then would he consider settling down.

Adventure had always been on the agenda, but this was hardly what he'd had in mind.

Luka watched as the dueños hurried about, preparing for their pilgrimage. It had been six hours since Alfie and Finn had disappeared into the realm of magic. Luka found himself constantly unfurling their shared parchment to look for a message only to find nothing. It was logical that traveling from one continent to the next, even magically, would take more time than traveling from point to point in San Cristóbal, but it was still worrying.

"So to be clear," Luka said to Paloma. "There are no tethers to transport us to this sacred place we're headed to."

Apparently they needed to go to some oasis where dueños could communicate with their dead brethren in order to ask how to stop Sombra once and for all.

Paloma shook her head. "You just said it yourself. It's sacred. We do not set up tethers to this place. Dueños usually make the pilgrimage on foot."

Luka's eyes widened. He looked down at his most modest pair of boots (low heel, a very subtle gold buckle, and pearl accents—very casual). "On foot?"

"But we do not have time to do things the traditional way," she said. "We will be leaving the palace and the city through the underground tunnels, then we will proceed on horseback."

In the chaos of the shadowless fleeing the palace the horses had been spooked, but the dueños had found them in the meadow between the palace and the Bow.

Luka was glad to hear they'd be using the tunnels. After his battle with the Tattooed King, he wasn't keen on returning to the city anytime soon, but still, there was a lump in Luka's throat. What would be left of the city when they returned?

Luka swallowed. He'd complained to Alfie so many times about how he felt trapped within the castle, how he yearned to leave, but now that he *had* to go he longed for another year, another early breakfast with the king and queen, another afternoon bothering Alfie in the library, another night sneaking lovers in under the guards' noses.

"Who will wait for Alfie and Finn to return?" Luka asked, his throat suddenly dry.

"We are leaving a retinue of dueños here to maintain the protections around the palace."

"And they will watch over . . ." Luka's voice petered out. He could hardly mention the queen without remembering how Sombra's influence had turned his surrogate mother into a murderer. "I don't want to abandon her."

"The dueños will watch over her and the others," Paloma said, a rare gentleness in her voice. "We are making this journey for her too. To reverse all that has happened."

Luka nodded, his throat burning. "How are you faring?" Like everyone else, Paloma looked worse for wear, but he had a feeling it wasn't just about Sombra's return.

Paloma looked annoyed that he'd noticed. "My colleague was traveling here by ship when Nocturna began."

Luka cocked his head. "Oooooh, your *colleague*. Svana, right? The Uppskalan dueña?"

Paloma narrowed her eyes. "Yes, my colleague. She knew I was in distress over the murders during the peace summit. She was coming to support me."

Luka blinked. The world had turned upside down so quickly that it was easy to forget about the chaos of the peace summit and Englass's betrayal.

"I had hoped she would get here before we left for our journey," Paloma went on. "I shared the news of our audience with the gods through our magicked parchment, but . . ."

"She hasn't responded," Luka said. It seemed everyone had loved ones to fear for. "I'm sorry." He didn't know what else to say.

"She knows to come to the palace for safety." Paloma looked away from him. "I trust that she'll be here when we get back."

"Of course." Luka nodded. Realistically, Paloma's girlfriend was dead. They both knew this. As a dueña she would not be corrupted by Sombra's influence, but she would have been trapped on a ship full of shadowless with nowhere to run. Then again, they were living in unrealistic times. Who could say that Svana wasn't still on her way as they spoke?

"Can't wait to meet her."

"Thank you, Master Luka," Paloma said, the ghost of a smile on her lips.

"Can I be of any use?" came a voice from behind Luka.

James stepped forward and bowed low to Paloma. Fully healed from his run-in with the Tattooed King, James looked refreshed. The dueños had thoroughly examined him—for how often do you meet someone who can somehow house four *propios* in his body? They'd gleaned little from their examinations but were glad to have him on Castallan's side for the journey.

Paloma eyed him warily. "Stay in Master Luka's line of sight until it's time to leave."

As the dueña walked away, Luka rolled his eyes. After they'd ventured to the Brim together to get the larimar, he was feeling more civil toward James, but that didn't mean he wanted to be the boy's babysitter.

James rocked on his heels, hands clasped behind his back. "Is there anything I can—"

"No," Luka interrupted. When James flinched, Luka's shoulders sagged. "I'm sorry. I didn't mean to get short with you. It's a stress-ful time and it—"

"It isn't any easier with an Englassen traitor in your midst." James looked down. "I understand."

A tense silence stretched between them. Why was it even more annoying that James understood? If he were a pendejo it would be so much easier to hate him.

"Is there anything you want to do before we go?" James asked, his eyes still on his feet.

The dueños had already packed everything they would need—weapons, healing draughts, food, and water. There was not much to do but sit and wait, but Luka couldn't stop his feet from carrying him down the maze of hallways and stairs to Alfie's rooms. James hovered by the doors as Luka paced. Now that Alfie might not come back, everything here—all his books, his writing quills, his bottle of sleeping tonic—had become precious treasures. Through the glass balcony doors their kingdom unfurled before him. From this high floor he could see over the rings of the city and make out the lush sugarcane fields that surrounded San Cristóbal. He stared at that shadowed patch of green in the distance. This was bigger than him and Alfie—there was a whole world to save. He needed to stay focused. But his fear overwhelmed him. Was that where he would be when Alfie died? Out in the wilderness, riding through the sugar-cane fields, unable to help?

"You're afraid for him," James said quietly. "Afraid he won't come home."

"Obviously," he said, feigning nonchalance, but the sound of his fears spoken aloud made his eyes burn. Luka was glad that James could only see his back as he faced Alfie's empty bed.

"It's hard being separated from family, not knowing if they're safe," James murmured. "It's strange. With everything that's happened over the past few hours, my life has at once become much better and much worse. Marsden and his family cannot torment me any longer. I don't feel any pain from my *propios*. I no longer feel as if my bones are going to splinter." He paused. "But I've also learned that my family is lost to me forever."

"I'm sorry," Luka offered. He wasn't great when it came to finding the right words at the best of times—and now certainly wasn't the best of times.

"I only mean to say, I spent many nights just as you are now, worrying, imagining every worst-case scenario. I would pray for the day that I wouldn't have to worry like that anymore. Now that day is here, and what I wouldn't give to feel that pain again, the pain of not knowing if things would work out, if we would see each other again. Because now I know we won't."

Luka jumped as James gripped his shoulder, his eyes soft with sympathy. "Embrace the pain of it, the anxiety you feel for him, because that means there is still hope, Master Luka."

Luka curled his shaking hands into fists. If this fear of losing Alfie and their family was a sharp blade, then he would lean into it. He would rather that than the alternative.

Luka felt the parchment become warm in his pocket. With shaking hands he unfurled it and saw Alfie's elegant script.

We've arrived safely in the Uppskalan wilderness. Will write more as soon as we secure the relic. Be well.

The knot in Luka's belly loosened. This expansion of Alfie's *propio* was incredible. Alfie's handwriting wasn't even rushed. Things must truly be okay on their end. They were safe.

Luka wrote back: *Good to hear. Be careful of your time and stay safe. We're about to leave too.*

According to the gods, they had just six days to keep their world from crumbling, and they were already well into the morning of the first. Luka didn't know if they could control how long it took to travel from one continent to another, but if they could, they ought to try.

"Master Luka." Dueño Eduardo stood at the entrance to Alfie's rooms, eyeing James with suspicion. "We are departing now. Are you ready?"

Luka steeled himself. If Alfie and Finn could brave the tundra hunting for Sombra's relics, then he could do his part. He tucked the parchment back into his pocket.

Luka gave Alfie's rooms one last look before lying through his teeth. "I'm ready."

THE DEAD

As the water gushed downward, the shirtless corpse rose from the ground, his limbs awkward with disuse. He reached for Sombra's stone head, but Alfie pulled it away, scrambling backward toward Finn.

Alfie's eyes were wide with fear. "Is that the same man from—"

"Yes," Finn said, her voice quiet with shock. "Yes, it is."

The man began a slow crawl toward them, his body thawing more with every shuffle. The water still tore through the ice, creating a mess of cold mud. Another body fell through the hole. Then another and another.

"How is this happening?" Finn asked. "They're dead. They've *been* dead!"

"Paloma warned us that Sombra's relics might have an effect on their surroundings," Alfie said. "This is it!"

It made sense because it *didn't* make any damn sense.

The shirtless man began to crawl toward them, his body moving with an unnatural, jerky rhythm. Finn pulled Alfie close.

"I'll be damned if I get murdered by a shirtless fool. Hold tight, this is going to get messy," she said. With Alfie's arms wrapped securely around her, Finn focused on the night Ignacio had caught her escaping and led her home. On the relief that had pooled in her stomach even though she knew a beating was coming. Fueled by that horror, she shaped the earth beneath them into a raised square. With a thrust of her hand it moved, carrying them bumpily back out the way they'd come. They surged out of the tunnel and plopped onto the snowy ground.

Finn stood over the hole, arms outstretched and fingers splayed. She reached for the walls of the tunnel they'd so hastily dug and then, as she curled her fingers into fists, the earth collapsed downward, blocking anyone else from leaving.

If there had been time to think, she would've worried about how good she was getting at dwelling on those thoughts and using them to fuel her magic, but luckily they only had six days to save the world. Time was at a premium.

"There," Finn said, shivering under the moonlight. "All taken care of."

"Finn," Alfie said uneasily.

Slowly Finn turned, dread pooling in her stomach. The hulking figures of more dead men were closing in, ten or fifteen paces away at best. They'd walked up the mountain. Finn wasn't one to wait for a fight to come to her. She gripped a dagger in her hand and ran forward.

"Finn! That's no use, they're already dead!"

Finn thrust a dagger into one man's chest. "What exactly should I do, then? Dance with them?" The man was unfazed as she pulled the dagger out of his chest and plunged it back in for good measure. "Congratulate them on their second chance at life?"

"*Fuerza!*" Alfie shouted, but his magic seemed to have no effect on the men, as if being so close to Sombra's relic gave them new strength. When the prince froze them in blocks of ice, the corpses just broke through, gathering speed and strength as they went. They advanced in deafening silence, but Finn supposed that their ability to speak had died long ago. Their bodies moved with no soul, no heart. They reached for the stone head like moths to a flame.

"What now?" Finn said, her heart racing. If she couldn't kill them and the prince couldn't keep them at bay, what was left to do?

Behind them an arm burst out of the sunken dirt tunnel. Collapsing it had done nothing to stop the corpses from seeking their treasure.

"I've got an idea," Alfie said as the dead closed in, their limbs twitching with excitement at the sight of the stone piece. "You're not going to like it."

"Will I like it more than being overrun by dead fools? If so, I'm good."

Alfie winced. "Questionable."

"Whatever, just do it!" Finn sniped.

As the dead lurched forward in their uncanny silence, Alfie pulled her close and waved his arms artfully through the air. At first, nothing happened.

Alfie cursed and tried again, his eyes closed in concentration. Finally the snow responded, curling upward until they were encased in a ball of it.

"Coño," Finn screeched as the cold sank in. Their coats could only do so much.

"I know, I know," Alfie said, his teeth chattering.

But before the prince could do whatever he'd planned next, a hand burst through the snow behind Finn, gripping her by the back of the neck. She reached back and grabbed the forearm with both hands, but the cold fingers wouldn't budge.

"Finn!" Alfie shouted, gripping the arm himself.

"Don't!" Finn wheezed. Over the prince's shoulder, other frozen arms and legs were breaking through. He needed to protect himself. "I'll handle it."

Alfie jolted at the sight of the limbs breaching the snow barrier in front of him, speaking words of magic and water charming to try to push them out, but using magic wasn't as instinctual as it used to be. She watched him try and fail more times than he succeeded.

While the prince had lived his life with his nose in his books, Finn had lived hers with her fists raised. She could rely on other skills to keep these pendejos at bay. She wrenched herself forward, tugging on the arm at its elbow. There was a brittle snap, and Finn fell to her knees, the hand still wrapped around her throat—though it seemed weakened now that it was severed from the body. Finn pried the fingers off her neck. The dead hand skittered like a spider at Alfie's feet.

"I am so tired of random body parts doing this around me!" she shouted. Sombra's stone arms had been bad enough in the palace months ago. Finn slapped away yet another dead, frostbitten hand. "Whatever genius plan you have, Prince, get to it!"

Alfie thrust his hands forward, and the great ball of snow began to roll down the mountain. As it picked up speed, Finn and Alfie tumbled within the ball of snow, slamming against each other as it rolled.

They'd been rolling less than a minute when they struck something hard. The sphere of snow cracked like an egg, sending the two of them flying out to land on the powdery snow.

"You're right." Finn spat snow from her mouth. "I hated that."

At least they'd made it halfway down the mountain. In the distance she could see the glimmer of the frozen lake at the base.

"The corpses," Alfie said, breathless. "They're magicked to guard the piece! The original magic on the pond must have compelled any human nearby to protect them—now it compels the dead ones too!" His eyes widened as he looked over Finn's shoulder. Far behind them, the dead were still pursuing.

Alfie raised a platform of snow with a curved front for them to brace their feet on, like a child's sled. "Get in, we've got to—"

A hand jutted out from the snow, gripping Finn's ankle. She yelped, wrenching her foot away and clambering onto the sled. All around them bodies began to burst free of the snow, clawing their way into the daylight. Now that they'd brought the stone head down with them, Sombra's magic was also affecting the dead on the lower parts of the mountain. How many men had died here? Dozens? Hundreds?

"*Go, go, go!*" Finn shouted.

With a thrust of Alfie's arms, the sled darted down the steep mountain. As they moved, the dead broke free from the snow like flowers bursting out of the dirt. Alfie nearly lost control trying to avoid them.

They flew off the mountain, skidding onto the frozen lake.

"Well," Finn shouted as the sled slowed to a halt. "At least we're off Dead Men's Mountain—"

A loud *crack* sounded beneath them. Finn looked over the side of the sled to see a ghastly face with no nose pressed against the glass, its ravenous mouth open. Then came the roar of shattering ice as men began clawing themselves out of the lake. Their skin wrinkled and wet, they reached toward the sled with blind hunger. Two of them began pulling themselves over the side of the sled closest to Finn, but before she could move to stop them, Alfie had pulled her toward him, his gaze intense and fixed on the moving corpses.

The prince grimaced, looking almost pained before shouting, "*Fuerza!*"

The wet, dead men flew all the way back to the base of the mountain, disappearing into the snow. Finn stared at him. What memory did he use to fuel the magic he needed to send them flying like that? But there was no time to ask. More and more corpses were breaking out from under the ice, clawing their way up the sides of the sled.

"Shit, shit, shit!" she cursed. "What do we do?"

"I don't know," Alfie shouted back, but then his eyes brightened. "The bag!"

"What?"

"Once the bag sends the relic back to Castallan, they'll have no reason to chase us anymore!"

Alfie wrenched the sack off his shoulder and thrust it into Finn's hands. She held it open as Alfie grabbed the stone head from where it lay at his feet and began shoving it into the bag. All the while, dead explorers continued bursting from the lake, shards of ice erupting underfoot.

When one crawled over the edge of the sled, just behind Alfie, Finn dropped the bag to kick him in the face, sending him skipping across the frozen lake like a stone.

"Hurry up!" Finn shouted, turning this way and that to watch the lumbering dead close in. Who knew if the stupid bag would actually work. Paloma had said they'd used the dueños' strongest magic, but that guaranteed nothing.

"I'm moving as fast as I can!"

The bag looked far too small at first, but just as Paloma had promised, it seemed to stretch to accommodate the head before the stone finally disappeared inside, transported back to the palace where some of the dueños waited.

In the space of a breath, it was gone. Finn stared at the lake, where the dead were still crawling out of the ice. Slowly they came to a halt, frozen once more.

"Well," Finn said as Alfie cradled his head in his hands. "That's one piece down."

THE COLLEAGUE

Svana washed onto the shores of Castallan like a message in a bottle—her thoughts and feelings carefully inscribed, waiting to be found and uncorked by the one they were meant for.

She sputtered on all fours, puking seawater. The beach stank from the countless dead fish that had been washed ashore, boiled alive in the ocean. Her pale skin had been scorched pink. When she had boarded the ship, she'd hardly expected to find herself leaping overboard into searing seawater, but life was full of surprises.

The journey had been nothing but smooth sailing until Sombra disrupted the balance of light and dark and Nocturna began. Svana had been lucky to be alone in her cabin instead of the crowded areas of the boat when chaos erupted on the ship, but not lucky enough to leave unscathed.

She'd been asleep when a man had burst through her door, demanding her valuables. Waking up to the sight of an angry, shadowless stranger had been so shocking that she froze. The man leaped on her and began to choke her. Dueños were not trained in combat.

To be a scholar of magic was to use it as a resource of knowledge, not a weapon, unless absolutely necessary, and Svana had spent her life avoiding situations that would make it necessary.

Until now.

When she'd tried to push the man away from her, he bit two of her fingers clean off.

Svana looked at the two stubs where her pointer and middle fingers used to be. She'd healed the wounds as best as she could, but there was little else that could be done. She frowned. Paloma had always told her she had beautiful hands.

Svana pushed that thought away. Now was not the time for vanity.

When she'd escaped the shadowless man and emerged on deck, she'd been shocked to see the moon splintered in the sky. She'd been even more shocked when she'd grabbed a lifeboat, lowering it and herself into scorching-hot water. Steam came off the waves in hot tendrils that stank of the dying creatures below. Thank goodness she'd made it as far as she did before her boat capsized. She'd been tossed around the hot waves like the sea was a cat playing with a mouse before devouring it whole.

But she'd survived. The sea had spat her onto the shore. She could help Paloma balance the world again, and if they couldn't manage that, then at least they could die together.

With difficulty, Svana pulled the parchment from the pocket of her robes. She thanked the gods that she had enchanted it to be water resistant. She'd hardly had time to open it and respond to Paloma's messages because she was too busy fighting for her life. At this time of the month the sea should have been gentle, but it seemed that the imbalance had not only affected the temperature; it affected the tides too. She supposed that made sense, since the moon was broken.

The last thing she'd read from Paloma was the prophecy from their audience with the gods, and the prince and thief's plan to retrieve Sombra's relics. She began to unfold the parchment, desperate to know if any progress had been made in their quest to end Sombra.

"Well, well, well. Look what we have here."

Svana startled as two men crept out of the darkness. She could tell from their clothing that they were fishermen—or at least they had been before Sombra had robbed them of the light.

"Look at those robes. Sombra will be pleased when we bring this one to him," he said, looking her up and down.

The sea had wrung her of energy, but she needed to get to Paloma. If she had to hurt these men to do so, then so be it.

With a thrust of her arm, streams of hot seawater struck the men in their bellies, sending them flying up the shore. She'd sensed Sombra's return and knew what needed to be done to access magic. She gritted her teeth and fell into her shame of loving another when it was against the laws of the dueños to distract oneself with such things. She burrowed into the years she'd spent denying herself before she'd finally shed her guilt and taken Paloma's hand in hers, a question in her eyes that the other dueña had warmly answered. She could feel the magic moving through her, uncomfortable and unpleasant as finding a hair on your tongue.

She would hurt these shadowless only as much as she needed to. It wasn't in her nature to press it further.

But she didn't see the shadowless woman coming up behind her.

As the stranger struck the back of Svana's head with the hilt of a dagger, she fell face-first into the wet sand, her mind going blank.

The woman dragged Svana away, and the parchment the dueña shared with Paloma was carried off by the current—a message without a bottle.

THE DRAGON

Finn had never thought she'd feel such a sense of triumph while surrounded by frozen corpses, but here she was.

The shattered moon shone its strange light over the white snow, reflecting on the frozen lake.

"Wow." Her head dropped back as she let out a laugh.

"How could you possibly be laughing at a time like this?" Alfie asked, exasperated. His hands were gripping the sides of the ice sled so tightly it had begun to crack. She and the prince had fought for their lives together before, but having to focus on their darkest memories while they did so had taken things to a whole new horrible level.

She thought of when he'd blasted those corpses all the way from the frozen lake back to the base of the mountain. She hadn't seen him perform such powerful magic since before Sombra's return. She wondered what memory had given his magic that kind of power.

Finn shrugged, pushing those thoughts away. "Because for a second there I wasn't sure I'd ever have a chance to laugh again."

Alfie must've found that answer acceptable because he let out his own sigh of relief. He let go of the sled and pulled the parchment out from under his chest plate. "Luka and the dueños are about to leave. Or they were when he sent this." He wrote a note back to Luka before pulling out his pocket watch. "It's nearly six in the evening. We've been here for six hours."

Finn swallowed. Their first day was almost done.

"Well then, we've got no time to waste," Finn said. "Let's get to the next relic."

Alfie tucked the parchment and pocket watch back under the chest plate of his armor. Then he rose from the sled, holding out his hand for Finn to take.

She swatted it away and hopped out. "I'm a thief, not a lady."

Alfie gave a small smile. "Why not both?"

"If you want an excuse to hold my hand, just say so," Finn replied with a smirk.

Alfie took her hand in his, interlacing their fingers. "Okay."

Her face hot, Finn looked anywhere but Alfie's eyes.

"Forgive me." Alfie pulled her up. "For a moment there I wasn't sure if I'd have the chance to do this again."

Warmth pooled in Finn's belly.

"You seem tired," Finn said, quick to change the subject. "Should we rest a bit before the next round?"

He looked as if he might fall right where he stood. She wondered how much transporting them from Castallan to Uppskala had taken out of him.

Alfie bit back a yawn. "While that sounds lovely, time is not on our side."

He wasn't wrong. They had until their birthday to stop Sombra for good. There was no time to waste. Alfie pulled the doorknob out of his pocket, weighing it in his palm. At least, since this was his *propio*, he wouldn't have to dwell on his own sadness to get the magic to work.

"All right, but remember that your expectations affect how the magic will look when we get there. So don't let your imagination get the best of you." She rose on her tiptoes and tapped his forehead. "I don't want to step in there and suddenly burst into flames or something."

"I'll make sure I behave this time." He let the doorknob fall from his hand onto the frozen lake. It spun and sank into the ice, waiting for the prince's touch.

The pair crouched, and with his free hand Alfie turned the knob. Finn bit back a scream as the ground opened beneath them and they fell into the dark. She braced herself to smack into a hard surface but was surprised when they landed on a soft floor.

Alfie tapped his forehead just as she had moments ago. "I used my imagination for good this time. Just imagined us landing in my bed—" He broke off, looking embarrassed.

Finn looked away too, not because she was embarrassed by what happened between them (after all, she'd been hoping for an encore), but because of how much it meant.

And how it could never last.

She hurriedly got off the soft patch of ground and took in their surroundings. The prince had done well. All the strings were still black, but at least they weren't knotted again because of his ever-climbing anxiety.

They stripped off their sealskin cloaks and boots in favor of lighter clothing. With Uppskala behind them, they didn't need them anymore.

"I've imagined a condensed version of the world's strings," Alfie explained, rubbing the back of his neck. "The same system as usual but shrunk down so that the strings from different kingdoms won't be too far out of reach. Your guitar method was brilliant, but this will make it easier to try to find the right one. Now I can walk through them and feel the person connected to each string. This way finding the right one will be a quicker process." Alfie looked at the crisscrossing of strings around them. "In this miniaturized representation of the entire world, each kingdom is more or less equally close to us."

Finn nodded. His logic was sound. "Where to next?"

Alfie's face soured as he pointed behind him. "This way, unfortunately."

"Why unfortunately?" she laughed as Alfie began his walk through the strings.

"Next we have to retrieve the torso," Alfie said stiffly. "We're walking through the strings of Englass now."

Finn's eyebrows crept up into her hairline.

"I'm fine," Alfie said, sensing her thoughts. "There's no way around it, but I'd appreciate some distraction while we walk there, if you're willing to keep my mind off it."

"Sure." Finn jogged to keep up with him and his annoyingly long legs. "What do you want to talk about? I've got a lot of info on daggers and blades that I can—"

"I was thinking of something else," Alfie said carefully.

Finn shrugged. "Name it."

"Could I ask you something?"

Finn rolled her eyes. "Spit it out."

"I thought we should talk about . . ."

Finn's stomach dropped. He was going to ask about the night they'd spent together. She knew it. In his eyes was the same soft look he'd given her then, when he'd cupped the back of her head and slowly lowered her, as if she were too delicate to even touch the pillow. When she'd held him as close as she'd wanted because she'd thought it was the only night they'd have together.

It was strange to so badly want to return to a moment yet simultaneously want to never speak of it again.

"I don't want to talk about last night," Finn blurted.

Alfie nearly tripped over his feet. "I was going to ask to talk about your *propio* not working."

Finn stared at him. "Oh." Yet another topic she didn't want to think about.

"Does what happened between us scare you that much?" Alfie asked gently, his steps slowing.

When she said nothing, Alfie stopped moving.

"Finn," he said. "*Propio* magic is related to emotion. They can become difficult to use if you have an—"

"Internal blockage," Finn interrupted him, recalling Dueño Bruno's words. "I know. That doesn't mean I have to talk about it."

Alfie blinked. She could tell he wanted to ask how she knew that. "You don't think that maybe that internal blockage could have to do with how you're feeling after that night?"

"You don't know how I felt after that." Finn picked up her pace,

Alfie trailing behind her.

"I know that you're running."

Finn turned on her heel and faced him. "I am not running. I—" Finn took a step back. "Something's under your shirt," she said, her eyes on the small bulge beneath his collar. It was just above where the flexible plate of armor began, and it was *moving*.

"What?" Alfie said. "Finn, please don't change the subject."

"Alfie!" she said. "I'm not joking, there's something there!"

Alfie looked down, seeming to finally feel the thing moving about. He yelped in alarm.

Alfie popped open the top buttons of his shirt to find the toy dragon walking on his chest.

"How can this be?" Alfie asked as the dragon sat on his palm. Dezmin was the only one who could animate these carvings.

Alfie's heart sputtered in his chest.

"Hello, hermanito." Dezmin's voice rang from the toy, brittle with emotion. He sounded uncertain, almost afraid. As if it had been a lifetime since he'd spoken to someone he loved.

But then, hadn't it been?

Finn stared at Alfie, suspicion in her eyes. She needn't speak; he knew what she was thinking from her gaze alone.

"How do I know it's really you?" Alfie forced himself to ask the dragon. He didn't want to believe that this was a trick. If it was, then the pain of this memory could fuel thousands of spells. Still, he had to ask.

Silence reigned for a moment, then the dragon spoke.

"When you were a little boy, you insisted that we give our little sister a name starting with 'B' or 'C,' so that it would be between our names in the alphabet. You said that it made sense because we'd always be on either side of her, to protect her."

Tears sprang into Alfie's eyes. Dezmin was the only person Alfie had said that to as they waited for their sister, who would be born silent and still. His hand flew to his mouth. "Dezmin," he said to Finn. "It's Dezmin."

"What?" she asked, staring at the dragon. Then her eyes widened.

"Dezmin is the dragon," Alfie said, and the dragon nuzzled his palm. "*Journey under dragon's wing.* It was a part of the prophecy." Hot tears poured down his face.

"I'm not sure of what that means, but I can't stay long," Dezmin said. "I can only do this while Sombra's attention is elsewhere. If I disappear it's because he is no longer distracted, and I'll try my best to come back when I can."

"Are you okay?" Alfie asked. He could barely speak over the burning in his throat. "Are you in pain?"

"I'm the eldest," Dezmin said. "I worry for you, not the other way around."

It was that familiar protectiveness from his older brother that undid him.

"I looked for you," Alfie sobbed. And he had. He'd looked for Dezmin in every tome in the library, at the bottom of bottles of rum, in illegal card games in the Pinch. "I looked for you every day but I couldn't find you. I couldn't save you, I couldn't—"

"I know you did, hermanito, I know." And though Alfie couldn't see his brother, he heard the strain in his voice, the strain of trying to stay whole even as what you were feeling threatened to pull you apart.

Finn gripped his shoulder and Alfie knew that if not for her he'd have fallen to his knees. His brother was speaking to him—his brother was *here*.

"Sombra has me trapped in my own body, but I can see into his mind," Dezmin said.

"Can he see into yours?" Finn asked.

Alfie had been so excited to hear from Dezmin that he hadn't wondered if Sombra would be able to pry whatever information passed between them from Dezmin's mind.

"He is far too vain to look into my mind," Dezmin said. "I'm a vessel for him, nothing more. But just in case, you two should keep your secrets to yourselves."

"What is he doing now?" Alfie asked.

"He is using his magic to summon more larimar," Dezmin said. "He knows that you used larimar to summon an audience with the gods and he is looking for ways to learn what you discovered."

Alfie opened his mouth to speak.

"Don't tell me," Dezmin said, the toy dragon's tail straightening sharply. "I can't let him use me against you. But I wanted to see you . . . and to tell you that I'm sorry. I'm so sorry. If not for me, he would not be here."

"What happened?" Alfie asked, rubbing his eyes with the back of his free hand.

"Telling you would take far too long," Dezmin said. "But I think I can show you."

THE BETWIXT

The toy dragon curled into a circle on Alfie's palm, as if trying to get as close to the skin as possible, and in the space of a breath Alfie was transported into his brother's memories.

Dezmin floated in the darkness, his body immobile, his soul dying slowly, while his body stayed resolutely alive.

He had spent so long in silence. First begging for salvation and then begging for death. When he finally heard the sound of another's voice, it was painfully loud.

I can help you move again. I can help you speak again. I can help you live again. You need only ask. Ask me to give you my strength and house me in your body.

Dezmin had studied all his life with the goal of becoming a good and just king. He was no fool. But the voice had awakened something desperate and dangerous within him—hope.

Hope had held his mind together by a thread when it would be kinder to simply go mad. Hope had held him in place when he wanted to crawl so far into the recesses of his mind that he would cease to exist. Hope had been his only company in the vast darkness—his companion and his sworn enemy.

He hated hope. But Dezmin couldn't help it—he was hopeful now.

Invite me in, the toy whispered.

With all his might Dezmin thought, *I invite you in. Please.*

A stream of obsidian smoke wafted from the toy dragon. Even against the darkness of the void, the smoke stood out. It made the gloom around it look lighter in comparison.

The smoke crept up his nostrils and slithered down into his body. Dezmin felt a surge of power building within him, as if he were housing the sun itself. It felt unnatural, painful, as if he were being seared from the inside out. He lay suspended in that pain for what could have been an eternity, burning and breaking.

In the throes of the pain, his body began to thaw and move. First his fingers and toes, then his arms and legs moving of their own accord, his tongue rolling over the edges of his teeth. When his throat had become raw from his cries, the pain finally began to subside. It was as if his whole body were a cauterized wound and the searing brand had been pulled back at last.

"I'm here, I'm here. I'm alive!" He patted his body down with his hands, afraid that it wasn't really there. Tears slipped down his nose and cheeks. "I want to go home."

And you will, the voice said soothingly, but its next words were sharp. *But there is something we must do first.*

"What is it?"

Promise me that when the time comes, you will do what must be done to leave this place.

"I promise," Dezmin said.

It no longer mattered what the promise entailed so long as there was someone here to make a promise to.

Alfie watched as the memory shifted. They were still in the void, but they were moving.

Dezmin listened to the voice, letting it lead him through the darkness.

He did not know how long they'd been walking or how much time had passed since he'd fallen into the void, but the voice was certain this was the way to complete the task that would let them back into the world.

There was no floor, but when Dezmin stepped forward his foot landed on a circle of invisible ground. As he stepped off and onto the next, the first one disappeared.

"How?"

I am weak, the voice said, exhaustion muffling the sound. *But I have enough strength to provide a path.*

"Why are you weak?" Dezmin asked as he walked farther and farther into the dark.

Before I was banished to this place I was injured by a great enemy.

Dez frowned. This voice had given him movement, given him life again. Who would choose to hurt it?

Dezmin pushed those thoughts away. There was no time for such concerns. He picked up speed, moving through the dark like a stone skipped across a black lake. He hurried, seeking only a way home, not destruction.

As fate would have it, he'd find both.

The memory switched yet again. Alfie couldn't tell how much time had passed, but Dezmin was still walking into the dark, the toy dragon floating at his side.

We're close, the voice said. *Keep moving.*

Dezmin ran on, his eyes searching for whatever the voice was guiding him to, but there was nothing but inky black emptiness. He was beginning to fear that the voice was mistaken, that he was running nowhere. Everything looked the same; there was no way to tell.

I feel your doubt, the voice said. *It is understandable but misguided. You must trust me.*

"I trust you," Dezmin replied.

They moved forward in silence and at first Dezmin thought there was something wrong with his eyes—they were burning and watering. He gasped. There was light in front of him. Real light. It had been so long that his eyes couldn't bear it.

He raised his hand against the glare, shielding himself.

We are here, the voice said, excitement making it speak too fast. *Open your eyes.*

Dezmin obeyed and blinked at the light before his eyes finally began to focus.

Before him, floating in the dark, was the shape of a woman

made of pure light. At her feet stretched a shadow in the shape of a man. There was an air of serenity around them that Dezmin did not want to disturb. Something told him he wasn't supposed to, the way a child knew not to touch a hot stove.

You see the light, the voice said. *You must destroy it.*

Dezmin jumped where he stood. "What?"

This is the price of leaving this place.

Fear pooled in Dezmin's belly. He couldn't return to the stillness and silence. He couldn't. But something about the man and woman before him felt familiar. He just couldn't place it.

"There's something wrong," Dezmin said. Hadn't there been a story about this?

Focus, the voice interrupted. *This is what must be done, what we have traveled so far for!*

What was that story about? In his mind's eye he saw a younger version of himself and Alfie listening intently as Paloma read it to them. But the words eluded him. For a moment they seemed solid, easy for him to grab, but once his fingers wrapped around the memory they turned to water, flowing out of his grasp. Why couldn't he remember?

Dwelling alone in the dark, all Dezmin had were his memories. He'd done nothing but rehash them over and over, until the memories had become blurred with overuse—a picture he'd folded and kept in his pocket, reopening it again and again until the image was marred with creases and age. His mind was a scramble. Had this happened or had he imagined it? Was that a memory or a story he created to soothe himself as he suffered through yet another eternity of darkness?

My strength is waning, the voice begged, and Dezmin could feel the ground that the voice had created for him to walk on becoming unstable. *If you do not do it now, we will never be free. Reach into the light and pull out her heart. Do it or return to the silent darkness.*

Panic chased the memory away. Dezmin couldn't stay here, couldn't return to a life of silent suffering.

But would the being of light fight back?

She won't, the voice said hurriedly. *She cannot move or harm you.*

His hand shaking, he reached for the chest of the woman made of light. He'd expected to feel something solid, but his hand sank right through as if she were made of nothing but air—until he reached her heart. It was painfully solid, beating against his fingertips with a steady thrum. Again, Dezmin had the feeling that he was about to do something terribly wrong.

Tendrils of the story were returning to him, faint and quiet: Their embrace created mankind as it was always meant to be—a balance of light and dark. And should the balance ever be disturbed in favor of Sombra . . .

Crush it! the voice shouted. *Destroy it or you'll never return home!*

Dezmin knew that this was wrong, that the voice could not be good if it asked for the destruction of anything, let alone something so beautiful. But his desperation overrode his conscience. He would not stay here, could not. How could the right choice be to stay in this agony?

The faces of his loved ones flashed before his mind's eye. He didn't know if they would forgive him or condemn him, but he couldn't bear the thought of never finding out.

He gripped tighter and tighter until it shattered in his hand, the light snuffing out with it.

The voice gave a sigh of relief and Dezmin could feel its strength growing inside him, a sapling quickly becoming a forest. The shadow that once lay at the woman's feet rose up in the dark and swelled in size until there was no void, only this man of shadow taking up all the space as far as the eye could see.

Dezmin's heart hammered in his chest as the shadow raised its arms high. For a moment Dezmin thought it was stretching, but when fissures sprang in the ceiling of the void he knew what it was doing—it was cracking the void open like an egg.

The voice laughed. *Finally!*

It was suddenly much louder than it had been, growing in sound and power just as the man of shadow had. Dezmin could barely hear himself anymore; the rush of thoughts flowing between his ears was no longer his. It was as if he had been locked in the attic of his body and he had to press his ear to the floor to hear what was happening in his own home. To hear an intruder making himself comfortable.

He'd made a terrible mistake.

Smile, my child, the voice laughed as the void shattered. Shards of shadow rained on Dezmin's head. *You're almost home.*

Alfie blinked as the string of memories ended. He looked at Finn, his face wet with tears.

"I'm sorry," Dezmin said from within the toy dragon. "If I hadn't—"

"No," Alfie said, cradling the dragon in his hands. "I would never blame you for wanting to be free of something so horrible." He'd seen how numb and empty Dezmin's existence had become. How could anyone blame him for trying to leave?

The dragon nuzzled Alfie's palm, and Alfie wished once again that he could embrace his brother.

"What happened?" Finn asked. "What did he show you?"

"Xiomara's void," Alfie said, finally understanding. "It isn't just any place. It's the Betwixt."

Finn stared at him. "The what?"

"There are countless magical theories about how the balance of light and dark works and how it stays hidden, but no one has ever known for sure since no mortal has ever seen it." He looked mournfully at the dragon. "Except Dezmin."

"All right, how does Xiomara's void matter in all this?" Finn pressed.

"One theory is that there is a vacuous pocket of space surrounding the woman of light and the man of shadow. A place devoid of life and untenable for any living thing. This space would keep mortals from ever being able to find and corrupt it. The void is like a protective layer to keep people out. Magical theorists called that empty space the Betwixt."

"So Xiomara's void was that protective layer around the balance." She stared at him, the weight of it settling in her mind. "Like an eggshell."

Alfie nodded. "Yes, just like that."

Finn looked at him, her eyes wide. "We delivered Sombra

straight to the heart of the world—the sacred place where the balance of magic is hidden."

Alfie swallowed thickly. "We did."

"And I carried him the rest of the way," Dezmin said, solemn.

"You didn't—"

"I must go," Dezmin said hurriedly, cutting him off. "Sombra is finishing his work with the larimar. Protect all that you learned from the gods, because he is looking for a way to find out what you know."

Alfie was so shocked by the thought of losing his brother once more that he could barely speak. "Wait, don't—"

But the dragon had already fallen still, and Alfie feared his heart would too.

THE GREAT OUTDOORS

Luka was not a nature person.

He'd been to a botanical-themed party once where the cocktails were named after and served in flowers, but that's as far as he got when it came to enjoying nature. Even his childhood riding lessons with Alfie and Dezmin had been the bane of his existence. Luka had wondered whether he might come to cherish the great outdoors with age, as their riding instructor had claimed he would, but as he rode through underground tunnels away from the city with the dueños and James, Luka knew the man had been wrong.

The torchlit tunnels were tight, allowing only three horsemen side by side. Their caravan of twenty rode slowly, with Luka sandwiched between two dueños just behind Paloma's horse.

As he tried to take a deep breath of hot air, Luka inhaled a buzzing cave fly. In a flurry of panic, he spat the bug right onto the cheek of the old dueño riding to his left.

"Excuse me!" Eduardo shouted, jolting in his saddle.

"What?" Luka demanded, wiping his face. "Did you expect me to eat it?"

The hairy-nosed dueño glowered at him. "No, but I'd hoped you'd keep it away from my face."

"Consider it a kiss," Luka said with a wink.

"Would you like a handkerchief?" James offered from the row behind Luka. He seemed to be trying to be as helpful and quiet as possible in the company of Castallanos, who still didn't quite know what to do with an Englassen ally.

As the old man snatched the handkerchief from James's hand, the two boys met eyes. Luka granted him a small smile and James looked grateful to receive it.

Luka's feelings about the Englassen boy hadn't changed, per se. But James had followed Luka into an unquestionably dangerous situation without hesitation. There was something to be said for that. James could've tried to escape when Sombra returned, but he'd chosen to stay and help. To atone for what he'd done. Luka didn't know how to stay distrustful of him. He didn't know if he even wanted that anymore.

Embarrassment pooled in his belly as he realized that he'd been staring at James for far too long. Feeling the familiar warmth of the parchment in his pocket, Luka looked away from the boy and wrenched it out. He read the message like a starving man devouring a piece of stale bread—it wasn't the same as speaking to Alfie in person, but it was something.

"They've secured the first of Sombra's relics!" he said excitedly, his voice echoing through the tunnel.

Paloma turned in her saddle. "And they're safe?"

Luka gripped the parchment in his shaking hands. "Yes, they're all right." At least he hoped they were. He knew that Alfie would try to keep the worst details of their adventure from everyone else. He found himself wishing that he'd set up another parchment only with Finn. She wouldn't shy away from the gory details. Then again, maybe Luka didn't want to know.

Luka wrote: *We're in the underground tunnels on our way to the oasis. Good to know you're both alive.*

A reply appeared immediately.

We're glad to hear you all made it out of the city in one piece. We'll be traveling now to find the next relic. Please take care of each other until we can be together again.

Luka rolled his eyes at Alfie's sappy words but felt a burn at the back of his throat. When *would* they all be together again?

"They'll be stepping back into the realm of magic to find the next relic," Luka said.

As if fate were attempting to match his mood, weak beams of moonlight began to fill the tunnel. They were finally getting out of this stuffy, gods-forsaken underground nightmare! The horses nickered in excitement, and even the dreariest, most straitlaced of the dueños perked up at the sight. According to Paloma, the tunnel would lead them into the sugarcane fields surrounding the city. Luka had always known the underground tunnels existed—after all, the royal family needed to have escape routes in place—but he hadn't known where they would actually take them.

"I hope it doesn't take as long for them to travel to the next one," James said quietly from behind Luka. He too rode between two dueños, who looked far from enthusiastic to be babysitting the Englassen.

"Me too," Luka agreed as they finally approached the mouth of the tunnel. Hours spent in the realm of magic could be the difference between victory and the end of all they knew. Luka pushed those bleak thoughts away. They were finally leaving the tunnels. He could be optimistic.

Moonlight fell over him like a curtain of joy as Luka's horse emerged into the fresh air, but his jaw dropped at the sight before him.

Where there once had been tall, green-leafed sugarcane stalks as far as the eye could see, now the stalks were black, curling in on themselves. On first glance one would think they'd been burned, but when Luka looked closely, the difference was clear. They hadn't been burned; they'd had the life sucked out of them, leaving only blackened husks. The horses whinnied in distress, and the caravan came to a halt at the mouth of the tunnel to calm them.

Luka reached for a stalk and watched it crumble to dust in his hands. "They were still alive before we left."

Luka had seen the green fields from Alfie's balcony while they were preparing for the journey. He'd *seen* them, a green halo that surrounded the city. It didn't make any sense.

"This is what happens to the world when the balance is disturbed," Paloma said, her face grim. "The power of darkness left unchecked. This is Nocturna."

Luka's jaw tightened. What was once sweet and alive had become soot on his palms. If the sugarcane was dying, would all the other crops follow? Would humankind starve in its final days in this world as Sombra laughed from his palace in the sky?

He and James met each other's gaze. The Englassen had been right to worry about Alfie and Finn's timeliness. Time was burning away into nothing, just as the sugarcane had.

"We don't have the luxury of stopping to mourn," Dueño Bruno said, but even he looked shaken, his hands gripping the reins of his horse tightly. "We must get to the oasis if we are to stop this destruction from spreading any farther."

"He is right," Paloma said. "We must make haste while we still can."

With that less than inspiring speech, the caravan broke into a canter, following Paloma's lead deeper into the dead fields. Luka scanned the rows of blackened stalks for signs of the shadowless, but there was nothing but salted earth and the picked-over corpses of animals that had died along with the sugarcane. He supposed there wasn't any reason for the shadowless to leave the city for empty sugarcane fields.

Hours passed, slow as syrup.

It was hard to tell how much time had gone by because the world stayed in an endless night.

Luka was struck once more by how quickly Sombra had taken this world into his hands and bent it into something else entirely.

Not only did the sky never change, but neither did the scenery. Luka had hoped that perhaps things would be better the farther away they got from San Cristóbal. But whether they were galloping quickly or stopping to rest the horses, nothing but blackened countryside surrounded them. There weren't even any animals milling about. They had either fled in search of someplace habitable or died along with the plants.

Tired of the silence and the bleak scenery, Luka brought his horse into a canter beside Paloma's. "What's the plan once we get to the oasis?" he asked her. "How will you get to the spirit realm to speak with the dueños?"

Paloma and her colleagues had merely said that the oasis was a sacred place where they could commune with the dueños of the past, but they hadn't explained how they'd do it. Luka supposed that he didn't *need* the details. After all, he wasn't going to play any role in the process. But still, he wanted to know.

"It's difficult to explain to someone outside our ranks," she said stiffly.

Their horses crunched over the withered remains of what should've been a field of flowers. He could see the corpses of bunches of morivivi and flor de mantequilla. This field should've been bright with color—pinks and sunny yellows, orange and magenta. The butter flowers had been his mother's favorite. "Try me."

"It requires a bit of meditation," Paloma explained. "A dueño enters the oasis and floats on its surface. They must let their mind fall silent, free of wants and desires. Then, if the dueños of the past so choose, they will make contact."

Luka grimaced. Making his mind silent and not wanting things were not his strengths.

"The dueño's mind will ascend to the spirit realm as the others keep watch to make sure nothing happens to them while they are on their mission," Paloma explained. "It's a vulnerable state."

Luka's brows rose into his hairline. Alfie had meditated in front of him, but it had never occurred to Luka that he might be so far gone that he was left unable to protect himself. But then, the two of them had spent their lives surrounded by tall palace walls and guards; they never had to worry much about being vulnerable to attack. Not until recently, anyway.

He smothered those thoughts, grounding himself in the present.

"Will it be you who does it?" Luka asked.

Paloma nodded. "The process takes a great deal of energy. As I am one of the youngest, it makes sense for me to attempt it first. Should I fail, the elders will try."

"Well, you won't," Luka said easily.

"What makes you so sure?"

Luka was surprised that she'd asked. Paloma didn't usually entertain conversations about hypotheticals. She dealt in logic and reality. But maybe she needed a distraction too.

Luka shrugged. "You just don't seem like the type who fails."

Paloma kept her eyes on the dim horizon. "Anyone can fail."

Luka's grip tightened on his reins. He wasn't sure what to say to that, but as it turned out he didn't need to say a word. Paloma's eyes widened at the sight of something ahead. Luka followed her gaze and there, in this endless graveyard of nature, was a patch of lush green.

Life.

It was an acre of farmland. Luka could spot a green field for grazing, row upon row of crops—corn, plátanos, sugarcane—all alive and vibrant. At the far end was a simple farmstead sandwiched between a large chicken coop and a grove of trees. He couldn't tell if they were mango trees or limoncillo trees, but it didn't matter—the sight of any living tree was exciting.

It looked foreign and unnaturally bright surrounded by so much death and darkness. Only a day had passed since Sombra's return, and still Luka found himself marveling at it, thinking, *That's how the whole world used to look?*

The dueños looked at each other in silent shock. Maybe his childhood riding instructor had been right. Maybe there really was something to love in nature.

"Is everyone seeing this or have I lost my mind?" James called from his horse.

"We see it!" Luka laughed. "It's there!"

Luka wanted to spur his horse into a sprint and roll in the grass (well, maybe not roll in it. Stains), but the dueños did the opposite. They began to slow their horses down.

"We don't know why this area is unaffected, Luka," Paloma said. "It might be best to skirt around it and carry on."

The dueños were talking among themselves, looking concerned. Only Luka and James looked at the oasis of green with unabashed longing.

"Let's go!" Luka shouted. "What are we waiting for?"

"Why should we go there?" Eduardo asked.

Luka stared at him. "Because it's *alive!*"

"Something's wrong," Paloma said. "Where are the cattle? The people?"

Luka gritted his teeth against their pessimism. "The people became shadowless and ran off, and the animals probably got spooked when their masters lost their shadows and their minds!"

He knew he was making sense because no one rolled their eyes.

"Maybe we should just keep going," James said, giving in. Luka was shocked that a boy who had killed with his bare hands was so conflict avoidant.

"It is suspicious," Dueño Bruno said, his voice gravelly with age. "But it may be worth the risk. The plants aren't the only things dying." Reaching into his bag, he pulled out a mango, spots of strange black mold riddling its bright skin. Sombra's influence knew no bounds.

"What?" Luka reached into his own satchel and pulled out the bread he'd brought. It'd been fresh from the kitchens, but it too was already starting to rot. Luka tore off the dark, fuzzy bits and tossed them to the ground.

The others checked their own food stores and confirmed the same.

Dueño Eduardo finally relented. "If our food is rotting at this rate, then it would be prudent to collect more for the remainder of the journey."

Luka's heart leaped in his chest. "And I bet there's a place to water the horses too."

Paloma massaged the bridge of her nose, but Luka knew the decision had been made.

"If you're nervous," James offered to Paloma, "half of us can stay here while the rest go in—myself included, of course."

Luka watched as the dueños stared James down. Even when he offered to hypothetically risk his life, he was still an Englassen traitor.

"I think that's a very smart idea," Luka said diplomatically. "Compromise."

James shot him a grateful glance. "Once we confirm that the place is safe, perhaps the rest of you will want to join us."

Luka stared at the lush farmland. "Maybe this is proof of the world fighting back, fighting against Sombra's grip to stay alive. Why can't it be something hopeful instead of something bad?"

Paloma didn't respond to that. She and six other dueños volunteered, roughly dividing their caravan of twenty in half.

Each volunteer picked a task. Luka chose grabbing corn and plátanos from the field. Some sweet corn on the cob would lift their spirits on the journey, and the plátanos would make a hardy mangú that would keep them full for hours. So long as they didn't rot too fast. Plus, he wanted to ride his horse through the field, letting the stalks whip past him.

"We ride through and grab food for the journey." Paloma looked at Luka. He felt like a child being told to behave before company came over. "No loitering or exploring. We grab fruit from the trees and the fields, eggs from the chicken coop. We move quickly, is that understood?"

Luka forced himself to nod. Was it still lying if you didn't speak? Because Luka was going to luxuriate in that verdant garden for as long as he could.

"And remember that magic no longer works as it once did. You must focus on darker emotions or you will not be able to access it," Paloma reminded them.

Luka shifted uncomfortably on his horse. He hadn't practiced using spoken or elemental magic since his fight with the Tattooed King. Thinking of his dying family had been the only way to summon the magic, and he did not want to return to that sad, hopeless place. But what stood before them wasn't an enemy like the Tat-tooed King; it was a lush paradise. There was nothing to fight aside from the dueños' paranoia.

"Very well, if we are all ready." Paloma held his gaze for a long moment before relenting. "Let's go."

They rode in a tight formation with Paloma, Luka, and James leading and the rest following in two rows. The group split off into different sections and Luka dug his heels into his horse's flanks, tak-ing him right into the cornfield. He dropped the reins and held his hands out, his fingertips brushing over the heads of the stalks.

As they reached the center of the field, he pulled his horse to a stop and dismounted. He wouldn't loiter, but he could still enjoy things for a moment. While his horse sniffed at the greenery, pull-ing grass from the ground, Luka surveyed the crops. They looked vibrant and strong in the weak moonlight. Whoever the farmer was, he'd taken great pride in his work. But there was one stalk in par-ticular that was larger than the others. It stuck out like a sore thumb, thicker and taller in the otherwise uniform row. Luka approached it, staring. He snorted—as if he had the agricultural knowledge to figure out why it was growing so well! But still, it was strange.

Luka scanned the stalk from head to toe. There was a dark cir-cle at its base, as if it'd just been watered. Luka scanned the ground. None of the others in his sight line were like this. Why would the farmer water a single cornstalk in the middle of the field? He squat-ted and moved the long, thick leaves to get a better look.

For a moment he didn't understand what he was looking at. He couldn't process it. No one should have to process it. But the lips stretched into an eternal wail were unmistakable.

Luka fell onto his backside, a scream perching on his tongue.

The cornstalk was growing out of the open mouth of a man. Leafy weeds sprouted from his eye sockets, and out of his ears. The circle of moisture around the stalk wasn't water—it was blood.

The empty farmhouse and cattle fields made sense now.

"*Paloma!*" Luka shouted.

As if it knew the jig was up, the land sprang to life.

Thick roots erupted from the ground, snaking around Luka's ankles. They flexed, their movements muscular and vigorous. Luka could feel them pulsing with life. They tugged him backward until he fell onto his stomach, smacking his face into the dirt right next to the corpse's open mouth. His horse reared back on its hind legs, whinnying in fear. Roots were wrapping around it too, pulling it to the ground as it bucked and writhed.

Luka could hear screams erupting from other parts of the farm, but he could see nothing beyond the rows of corn. Small tendrils sprouted from the ground and forced their way up Luka's nostrils. He choked and gasped. He could feel them tickling the back of his throat, seeking a new place to root themselves.

"No!" he yelled, jerking his head back. He gagged as the tendrils shot back out of his nose.

Luka reached for the root around his right ankle, but another root shot from the ground to wrap around his wrist. Adrenaline surging through him, he fought the pull off the root and jerked his arm to the left. The root snapped.

He'd never been more grateful for the strength he'd gotten from Sombra.

He tore his other ankle free and shot to his feet. He turned to mount his horse, but it was too late. It was lying on the ground, glassy-eyed, as roots wormed its way into its flesh.

Luka took off at a sprint, the cornstalks whipping him in the face. Roots sprang up underfoot, and Luka jumped and dodged until he finally burst out of the cornfield. Still he kept running. He nearly tripped over the body of a dueño as it was pulled down into the dirt. So many roots filled the man's mouth that his lips tore at the corners.

He needed to find Paloma and James. They needed to get out of here.

His feet carried him to the thicket of limoncillo trees. He could see Paloma and another dueño shouting words of magic to stop the branches from swiping them, but this was Sombra's world now, *his* magic. They couldn't hope to beat the darkness at its own game. Paloma's words rang in Luka's head:

We will never be able to lean into our worst selves the way the shadowless can. So even if you can *access it, your magic will be substantially weakened.*

He opened his mouth to shout her name, but the sight before him killed the words on his tongue. A branch of a limoncillo tree gripped the other dueño by the neck and pulled him off the ground. He kicked and yelped, gripping at the vise around his throat. The limb snapped to the left, and Luka heard the telltale *crack* of a broken neck. It killed quickly and efficiently, like a butcher, numb to the shrieks of the dying.

The branch pulled the corpse flush against its trunk. Veiny roots broke free of the bark and weaved through the man, pegging him to the tree in a web of stringy brown roots. Luka tasted the acid burn of vomit at the back of his throat.

The trees were *feeding* on the corpse. This was how the land stayed green and lush. It was fertilized with blood.

Paloma stood, paralyzed. Luka tackled her just as a branch reached toward her waist, sending them both tumbling to the ground.

"Up up up!" Luka shouted, pulling her onto her feet. "The ground's not safe!"

But where *was* safe? They certainly couldn't climb a tree.

"Luka!"

Luka followed the sound of galloping hooves and saw James riding toward them. Was he covered in . . . feathers? It didn't matter now. They could jump on his horse and get to safety.

As if the land could read his mind, more roots surged out of the ground and wrapped around the horse's back legs. The steed was jerked to a halt and James went flying.

"Shit shit shit," Luka cursed.

James skidded on the ground like a stone skipped across a lake. But in the blink of an eye, he was gone. For a moment, Luka thought he'd lost his mind. But no—James was using his speed. Luka felt the tickle of roots slithering up his pant leg and jumped, slapping at his trousers.

Before he could scream, James got to him, lifting him off his feet. For a moment the world became a blur of green. Then he dropped Luka unceremoniously on the blackened ground and disappeared again.

Luka had never been so happy to see dead plants.

A long moment later James returned, Paloma in his arms.

He set her down before falling to his knees, gasping. Luka could see the scratches on his face and arms. Blood poured over his left eye. Even with his speed, he hadn't been able to avoid the roots.

With quivering fingers Paloma plucked a thin piece of root from her mouth and pulled, gagging as she dragged it up from down her throat.

"Where are the rest?" she asked, her voice hoarse. "*Where?!*"

James leaned forward, palms pressed against the ground. He shook his head.

THE STRANGER IN THE WINDOW

Dezmin didn't know how much more he could take, how much more he could watch.

But he had no choice.

A man stood before Sombra, his eyes still white at the edges, shadow quivering at his feet. Urine soaked his trousers, pooling around his shoes. Much like the victims who had come before him, Dezmin could see he was too afraid to speak, too afraid to move.

Frustrated that Dezmin's body became depleted, almost to the brink of death, whenever the god used his magic, Sombra had decided to feed to keep the body from collapsing. And Dezmin would be a witness to it all.

"Come now, don't be afraid," Sombra said gently, gripping the man by the shoulder, like a father soothing a child. The man looked up at Sombra hopefully, his shadow calming slightly. Dezmin wanted to tell him this was Sombra's favorite part—stoking his victim's hope before snuffing it out. "This world will end regardless. I will give your death righteous purpose."

The man tried to step back, but the god's fingers curled tight over his shoulder, holding him in place. Dezmin could feel the excitement welling up in Sombra. Their fear whetted his appetite, seasoned the meat.

Sombra could not feed on the shadowless—they were extensions of him, the equivalent of gnawing on his own arm. So he'd demanded that the shadowless bring him any Castallanos with *propios*. This man was not the first and Dezmin feared he would not be the last either.

The man began to panic, his nose running as he begged. "Please, please, no! I—"

Sombra took in a deep breath and the man's voice faded into a croak. Ribbons of light flowed out of him, turning black as they poured down Sombra's throat. He fed off the corruption of the light. Nothing else could sate him. The man's body began to gray, drying out until it was only a husk. When Sombra pulled his hand back, the man collapsed into gray dust.

The throne room floor, once as white as the clouds it was made of, was now gray with dried flakes of flesh and bone.

Sombra gave a satisfied sigh. "Much better."

The god had found a way to fortify himself, to stave off destruction until he secured all the relics and assumed his immortal form. Now there was no hope of Sombra destroying himself and Dezmin from the strain of it all. Nothing to stop him from hunting Alfie.

Dezmin wondered how his brother was faring. Was he still alive? Dezmin wanted to try to reach out again, but if Sombra wasn't sufficiently distracted he'd be caught. And then he'd have no chance of warning Alfie.

The sound of heavy footsteps rang out from the hall beyond the throne room. Two shadowless strode through the doors, dragging someone by the shoulders. Dezmin was surprised to see long hair so blond it was nearly white. The woman wore the winter kingdom's dueño robes, white as the snow they loved so much. How—and where—had they found an Uppskalan dueña? The woman raised her head and Dezmin's heart froze.

It was Svana.

When he was just a boy, he'd once caught her and Paloma in a kiss and had simply snuck away, never telling a soul. She was a kind woman who'd squatted before him and marveled at his *propio* of bringing objects to life. She'd called him a special boy.

She and Paloma had always stayed in close contact. She might know what Alfie had learned from the gods. Dezmin prayed that Sombra wouldn't think to interrogate her. There was a chance he wouldn't—after all, she was a foreigner. So long as he didn't know that she'd interacted with Castallan's royal family, he would see no use for her aside from feeding.

Guilt clotted in Dezmin's stomach. The world had become a terrible place if he was desperately hoping for this woman's quick death instead of her salvation.

"We've brought you a dueña, my king!" the woman said. "Just as you asked!"

Svana let her head hang low and Dezmin wondered if she was trying to look uninteresting, inconspicuous.

Sombra's footsteps were slow and measured, the gait of a man who knew his own power.

With surprising gentleness, he gripped Svana's chin, lifting her head.

Please don't give it away, Dezmin thought fervently. *Don't recognize me.*

"Prince Dezmin," Svana gasped, her words slurred. She seemed to be drugged.

Dezmin's blood ran cold. Still, knowing his name, recognizing his face, wouldn't necessarily give away that she knew him.

Disappointment boiled in Sombra until it settled into quiet fury. "You brought me a dueña from Uppskala," Sombra said carefully to the two shadowless.

The woman sputtered. "Yes, but we—"

Dezmin flinched at the brittle *snap* of broken necks. Not because of the brutal quickness of their deaths, but because he could feel himself getting used to the dry pop of cracked bone.

With the shadowless who carried her dead, Svana fell on her face, her white robes stained with gray.

"Perhaps I should've been more specific," Sombra sighed. "Though you may serve a purpose yet. Why would an Uppskalan dueña be in Castallan?"

Svana floated off the floor, held upright by Sombra's will, until they were eye-to-eye.

"And you didn't speak the prince's name as if you knew *of* him, you spoke it as if you *knew* him," Sombra said, and a terrible panic threaded through Dezmin. "*Did* you know him? Were you close with the royal family?"

Svana held his gaze but didn't speak, her eyes still glassy from whatever the shadowless had used to incapacitate her.

"A quiet one, are you?" Sombra cocked his head to the side. "Well then, I'll have to learn for myself. Forgive me," he said as he placed his hand on the crown of her head. "I'm not at my best so this will likely be more painful than it ought to be."

Sombra did not move his hand, but Dezmin could *feel* his fingers searching her mind, prying her memories apart and inspecting them. The god ripped them from her head like pages from a book, her whole childhood crumpled and tossed over his shoulder.

The dueña's shrieks echoed through the throne room, and Dezmin wanted to put his hands over his ears, wanted to hide from the atrocities committed by his own body. But he'd given so much to Sombra that he felt a part of himself enjoying it, drawing it out.

"Ah," Sombra said. "Here we are."

Svana whimpered as Sombra found her memories of the Castallano palace, of Paloma, and finally of the information he sought—a prophecy from the gods.

Lifting his hand off her, he withdrew from her mind—but the damage was done. Svana's head sagged to the left, saliva dripping down her chin.

Sombra smiled at her. "Who knew I'd have to import the truth from abroad?"

With a flick of his wrist, he tossed her aside.

Dezmin wept within the prison of his body as he felt the violation of her mind, the glee that Sombra felt upon tearing her precious memories to shreds. And Dezmin would always remember the woman's last thought, just before Sombra tossed her away like garbage—Svana was a child of twenty again, new to her robes and responsibilities. She looked up, and seated in the window of the library was a stranger. A tall woman, a dueña from Castallan. She was reading a book, her brown skin bathed in the buttery glow of the sun.

Locked inside Sombra's mind, Dezmin stared at Svana's discarded body as it twitched on the ground.

"Finally," Sombra sighed.

Dezmin felt a wave of relief pour through Sombra. Not knowing what the other gods had said behind his back had been maddening to him, but now he knew the truth of it all and so did Dezmin.

Sombra's elation at learning the prophecy was chased by an undertow of panic.

He'd thought that Alfie and Finn trapping him in the toy dragon had been mere luck, but now he knew they were prophesied to destroy him.

He would have to destroy them first.

Sombra also knew the reason for his weakness now. Wearing the arms had done nothing but put a strain on Dezmin's body and hinder Sombra's own abilities. But he could not remove them—he'd committed to this vessel. He'd need to keep feeding to keep Dezmin's body alive until he could obtain the rest of his body and assume his true form once more.

"I will not fail," Sombra said, a promise to himself that Dezmin hoped he could not keep.

Dezmin could see the consequences run through Sombra's mind. If this world ended before Sombra retrieved his full body, he would be trapped in Dezmin's until it withered to nothing. He would be a disembodied spirit with no vessel. He'd have to go to the gods who'd betrayed him and beg them to restore his body.

Sombra gazed up at the heavens through the transparent ceiling. "You thought you could help these fools by making their *propios* a little more powerful?" He gave a sharp laugh, a sweltering anger burning inside him. "I will find my relics and restore myself. I will destroy what you hold so dear."

He would need to keep Dezmin's body safe from harm, so he could not retrieve the relics personally. But perhaps he could find others to do it for him. . . . Dezmin saw the plan unfurl in Sombra's mind, the monsters he planned to create, the horrors to come.

In that moment, Dezmin knew that he'd given too much of himself to Sombra, because a single tear rolled down Sombra's face.

The god didn't notice, not even when it crossed his lips, stinging his tongue with the taste of salt.

THE DANCE

Luka would never forget the feeling of roots squirming up his nose and down his throat.

The moment flashed in his mind over and over—vines slithering and flexing around his ankles, the sight of the corpse with a cornstalk growing from his ruined mouth.

"Stop," Luka mumbled to himself. "Stop thinking about it."

Luka looked around, focusing on his surroundings to ground himself. He was sitting cross-legged in the dry dirt. Before him was a dwindling campfire surrounded by a circle of stones to keep it from spreading. Over to his left, the remaining dueños were setting up their tents.

After losing six dueños and three horses, their now-smaller group rode for hours, putting distance between themselves and the patch of green land. They rode until people began falling asleep on their horses, exhausted from travel and all that had happened at the farm.

Luka stared at the strange, dim fragments of moon in the sky. It was just past midnight. The first day had passed—only five left to put a stop to Sombra.

He'd asked Paloma if that cursed acre had been a trap set by Sombra, but her answer had been even more horrifying.

"I don't think so," she'd said. "Sombra has infected the world's very core with his will, and his greatest desire is for this world to destroy itself. He does not need to command parts of the world to self-destruct; it will simply happen. He doesn't need to actively set traps. We are lucky we haven't run into anything worse."

Luka grimaced. He'd overheard the dueños talking. There were reports that the Suave was boiling. An entire ocean bubbling and steaming, killing every last creature in its depths.

Luka had assumed that if the world was going to end in five days, it would all happen suddenly, at the very last moment on the very last day, an explosion that sent their world into oblivion; but now he understood that it would be gradual. They would be forced to witness their world fall apart, piece by piece.

James sat beside him, staring at the fire. Luka cocked his head, spotting something caught in James's hair. The Englassen flinched when Luka plucked a feather from just behind his ear.

"I went to check the chicken coop," James said as Luka let the breeze carry the bloodied feather away. "I thought there might be chickens or at least eggs for us to boil. But it was dark and quiet there. Then I heard . . ." He suppressed a shudder. "I heard a strained cluck. There was a hen twisted in the plants. Still alive." He shook his head. "I tried to get out, but the roots trapped me in the coop, bloody feathers everywhere."

Luka couldn't stop himself from imagining the mangled hen, intertwined with the roots. It was his fault they'd gone to the farm, his fault they'd had to witness such horror.

"I'm a fool." Luka cradled his head in his hands. "I shouldn't have insisted on going. I walked those dueños right to their deaths."

"Master Luka." Paloma's voice rang out behind him, and Luka startled. Her voice was still rough from the roots—the ones that had gone down her throat had been thorned. Luka had seen her spitting blood after James had rescued them. "You're overestimating the amount of influence you have."

Luka stared at her.

"We dueños decided to go there to get more food. We didn't go because you wanted to," she explained. "We would have gone regardless."

Luka turned his gaze to the dying flames of the campfire. The wood kept needing to be replaced. The blackened sticks they had found didn't last long and the smoke smelled cloyingly sweet, like fruit gone rotten.

"Still, I wish—"

"Wishing will get us nowhere," Paloma interrupted. "Every dueño on this mission knew the chance of death was high." Her face was drawn and somber, and Luka wondered if she'd been close to any of the men who died. They'd been much older than Paloma, but still, they must've spent a fair amount of time together. "We will mourn them properly when the world is safe once more."

Traditionally, dueños were cremated in their robes. But there were no robes or bodies to burn, so each surviving dueño had torn a strip from their own robes and burned that instead.

"All right," Luka relented, but guilt still twisted into a tight knot in his stomach.

He knew Paloma could tell that he was far from absolving himself, but she looked too tired to fight him on it. Instead, she turned to the Englassen. "James."

The boy froze, his arm outstretched to drop another flaky, blackened log into the fire. Luka was pretty sure this was the first time Paloma had used James's name on this hellish adventure.

Wide-eyed, James looked at her. "Yes?"

"I thank you for using your abilities to carry Master Luka and me to safety," Paloma said. Even when thanking someone for saving her life, her voice was deadpan. But Luka knew her well enough to sense she wasn't particularly happy to be thanking him. "I owe you a great debt."

James was still frozen, clearly unsure of what to say. "You're welcome; anytime."

Luka snorted.

Paloma stared at the boy for a long moment (Luka was certain that James had died three full times in that silence) before changing subjects. "We will sleep in shifts. You two can take the first."

The dueños had hobbled off their horses, rubbing their lower backs. It hadn't occurred to Luka how much of a strain this journey would be on an older body. That, and the dueños had to continuously work to maintain their balance through meditation and focus, while Luka and those with *propios* maintained it naturally. So instead of making a joke, he nodded at Paloma. "Of course. Get some rest."

The dueña strode away, disappearing behind the cloth flap of a red tent.

As the dueños slept, Luka and James sat facing each other on either side of the fire, scanning their surroundings. After riding through miles of blackened grass, they'd settled in a clearing. When the wind flowed through the grasses they made an awful dry sound, the sound of dead things rubbing against other dead things. Luka shuddered. To Luka's left was the field of tall grass bathed in shadow, to his right more open land.

For the first hour of their watch, they sat in silence. James wrung his hands while Luka snacked on a mango (after cutting the rotten bits off), both feeling far too awkward to talk. What did one say during an occasion like this? "Nice weather we're having" didn't seem to cut it when you'd just seen a cornstalk planted down a man's throat.

"Have your *propios* gotten any stronger?" Luka finally blurted out just to kill the silence.

James cocked his head. "I think my version of the enhancement is that I can carry it all without pain, but none of the actual *propios* are more powerful than before."

"Ah."

More silence.

"Did the dueños tell you anything about what we need to do when we reach the sacred oasis?" James asked.

"Yeah. The dueños are gonna have to meditate in some pond."

The specifics of it all remained a mystery, though. Like what would they see when they crossed into the spirit realm? Which dueños would they speak to? Could they ask any question they wanted? Luka supposed it wasn't his business anyway. Just dueños doing their dueño thing.

"Communicating with the dead through some pool seems absolutely ridiculous, but I suppose just about anything is possible right now," James said.

"Everything but peace," Luka sighed, his eyes on the fire. "I miss life as it was before."

"Before Englass arrived?"

Luka shook his head. "No, things were already falling apart well before then." To James, the chaos in Castallan had only begun when the Englassen royals came for the summit, but the dominoes had been falling ever since Luka had drunk the poisoned sleeping tonic meant for Alfie, and Alfie freed Sombra's essence to save him. Though that wasn't even when it had really begun, was it? The diviner had implied that Alfie releasing Sombra had been written in the stars long before any of them had been born. But as far as Luka had known, life had been perfectly normal until that moment six months ago.

"What do you miss most?" James asked, his eyes on the crackling fire.

Luka tilted his chin back and stared at the sky. "Hard to narrow it down, but I'll start with dancing."

"As do I," James said.

"*Pfffft.*"

James's green eyes narrowed. "What?"

"How could you miss dancing when Englassens don't dance?"

Luka and Alfie had been tasked with learning some popular Englassen dances before the summit, and it had been an odd, rhythmless slog. The instructor kept swatting at Luka to keep his hips from moving.

"We *do* dance," James argued. "The Englassen waltz is lovely and—"

"Boring," Luka interjected. "Boring and slow. You barely move! It's more of a walk than a dance."

"What do you mean?" James frowned. "There's plenty of movement. It's a classic box step." He stood and demonstrated with sure steps forward, to the right, then back and to the left. Like most Englassens he'd seen dance, all the movement was in James's feet. The rest of him was as still as a statue.

"Exactly," Luka said. "You're not moving. Castallano dancing requires full-body movement."

James rolled his eyes. "I can do Castallano dances just fine, thank you." He moved into a tense version of a merengue that looked more like a march, and then a stilted bachata where his hips did not move an inch.

"You're not doing it right," Luka said with a laugh. He stood in front of James to demonstrate. "In bachata and merengue there's a slight bend to the knees with every step that makes your hips move. If you don't have that you might as well just walk around in circles. See? You try."

James tried, but it only looked like he was doing a squat with each step. "Oh, hush," he said as Luka bit back a laugh.

"All right, maybe we need to pull back. You're not ready to move your feet yet. Just try standing still and moving your hips in a circle. Get loose," he added, though he didn't think Englassens knew how to get loose.

"All right, how's this?"

Luka squinted. "That's not a circle. It's more of a square."

"And now?"

"More of a rhombus?"

James let out a bark of laughter. "Surely I cannot be that bad."

"I'm afraid you can. It's a cultural barrier that an Englassen simply cannot pass—fluid hip movements."

James shot him a look. "I assure you, we do just fine with our hips when the occasion calls for it." Seeming to realize what he had said, James's face grew red.

Luka found that he liked the look of him blushing.

Luka had always tended to pick lovers who matched his own swagger. Ones who, when faced with the filthiest of innuendos and propositions, wouldn't so much as bat an eye. He enjoyed the chase, the struggle of trying to throw them off their game. But there was something refreshing about a boy who made himself blush with the smallest suggestion of an innuendo. There was no game, no power play, no facade—just honesty.

Wait, why was he comparing James to his lovers? Luka promptly pushed that thought down a well.

"Could I ask you something?" James said.

Luka shrugged. "Why not."

"If we survive—if we save the world from Sombra," James said, and Luka couldn't blame him for using "if" instead of "when." Even with his own constant optimism, things looked bleak. "What do you think will happen between Englass and Castallan?"

Luka cocked his head. He hadn't given it much thought. Worrying about inter-kingdom politics seemed like a luxury now. "Well," he began uneasily. "Now that the Englassen royals have been killed, I have no idea who the crown goes to, succession-wise . . ."

"Do you think Prince Alfehr will go to war with us over what happened?" In James's eyes Luka saw real fear, and he wondered if that was what Prince Marsden had told him would happen if James didn't comply. "Over what they did. What *I* did," James corrected himself. "I don't want him to think that everyone in Englass is deceitful and deserving of punishment. If my actions sentenced others to death I would—"

"James." Luka gripped the boy by the shoulder. "Alfie is angry because of who we lost." Luka swallowed thickly, unable to utter the king's name. "But he was willing to marry Princess Vesper to keep your people from suffering. I don't know exactly what will happen after the world is saved, but I know Alfie. He is unfailingly kind, even when he shouldn't be." Luka looked away, his eyes burning. "He will be merciful. He always is."

James's shoulder relaxed under Luka's hand. "I'm grateful for that. Thank you."

Unsure of what else to say, Luka just nodded, pulling his hand back.

Paloma had made it abundantly clear that James would be tried for his crimes after Sombra was dealt with, and the odds certainly weren't in his favor, but James hadn't asked Luka to convince Alfie to grant him clemency. He'd only wanted to look after his people.

The longer Luka spent with this boy, the more James revealed himself to be painfully selfless.

It reminded him of Alfie.

"Do you think there's a future in which Englassens and

Castallanos can be friends?" James asked quietly, and when they met eyes Luka knew he wasn't asking about a hypothetical Castallano and a hypothetical Englassen. He was asking about them.

Luka opened his mouth to answer.

"Hello? Is anyone there?" called a soft voice from the dark.

Luka and James startled at the sight of a little boy emerging from the tall grasses at the edge of the clearing. He couldn't have been more than ten years old. His eyes were undarkened, his shadow moving at his feet—which meant he must have a *propio*.

Luka rushed to the child. "Are you all right? Where are your parents?"

The boy shook his head, his lower lip quivering.

Luka remembered what it was like to lose his family, how the sickness had crept through his house until all the rooms were quiet and the air was stale. How many people were experiencing that terrible feeling thanks to Sombra?

Luka knelt in front of the boy. "You're safe here with us." Without hesitation the boy threw himself into Luka's arms. Luka lifted him and balanced him on his hip, rubbing his back. Luka needed this hug just as much as the boy did. "What's your name?"

But the boy's eyes were on the ground where James's shadow swayed. "You have a *propio*?"

"He does," Luka said. "Just like you."

The boy's eyes sharpened, and Luka wondered if he was afraid to trust them. After all the child must have seen since Sombra's return, Luka couldn't blame him.

"Does anyone else here have one?" the boy asked.

Luka shook his head. "Just James. We're here with our dueño

friends." The boy's eyes brightened. "They know all the magic in the world and will use it to protect you. You didn't tell me your name, little one."

"Luka," James said, warning in his voice.

"What?" Luka asked. Why would James be so suspicious of a child?

The little boy raised his hand, his index finger in the air. "One with *propio*!" he shouted. "And a group of dueños!"

The little boy scrambled out of Luka's arms, and before Luka could speak a word, a group of the shadowless leaped out of the tall grasses armed with machetes and cruel grins. They looked upon the campsite as if they'd stumbled upon a lost treasure.

The realization struck him like a slap—the child wasn't shadowless, but he was working for them, scouting prey. But why would he help the shadowless? Shouldn't he be terrified of them? And why would the shadowless be out in the wilderness when there were cities to wreak havoc in? He'd been wrong to assume they were safe here.

"Luka!" James called out, but before Luka could find him he was tackled to the ground. The shadowless descended on the campsite. Screams erupted as the dueños were dragged from their tents.

Luka shoved the man off him, but another quickly took his place, and then another and another. He thrust out his arm and desperately tried to summon flame to light his way.

Nothing came.

Luka's mind scrambled, trying to cling to a dark memory to give him access to the magic, but he was too frantic to focus on one.

"Keep still!" one of the men said before holding a strong-smelling handkerchief over Luka's nose. "We've caught ourselves a strong brute, muchachos!"

Luka's head swam as he inhaled the acidic scent.

The last words he heard before he fell into the dark were worse than he could have imagined. Worse than a promise of death or torture.

"A group of dueños and two white-eyed boys. Sombra will be pleased."

THE FOREST

Alfie and Finn stood in the quiet of the realm of magic, dumb-founded by what they'd learned.

Dezmin had found a way to communicate with them through the dragon, if only for a moment. Alfie had heard his brother's voice—not in his memory or in dreams, but here in real life.

Alfie stared at the figurine in his palm, willing it to move again.

"Dezmin?" Alfie breathed, his voice desperate. "Please . . ."

"Prince." Finn gripped his shoulder. "He'll be back when he can. He said he would be."

"What if he isn't?" Alfie asked.

Alfie hadn't told his brother how much he loved him. Or how every time his father laughed, he could see Dezmin in his face. How he'd relished those moments of dual joy, of seeing his father smile and seeing Dezmin alive and well in his features. Alfie hadn't told him about all the nights he'd spent in Dezmin's rooms, sitting in front of the cabinet that held his carvings, begging one to move.

"What if that was all the time I had left with him?" he heard himself whisper.

"It's not," she said firmly. "The prophecy said to journey under dragon's wing. He's got more to tell us, more time to spend with you, I know it."

"Thank the dioses that Luka gave me the dragon before I left." He froze. "I have to tell Luka!" Everyone needed to know that Dezmin was all right, that there was hope.

He pulled the parchment out of his bag, unfurling it with shaking fingers.

"Wait," Finn said, gripping him by the wrist. "I don't think we should tell them."

Alfie stared at her. "Why could I not let Luka know that Dezmin has made contact?"

"Your brother said that Sombra is trying to find out what we know. If he knows we had the audience with the gods, he'll be looking for anyone who might have been there," she said. "If I were him, I would be looking for the dueños."

Alfie's grip on the parchment tightened. "But Sombra is too vulnerable to leave the pala—"

"We don't know that for sure. He could send someone else to hunt them down now that they're outside the safety of the palace," Finn pressed on. "And if he finds out your brother is somehow communicating with us, he might find a way to stop it."

Alfie's heart dropped. Dezmin himself had asked them to keep everything they knew to themselves so that Sombra would never be able to use Dezmin against them.

"You're right," Alfie sighed, but it felt like a betrayal. He and

Luka had suffered the loss of Dezmin together. He deserved to know, and Paloma did too, but if there was the slightest chance that Sombra could find out, then it was best to keep this knowledge to themselves until everyone was safe in the palace again.

"We'll tell them in person when we get back," Finn promised.

"When we get back." Alfie nodded. "But I still want to tell them to be careful. If Sombra catches any of them, he will learn of the prophecy and we'll lose any advantages that we have."

"That works," Finn agreed. "Just don't tell them *why* you're feeling that way."

Alfie scribbled a quick note, then rolled the parchment back up and placed it in his bag before he could give in to the temptation of telling Luka everything. He stared at the dragon in his hand. It had been so full of life before, but now was stiff and still. He couldn't tear his eyes away, waiting for it to make the slightest movement again.

"We've got to move on to the next piece," Finn said gently. "We've been in the realm of magic even longer than last time. Who knows how much time has passed in the outside world."

She was right. The conversation with Dezmin had kept them here longer than they'd intended. Alfie pulled out the pocket watch to see how much time had passed, but the clock's hands were frozen. They wouldn't know for sure until they left the realm of magic and the clock's hands zoomed into place. He swallowed. He hoped they hadn't wasted too much time.

"You're right," Alfie said. "Let's go."

With Finn at his side, Alfie refocused and the web of strings returned. He resumed walking through the strings, Finn following close behind. As he moved, countless Englassen voices poured over him. He fought to keep his head above water, to not get overwhelmed, but feeling through the entire population of a kingdom was no small task. Especially when simply hearing the language made him angry.

Alfie took a breath and forced those thoughts away. It hadn't been the Englassen commoners who had plotted to enslave his country; it was the royals, and they were all dead.

He didn't know how much time had passed when he finally walked through the right string. Sombra's darkness flowed over him, a trickle of ice water down his spine.

"It's here," Alfie said uneasily. He plucked the string with two fingers and looked at Finn. "Are you ready for the next one?"

"I wasn't ready for the first one." After a moment's hesitation, Finn grabbed the string.

Alfie and Finn clung to each other as the realm of magic pulled them into the swirling dark. Finn knew better than to scream, but Alfie could feel her stiffening in his arms. She held him tightly, something that he knew she would be too embarrassed to do on any other occasion.

The magic spat them out at the edge of an Englassen forest.

They landed on their sides, still gripping each other. As they disentangled, Alfie rubbed his sore shoulder and took in their surroundings. It looked nothing like the drawings of Englassen flora and fauna that he'd seen in his books. The forests should be lush and green, full to the brim with oak, birch, and sweet chestnut trees. Especially considering that while Castallan was moving toward winter, Englass was in the thick of its spring.

But this forest contained only naked, blackened trees. Their gnarled branches looped around one another in tight knots. It wasn't just the look of the forest that gave Alfie pause, it was the *feeling*. These trees didn't reach up toward the shattered moon, they curled inward as if the light were offensive to them. It was as if they wanted to pull themselves back into the cold ground. The forest was so thick with darkness, he could scarcely see more than a few yards in. Alfie shuddered.

"Do you think it's like this everywhere?" Finn eyed the bleak scene before them.

Alfie swallowed. "If it's not already, it will be soon."

Sombra's corruption was destroying their world from the root. Soil that was rich with nutrients, built to support a forest generations ago, was decimated mere days after his arrival. The world would become unlivable if this went on much longer.

As he and Finn dusted themselves off, Alfie couldn't help but feel grateful for the location of the relics. Once again, they'd been lucky that Sombra's relic wasn't in the center of a city's chaos. They were alone in the Englassen countryside. He supposed that made sense. Why hide something where there were people around to find it? But they'd learned in Uppskala that there were still foes to be found in these remote places.

"How long did it take to get here?" Finn asked.

Alfie pulled out the watch again and together they watched the hands spin. Alfie's eyes widened when they finally settled in place. "We left at six in the evening. Now it's half past five in the evening." He stared at her. "It took us nearly twenty-four hours."

Finn stared at him, wide-eyed. "*Qué?*"

"We're nearly done with our second day." Getting from Castallan to Uppskala had only taken six hours. Had their conversation with Dezmin been that long? He knew that time moved differently in the realm of magic, but still, a whole day lost. In a matter of hours they'd only have four days left to stop Sombra.

Alfie pulled out the shared parchment. Luka still hadn't responded to his previous message warning them that Sombra could be finding ways to seek out him and the dueños now that they were outside the palace. Luka's lack of response worried him, but Alfie knew he couldn't focus on that. As bleak as it sounded, there was nothing he could do for Luka from here. He wrote a note saying that they'd just arrived in Englass and tucked the parchment away. He had to concentrate on what he could actually control—finding the relics.

Finn was still staring at the pocket watch as if it'd betrayed her personally.

Alfie put it away. "We don't have time to figure out why time is passing the way it is."

Finn nodded nonchalantly, but he could see the tenseness in her jaw. "Right."

"I need to figure out what kind of magic was used to protect the relics before we walk into the forest," he said. "We got lucky that the magic was so obvious last time. Here, we don't know where the spellwork begins and where it ends."

This already felt different from the enchanted pond. In Uppskala, Sombra's presence hadn't felt this strong until they'd made it all the way up the mountain, but here the dark aura was already upon them—and they hadn't even entered the forest yet. Alfie's skin was speckled with gooseflesh, his eyes scanning ceaselessly around them. It was like walking alone and suddenly knowing someone was lurking too close for you to put a stop to it; there was only time to feel the fear and wait for them to strike.

"All right." Finn rubbed her arms, staring warily at the trees. "How do we figure out what protective magic the dead dueños placed on the relic this time?"

Alfie had no answer. There was no pond covered in dead starlings to act as a clue, only bare trees. They wouldn't be able to figure it out by just looking.

"Give me a moment," Alfie said. He engaged his *propio* and looked around. He could see that a barrier of magic had been placed around the entirety of the forest. Though he knew it once had been other colors—the colors of the magic possessed by the dueños who had cast the spellwork—now it was covered in shifting shades of black.

Sombra's color. The color of a world unbalanced.

Alfie raised his hand to the barrier, attempting to match Sombra's color, but it was shifty, difficult to mimic. It reminded him of how Finn's used to slip between different shades of red, before she lost the ability to access her *propio*. He wondered if that was Finn's role in their destiny, to help him match Sombra's magic, but he wouldn't say that out loud. She was already upset enough about losing her *propio* and her magic going flat without him pointing it out.

He usually was able to match his magic perfectly to another's, which would have allowed him to read the spellwork like a book—but this one only provided snippets, its full story hidden. If this spellwork were a necklace, it would be full of different colored beads. Not only did he need to match with Sombra's shifting shade of black, he also needed to match the colors of the dueños who had contributed to the spell. If he went color by color, bead by bead, it would take hours. Alfie forced himself to focus, to try.

For a brief moment, he could feel the intentions the dueños had breathed into the magic.

Stop, they seemed to chorus, only to be interrupted by Sombra's own presence emanating from the stone relic. Then again. *Stop*.

But stop what? He tried to sink deeper into the magic, to dig deeper . . . and there it was! He struck a new word that the dueños had threaded through the enchantment: time. *Stop time!* He got it. But the effect of Sombra's magic on it was lost to Alfie. He pulled his hand away, frustrated.

"The original magic was designed to stop time for anyone who walked into the forest with the intention of taking the relic, but it's been changed." He chewed the inside of his cheek. "Nocturna has altered it, but I don't know how."

Finn threw her hands up in exasperation. "Then what are we supposed to do?"

Alfie thought for a long moment. The intention of the magic—to protect the stone pieces by freezing those who sought them out—was clear when Alfie matched its color, but it was interrupted by flecks of shifting black, making it unable to do its job.

"I don't think the magic will be able to freeze us," Alfie explained while Finn gripped a dagger. "It's like the dueños' magic is a song, and the darkness from Sombra's influence is erasing notes and verses. I don't think it can do its job of keeping us out of the forest the way it should have. The song's changed, but there's no way to know for sure." It wasn't as if they could toss a rock like they had over the pond in Uppskala. "I can't match Sombra's magic; it's shifting shades."

"The way mine used to." Finn stared at him. "If my *maldito propio* still worked and we combined our magic, you could match Sombra's magic and figure it out, couldn't you?"

Alfie could see the gears turning in her head, her guilt at not being able to help. "Finn—"

"Well then, there's only one thing to do. If we want to figure out what song it is, we gotta dance to it." Without another word, Finn took off running straight into the trees.

"Finn! Wait!" But the thief had sprinted into the wood, disappearing into the dark.

"Finn?" he called again, only to be met with silence. Was he wrong—had she been frozen? The magic was meant to stop anyone who intended to take the stone torso from even entering the forest. Maybe the magic didn't take effect until a few yards in.

Before he could panic any further, Finn raced out of the trees, her eyes alight. "Nothing happened! I ran in pretty deep too."

Alfie reached for her and pulled her close, his heart hammering against his chest. "Did you have to do that without discussing it first?"

"Prince, if one of us was gonna try it, it had to be me," she said, her head tucked beneath his chin. "If I can't help with my shifting magic, I'm going to find another way, and you're the desk magic expert. If something went wrong, I would have needed you to get me out."

"Nothing happened? You didn't feel yourself beginning to freeze as you ran farther in?" Alfie asked, looking her over carefully to be sure she wasn't hurt.

She shrugged. "I felt nothing. There wasn't any resistance or anything. It's creepy and quiet in there but seems all right otherwise.

At least there are no frozen, dead explorers."

Alfie nodded thankfully. Dead Men's Mountain in Uppskala had been a place where many had perished, but this was just a regular forest—it was blackened by Sombra's magic, but a regular forest nonetheless.

"Good," Alfie said. There was no more time to waste. "Then let's go."

Together, the prince and the thief stepped into the forest's dark embrace.

Gooseflesh erupted over Alfie's skin as they stepped deeper into the forest. There was no breeze, no sound. Only the crunch of dead leaves under their feet. This place should've been bursting with life: the sounds of birds nesting, plants growing and dying. But there was nothing here. It should have been an ecosystem, but it felt like a graveyard. The quiet was too unsettling. Alfie found himself looking over his shoulders for a foe hiding among the trees.

"*Luz*," he said, summoning a ball of light.

Finn wrinkled her nose. "What is that smell?"

It took a moment before the rancid stench hit Alfie. "It smells like something—"

"Rotting," Finn said, pointing and walking eastward.

A family of deer lay still on the forest floor. Finn squatted next to a young, white-spotted doe. "They all look healthy." The deer weren't wounded, nor did they look sick. They almost looked like they could be asleep.

"The imbalance." Alfie's face was grave. "It's killing the animals."

Finn looked up at him, her eyes wide. "*All of them?*"

"I don't know," Alfie said, feeling useless.

How would anyone survive if animals were dropping dead? And if forests were dying, then so were crops. Would the world starve to death before it even ended?

Finn sighed and stood up from her crouch. "I really don't want to go vegetarian."

"We need to hurry," Alfie said. "Come on."

The deeper they walked, the more corpses they found. The forest floor was littered with the brittle-boned bodies of dead birds and rabbits and foxes. If they defeated Sombra, would the animals come back? Or was this permanent? There was no way to know.

At first Alfie had been afraid that finding the stone relic would be difficult, but, just like in Uppskala, he could feel its presence, could sense which way to go. It was like following the scent of soured fruit or chasing a voice in the dark that promised sweets but held a knife instead.

"You can feel it too, can't you?" Finn asked.

Alfie nodded. "I can." Everything inside him wanted to turn away from the call of Sombra's relic, but he knew they must get it and send it to the dueños in the palace. They must protect it from Sombra until Luka and Paloma learned how they could use the relics to stop him. Alfie picked up the pace, moving faster while his shadow stretched backward in the opposite direction. "The sooner we get it the sooner we can leave this place."

Finn matched his speed, wiping the dead leaves off her trousers, and Alfie stared down at her. She looked smaller than usual next to him. It was probably because they were surrounded by so many gargantuan trees. Anyone would look shorter here.

As they walked farther into the forest, the silence became overwhelming, as if the closer they got to the stone piece the more insulated from the rest of the world they became. Alfie felt as if his ears were filled with cotton. He needed to hear something, anything.

"Can we talk?" Alfie said. "I can't take the quiet any longer."

Finn kept her eyes on the horizon. "About what?"

"Do you remember when I blasted the dead men away?" he asked, his voice hushed.

Finn looked at him. "Yes."

"I had one particular memory that could power that much magic." If he didn't say it, he would explode. Especially after he and Dezmin had finally spoken.

Finn slowed her steps. "You don't have to say it."

"I do," he admitted, his eyes burning. "When the diviner first told me that I had no future to speak of, I felt so much anger and jealousy toward Dezmin." The words felt just like Sombra's tainted magic—unnatural and wrong. "The diviner said that his reign and his influence would be eternal, while I was nothing." Alfie's hands squeezed into fists, his nails digging into his palms. "I wished he had never been born so that I could have his destiny instead."

"Prince," Finn said, her gaze meeting his. "You were a boy."

"I still wanted it. I wanted him gone just so I could take the spotlight." Tears slipped down his nose. "And when he disappeared, I wondered if I'd somehow made it happen—"

"Alfie, you know that the chain of events that led to Dezmin being lost was complicated." She gripped his wrist, pulling him to a stop. "We learned that from Xiomara herself. You didn't make it happen. You're creating that shame for no reason."

Alfie felt the guilt ease as she spoke, her grip on his hand anchoring him here to the present. But the look on her face told him that she had more to say. She was frantic to tell him that he was blameless, that he didn't deserve to hate himself, and yet Alfie knew that she was just as quick to tell herself the opposite.

"And you?" he asked. "Do you think you deserve the shame you feel?"

Finn blinked, her jaw working as she dropped his hand. "This isn't about me."

Alfie tried to reach for her again, but she stepped back. "Finn, I watched your face when you used your stone carving to dig under the pond. I don't know what memory you had to think of, but I know it wasn't fair to yourself."

"Oh?" Finn sniped. "So you can read minds now?"

"No, I can't." He trailed behind her as she turned on her heel, striding away from him and toward the pull of Sombra's relic. "But when it comes to you, I wish I could."

"Well, until you can, you'll have to stay out of my business!" she shouted over her shoulder. "I don't want to talk about what thoughts I used to fuel the magic. I don't want to talk about my *propio*. I don't want to talk about what happened that night. Leave. It. Alone."

"I can't just leave it alone. We *need* to talk about it," he insisted. "All of it."

"Why?" Finn said, finally stopping and turning around to face him. Alfie stumbled to a halt, nearly bumping into her. "My *propio* is my business, my memories are my business—"

"Fine!" Alfie threw his hands up. He knew that her emotional turmoil was part of what was flattening the color of her magic and blocking her *propio*, but she had a fair point—technically they weren't his business. "Fine! Then let's talk about the other night. That was my business too, wasn't it?"

Finn glowered at him but said nothing.

"I thought we'd only have one night together," Alfie said, a fissure of hurt in his voice that made her look away. "That I'd be betrothed the next morning and we'd never see each other again. Now there's a chance for more time and I'm so happy about that. But you don't seem to feel the same."

"I don't know how I feel about it!" she shouted in the silence of the forest. "That's the answer!"

Alfie stared at her, pain etching itself on his face. How could Finn not know how she felt about it? How could it have been anything but wonderful?

Finn threw her hands up. "See, that's why I didn't want to tell you. Because I knew you'd look at me like that."

Feeling utterly exposed, Alfie fought the urge to look away. "How am I looking at you?"

Finn gestured at his face. "All sad and upset!"

"Should I not be sad about you feeling unsure about what I thought was one of the best nights of my life—"

"Maybe it was great because it was only once!" she blurted. "Maybe it was only supposed to happen once."

Alfie tried to mask it, but it was no use—he could feel his face crumpling.

The flush of anger and defensiveness drained out of Finn in a quick rush until all Alfie could spot on her face was regret. Regret that she'd hurt his feelings or regret that they'd slept together, he couldn't be sure.

"I—" she began, then stopped. Her gaze clung somewhere above his forehead.

Frustration bubbled up inside him. Was it *that* odd that he wanted clarity on what had happened between them? Why was she staring at him like this?

"What?" he finally asked.

She kept staring. "Your hair."

Alfie touched his curls. He didn't have a mirror to see it. "What's wrong with it?"

"It's gone white." She got on her tiptoes to touch a patch of hair at his hairline.

Alfie blinked down at her. "And you've gotten shorter." He hadn't been imagining it. She had never needed to stand on her toes to touch his hair before. Her face looked a little rounder too, padded with an extra layer of baby fat that hadn't been there before.

Finn looked down, taking stock of herself. "What's happening?"

The answer bloomed in his mind, so painfully obvious that he felt foolish for missing it.

"The magic is still working," Alfie said.

Finn squinted up at him. "But it isn't freezing us?"

"No, it's mutated just like at the pond, but not in the same way," he explained. "And it's working differently for each of us. Time is moving quicker for me; I'm aging."

Finn's jaw dropped. "And it's moving backward for me. I'm getting younger."

Alfie nodded, watching the weight of it dawn on her.

"What do we do?" she asked. "How do we stop it?"

Alfie shook his head. "We don't. We keep moving and hopefully once we send the pieces to the dueños the effect will reverse itself."

It made sense. After all, once they had sent the Uppskalan relic to Castallan the dead men had stopped moving. But it was hard to rely on logic when magic was behaving so oddly. What if this didn't wear off?

What if they were stuck this way forever?

"No more talking," Finn said, resolute. "Let's get this over with before you turn into an abuelo."

Though he wanted to talk more about what she'd said, Finn was right. They needed to finish this before the magic got the best of them. They moved more quickly, saying little as they followed the pull of Sombra's darkness. Alfie walked ahead of her, not wanting to watch her back and think of all the questions he shouldn't ask now—did she ever love him? Had he made it all up in his head? Had everyone seen him as a foolish boy pining after a girl who would grow tired of him after one night? His eyes stung, humiliation pooling in his belly. He couldn't think of this now, not when so much was at stake. He swallowed down his hurt, letting it scratch his throat all the way down. He needed to focus. Alfie squeezed the dragon in his hand, letting it anchor him to the present.

Perhaps it would've been better to let himself be driven mad by the scenarios in his head than to be destroyed by her words.

A GAME OF FETCH

Dezmin could not forget the look on Svana's face as Sombra tore the prophecy from her memories.

The god had cracked her mind open like an egg, and it was Dezmin's hands that were covered in yolk and shell, his body a tool for destruction. He felt disgusted with himself. He clung to that disgust—it was better than sinking into the elation Sombra had felt as he'd destroyed her.

Now Sombra knew what secrets the gods had told Alfie and Finn—he could not simply adorn himself with the relics of his immortal body, one by one, as he had before. He needed to don them simultaneously. When he did so, Dezmin would disappear and only Sombra would be left.

But until then he could not leave the palace to pursue them. He'd feasted on the souls of the innocent to keep Dezmin's frail human body from falling apart, but that would only last so long. And Dezmin was grateful for that. It would give Alfie more time to find the relics. But still, Sombra had options.

Sombra looked at the shimmering larimar inlaid in the walls of cloud. He hoped the other gods were watching.

"Your Highness," a voice came from behind him. "Tell us your will. We only wish to serve."

Sombra turned and looked upon the four men before him. Each was on his knees in a bow, forehead pressed to the ground, arms outstretched.

Dezmin knew what Sombra intended to do to these men. He could see it in the god's twisted mind. The mere thought of it chilled Dezmin to his bones, but he knew witnessing it, feeling his own body command it, was going to be much worse. It would destroy something within him that could never be repaired.

And there was nothing he could do to stop it.

Sombra smiled as the men shook where they knelt. "I am looking for men to help me fulfill my great purpose," Sombra said, cocking his head. "Can I trust you?"

"Of course, Your Highness!"

"Please," one begged, desperation straining his voice. "Please choose us."

Dezmin pitied this man who begged so genuinely for his own destruction.

"Rise," Sombra said, and the men shuffled to their feet, meeting his gaze with their blackened eyes. Sombra did not see human bodies as a home for the soul; he saw them as limitations. Flesh that could tear, bones that could snap, hearts that could leak and falter. These men's shadows had curled into their bodies—the dark in its purest form. Sombra needed *that*, not the useless shell that surrounded it.

Sombra flexed his fingers. The snapping of bones echoed

through the throne room. Shrieks of agony stretched the men's mouths wide as Sombra broke them apart from the inside out.

Dezmin could not turn away. What Sombra saw, he saw. The elation that Sombra felt as the men suffered, Dezmin felt. His body and mind felt tainted, forever changed by their proximity to Sombra.

The god's voice bloomed in Dezmin's mind.

Your existence does not have to be one of suffering and mediocrity. You are fighting the natural way of things—the dominant force absorbing the submissive. Let go. Let yourself become a part of me. You will live an endless life of glory.

He could disappear, leave this pain behind—he just had to let go. Dezmin let the current of Sombra's power pull him under, stripping him of more layers of himself. The longer he stayed, the more the pain dulled. He was disappearing, collapsing into sweet nothingness.

But what about Alfie? He must protect Alfie.

Dezmin fought the current and broke free, forcing himself to look at the horrid scene before him. He had to help Alfie and save this world.

"Your potential is trapped in a prison of flesh and bone," Sombra said over the men's cries for mercy. At his command, the broken bones tore through their flesh. "But I can help you, as only a god can."

When all was said and done, the floor was littered with wet hunks of flesh that brought to mind a butcher's table.

Before Sombra stood four dark forms, like shadows made solid. Their bodies were fluid, the shape of man a mere suggestion. They were taller than any human, their fingers long enough to drag on the ground behind them as they moved. They had no faces, no will. Sombra had stripped them of that. Now they were only extensions of him, of his desire to find his relics and claim his new world.

They would not eat, they would not sleep; they would only seek.

Sombra needn't tell them what he wanted, for they already knew—*find the prophesied pair, stop them from taking what is mine, return my relics to me*.

He could tell them to kill the prince and his companion, but Sombra wanted to do that himself. He wanted to look into the boy's eyes as he plucked every last petal of hope he had of saving his brother.

Dezmin hoped and prayed that Alfie and Finn were ready for what was to come.

Sombra stumbled back onto his throne, blood pouring from his nose. Dezmin leaned into the pain that racked his body, clinging to it. He needed it to keep him awake, to keep him from slipping under into the abyss of Sombra's power.

"Now," Sombra said to the quartet of monsters, his breath labored and wet with blood. "Go fetch."

THE CHILD

"I hate this maldito forest!" Finn squeaked, then bristled at the sound of her voice. "For fuck's sake."

Even in his heartbreak over their last conversation, Alfie couldn't stop a laugh from bubbling up. As they roamed deeper into the silent forest, he watched Finn shrink from a young woman to a child. He watched her face get rounder, her limbs shorten, her eyes grow larger in her little face. She had physically transformed into a twelve-year-old, but her mind was still the same. She shuffled beside him, holding up her trousers lest they fall off.

It was honestly nice to have something to laugh about. Sombra's unsettling essence called them forward through the gnarled, blackened trees, and they had no choice but to follow, though everything inside them wanted to run.

"It's not funny, old man," she sniped. She had to tilt her head all the way back to make eye contact with him as they walked. She was scarcely taller than Alfie's hip at this point.

"No," Alfie agreed, rubbing his lower back. "It isn't." He promised himself that when he returned to normal, he would never take his mobility for granted ever again.

If they returned to normal, his mind corrected.

That "if" loomed over their heads like a guillotine. They could be stuck this way forever.

Alfie felt his bones aching in protest, begging him to slow down. He had no mirror, but the sight of the liver spots on his hands told him that he was nearing the age his grandfather had been when he'd passed.

"I think I need to slow down," Alfie said. His own voice had become raspy and unfamiliar.

"Why are we even here?" Finn asked, matching Alfie's stilted pace.

Alfie stared down at her. Was she joking? "To find the relic."

Finn blinked, her face softening with confusion. "Right."

"Are you all right?" he asked. The weight of the magic here was heavy, but that was still an odd question to ask.

"I'm fine," she said. "I'm just tired. We've been in here too long."

"Okay," Alfie said. She wasn't wrong. They'd been here for two hours already, but still. It was an odd question. He watched her carefully as they walked on in silence.

"I'm fine," she bit out, crossing her little arms. "Stop watching me."

"Fine." Alfie looked away. "I'm sorry."

The tension from their last conversation still hung in the air.

Alfie wanted to dispel it, but after what she'd said, he wasn't even sure of how to.

Maybe it was great because it was only once! Maybe it was only supposed to happen once.

Alfie flinched at her words. How could she even think that? Did she really see him as some sort of dalliance? A one-night conquest? An itch to be scratched, then forgotten?

His throat burned. How could he have read everything so wrong?

He knew that she needed space, that pushing her to talk wouldn't help. So instead he forced himself to focus on the pull of Sombra's relic and the sounds of the dead leaves crunching underfoot. He had to. She seemed to think there was nothing left to say to each other, and he would not try to make her feel otherwise.

Alfie still held his ball of light, searching the darkness for danger. After a painfully silent stretch of walking, he spotted a stump. Finally, something for him to sit on and rest his weary bones.

Alfie quickly hobbled toward it, leaving Finn to follow. "*Ahhh,*" he sighed as his bottom hit the wood. "Let's take a break for a second."

He waited, expecting Finn to protest, but heard only silence. Alfie raised the globe of light and scanned the thicket of black trees around him.

Finn was nowhere to be seen.

"*Finn!*" he shouted, his voice echoing in the dark. She was gone.

He grabbed a blackened stick from the ground, tall and thick enough to work as a cane. It felt as if in the last few minutes his back had hunched terribly. The magic was taking its toll faster now. "Finn!"

Panic surged through him. Where could she have gone? Had something taken her? Were they being hunted here like they'd been chased by the dead men in Uppskala?

Alfie's palms began to sweat, panic overtaking him. He gripped the toy dragon to his chest and took a breath. "I'll find her," he promised himself and Dezmin too. "I'll find her."

At the sound of quiet crying his heart leaped with hope. He followed the noise, and there she was, huddled into the hollow of a tree. When his light shone on her, he could see that she was even younger now.

"Finn," Alfie said as he slowly crouched, his knees shouting in protest. "Why did you run? Are you okay?"

"Who are you?" she asked, retreating deeper into the hollow.

Alfie stared at her in confusion before the truth struck him. The forest's magic wasn't only aging them physically, it was affecting their memories. Finn had aged backward to a time before she knew him. Her mind seemed to have caught up to her body now and she'd forgotten him. Alfie was aging forward, so he still remembered everything, but even his recent memories seemed blurry and strangely far off, as though he'd lived decades beyond them.

"I'm a friend," Alfie said gently. "Here to help you get out of the forest and go home."

"I don't want to go home to him." Finn shook her head. "I won't. It's better here."

Alfie didn't need to ask to know she was speaking of Ignacio. His heart dropped at the fear in her eyes as she tucked her knees under her chin. Ignacio had hurt her so deeply that she'd rather stay in a dying forest than go back.

"We're not going back to him," Alfie promised. She watched him with large, skeptical eyes. She didn't look at him with the inherent trust most children had. "We're going to find a new home." Alfie extended his hand to her. "Together."

She looked at his hand but did not move to take it. "Where?"

"Where do you want to go?" Alfie asked. He knew that Ignacio had controlled her, given her no agency. Maybe the way to get little Finn to follow him was to let her make some choices.

"San Cristóbal," she said, her eyes alight. "I wanna see the Equinox festival."

Alfie smiled down at her. "That sounds perfect." He slowly stood and extended his hand again. "Let's go."

This time, Finn took it and stood. She'd taken off her pants—they were far too big for her now—and was wearing her shirt as a long dress. Alfie folded her trousers and placed them in his satchel, then he took her satchel too and tucked it inside his own, letting the enchanted bag swallow it whole. Under normal circumstances the extra weight would've been nothing to Alfie, but now it nearly sent him falling to the ground.

"Here," Finn chirped from below, holding his cane.

"Thank you, little one," he said, and the two set off, deeper into the forest.

"Why are you here?" Finn finally asked him, her eyes scanning the silent trees.

"*We* are here to find a secret treasure," he said, unsure of what else to say. In a way, it wasn't a lie.

Finn brightened. "What kind of treasure?" Even as a child, Finn had a spark to her, a longing for adventure.

"We'll have to find out, won't we?"

Finn squeezed his hand. "He's not here, is he?"

"He's not," he assured her. This was one gift he could give to Finn's child self—safety. "He's gone."

"Are you sure?" She looked over her shoulder, and Alfie's heart broke at the terror in her face as she searched for Ignacio in the trees. "He wouldn't like it if he found me here with you."

"I'm sure, little one," Alfie said to her. "You're safe."

"He doesn't like it when I'm with other people."

"Why is that?"

"Because a good daughter only needs her father," she said, shifting closer to him.

"I don't think that's true," Alfie said. He bit the inside of his cheek. The amount of damage that man had done to a child was more unsettling than any dark magic he'd witnessed.

"He said I only think that way because I'm bad," Finn admitted. She said it casually, as if she were commenting on the weather.

"You are not bad," Alfie insisted.

She didn't seem to hear him. She had reached for her face, and after feeling it for a moment, she began to panic. "Why can't I change my face?" she cried. "I want to change my face!"

Alfie watched tears fall from her eyes as she grabbed at her face, trying to change it by pulling, hurting herself. It was so clear now how much Ignacio had made her hate herself. How much he made her want to be someone else. If you told a child they were bad, of course they would use their abilities to change their face, become someone else.

Overwhelmed, Alfie remembered when she'd first shown him

her true face. How afraid she'd looked, as if Alfie would reject it when in truth all Alfie had wanted to do was kiss it. She'd been afraid to be herself because of Ignacio. Afraid to be loved.

"Stop, little one," Alfie said, pulling her hands from her face. He couldn't stand watching her hurt herself. "Breathe. Your *propio* is just taking a break, because you're tired," Alfie lied, his voice thick, his eyes stinging. "It'll be back."

"But I want to change," she said tearfully. "I want to look different."

Alfie gathered her in his arms, his throat burning. "You don't need to," he said gently. "I like your face. It's a nice face."

Finn looked up at him, her tears forgotten for a moment. Children's emotions changed so quickly. "I like your face too. It's really old."

Alfie snorted. Oh, to be a child again and have no concept of manners.

"Let's keep going to find the treasure, shall we?" He held out his hand and she took it.

Alfie marveled at how different she looked. Not just physically, but in spirit. Paloma had once told him that people were like clay. Malleable and soft at first, but with time the clay dries into one shape and can no longer bend as it once had—it becomes brittle, immovable. Finn at this age was still moldable, still open. She had not dried into secrecy just yet. As a child, she spoke plainly about how Ignacio had made her feel. If she were her regular self, Alfie would've had to drag each word from her.

"What if I told you Ignacio was wrong," Alfie offered. "That you're good—wonderful even. Some people make you feel bad in order to control you." She tilted her face up and their eyes met. "Don't let him. There are people in this world who will love you truly." He swallowed thickly. "People who love you now and will never think of you as bad."

Finn's brow furrowed. Alfie didn't know if it was the right thing to say, but he couldn't regret saying it.

"Ignacio says that he can love me *and* hurt me." She looked up at him, as if she were trying to teach him something, save him from heartbreak. "Those things always go together."

Sadness closed around him like a fist. She might never be able to disentangle herself from that belief no matter what Alfie felt for her. He flushed, embarrassed. It was vain for him to think his love would be enough to heal such deep wounds.

Shame pooled in his belly. He felt stupid for having been so blind, for not seeing her truth when she'd been speaking it so plainly with her actions. How could he ask so much of someone who had been forced to see herself as an unlovable monster? How could he see her fear of love as an insult to him rather than a wound inflicted upon her by Ignacio? He'd wanted her love so badly that he hadn't thought about what it would take for her to give it. He hadn't been thinking about her at all; he'd only been thinking of what he wanted and what future he imagined for them when he needed to meet her where she was.

It had taken her turning into a child for him to understand her as a young woman.

As they moved through the forest, their strides slowed, Alfie growing ever older and Finn becoming younger still. She was a toddler now, babbling, carefree, squeezing his hand tight while she laughed. This was who Finn had been before the pain that Ignacio had inflicted on her. Alfie mourned for who she could have become if that monster hadn't found her and taught her to despise herself.

Finn continued getting smaller until soon Alfie was carrying an infant in one hand and his globe of light in the other. She yawned, a dozing baby, unbothered by the weight of their prophecy or Ignacio or the fear of death. Alfie hobbled, his back hunched, his bones aching. He sweated from the effort of just holding her.

But still, he smiled. He was glad she would have this moment of solace, even if she wouldn't remember it when they retrieved Sombra's relic and, hopefully, returned to their true ages.

"I'm so sorry that I asked so much of you," Alfie said, surprising himself with how low and soft his voice had become with age.

Finn looked at him, her dark eyes wide and curious.

"I love you," he said to her, and he could hear a naked earnestness in his voice. A level of honesty that he could only have with her here, now. "I love you very much. And I was so excited to have more time with you, to be with you, that I asked for your love as if you could just pull it out of your pocket and hand it to me." He shook his head at his own naïveté. "But you haven't had the kind of life where you carried love in your pocket, ready to share it with another. Instead you carried daggers to protect yourself, to feel safe.

"You've experienced so much—so much that I cannot understand," Alfie admitted as he walked. "You may never be able to love me as I love you. But that's all right," he assured her. "I'll be here." He adjusted her in his arms, and she reached up to grab his nose. "To love you as you are, right now, and as you will be, for as long as you want me to. Would that be all right?"

Finn snuggled against his chest and Alfie hoped part of her, somewhere, understood him. He switched her to his other arm. She weighed little but he had grown weak with age. If they didn't find the stone pieces soon, he wouldn't be able to keep walking, let alone carry her.

As if in answer to his question, the overwhelming pull of Sombra's magic seemed to reach a crescendo. Alfie approached a clearing. All the trees here had fallen to dust, and the shattered moon lit the ground, unencumbered by branches. This had to be it.

"See that," he said to Finn as she dozed in the crook of his arm. "We're going to make it."

Alfie let the pull of Sombra's essence lead him to the center of the clearing. Gooseflesh burst over his skin, and he knew he was standing in the right place. The relic was buried beneath him. The plan had been to have Finn use her stone carving to unearth it, but in her current state that was hardly an option. Alfie slowly knelt and placed Finn on the ground, wrapped in a bundle of her clothing.

"I'll just be a minute," he said to her as she gripped at his fingers.

With Finn a safe distance away, Alfie stepped back onto the spot where the pull of Sombra's influence was strongest. He looked at the ground and grimaced. He'd need to break into the earth to find Sombra's relic, and since Finn using her stone carving was out of the question, he'd need to use magic himself.

Alfie closed his eyes and sighed through his nose. He needed to feel shame and anger to use magic. He let his mind drift back to the Blue Room, to the day he'd lost Dezmin.

He'd watched Dezmin fall into the darkness and he hadn't lifted a finger. He'd been too afraid to move, too shocked by the sight of the dead guards that Xiomara had left in her wake. He hadn't even thought to fight, he'd simply been paralyzed. Nothing but a weak, spineless coward.

Alfie drowned in that shame, letting it swaddle him tight until the magic flowed through him, steady and sure.

"*Fuerza*," he said. The ground cracked with less vigor than usual, but still, it cracked. He thought of Dezmin's face as he fell. "*Fuerza!*" The ground cracked again, deeper this time. Alfie's eyes burned as he thought of how his mother had gripped him by the shoulders and asked him what had happened, and all he could do was weep instead of telling her he'd failed to protect her firstborn. Magic roared in him, wild and angry.

"*Fuerza!*"

He shouted it over and over again, the fissure in the earth widening and deepening with each round. Beads of sweat were rolling down his forehead when he finally saw Sombra's stone torso buried in the dirt. The hole was so deep that Alfie himself could have jumped down into it, and, even with his height, he would've had trouble climbing out.

He rubbed his wet eyes with the back of his hand, his breaths ragged. Finn had fallen asleep in her mound of clothes, and Alfie almost didn't want to get the stone piece and send it away. Once he did, the spell would break, just as it had in Uppskala. And Finn would no longer be blissfully unhindered by memories of Ignacio.

But he could not protect her from what had already happened. He could only be there for her as she moved forward—and, hopefully, she wanted to do that together.

"*Venir*," Alfie said, his gaze on the stone. It levitated out of the ground into Alfie's waiting hands. The torso of the dark god was intimidating to say the least—muscular and wide, the body of a conqueror.

"You will not win," Alfie said. In a way, Sombra was just like Ignacio, but instead of trying to control Finn, he wanted to control the whole world. "I won't let you. I will save this world and my brother. I was too afraid to protect him before, but this time, I will make it right."

Alfie pulled open the bag and forced the stone torso in, letting it drop through the bag to Castallan, where the dueños waited.

In the space of a breath, Alfie felt the vigor returning to his body. Before his eyes the wrinkles on his hands grew smooth. But while his joints ceased aching, the forest did not change. It stayed bleak and silent. He had hoped that sending the relic away would reverse this damage somehow.

"Prince?" Finn said. And there she was, back to her normal age. Alfie had scarcely seen a more beautiful thing. She was clutching her clothes to herself, picking dirt out of her hair. "Why am I naked?"

"You became a baby," Alfie said. There was no other way to explain it. He pulled her trousers out of his satchel and tossed them to her.

Her eyes widened. "Qué?"

"It's a long story," he said, his gaze on her. "But you're safe now."

Finn cocked her head, and Alfie hoped she knew that as long as she wanted him around and not a moment more, he would do his best to keep her safe.

From beyond the clearing came the sound of heavy-footed bodies breaking through the brush. Finn's eyes darted toward the noise, her hand searching her clothes for a dagger.

"What is that?" she said. "Were we followed?"

"I don't know," Alfie said, fear pulling his stomach tight. "I—"

Four hulking masses of black burst through the ring of trees surrounding the clearing. They were tall, their backs hunched, their skin a crisscross of dark, pulsing veins.

"What *is* that?" Finn shouted. She threw her dagger with precision and Alfie watched in horror as it sailed right through the creature, as if it were made of smoke. It didn't even seem to notice.

"I don't know!" Alfie called back.

The creatures' bodies only had the merest suggestion of humanity—they had two arms and two legs, a lump for a head, but no faces. Their fingers were horrifyingly long, dragging behind them as they moved, twitching against the dirt ground. They moved with the fluidity of water, but Alfie could not use his water charming to manipulate them the way he had the Tattooed King's beasts of paint.

The monsters tore toward Alfie, reaching for him as he stumbled back. One gripped him by the neck, its long fingers wrapping around him twice over and raising him high above the ground. Alfie could feel the cold veins slithering and pulsing on his neck as he struggled to breathe.

Images flashed in his mind—skin peeling, bones breaking, and a throat left raw from screaming. Then darkness drawn out of the bloody carnage like water from a stagnant well.

This creature used to be *human*.

Then he saw Sombra puppeteering Dezmin's body, his dark intentions smothering Dezmin. His lust for finding his relics and returning to his former glory. He was not just giddy to reclaim his immortal form, but also to humiliate Alfie and Finn for the audacity of being prophesied to defeat him.

These monsters weren't part of the forest's mutated magic; they'd been sent by Sombra himself.

Alfie choked, grasping at the monster's hand, his globe of light extinguishing and plunging them into darkness. Only the slim bars of moonlight traced the creature's hideous form. Its skin squished under his grip but wouldn't break, and as soon as he released his hold, the cold arm expanded again.

Finn had managed to throw her shirt on before appearing at Alfie's side, a globe of stone encasing her fist. She swung it at the creature closest to Alfie, but when she made contact with the monster her fist sank in, as if pulled in by quicksand. Somehow both solid and fluid.

"Mierda!" she shouted as she tried to pull her arm out.

Alfie's vision began to blur. The touch of these monsters was pulling the strength from him, cracking him open and slurping out the marrow. He would die if he stayed in its grip much longer.

Alfie's satchel fell from his shoulder, plopping onto the ground.

Like a dog at the sound of a whistle, the creature dropped Alfie and dove onto the bag, tearing through it. As it lurched away, Finn's stone fist slid out of its body.

Alfie gasped, gripping at his neck to make sure it was still there, still whole. He watched the creatures converge on the bag, paying him no mind. They didn't care about Finn or Alfie any longer; they were only after Sombra's relics. The bag probably still had the stink of Sombra's influence on it.

"Finn!" Alfie croaked, but she was already ahead of him.

"I've got it!" she shouted. "Get the doorway ready!"

All four of the creatures were trying to grab at the bag, fighting each other to get to it. Finn reached out a hand and the ground opened and pulled the satchel beneath the earth, out of the creatures' reach. They slammed themselves against the dirt trying to find it, breaking the ground apart with every attack. Finn's hand twitched and Alfie knew she was moving the bag beneath the ground. The creatures followed until they were twenty paces away from Alfie and Finn, beating at the ground for the bag.

Still catching his breath, Alfie pressed his palm to the ground and opened a door into the realm of magic.

"I'm ready!" Alfie shouted.

With a jerking motion of her arm, the satchel shot out of the dirt and into her arms. The creatures turned, furious even in their silence, and made a mad dash toward Alfie and Finn.

Alfie gripped her hand, but he was so shaken by all that had happened that he kept failing to match the colors of their magic. The realm of magic wouldn't let her in if she didn't match him.

"Hurry!" Finn shouted as the creatures drew closer.

"I'm trying!" Alfie said. Finally he and Finn were the same shade of purple. He grabbed Finn by the shoulder and jerked her out of the monsters' way, falling backward into the realm of magic.

As the prince and thief fell, one of the creatures swiped at them, its long, cold finger skimming the tip of Alfie's nose just before they disappeared.

THE CAPTURE

Luka's head swam as he woke.

He was uncomfortable, his body in a strange, curled-up position. The world rocked beneath him as his eyes stared up at a cloth canopy of sorts. He was in . . . a wagon? A headache pounded behind his eyes.

He turned his head to loosen the crick in his neck and bumped noses with a cold corpse.

Luka bit back a scream as he leaned away from it. It was Eduardo, the dueño he had accidentally spat a cave fly at. The man's face was slack; all the disapproval and annoyance it had shown before was now extinguished.

A flood of memory coursed through Luka.

He'd been teaching James how to dance. Then that little boy appeared, and after that—darkness. Why hadn't the shadowless just killed them? When he'd gone into the Brim to retrieve the larimar, they'd seemed more concerned with their own pleasure than kidnapping people.

"Sombra wanted living dueños, *living*!" one of the shadowless complained.

Luka turned to see a pair of them seated at the back of the wagon, their feet hanging over the edge. A second wagon was following closely behind, no doubt carrying the rest of their camp. "What's he going to do with all these dead ones!"

Luka's stomach tightened. Had they killed everyone but him?

They'd already lost half the dueños at the farmstead, and now this. They needed to get to the oasis so they could figure out how to kill Sombra and save Dezmin. That was of the utmost importance, of course, but beyond that, he had known Paloma since he was that tiny hopeless child brought to live in the palace after his family had perished. He'd hated her endless lessons and homework, but he could not deny that she had, in many ways, raised him, grounding him in study and routine when he was in danger of being swept away by grief. Was she even still alive?

And then there was James.

James, who had finally come out of his shell when they'd danced the night before. Who had saved him and Paloma at the farm. Was he finally free from Marsden's cruelty only to die now? It wasn't right.

"Well, we've still got a few live ones," the other said, and hope sparked in Luka's chest. "And who knows, maybe he'll have use for the dead ones too."

"Use for the dead ones?" one laughed. "You think he wants to make dueño sancocho?"

"Mira, all I know is Sombra promised he'd give us treasure and glory if we brought him dueños and any people who still have their shadows. And we're bringing him both."

Luka bit back a curse. Of course Sombra was offering bounties for the capture of those who could resist his magic. He was trying to hobble Finn and Alfie by enlisting the shadowless as hunters.

Luka needed a plan. They had only bound his wrists and ankles in rope. He could free himself quietly and still have the element of surprise. They wouldn't have time to knock him out with whatever they'd soaked that handkerchief in. Not if he got to them first. Wait. Luka flexed his toes. Why was he in just his socks? Where were his boots? And his cloak?

The shared parchment was in his cloak.

"One's awake!" a voice cried, its pitch higher than the others.

In the back corner of the wagon, close to his bound feet, sat the very boy who'd tricked them. Luka's eyes narrowed. The shadowless had used the boy as bait, had him figure out how many *propio* users were in the camp so they'd know who to take out first.

One of the men crouched over Luka. "How are you even awake? We gave you a nice kick in the skull after we knocked you out."

"Might need another to put him back to sleep," the other called. He hadn't even moved from his post. Clearly neither of them was worried about Luka escaping.

Luka would make sure they regretted that.

"This was the one with the fancy boots and cloak," the crouching man said. "We got a nice price for that, didn't we?"

Luka's heart froze in his chest. If the parchment was too far away he wouldn't be able to get it back with magic. How would he communicate with Alfie?

"Oh, look how sad he is." The man grinned. "Poor rich

muchacho lost his favorite outfit."

The men burst into laughter, and Luka felt something inside him break open.

He wrenched his wrists and ankles apart, snapping the ropes in two.

The shadowless cried out, stumbling back.

With quick movements Luka punched one man in the jaw, the bones cracking beneath his knuckles. The man shrieked, gripping his face in pain as he cowered on the ground. The other man tried to leap out of the wagon, screaming for help, but Luka grabbed him by his collar and dragged him right back in. These men didn't have powerful *propios* like the Tattooed King did. They were just smugglers and thieves, and Luka was grateful for the ease of it.

"Please don't—" the man began, but Luka kicked him in the stomach with such force that he flew straight through the fabric covering the side of the wagon and out of sight.

"*Oye!* What's going on back there?" Luka heard the driver shout.

Luka darted deeper into the wagon, carefully stepping over the bodies of half a dozen dueños, some of them asleep, some of them dead. Paloma and James were nowhere to be seen. They must be in the other wagon. They would be fine, Luka reassured himself as he tore through the canopy and grabbed the driver by the back of the neck. The man shouted as Luka pulled him into the wagon and slammed him to the ground. None of the men were dead, but if they tried to fight Luka again, they'd wish they were.

Without a driver, the horses meandered to a stop. Then came

the jeers of the men in the wagons behind.

"Why have you stopped?"

"Keep going, fool!" another shouted.

Luka turned to the little boy in the corner of the wagon. His eyes were wide with fear. If not for him tricking them, they wouldn't have been captured and he'd still be able to contact Alfie. But still, he was just a boy. Luka released a gust of a sigh.

He crossed his arms and stared at the child, hoping to conjure some form of parental disappointment. "You stay here."

"You hurt Papi!" the boy said with a glower too strong for someone his age. His gaze flickered to the passed-out wagon driver. "I don't have to listen to you."

Luka frowned. He wanted to be angry with the boy, but what child wouldn't listen to their parent, even if that parent no longer had their best interests at heart?

"You know that man isn't your father right now." Luka thought of his own panic at seeing Queen Amada infected with the darkness. How shattered would he have been to witness that as a young boy? "He's changed."

The boy said nothing, though his eyes shined with unshed tears.

"But my friends and I are going to figure out a way to change him back," Luka said. He didn't know if it was possible, but he had to give the boy hope. "And we'll keep you safe until we can fix everything, all right?" When the boy finally nodded Luka asked, "What's your name?"

"Jorge," he said.

"You wait here with your papi, Jorge. I'll be right back."

Luka parted the wagon's cloth opening and leaped out of the back. Now he could see that there were two other wagons full of kidnapped people behind them, both driven by pairs of black-eyed men and women. At the sight of him, they reached for their weapons. As his strength flared inside him, Luka promised himself that he would reach for restraint to keep them alive.

After the shadowless poachers were knocked out, disarmed, and hog-tied with their own rope, Luka went through each of the wagons.

The poachers had not only kidnapped their camp, they'd kidnapped any civilians with *propios* that they could find. Even children.

After the incident at the farmstead, there had been only ten dueños left. Now five more were dead, but thankfully both Paloma and James had been spared. The Englassen, like Luka, had simply been knocked out, leaving an angry red welt on his temple. Paloma, on the other hand, was not so lucky. The dueña had been stabbed in the side with a poisoned blade, and after hours in the wagon, infection had seeped in. Healing it was beyond Luka's skills. She needed potions from the palace infirmary. The remaining dueños had been dosed with a magic suppressant of sorts, leaving them groggy and their magic weak. Such precautions hadn't been taken for Luka, James, or the civilians. It seemed that the poachers had only feared the dueños' magic. Now they all stood on a dirt road, each side flanked by dead grass. Luka surveyed the line of wagons, their occupants either knocked out, dead, or milling about as they caught their bearings. When Luka tried to summon the shared parchment, his fears were confirmed. It was too far away to recover. His connection to Alfie was lost. How would he know if Alfie and Finn were okay?

He fisted his hands to keep them from shaking.

"We need to go . . . ," Paloma said weakly, her eyes glazing over. "The oasis. We need to go to the oasis. There are only three days left. . . ."

Paloma's pocket watch confirmed how much time they'd lost. It was just past noon on the third day. They had only three left to stop Sombra.

James had found some blankets and fashioned a bed for Paloma, and Bruno had cleaned her wound, but that could only do so much.

"No, you can barely string a sentence together." Luka put his hand on her shoulder when she tried to sit up. He knew what had to be done, what responsibility he needed to take on, though he really didn't want to. "You and the remaining dueños need to return to the palace."

Paloma stared at him. "Are you out of your mind?"

"No, you're out of your mind if you think you can keep going." Luka crossed his arms. "You're gravely injured, and we've got three caravans of civilians who need to be taken to safety. Tell me what needs to be done at the oasis and I will do it." Luka tried to sound more confident than he felt, but the bar was depressingly low on that front.

Paloma stared at him, her eyes focusing for a moment. "Luka—"

"Alfie *needs* you," Luka interrupted. "He will need you and the dueños in the final battle against Sombra. If he returns with the relics and all of you have died, what then?" He gestured around them, where Paloma's brethren groaned in pain from their injuries.

When Paloma fell silent, Luka knew that he was right. A pit formed in his stomach. He had been kind of hoping not to be right.

"The poachers said that Sombra offered glory to the shadowless who brought him dueños and anyone who resisted his influence," Luka said. "You are in danger."

"And so are you," Paloma said, insistent. "You've resisted Sombra's influence. You still have your shadow—you could be targeted."

She wasn't wrong about that.

"Still, I'm not as important," Luka said. He hated admitting it. From a young age, Luka had loved being the center of attention, and growing up in the palace had only stoked the flames of his ego. But if this adventure had taught him anything, it was that he was a very small speck in the fabric of this world. He was not the most gifted or the most important. If he had to sacrifice himself to save the world, it wouldn't be a high price; it'd be a bargain.

Luka didn't have the magical prowess or the knowledge of the dueños. He wanted to see Alfie again, wanted to be there for him to stop Sombra, but if it was a choice between him or the dueños, he knew Alfie would need the dueños more. "Alfie will miss me if I die," Luka said, his voice thinning with emotion at the thought. "But if *you* die, the whole world will suffer."

Luka held her gaze until Paloma finally closed her eyes, sighing through her nose.

"I'll go with him," James said, stepping forward.

Luka looked at him with gratitude. At least he wouldn't have to do this alone.

"Fine," Paloma bit out, sweat rolling down her forehead. "Before you leave, you and I will share a parchment . . . so you can send us the information that you receive from the ancient dueños—"

"In case we don't make it back, I understand," Luka said grimly.

"While we do that, you and your comrades can take the civilians to the palace for safety."

There were dozens of them gathered around the wagons, confusion and fear in their eyes.

Dueño Bruno came to stand beside Paloma and nodded in agreement. He looked feverish and there was blood in his white beard from the fight, but he still looked coherent. "We'll use the wagons to take them."

It was all the more reason for the dueños to retreat to the palace. If they all went to the oasis, who would lead the civilians to safety?

"Good," Luka said, his eyes straying to little Jorge, who sat with an elder dueña as she shared a piece of bread with him. They picked off the mold together, flicking it into the blackened grass. "Now tell me what I need to do once we get to the oasis."

"The oasis would usually not allow the presence of a non-dueño," Paloma said, her voice syrup-slow from her weakness. "But the world is different now. The balance . . ."

"I know," Luka assured her. Now that Sombra had upended the world's balance and Nocturna was here, anything was possible. "How do I use the oasis to reach the other dueños?"

"Meditate, mental clarity." Just speaking those three words took so much strength from her.

Luka held back a curse. Neither of those were his strong suit.

"If I fail, can James give it a go?" Luka asked, desperate for a backup plan.

James was startled. "I could never—"

"No," Paloma said, and even in the thick of her fever, she

managed to shoot him the same look she'd given him during his childhood lessons. "It needs to be a Castallano. You."

"Coño," he sighed.

"What exactly do we need to do?" James asked. "How can I be of help?"

Paloma slowly explained that Luka would need to enter the oasis, clear his mind, and float on his back, but when the spirit realm accepted him, his body would remain in the physical world, defenseless. James would need to guard his body until he returned.

"How long will I be in there?" Luka asked, ignoring the part of his mind that doubted the spirit realm would even accept him in the first place.

"Hours, days," Paloma said. "Depends on you."

Luka stared at her, wide-eyed. Days? "How would my body live without food and water that long?"

"It won't," Paloma said.

"Is there a clock in the spirit realm?"

She cut her eyes at him. "Stay cognizant of your goal and you'll be . . . fine."

"Can I wake him if he's there too long?" James asked, concerned.

Paloma shook her head, and when she met Luka's eyes he knew she was about to say something that would make him even more nervous than he already was. "The spirit realm will challenge you . . . tempt and distract you from your goal. Remember why you are there. For answers, for this world, for Alfehr. Else you'll find yourself stuck there forever."

Luka forced himself to nod. "I will."

"I'll ready some horses for us," James said, leaving Luka and Paloma alone.

"In my robes," she said with great difficulty. "A map and the pocket watch to keep time."

Luka hesitated before reaching for her clothes. A dueño's robes were sacred—and even if Paloma weren't a dueña, it'd be weird to be reaching into her clothes. But now was not the time for decorum. Luka carefully parted her robe and reached into the inner pocket. Inside were the watch, a map with the oasis marked, and a few sheaves of blank parchment. With spoken magic, Luka clumsily paired two pieces of parchment so that they could communicate.

"It should be you doing this," Luka said as he folded the map. "You aren't the type who fails." A quiet, fearful voice in his head whispered, *And I'm the type who does.*

With a quivering arm, Paloma reached out and took Luka's hand in hers. Her skin was clammy, too warm.

"I already told you, anyone can fail." She squeezed his hand. "Which means anyone can succeed too."

Luka curled his free hand around her knuckles, cradling her hand between his palms. He should say something poignant now, something memorable, but he could do nothing but hold on to her the way he had as a little boy.

Luka wasn't sure how long they stood like this, but soon James reappeared with a pair of horses, and Luka knew there were no more excuses to linger.

"Be safe," Paloma said, withdrawing her hand from his. "Be as smart . . . as I've always known . . . you are."

Luka's throat tightened, and he moved quickly to change the subject.

His eyes darted to Jorge, the little boy who looked lost and ashamed. "The boy is named Jorge," Luka said to her. "His father is one of the poachers. Take care of him, please."

Paloma nodded.

Luka turned to Bruno. "Keep her safe."

"Of course," he said.

With nothing left to say and so much to be done, Luka and James mounted their horses and rode into the barren countryside.

SAVED FOR DESSERT

With a painful *plop*, Finn and Alfie landed in the realm of magic once more.

"What were those things?" Finn gasped, her heart pounding against her ribs. She stared at the strings of magic blinking in and out of existence around them as Alfie groaned on the ground, clearly too winded to influence how the realm of magic presented itself. Slowly he took in deep breaths, and the strings began to solidify.

Alfie rubbed his throat with shaking hands.

"Prince," she said, crawling over to him. "Are you all right?"

"I don't know." Alfie's voice shook. "When that thing touched me, something felt *wrong*. When you punched it, did you feel how cold and awful it was?"

"My hand was covered in stone," she said. He looked terrified. "It didn't touch my skin." She tugged at his hand. "Let me see."

The prince dropped his arm from his neck, and there, wrapped around his Adam's apple, was the dark imprint of the monster's long fingers. It looked as if a soot-covered hand had grabbed his throat, but the stain wouldn't come off when Finn wiped at it.

Alfie's eyes widened at the sight of her grimace. "What is it?"

It wasn't a bruise—it was as if a piece of the monster had clung to Alfie's skin. "It left a mark."

Alfie touched it, wincing.

"How does it feel?" she asked.

"Cold," he said, his brow furrowing. "Cold and sore."

"Can you heal it?" Finn asked.

Alfie wrapped a free hand around his marked neck. "*Sanar.*" Nothing. "*Sanar!*"

The prince tried over and over, to no avail. The mark remained a stain on his brown skin.

"We don't have time to fret over it," Alfie said as he shakily stood. "We need to head to Weilai to get the next relic."

Finn watched him warily. "Did Sombra send those things?" Only a god could create something so ghastly, and the monsters had seemed keen on searching their bag for Sombra's relics.

Alfie nodded. "When it grabbed me, I could see where it came from, its past." His voice was low with fear. "Sombra took men and turned them into those things."

Finn's blood ran cold. Those creatures had once been men? It didn't seem possible. "How?"

Alfie just shook his head.

Finn wasn't so sure she wanted to know the answer to that question anymore. "What else did you see?"

"He's sent them to collect his relics for him. He's too weak to come himself," Alfie explained. His hand passed over the mark on his neck, and Finn could've sworn she saw it move, almost as if something were wriggling beneath the skin. But when she focused, it was still again. "He wants them to get the relics. And he wants us alive to the end so that he can humiliate us and the gods when he returns to his immortal form."

Finn's jaw tensed. "He's saving us for last."

Alfie nodded, his face grim.

"Well, I'm no maldito dessert," Finn said, crossing her arms. "If he tries to take a bite of us I'll make sure he chokes."

Alfie's eyes lost focus, glazing over. He stumbled sideways, and Finn rushed to catch him before he fell.

"Prince!"

Alfie leaned against her. "I'm all right," he said. "We don't have time to stop. We don't know how quickly those creatures will get to the rest of Sombra's relics. And who knows how long it'll take us to reach the next location."

After he steadied himself, Alfie pulled the shared parchment out of his armor and unfurled it. Finn hoped that Luka had responded. The prince could use a win.

His face fell.

"Nothing?" Finn asked.

"Nothing." He looked at her, his brow furrowed with worry.

"They're probably just busy," Finn reassured him, though even she was beginning to worry. "We don't know what he and Paloma are up to. For all we know they're having a tea party with the dead dueños."

Alfie didn't laugh.

"And Dezmin hasn't come back either." Looking more tired than she'd ever seen, he weighed the dragon in his palm before tucking the parchment back into his armor. She knew it wasn't the jumping from continent to continent that drained him—he would do that all day if it meant saving the world and his brother. It was the fear for those he loved. And there was no joke Finn could tell to help with that.

But she could try something else.

Finn gripped the prince by the chin, rose onto her toes, and kissed him.

It wasn't searing with passion like their kisses had been the night before the betrothal ceremony. This kiss was gentle, one that calmed instead of smoldered, whispered instead of shouted. A kiss that was the eye of the storm, a pocket of peace in the chaos.

She couldn't remember it herself, but she knew that Alfie had protected her when she'd turned into a helpless baby in the forest. If he could do that for her, then she could take the hard stone of this terrifying adventure and carve out a moment of hope for him.

She pulled away slowly. "Everything will be fine."

He leaned into her touch, folding his hand over her own. "I believe it when you say it."

They held each other for a long moment, the realm of magic quiet around them, until Finn finally murmured, "We have to go."

"I know," he said, his voice heavy with exhaustion. He stepped away, swaying on his feet for a moment. He took a deep breath and focused, his brow furrowing as the strings of magic appeared around them once more.

"Which way should we go?" Finn asked, eager to get the next one over with.

Alfie didn't answer. He appeared to be lost in thought as he rubbed the strange bruise on his neck.

Finn waved her hand in front of his face. "Hello?"

He looked at her, surprised. "Don't you feel it?"

She shook her head. "Feel what?"

"A pull," Alfie explained. "Similar to what we felt standing at the base of Dead Men's Mountain and in the Englassen forest. We go this way." He pointed eastward.

Finn quirked a brow. She'd felt the presence of Sombra's aura back then because they were close to the relic's resting place in the pond. How was it possible that they weren't even in Weilai yet, but Alfie already felt it? She never felt Sombra's pull while here in the realm of magic. Then again, who was she to question it? Maybe this was an example of what the gods meant when they said that Alfie and Finn had been born with the ability to stop Sombra.

"I don't feel it, but lead the way," she said with a shrug. Maybe the prince's *propio* made it possible for him to sense it now. She threw in a pantomime of a formal bow. "After you."

Alfie rolled his eyes but smiled all the same. "I thought I'd have to move through the strings blindly again, but now I can sense it, which'll save us some time." There was a hopeful lilt in his voice. He picked up his pace as they walked deeper.

Finn watched his back, questions brewing in her mind. Because of the monsters, she hadn't had time to ask him to fully explain what happened in the forest. She knew that she'd aged down to a baby, which was embarrassing enough, but what else had happened? What had she told him when she was too young to know better?

"Whatever nonsense kid Finn told you, you can just ignore it," she blurted, her eyes anywhere but on his face.

"I liked kid Finn." His hand found her shoulder and squeezed, lingering just long enough for her to lean into it. "I learned a lot from her."

Finn wrung her hands. "What did she say?"

Alfie was quiet for a moment, and Finn was in agony for each second. "She told me that she was scared."

What a stupid thing to say. "Of what?"

"Of not being enough," he said. "Of the people who have tried to hurt her and what they made her believe about herself."

Ignacio's face flashed in her mind.

"She was nervous to tell me at first. I think she worried I'd judge her," Alfie said, glancing at her. "I wish she knew that hearing her say it made me feel better, because I feel the exact same way."

Finn met his gaze.

"It made me understand her more too," he went on. He looked exhausted, but somehow he was still able to muster the energy to comfort her. She was stunned by how he could balance the weight of the world in one hand and her heart in the other. "She might think it made me like her less, but it did the opposite—it made me like her more. Something I didn't think was possible."

Finn wanted to say something to ruin the moment, just as everyone (herself included) expected. But she didn't.

"I'm sorry that I pushed you to tell me things you weren't ready to talk about," Alfie said. "We don't have to say anything more about it—I just wanted to apologize."

Finn's eyes darted ahead, but she couldn't stop the warmth from flooding her voice when she said, "Thank you."

She would regret it later. After all, wasn't she supposed to be keeping her distance from him? Shouldn't she stop this to save him the trouble—and save herself the pain? But instead she stayed quietly by his side, their knuckles brushing as they walked.

When Alfie finally found the string that would carry them to Weilai, Finn grabbed it, but not before she twined the fingers of their free hands first.

THE SPIRIT REALM

Luka and James rode for over half a day, their horses lathered with sweat.

After interrogating one of the poachers, they'd learned that their kidnappers had driven them away from the jungle and toward the city to deliver them to Sombra. Now they needed to make up for lost time.

Following the map, they rode south before dismounting at the edge of the jungle. By then, the trees had not only blackened; they'd also curled inward, interlocking with each other like fingers. There was no longer enough space to ride their horses through.

Luka flexed his sore feet. He'd stolen boots from one of the poachers, but they were a size too small and not half as stylish as his old pair.

"Well," Luka said as they stood at the rim of the dark forest. He should say something smart right now, something to rouse their spirits, but all he could string together was, "Let's get this over with."

Together, the pair stepped into the shadowed trees, ducking and squeezing between trunks and branches, which were stiff and cold to the touch. Luka conjured a globe of light to illuminate the way (using his flame casting could set the forest ablaze). He could only hope they wouldn't happen upon any foes lying in wait, but what they found was somehow worse—

Silence.

The jungles of Castallan were known for their biodiversity. There was no other place in the world with such a variety of flora and fauna. Scholars from other kingdoms would travel there just to witness the jungles' green glory and to collect plants to create salves and medicines. But now there were no colorful birds darting through the canopy of trees, no furry creatures foraging in the dirt for food, no breeze softly swaying the branches. The leaves had long perished, littering the ground with their corpses.

James held up the map. "The oasis is about two miles into the jungle."

"Two miles!" Luka sighed. They didn't have time for two minutes, let alone two miles. He checked the pocket watch. It was well past midnight, officially the fourth day of their journey. Only two left to save the world. "Let me see it."

James handed him the map and Luka looked at it, confirming the distance with a glance. "Damn it." For the first time he was thankful for those forced cartography classes he and Alfie had taken as children or else he never would've been able to read it at all.

Alfie.

The thought of his cousin struck Luka like a slap. Thanks to the poachers, he had no way of contacting him. Were he and Finn safe? Had they secured the relic in Englass?

Or had they died, far from home and the people who loved them? Had their lives ended before the world did?

Luka nearly tripped over a thick root that seemed designed to make him land directly on his face.

"Are you all right?" James asked quietly.

"I'm fine," Luka said, his eyes stinging. Why was that the very worst question you could ask someone when they were upset? And why did James have to ask it right now? "Let's just keep quiet until we get there. In case there are enemies afoot."

James looked around, the silence of the jungle deafening. "As you wish."

For once, Luka was happy to not talk.

As the two made their way deeper into the jungle, Luka tried his best (and failed) to stop worrying about whether he'd ever see Alfie again.

"We're close," James whispered, breaking over an hour of silence. Though his voice was soft, Luka startled at the sound. "Just beyond this brush."

Luka had been afraid they wouldn't be able to tell when they'd arrived at the oasis, but in the end, that wasn't the problem. James cut through thick, blackened brush and Luka stepped through to find not an oasis, but a dry hole.

"What?" Luka said, staring at the dirt. The oasis was ten men wide, but there wasn't a drop of water left. He knew the seas were boiling, so he'd expected uncomfortably hot water, but not no water at all.

"Oh no," James said. He carefully stepped into what would have been the shallows of the oasis and bent over to grab a handful of dirt. "Even the soil is bone dry. It's as if there was never water here to begin with."

Panic surged through Luka. "Paloma said I'm supposed to float in the sacred water to reach the dueños. What am I supposed to do now?"

James eyed the dirt, as if searching it for answers. "Maybe if we dig we can find some of the water."

Together, he and Luka walked to the center of the oasis and began to dig. With spoken magic and their bare hands they broke into the earth, but they found nothing but more dirt.

Luka sat on the ground, too distraught to care about how he was staining his trousers. If there was no water for him to float in, what hope did they have? He'd been afraid of failing Paloma, failing Alfie, failing the world, but in the end he hadn't even been given the chance.

James crouched beside him, his voice gentle. "I think you still have to try."

"How?" Luka asked, gesturing around them. Paloma hadn't mentioned floating in the water just for fun—it was clearly an important part of the process. "Do you expect me to levitate in here?"

"No," James said, annoyingly patient. "Maybe just being here is enough. Even without the water, this is still a sacred place."

Luka looked at the dusty, dried-out scab of land. "Is it, though?"

"Luka," James said, gripping him by the shoulders. "I know you're afraid, I know you didn't imagine having to do this part at all, but we have to try. We don't have a choice."

"I know," Luka admitted, his eyes stinging. "I know. I just . . ."

James's gaze softened. "What?"

"I just thought I'd be able to speak with him one last time,"

Luka heard himself say. "Or at least leave a message for him in the parchment."

He might disappear into the spirit realm, never to return again. He might die without getting to say goodbye.

James was quiet, his green eyes pensive. "I think I can help," he finally said.

Luka rubbed at his eyes with the back of his hand. "Unless you can turn back time and stop those poachers from selling my cloak, I'm not sure what you can do."

"I know it's a lot to ask, but just trust me." James stood from his crouch and held out his hand to Luka.

Luka let him pull him up. "What are you—"

"Close your eyes," James insisted.

Luka stared at him, skeptical.

"Close your eyes," James repeated. "Please."

"Fine," Luka said, closing them. "What now?"

Luka heard James take a deep, focusing breath. A long silence settled between them.

"Okay. Open."

Luka opened his eyes and before him stood . . .

Alfie.

James had a *propio* that let him create illusions, so Luka knew this wasn't truly Alfie. He knew this, but Luka still couldn't stop himself from extinguishing his light and pulling James into a fierce hug.

"I've missed you," Luka said, his eyes tearing as Alfie hugged back.

James didn't speak, and Luka was grateful for that because

his illusion could not capture the cadence and rhythm of Alfie's words—the thoughtfulness that came from years spent in a library. Luka kept his face buried in Alfie's shoulder.

"I love you," Luka said. "And if I never come back, I need you to know that I did everything I could. And if you're already gone," Luka said, his voice breaking, "then I hope I stay stuck in the spirit realm, because I don't want to live in a world without you."

He felt Alfie nod and hold him tighter still.

Luka forced himself to pull out of the embrace, and as he blinked the tears from his eyes, the illusion faded until once again it was just James standing there, lit only by the weak bars of moonlight penetrating the tangle of trees.

"I hope I didn't overstep boundaries—" James began, but Luka didn't let him finish.

He fisted his hands in James's shirt and tugged him into a kiss.

Luka usually was not one for a kiss so raw and vulnerable. A kiss where his mind wasn't abuzz with the tingle of alcohol and ego, but with gratitude and affection. And then, when James gripped his shoulder and kissed him back—passion.

After a long moment, he stepped back, letting go of James's shirt. "Thank you."

"You're very welcome," James said, his face flushed.

"You're right." Luka stepped away from him, his eyes on the dried-out oasis. "I've got to try. Even if there's no water, maybe it'll still work."

James nodded, the blush fading from his face. "One way to find out."

Luka figured that the center of the dried-out oasis was as good a spot as any. He sat cross-legged in the dirt. "If I somehow pull this off, be sure to write to Paloma once I've entered the spirit realm."

"I will." James took several steps back as if to give Luka space, and summoned his own globe of light to keep watch with. Did one need space to enter the spirit realm? Luka supposed he'd learn soon enough.

Luka drummed his fingers on his thighs. "I don't even know how to begin."

"Just try to let your mind go blank," James said.

Luka closed his eyes before he could roll them. "Easier said than done."

"And remember that Paloma said there'd be distractions, temptations to keep you from your goal," James added. "Don't forget why you're there."

Luka nodded, his eyes still closed.

He sat in silence, begging his mind to fall silent, but all his fears echoed between his ears. What if his inability to do this was the sole reason that the world ended? The jungle was completely silent, which made his thoughts that much louder, harder to ignore.

"Coño," Luka said, opening his eyes. He looked at James, who still stood ten paces or so away. "How long was I sitting there?"

"Five minutes."

Luka bit back a curse and massaged his temples. "It felt much longer. It's too quiet here. I can't focus."

James stared at him, confused. "You need noise to focus?"

"Yes," Luka said. "Silence doesn't work for me. It just makes my thoughts louder." It was part of the reason why he hated the library. It was impossible to distract yourself in the oppressive quiet.

"Maybe I can help again," James offered. "With my *propio*."

Luka cocked his head. "How?"

"I can create auditory illusions too," James said sheepishly, as if embarrassed by his own skill. "What's a sound that makes you feel relaxed?"

Luka didn't need to think for long before the answer came to him. "Being in the bathtub. The quiet drip and slosh of the water, the feeling of the steam."

"I think I can manage that," James said with a nod. "Let's try."

Luka closed his eyes and waited as the illusion carried him away.

He could feel the hot water on his skin, smell the scent of soap in the air. Luka's muscles relaxed, his shoulders dropping far from his ears. He reclined fully, letting himself float on the surface. He had to suppress a laugh at the thought of how apt Finn's nickname for him was. He truly did love a good bathtub.

He hoped she was all right.

Luka took a deep breath, inhaling the steam. He focused on the gentle sounds of the tub until those sounds were all that was left in his mind.

Luka blinked, opening his eyes. James was gone. The empty oasis had disappeared too. Instead he stood in an endless jungle, but not the bleak, dead jungle that Sombra had created—this was lush and full of life. Brightly feathered birds cawed as they flew between the trees. Luka could spot a river in the distance, running through the land like a blue ribbon. The trees were heavy with limoncillos and mangos. The sun hung in the sky, bright and lovely. How he'd missed it! He would never complain about sweating again. Luka could smell the earthy scent of growth, of sun-warmed dirt. His eyes stung. Sombra had stolen this beauty from them.

But he was here to return it.

He'd done it. He'd entered the spirit realm, and that was in no small part thanks to James. Luka thought of the kiss they'd shared. He'd told himself that it was out of gratitude for James helping him, but part of Luka had simply wanted to kiss the boy. And that was way too complicated a thought for right now. Luka tucked it away for safekeeping, promising to return to it.

"I'm here to learn how to stop Sombra." Complex romantic entanglements were more of a post–saving the world thing. "Priorities."

Luka wasn't sure which direction he was supposed to go in, so he picked one at random and set off.

"Hello! Anybody out there?" Luka called into the trees, but no one answered. How was he supposed to just find some old dueños? The thicket of trees in front of him and the one behind him looked identical. Even though Paloma had never implied it, part of him had expected something more obvious—a golden path winding through the jungles to lead him where he needed to go. But there wasn't a hint to be found.

With a shrug, Luka kept moving, swatting away low branches as he went. He walked for what felt like hours, but who even knew how time worked in the spirit world? What if time moved much slower here, and whole days had passed in the outside world? Luka stifled that panic before it could fully bloom. He needed to focus.

And then he heard a sound.

Laughter.

Familiar laughter.

His heart racing, Luka sprinted through the brush, following the melody of children playing. He'd seen nothing but trees and now he'd finally found someone, but he hadn't expected it to be *them*.

He burst through the brush into a clearing, and there they were—his family.

His four brothers and sisters chased each other about, his parents keeping a watchful eye on them.

Luka could barely breathe. He knew the spirit realm was where souls resided after death, but he'd thought that was metaphorical. He'd thought that maybe the dueños would be reachable because they were dueños. He hadn't expected to find his family, to hear them laughing, to watch them fall and wipe the grass off their knees before they continued their game.

"Luka!" Ana, his youngest sister, shouted. She was only four, just as she had been the last time he'd seen her alive. "You're here!"

His family turned in surprise. When Ana ran over and grasped his hand, it was no longer the hand of a young man but that of a ten-year-old boy. The age he'd become an orphan.

"Come play!" she said. "We didn't expect to see you so soon!"

Luka scrubbed his eyes with his knuckles. "Me either."

With each step, the memories of Sombra's tyranny and Paloma's advice grew quieter.

He was home.

He was splashing in puddles with his brothers and letting his sisters braid his hair the way he used to hate when they were alive. But now he would sit for every tea party, every play and puppet show. He could spend limitless lifetimes in this place.

Had he ever been anywhere else?

"Mi vida," his mother said as she crouched in front of him, cradling his face in her hands. Her brown skin was so vibrant, so different from how she'd looked when he'd found her body draped lifelessly on her bed, her lips crusted with sick. "You're too early."

Luka shook his head, panic seeping through him. Her words had triggered something, the memory of why he'd come here in the first place, and he worked to bury it. "What do you mean? I'm supposed to be wherever you are. Where else could I be?"

His father joined them, his hand rubbing comforting circles on Luka's head. "That's not why you're here, Mijo."

Luka shook his head furiously, tears dropping down his nose. "I don't care why I'm here, I want to be with you!"

"And one day you will be," his mother said. "Just not today." She took him into her arms, and when Luka pulled back he was no longer a little boy. He was a young man again, with a purpose—and with a world to save from the darkness.

The spirit realm will challenge you . . . tempt and distract you from your goal. Remember why you are there . . . else you'll find yourself stuck there forever.

He had known he'd be tested, but not like this. This was unfair, this was unforgivable—and yet it was one of the best moments of his life.

"You'll be here when I get back?" he asked them. "All of you?"

What if this was a one-time thing? What if even after he died, he never saw them again?

"Right here," his father promised with a nod.

"You're sure?" he asked, his voice thick with emotion.

"Yes." His mother kissed his cheek. "We're sure. And even if we weren't, you have a world to save. You cannot linger."

Luka nodded, unable to speak. Maybe there was a risk that he'd never find them again. Even if that was true, there was too much at stake for him to stay.

"Say goodbye to your brothers and sisters and we'll see you soon," his mother said as she ran her hand through his hair just like she had when he was a boy.

Luka took a tentative step away from them, the movement overwhelmingly painful.

"Wait," his father said, gripping his shoulder. "Before you go. It's not your fault, Mijo. It's not your fault that you lived and we did not."

"You just had more to do," his mother agreed. "That's all."

A broken sob parted Luka's lips. He wrapped his arms around them both, clinging to them for a long moment before he finally pulled himself away.

He turned toward the children and knelt on the ground. "Come give your big brother a hug!" he called, trying to smile.

The children rushed to him, throwing themselves into his arms and shouting an endless parade of questions.

"You're so big now!"

"Where are you going?"

"When will you be back?"

Luka looked tearfully back at his parents before saying, "Soon. I'll be back soon. You keep playing. I'll be here for the next round."

"Why are you crying?" Ana asked.

The question shattered him, and Luka bit back a sob. "I'm crying because I'm happy, hermanita."

He kissed their heads and let them play. The pain of their unfinished childhoods weighed on him, holding him captive. But, then again, here they could finish them. They had all the time in the world.

"Go, Mijo," his father said. "Your destiny is waiting for you."

Luka couldn't look at them a moment longer; he dashed away from the clearing, back into the brush. He ran until he could no longer hear their laughter. Until he couldn't breathe. Finally he skidded to a halt in front of a meandering river, sweat mingling with the tears on his face. He buried his head in his hands and sobbed, his knees meeting the soft ground with a *thud*.

This wasn't fair. None of it. Sombra's return, his use of Dezmin's body, the weight of saving the world on their shoulders, and now the spirit realm dangling his family in front of him like a carrot before a horse. He couldn't understand how the world could be so cruel.

"Where are you!" he roared into the quiet jungle, his voice hoarse. "I've passed your stupid test, so let me ask my questions!"

The least that the universe could do for him was help find the dueños quickly so that he could leave this place with his sanity and his heart intact.

"You needn't shout," a calm voice sounded ahead of him. "We are at your service."

Luka startled where he stood. A pair of dueños, a man and a woman, stepped out of the trees to stand on the other side of the river. Luka had expected them to look important in some way, but they looked like any other dueños he'd ever seen, just with different robes. They looked to be the same age as the king and queen, perhaps in their fifties. And, of course, they had the same stern look that Paloma constantly wore.

Luka took a steadying breath. "I'm here because—"

"We know why you are here," the woman said. "We were there the day Sombra was finally trapped, and we have seen what has happened since his release. You needn't explain."

"Then tell me," Luka begged. He couldn't stand being here a minute longer knowing that somewhere in the trees was his family. He needed to return to the real world before his desire to be with them tore him apart. "Tell me what we can do to set things right. Tell me how we can kill Sombra and free Dezmin."

"When we trapped Sombra," the man said, "we cleaved his spirit from his immortal form and separated it into stone relics. But that strategy will not work for you since Sombra's immortal form is already in pieces."

Luka nodded. They were working backward, in a way—if Finn and Alfie were successful in tracking down the relics, then they'd have to find a way to use them all against Sombra, whereas the dueños' solution had been to create the separate relics in the first place. "Then what do we do?"

The dueños looked at each other grimly, speaking volumes without uttering a sound. "You must return Sombra's pieces to him."

"Qué?" Luka's eyes widened.

The relics were all Sombra needed to return to his full strength. Why would they send Alfie and Finn on a deadly mission to retrieve the relics only to hand them straight back to Sombra?

"You can only defeat Sombra when he is in his true form," the man said. "This much we know."

"So there's no way we can just destroy the relics?" Luka asked, grasping at straws. "Or use them to perform some kind of god-defeating magic?"

The dueños shook their heads.

Luka fisted a hand in his hair, a hopeless sigh sagging out of him. What chance did they stand against a god in his strongest state? "Coño," he said even though you weren't supposed to curse in front of dueños.

"We cannot offer much insight beyond this. The prophecy states that the prince and the thief will end him. The way to defeat him lies within the two of them, but we do know that they must do it when he is in his immortal form."

Luka had never been so disappointed. The dueños of the past were supposed to be their way of finally figuring things out, but all they had was a nugget of information—and devastating information at that. They'd thought that getting to the relics before Sombra was part of the prophecy because they could use them to *stop* him from assuming his true form. Now, at best, all they could do was control *when* Sombra became immortal again.

"You cannot stay here for much longer," the woman warned. "If you have any other questions, be quick."

"Dezmin," Luka blurted. "Sombra is using Prince Dezmin as a vessel. How do we separate them? How do we save Dez?"

There was a moment of silence before the man spoke, decimating Luka's hopes once more.

"I'm sorry, my child," he said. "That, we do not know."

"When we defeated Sombra he did not have a human vessel," the woman explained. "We did not have to deal with this conundrum.

That problem will be yours to solve."

Luka hung his head. He wanted to scream with fury, but he was simply too tired.

"Farewell," the man said. "We wish you luck on your journey."

The jungle began to fade, winking in and out of existence.

"Wait!" Luka shouted, but the dueños were gone.

Luka gasped as he awoke, lying on his back in the dirt.

"Luka!" James said, crouching beside him, a look of relief on his face. His globe of light shone brightly over Luka's face. "Are you all right?"

Luka shook his head, a headache blooming between his ears. "How long was I gone?" His mouth felt gummy in the same way it did when he woke after a good night's rest.

"Just over fourteen hours," James said.

Luka blinked at him. So much time had passed. They were half-way through the fourth day. The end of the world was approaching too fast. "Shit."

"Did you find out what we need to do to stop Sombra?" he asked.

"Sort of," Luka said listlessly, and James knew better than to ask for details just yet.

He handed Luka the shared parchment with Paloma. Luka quickly scribbled what he'd gleaned from the dueños.

A jumble of text that added up to one simple truth—they were probably screwed,

THE END OF THE LUCKY STREAK

Thus far in their journey, Finn thought, she and Alfie had been pretty lucky. After all, they'd only landed in secluded areas, no legions of shadowless foes lying in wait.

But that lucky streak ended now.

The prince and the thief thumped down onto a hard, tiled floor, shouts of surprise erupting around them.

"Prince!" Finn said, but Alfie lay still on the floor, passed out. She shook him. "Alfie, get up!" He didn't move.

A flurry of whispers drew her eyes away from him.

They were in a sweeping chamber with impossibly high ceilings. A wide ring of shadowless knelt in prayer. Their hair was straight and dark, and they wore silk robes in bright purples, greens, and reds. The walls were lined with ceremonial scrolls in characters that Finn could not hope to read.

They'd made it to the kingdom of Weilai.

The sea of people stared at her and Alfie, shouting in Weilainese— which Finn, of course, did not understand. She'd thought Weilai was an ally of Castallan, but they didn't look happy to see her.

"I could really use your help right now!" Finn shouted at Alfie, shaking him again.

When one of the shadowless men tried to grab her, Finn crawled backward, bumping into something hard.

She gasped.

Behind her, on a jade pedestal, sat Sombra's stone legs, cut off at the feet. Alfie had managed to transport them right to the relics! How? She had no clue, but she was the last person to question something this convenient.

Finn stared at the sea of shadowless, panic thrumming through her as it dawned on her. These people were worshipping Sombra's relics. They *loved* Sombra. She and Alfie needed to grab the relics and go.

"Wake up." Finn shook Alfie again, and the prince finally started to stir.

Rushing to the pedestal, she hefted the heavy legs into her arms, nearly dropping them.

"We've gotta get out of here!" Finn shouted as Alfie sat up. If he opened a path to the realm of magic, they could just drop in with Sombra's stone legs in tow—but he needed to do it *now*. "This is not the time for a nap!"

"*Qué?*" Alfie said groggily, rubbing the back of his head. Something was wrong. He never fully passed out mid-transport like this.

"Take us to the realm of magic!" Finn cried.

But it was too late.

Something hard struck the back of her head. Her vision blurred, and for a moment she swayed on her feet before falling onto her side, dropping the stone legs. Someone with quick hands flipped her onto her stomach. They grabbed her arms and pinned them behind her back, shackling her by the wrists and then the ankles.

With a yelp, she was hauled onto her feet by guardsmen clad in red armor.

"Let us go!" Finn shouted as they did the same to Alfie. She fought against them, bucking as the guards dragged her. "Get your hands off me!"

The guards did not speak a word as they dragged Alfie and Finn toward a row of doors on the west side of the chamber. Finn could only wonder what fate awaited them on the other side.

HOMEWARD BOUND

Their horses galloping at top speed, Luka and James rode through dead cane fields, searching for the tunnel that would take them under San Cristóbal and into the palace.

They'd been riding for hours straight with no rest. Luka had already told Paloma what he'd learned through their shared parchment—that wasn't why Luka was rushing.

He needed to be there when Alfie came home. He needed to see him alive and well.

Before, Luka had been upset about the loss of the parchment he'd shared with Alfie, but now he was partly glad for it, because he didn't want to tell Alfie that the dueños knew nothing aside from the devastating fact that they'd need to return the relics to Sombra in order to defeat him.

He and James were less than an hour from the palace. Would Alfie and Finn already be there? How was he going to tell him? Would Paloma break the news without him? Luka couldn't decide if that was better or worse.

"There it is!" James shouted, pointing ahead. In the distance Luka could see the hill where the mouth of the tunnel sat, its dark maw their fastest way home.

Luka and James slowed their horses down. The tunnel would be tight, and even though Luka wanted to dig his heels into his horse's sides, he knew better than to try. They approached the tunnel at a slow trot, side by side.

As they entered, Luka used his flame casting to light their way.

"It's not as hot as it was last time," James said as they moved through the dark. The fire illuminated the path ahead by twenty paces or so.

Luka's brow furrowed. "Yeah, and it feels like the tunnels are wider?"

Luka could have sworn that the dueños had been packed shoulder to shoulder when they had ridden out. Now he and James had plenty of space. And there was a constant rain of dust falling on them, as if the skin of the tunnel walls was sloughing off.

Luka focused on the ball of flame, making it stronger until it cast its glare onto the tunnel walls. James reached for the wall on his side, running his hand along it, grimacing when his hand came away looking as if it was covered in soot.

"The rock and soil weren't like this when we first came through," James said. "It was still brown, still alive. Now it's dried out completely, just like the plants aboveground."

Luka cocked his head. It made sense. Perhaps Sombra's reach started at the surface, working its way down. "But I don't get how that would make the tunnels wider."

"The walls are so dry that they're flaking away," James said.

"That's why it's wider." He looked at the tunnel ceiling uneasily, wiping his eyes as dirt rained on his face. "I don't think it's going to be stable for much longer."

"What?" Luka asked. The tunnel suddenly felt too small. "Why?"

"We need to be careful and quiet and hope that it doesn't collapse on us," James said, his eyes scanning the path ahead. "The infrastructure is dry and weak. A loud noise could send it all tumbling down."

Luka swallowed thickly. There was no magic that would be able to save them if that happened. "All right, then we'll be quiet and tread softly."

Though every fiber of his being begged to gallop, Luka urged his horse to slow.

Their horses nickered and whinnied, but Luka and James kept them calm, and the rock walls held. Hours passed with no conversation between them, and Luka was left with nothing to do but ruminate on what was to come.

Not only would Alfie come home to the news that the dueños had no specific solution for how to defeat Sombra, but he would also learn that they didn't know how to save Dezmin.

Luka hoped that Paloma and her colleagues had had some kind of epiphany on their way back to the palace, or else Alfie would come home to nothing but disappointment.

Paloma hadn't responded to him on the parchment, and he wasn't sure if that was because she had nothing to say or because she was still recovering from her injuries. He wished she would write something, tell him that everything would be all right, that the path forward was clear.

"We're almost there," James whispered. Luka startled at the sound. Neither of them had spoken a word for ages. "Perhaps half an hour out."

Luka nodded and opened his mouth to speak when something landed on his head, furry and squirming.

James stared at him, "Luka, don't—"

But it was too late. Luka shrieked in disgust, slapping at his head and shoulders to get the cave mole off. The creature flopped to the ground, running between the horses' legs. The horses reared back, whinnying in fear.

The sound echoed through the tunnel, rebounding against its walls. Luka sat frozen on his horse, his eyes screwed shut as if the tunnel couldn't collapse so long as he couldn't see it.

For a breath, there was only silence.

Then came the grinding noise of rumbling rock. The air itself seemed to vibrate as chunks of stone and dirt began to break free of the wall.

"Fuck."

"*We have to go!*" James shouted, spurring his horse on. Luka followed as the tunnel behind them began to crumble, collapsing in on itself.

Luka pressed his heels into his horse's sides, urging him to go faster. A rock slammed into his shoulder. Another struck his temple, nearly knocking him off his horse. If he fell off, he knew he was done for. He was strong, but not strong enough to survive being buried alive.

As James rode ahead of him, Luka saw the rocks and clods of dirt striking him too.

"We're not going to make it!" Luka shouted, but as if fate itself wanted to prove him wrong, he spotted moonlight in the distance, beckoning them forward.

James and Luka burst out of the tunnel and onto the edge of the palace grounds. Luka's horse had scarcely gotten out before the rocks collapsed, sealing the tunnel shut.

"Whoa! Whoa!" Luka said, tugging the reins of his horse until it came to a skidding halt. James followed suit and for a long moment they simply sat there, trying to catch their breath.

When he and James finally met eyes, they both burst into laughter.

"I'm so sorry," Luka chuckled. "I really tried not to scream."

"It's all right," James said when he finally could speak. "We made it out."

"Can you imagine if, in this whole wild story, instead of dying at Sombra's hands in some epic battle we're crushed by a bunch of rocks?" Luka wheezed with laughter again and James joined him.

When they finally quieted and the adrenaline had burned away, Luka was left with the gravity of what was to come. When they'd left the palace, the grounds had still been green, but now they were black as ash. The broken moon hung in the air, casting its dim light over the dying earth. The palace looked strange. Such a beautiful structure in the middle of a wasteland. The moat was dry as a bone, and Luka wondered if whole oceans had also disappeared. The horses sniffed at the ground. Luka's tried to chew some grass before spitting it out and snorting in annoyance.

They rode across the grounds in silence. When he and James finally stood before the palace steps, Luka could not get himself to move. A potent mixture of dread of what was to come and relief at being home kept him paralyzed.

"Standing here won't change whatever you learned in the spirit realm," James said gently.

Luka swallowed. "I know."

When he still didn't move, James held out his hand.

Releasing a breath, Luka took it and let James lead him up the stairs. Paloma had magicked the palace doors to keep shadowless out and allow only a select few, James and Luka included, to enter. As he and James approached, the doors swung outward.

Luka wanted to cry with relief at being home, but there wasn't time. What would the dueños think about what he'd learned in the spirit realm? Were Alfie and Finn back yet? His mind buzzed with countless questions as he and James hurried down the empty halls.

They passed the banquet hall where the civilians were being kept, where Jorge lay sleeping among the children in cots on the floor. They passed the library, which looked wrong without Alfie standing in it. Finally, they turned a corner and found themselves standing before the doors of the meeting chamber where they'd gathered to hear the prophecy. He could hear the dueños and Diviner Lucila inside, waiting for him.

Luka pushed open the doors. As he and James stepped through, the conversation halted.

Paloma stayed seated in a chair. She wasn't fully healed, but she looked better.

Luka didn't say a word. He closed the distance between him and his former teacher and wrapped her in a gentle hug.

"Paloma," he said into her robes.

"Master Luka." The dueña stiffened for a moment before returning the embrace. "You smell."

Luka couldn't help but laugh.

The clock chimed, signaling the stroke of midnight. The fifth day had begun.

Luka's laughter quickly withered into quiet sobs.

THE JUDGE, JURY, AND EXECUTIONER

"Let go of me!" Finn cried as the guards dragged her and Alfie by the armpits.

Just their luck that they'd landed smack in the middle of the Weilainese palace, where people had been worshipping the relics of Sombra's legs.

The black-eyed guards didn't say a word, didn't even seem to hear her. She flexed her fingers, trying to use her stone carving to summon rock from the ground to clobber them with, but the magic wouldn't come to her. At first she thought it was because she hadn't focused enough on her shame to summon it, but the look on Alfie's face told her otherwise.

"Magic-suppressing chains," Alfie said weakly. He looked exhausted, and Finn could've sworn the dark mark on his neck had gotten larger, stretching its fingers toward his Adam's apple.

"What do we do?" Finn asked, and Alfie, the boy who held a million books in his mind, said something that she rarely heard him say.

"I don't know." Sweat rolled over his temples. "I don't know."

The guards dragged them toward a tall set of doors. They swung outward, and Alfie and Finn were thrust out into the weak light of a broken moon. The sound of jeering was so loud Finn wished she could cup her hands over her ears.

They were in an open amphitheater ringed with tiered seats full of spectators. There were so many that Finn could hardly separate one face from the next—a blur of black eyes and gaping mouths spewing hate in a language she could not understand.

"Dioses," Alfie murmured, his eyes wide.

Finn looked away from the crowds and followed his gaze, her stomach dropping.

At the center of the amphitheater stood a gallows. Three bodies hung from it, swaying by their bent necks.

Finn had always known that her short life might come to a quick conclusion at the end of a noose. As a thief, it came with the territory. But she hadn't expected it to happen in a foreign country, at the end of the world, with a prince about to hang with her.

The guards forced Alfie and Finn up the stairs, and Finn could see the faces of those who had been hanged, each contorted in a rictus of pain. The corpses were varied in age and size—the first a startlingly young girl with long dark hair, the second a balding old man, and the last a lanky boy—but they had one thing in common. Their eyes were not black. These people had resisted Sombra's influence and they'd been hanged for it.

The guards thrust Alfie and Finn toward the hangman, and he said something that Finn couldn't understand, but Alfie stiffened.

"What did he say?" Finn asked.

"'Cut down the old bodies,'" Alfie said, his voice threadbare with fear. "'We've got fresh meat to serve.'"

The hangman's servants swiftly cut the ropes, letting the bodies drop to the ground below, where they were silently tossed into a wagon to be taken somewhere that Finn hoped she'd never go. The scent of charred flesh and cloth wrinkled her nose, and Finn searched for the source. At the far end of the courtyard, behind the gallows, was a pile of something burning.

Not something—*someone*.

Bile burned the back of Finn's throat. That was where the bodies were going.

"Prince—" Finn began, panic taking root inside her, but her voice was muffled by a fanfare of drums. A procession approached the gallows, rows and rows of musicians playing their instruments with gusto. Behind them Finn could see a great palanquin, its red silk curtains blocking the person inside from view.

As the music ended the procession stopped, the musicians moving aside to clear a path. The palanquin was set down a good twenty paces from the gallows. Whoever was in there wanted to see the show, but from far enough away that they didn't have to face the reality of it.

"Coward," Finn spat.

A pair of servants parted the curtains and a woman stepped out.

She wore an extravagant red robe traced with a gold pattern. The long sleeves billowed as she moved, and the fingernail of one pinkie was astoundingly long. Her dark hair was swept in an elaborate updo. Her eyes were completely black from edge to edge.

"Empress Guo Wei," Alfie said so quietly that Finn could barely hear him.

The empress raised a silencing hand and the raucous crowd fell quiet.

"Prince Alfehr of Castallan," she said—thankfully in Castallano so Finn could understand—"and his accomplice have been charged with the heinous crime of—"

"Oye!" Finn shouted. "The name's Finn. If you're going to hang me, the least you could do is get my name right!"

Shocked murmurs echoed around them as the empress glowered at Finn.

"Finn," Alfie said warningly.

The hangman grabbed Finn by her hair, wrenching it backward so suddenly that she bit her tongue. "You dare interrupt the empress?"

"You dare steal from a thief!" Finn shot back, her eyes trained on the empress.

"Please don't hurt her," Alfie said, struggling against the guards holding him. Finn wished she could laugh. They were standing at the gallows and Alfie was asking for her not to be hurt. "Please, Empress, as the prince of an ally nation, I ask that you hear me."

"You will hear *me*, Prince Alfehr." The empress's face hardened. "You have been charged with the crime of attempting to steal the relics of the great Sombra." Guo Wei clapped her hands and servants quickly brought forth a pedestal and placed the stone relics of Sombra's legs atop it.

An eruption of furious jeers sounded around them, and the empress had to raise her hand again to quiet them.

"We meant no disrespect," Alfie said. "If we don't secure the relics, this world will end. And Sombra has sent monsters who are hunting the relics. These creatures will—"

"*Silence!*" the empress shouted. "Sombra is the king of this world, and you will pay for your crimes against him. You will be hanged from the neck until dead."

The crowd roared with excitement, the sound echoing throughout the amphitheater.

"No," Finn shouted as the hangman pulled the noose over her head. "Stop it!"

"Don't touch her!" Alfie said as Finn bit down on the hangman's hand.

The hangman screamed. She could feel the blood welling up beneath her teeth. When he finally pulled his hand free he slapped her across the face, smearing her cheek with his blood.

Finn spat at his feet. "You'll remember that long after I'm dead." She could feel the clock ticking down the seconds left in her life, and she had to leave her mark where she could, even if it was just teeth marks on a stranger's hand.

"I just want you to know," Alfie said to her quietly as the hangman roughly pulled a noose over his head, "you don't need to change your face or be anyone else, ever."

Finn stared at him, her eyes stinging. He leaned as close to her as the noose would allow, but it wasn't close enough to touch.

"The day you showed me your true face for the first time was one of the best days of my life." The words rushed past his lips. He could feel it too, their time coming to an end. "Seeing you, truly seeing you, was a gift."

"Stop," she managed to say. The earnestness of his words made her want to look away, but this might be her last chance to see his golden eyes.

Alfie didn't stop. "I would've spent the rest of my life making that clear if we'd had the time."

"I—" Finn began, but she didn't know what to say. When it came to Alfie, everything inside her was still a tangle. There was love there, to be sure, but there was also shame and fear that dragged all she wished to say away from her lips and his ears. But she needed to say something, to tell him how she felt before the noose silenced them forever.

"Alfie, I . . ." If her words were a well, it had run dry. "I—"

The floor dropped out beneath them, and Finn fell.

The moment seemed to stretch into eternity, long enough for her to know that she would die before telling him how she felt. Her jaw painfully tense, she waited for the jerk of the rope.

But it never came.

Finn's feet met stone. Two pillars of earth had risen from the ground beneath the gallows to catch them both, just enough surface area to stand on.

"What?" Finn shouted, adrenaline singeing her from the inside out. When one was faced with death, forced to look their own mortality in the eye, it was almost insulting to suddenly have to keep living. She couldn't help but let out a tearful, "*Shit*."

The hangman was yelling in Weilainese, gesturing angrily at the columns of earth that had saved them. The crowd booed, angry that they'd been denied their entertainment.

"What just happened?" Finn asked, her breaths ragged. She

stared at the stone beneath them that had saved them from certain death. "Who did this?"

With an earth-shaking *boom*, an explosion of shattering wood sounded at the far side of the amphitheater. The towering double doors that they'd been dragged through burst open, slamming into the outer wall of the palace. Finn scarcely had a moment to catch her breath before she caught sight of them.

Sombra's monsters.

There were two of them, their black-veined bodies pulsing, their eyeless faces turning toward where the empress still stood beside the pedestal holding Sombra's relics.

"Let us go!" Alfie cried. "They'll take the relics and everyone will die!"

But no one was listening; they were staring at the monsters in awe.

"Sombra has blessed us with his creations," the empress cried out, her face lit with joy. The crowd rushed toward the monsters as if they were their saviors. "They've come to collect the relics and bless us for keeping them safe!"

"No, pendeja!" Finn shouted at her. "They're here to take them and end the world!"

"*Now!*" a voice called out from beneath the gallows. A loud *pop* sounded below her, and a cloud of thick red smoke began to unfurl at the base of the pillars. Finn blinked, trying to see through it. A hand emerged from the smoke, gripping the chains that weighed Finn down by the wrists. She jerked away, her fists clenched.

"We're here to help you!" A wrinkled face emerged from the

smoke, a face with clear eyes. "We're the ones who stopped you from hanging!"

"Dueños!" Alfie said in relief.

Finn saw five figures emerging from the smoke in jade robes.

"They didn't hang all of us," another murmured as they quickly removed Alfie and Finn's magic-suppressing chains. "Been waiting for a moment of distraction to set you free."

Finn rubbed her wrists, grateful to move freely again.

"Go!" the one who'd freed them said. "Get the relics. *Go!*"

Alfie and Finn rushed out from beneath the gallows. From the east, the monsters were barreling through the adoring Weilainese crowds trying to bow at their feet. One creature gripped a man by the ankle before tossing him clear across the amphitheater. Soon prayers were replaced by screams of fear as the monsters threw the worshippers like rag dolls as they ran. They had to get the relics from the empress before those creatures got their long-fingered hands on them.

"Hurry!" Finn shouted, tugging Alfie along. The prince was slower, his face drawn. He wasn't going to make it much farther.

Together, they closed the distance between them and the empress.

"We don't want to hurt you," Alfie said as a group of guards moved to stand in front of the pedestal. "Let us have the relics and we'll leave."

"Protect Sombra's relics from the thieves!" the empress shouted. "Kill if you must!"

The guards drew long, thin blades from the scabbards strapped to their backs.

Finn glared at the empress. "Forget the relics. They're going to have to protect you from me." She'd already headbutted one queen this week; why not another?

A frenzy of fighting began as three guards rushed forward.

"*Parar!*" Alfie shouted, but the guards kept coming. Finn didn't know if it was because he wasn't using dark emotions to fuel the magic or because he was too tired.

Finn forced herself to think of Ignacio, of how even on his worst days, she'd longed to impress him. It was enough to pull mounds of stone the size of her head from the ground. She shot the stones forward into the stomachs of two guards, sending them skidding back.

Finn could see Sombra's creatures advancing through the crowd. She didn't have time to fight these men. She made a parting motion with her arms and a wide circle of earth opened before the rushing guardsmen, swallowing them whole—then sealed shut again before they could crawl out.

"Stay close!" Finn said to Alfie as they dashed toward the pedestal where Sombra's legs sat.

"Stop them!" the empress shouted.

"Forgive me." Grimacing, Alfie managed to pull water from the humid air and froze the empress's lower body, keeping her pegged in place.

Finn snatched one of Sombra's legs off the pedestal and watched in horror as long black fingers gripped the other.

"No!" Alfie shouted. He grabbed the creature's huge hand, trying to pry it off the relic.

"Don't touch it!" Finn said, but it was too late. Alfie's eyes glazed over as the creature shook him off, sending him rolling on his side far behind Finn.

"Hold on!" Finn shouted, hoping Alfie could hear her, but the prince didn't move. Had the creatures killed him? She didn't have the time to check. "Just hold on!"

Finn swallowed a lump in her throat and used her stone carving to pull two walls of rock from the ground, one on either side of the two creatures. She thought of Queen Amada telling her that she brought Alfie nothing but danger—with the prince lying unmoving in the dirt, it was enough to make Finn believe her. Magic surged through her, and with a cry of exertion, she slammed her hands together and the walls collided, smashing the two creatures, leaving only the long-fingered hand that had been gripping Sombra's other leg. Its fingers loosened and the hand fell to the ground.

Had she done it? Had she killed the things? They couldn't risk sticking around to find out. Finn grabbed the legs and turned to run. She made it only a few long strides before she heard a strange cracking sound. She fell, landing hard on one knee. Sombra's relics flew out of her hands and rolled to a stop beside Alfie. Still, the prince didn't move.

Finn looked down to see what had tripped her, but her mind couldn't process what she was looking at. The ground had opened and swallowed her leg, as if a spot on the earth had gone completely hollow, giving at the slightest pressure. A hole into the endless dark, wide enough for both her and Alfie to plummet through, had opened beneath her. She was lucky that she'd fallen forward so that her other knee landed on solid ground.

When Sombra had promised that the world would collapse in on itself like a dying star, she'd hoped he was being dramatic, but now she could see it with her own eyes. What once had been layers upon layers of earth was reduced to something as delicate as spun sugar, a hollow egg.

It was as if she'd tried to walk across a frozen lake and gotten unlucky. Her left leg hung in the abyss. It was neither hot nor cold, just empty. She'd thought the scariest thing about the dark was that you couldn't see what lay in wait, but knowing that there was nothing there, nothing to hear you scream? Somehow that was much worse.

The prince was still several long strides away, barely conscious. Finn looked over her shoulder. Thick, inky black fluid was squeezing out from between the stone walls she'd summoned, plopping onto the ground, and re-forming into Sombra's creatures. These things were indestructible.

Adrenaline burned through her veins. She was done running—and now she didn't need to. Carefully, she pulled her leg out of the hole in the universe, then skittered back from it like a crab as she watched more cracks branch out from the first. Pieces of earth kept chipping away and falling into the dark.

As the creatures re-formed, thickening and lengthening to their original shapes, Finn pulled a large boulder from the solid dirt behind her.

"If you want the relics," she shouted, "then come and get them!"

As if they could smell Sombra's scent on the wind, the creatures started after her.

Finn prayed to whichever god was listening that she got the

timing right. As the creatures approached the ground surrounding the hole, Finn slammed the boulder down. The cracked earth fell apart, revealing a wide, gaping maw into nothingness. The creatures fell through, disappearing into the chasm without a sound.

Finn breathed a sigh of relief—until the ground kept cracking, the chasm stretching farther and farther in all directions.

"Damn it!" she shouted as she dashed to Alfie, the ground crumbling behind her as she ran. Even the shadowless had the good sense to run for their lives. Finn skidded to a halt beside Alfie and the relics.

"Alfie," she said, shaking him by the shoulder. Behind her the chasm was still spreading, sheets of earth falling into the crevasse. "Alfie, wake up! Take us to the realm of magic!"

His eyes were unfocused. "I touched it . . . I saw . . . They already have the other one . . ."

"Hurry!" she shouted as the ravine stretched closer. Whatever he was trying to tell her would have to wait.

Alfie grabbed her hand to match the shades of their magic, his skin burning where it touched her. He was in no condition to perform magic, but there was no choice.

"Hold on," Alfie said weakly.

And just before they could fall into the darkness of the chasm, they fell into the realm of magic instead.

The portal had scarcely closed behind them when Alfie fainted in her arms.

THE FOX AND THE DRAGON

Finn landed on her back, Alfie's weight slamming into her lap.

Sombra's stone legs clattered to the ground beside them. They'd have to carry the relics home themselves, since the Weilainese guards had taken their magicked satchels.

Finn looked around her and saw only darkness. There were no strings here. With Alfie passed out, there was no one manipulating how the magic presented itself.

"Prince," Finn said, shaking him by the shoulders. "Get up!" She pulled him up into a seated position, hoping it would do the trick, but he only slumped forward, his forehead on her shoulder.

"You've got to wake up," she said, desperation tightening her voice.

When they were about to be hanged, he had looked her in the eyes and told her that she never needed to change her face again. And she couldn't say a word.

If not for those Weilainese dueños saving them, Finn would've died without telling him how she felt. Her eyes stinging, she lifted his head from her shoulder. "Prince, you need to wake up," she begged. "We have to save the world, and there are still things I need to tell you."

"Why won't he wake?" a voice asked. Finn jumped at the sound. It was close to her and Alfie, but there was no one else with them in the realm of magic. "What happened to him?"

"Dezmin?" She blinked. There on Alfie's shoulder was the toy dragon.

It had been days since Dezmin had last communicated with them after they'd gotten the relics from Uppskala. Alfie had been so anxious to hear from him again. It was a shame that he wasn't awake now.

"Yes, I'm here," Dezmin said. He sounded different from before. Where his words had once been alive with urgency, now he sounded tired, lost, but underneath that was an undertow of fear. "I couldn't come back for a while. But now he's distracted, he's . . ." His voice petered out for a moment. "He's feeding."

Finn stared at the dragon, unsure what that meant.

"What happened?" Dezmin asked. His voice had a little more strength now, as if he was just waking up. "Why is Alfie like this?"

"I don't know." Finn shook her head. "We got the relics and Sombra's creatures chased us—"

As she spoke, Alfie's head lolled back, revealing his neck. She gasped. The mark was darker, larger. When she touched it, he twitched, groaning in pain.

With her hand cupping the back of his head, Finn carefully laid him down and examined the dark handprint. She touched it again and, sure enough, the mark *moved*, rippling under Alfie's skin. He was burning hot. When Finn removed her palm, it was stained with dark liquid.

It was leaking from Alfie's skin.

"It's inside you." Her fingers shaking, she grabbed Alfie's hand, and there was another black mark staining his palm. This was why he was sick. He'd been infected twice—first in the Englassen forest when the creature grabbed him by the neck and again when he had tried to stop the creature from taking the relic in Weilai. He'd grabbed the thing's arm without thinking.

"The creatures," Dezmin said, his voice grave. "They touched him?"

"Twice," Finn admitted. "Do you know what this means?" She gestured to the black marks. Dezmin lived inside Sombra's head. Maybe he knew something.

"I don't," Dezmin said, his voice ringing with the same guilt that Alfie's did whenever he didn't have an answer. It was strange how she could tell they were brothers without even seeing Dezmin's face. "Though I live in Sombra's mind, it is a jumble. I cannot simply conjure information."

Finn's mind ricocheted from hope to hope, searching for an answer. "Well, if you can access Sombra's power, can you use it to pull this stuff out of Alfie?"

Dezmin hesitated. "I'm not sure. I've only ever used Sombra's power to reach you two. It's hard to explain, but it's as if I have to whisper to make sure Sombra doesn't hear me. If I try to do anything more, he'll notice what I'm up to."

"Mierda." So she was truly on her own. "Okay. Think, think,

think." She didn't know any desk magic to fix this. What would happen if she didn't get it out of Alfie? Would he die? Would he turn into one of those *things*?

With a shake of her head Finn forced those thoughts out of her mind. She would never find out because she was going to save him. Now.

Up her sleeve, fastened to her forearm, was a dagger. The last one she had left since the Weilainese guards had taken the rest.

"Be careful," Dezmin whispered. The dragon toy walked over Alfie's collarbone toward where Finn poised her dagger. She could feel that sense of protectiveness from Dezmin that she'd always imagined when she'd wished for an older brother.

"I know," Finn said before turning back to Alfie. "I'm sorry." Finn made a careful cut in the prince's neck, avoiding the arteries, but no blood flowed out, only liquid shadow.

Finn had spent her fair share of time living off the land when things got rough. She had to hope this could be handled like a snake bite because she didn't have any other ideas. But if she did this, would she be infected by the darkness too? Finn pushed that thought away. There was no time to be afraid if she wanted to save him. She'd burn that bridge when she got to it.

She tilted his chin up and sucked the wound on his neck, spitting out the sour black goo, then returning for more. She could feel it staining her teeth and tongue in a thick film.

She repeated this several times, until only clean blood dripped from the wound. The prince would have to heal himself when he woke up.

If *he wakes up*, her mind whispered uneasily.

"He's going to wake up." She rubbed her eyes with the back of her hand. "He will."

"His skin is cooling," Dezmin said, hope in his voice. "I can feel it."

Finn looked at Alfie. His breathing had calmed a bit, and his brow had unfurrowed. Dezmin was right; he already looked a little better.

"On to the next, then." Finn cut a clean wound in his palm and sucked until his blood ran red again. Satisfied (and disgusted), Finn gently put his arm down. She'd never been happier to taste the copper tang of blood.

"You scared me for a moment there," she admitted to the sleeping Alfie.

"Thank you for saving my brother," Dezmin said to her, and Finn was glad he was locked in that toy because the look on his face would've been so heavy with gratitude that she wouldn't have been able to look him in the eyes.

"He's done it for me before," she said. "Many times."

She remembered when they'd faced Ignacio together, half a year ago. How she'd woken up after the battle to the sight of him kneeling over her, his soft gaze willing her back to life. Even though she'd never been closer to death, she'd never felt safer.

"Do you love my brother?" Dezmin asked.

Finn choked on her own spit. When she caught her breath, the dragon was still staring at her, its head cocked as it waited for an answer.

"Why are you asking me that?" was all she could think to say.

"I only wish to know that my brother is in the hands of someone who loves him while he endures what I have unleashed. And, you know," he went on, amusement in his voice, "answering questions with questions is a lot more transparent than you think it is."

"What I feel isn't anyone's business but my own."

"That is true," Dezmin admitted. "Perdóname if I've been too blunt. It's been a long time since I've had a conversation with someone—anyone—else."

Silence stretched between them, and Finn thought of how agonizing it must have been for him to be trapped alone in silent darkness for so long.

"How did you survive that?" she asked.

The dragon was quiet for a long moment. "I'm not sure I did."

Finn nodded. Life could be cruel, and she herself had lived through things that she could've sworn would kill her, that she wished *had* killed her. Ignacio had buried her corpse every day for years, yet here she was. "Sometimes I'm not so sure I did either."

Dezmin had the good sense to not ask for details. "How do you go on?"

"Honestly?" She shrugged. "With great difficulty."

A bark of laughter came from the dragon. It was a nice sound, lower and fuller than Alfie's laugh. Finn imagined that this sound had colored Alfie's childhood.

A flood of memory found her, Alfie's voice blooming between her ears. She'd been recovering in the palace after defeating Ignacio and had tried to return the fox figurine she'd stolen. *You should keep it*, he'd said. *Dezmin would've liked you.*

"I'm glad he has you," Dezmin said. "Alfie can be so somber at times."

"Yeah, well," Finn said, her eyes tracing the contours of Alfie's face. "It's part of his charm."

She knew the clock was ticking, but she would've been content lying down next to him in the darkness for a long moment before he woke up and they carried on to the final relic.

"Sombra is finishing his magic," Dezmin said hurriedly. "I have to go."

"You can't stay until he wakes up?" Finn asked. The prince would be devastated to have missed his brother.

"I cannot. Please tell Alfie—"

Something moved in the dark.

Finn stumbled to her feet, standing guard over the sleeping prince. "What was that?"

"What was what?" Dezmin asked.

"Something moved," Finn said, her eyes scanning. If Alfie wasn't awake to influence the realm of magic, then where had that come from?

Something slithered over her shoe.

"Mierda!" Finn jumped.

The black goo that she'd removed from Alfie was forming into a pile on the ground.

"Hello, Finn," a low voice came from the black sludge as it grew, forming arms and legs until Finn was looking at the mirror image of herself—but with blackened eyes. A shudder of fear prickled over her skin. "You and I have things to discuss, don't we?"

Finn stumbled backward. "What are you?"

"What a silly question. I'm you. Even if you could change your face," the other Finn said. "You can't avoid yourself now, can you?"

"Finn." Dezmin's voice came in a nearly imperceptible whisper. "Sombra's magic works to bring out the worst in mankind. That is what it's doing right now."

"You're still here?" she murmured to the dragon that still stood on Alfie's chest. It nodded. Wouldn't Dezmin get caught now that Sombra wasn't distracted? Still, Finn was glad to have him here with her, even if he couldn't say much.

The other Finn paid the dragon no mind. She cocked her head, her black eyes bright.

Finn swallowed. "What do you want?"

"To help you get to know me," the other Finn said, taking a step forward as Finn took a step back. "To get to know yourself, really. To see the reality of the situation."

"What are you talking about?" Finn asked, her palms slick with sweat. This monster looked at her just like Ignacio had—as if he had all the answers. As if he knew every cruel thing she'd ever done and would do.

"Do you really think you're any good for him?" the other Finn said, pointing at the sleeping Alfie. "A nice boy with a big heart like that'll be nothing but target practice for you."

"You don't know me," Finn said, and she knew she was trying to convince herself as well as the black-eyed clone in front of her. "You're just Sombra's spit-up."

Finn took another step away and was relieved to see the monster mirror her with a step forward, away from Alfie.

"Ah, don't worry about the sleepy prince," the other Finn said. "Why would I hurt him when you're going to do that yourself?"

"You don't know what the fuck you're talking about," she said. "I'd never hurt him."

"But you will," Other Finn said. "Everyone says so. Even his own mother."

In the blink of an eye it transformed into Queen Amada, its voice changing to match. "You have brought my son nothing but violence and danger. Alfehr was sheltered and protected before he met *you*. He stayed out of trouble. I lost my baby the day he fell into your hands."

"Don't listen," Dezmin's voice came again, so quiet it could've been the wind. She knew how much those two words had likely cost him. How dangerous it was for him to speak. But his voice could barely reach her now. Not when Amada was standing in front of her repeating those terrible words.

"Stop it," Finn said. "*Stop it.*"

Queen Amada disappeared, re-forming into Paloma. "If you intend to hurt him, wait until the mission is complete . . . he's been hurt enough today."

"*Stop!*" Finn shouted, her hands clapping over her ears.

"The most important people in his life are terrified of you destroying him," the monster said. "What do you think that means?"

"It doesn't mean anything," Finn shouted. "It means they're wrong."

"There's no need to lie. Sombra knows your true nature. All of it. *And so do I.*" It sounded just like Ignacio. He'd once told her that he could see her future written before her. A future of filth that no one but him would tolerate.

"I don't need to hear my own life story," Finn sniped through gritted teeth. "I'm the one who wrote it." But she could hear her fear leaking through the bravado.

As the creature approached, she stepped backward until her back hit a wall. Finn startled against it. This realm was supposed to be endless, but the realm of magic still recognized her as an extension of Alfie. Her fear had made it small, stifling.

"Why not let me in," it said. "Why not let yourself be who we actually are instead of fighting so tirelessly?"

"There is no *we*," Finn gritted out.

She had no time to beg it not to before it transformed into Ignacio. He surveyed her, his smile sharp, lethal. "We're both monsters, aren't we?" he said with a cruel laugh. "You and the prince? Poor thing, you thought that once *I* was dead, you'd like yourself more. That all of the pain would go away. But it *lives* in you. It was never about me and how I raised you; it was about the part of you that has always known exactly what you are—irredeemable, monstrous filth. And you're proud of it too, sin vergüenza."

The walls were closing in further, and Finn had to slide down the wall to the floor to stop the ceiling from crushing her, her knees pulled up under her chin.

"It's all right." The monster crouched in front of her. "I know it's hard. I know you're tired."

Finn's eyes stung. She *was* tired.

"Let me in," it whispered. "It'll be just like falling asleep. Quick and easy."

Nothing in Finn's life had been quick and easy, but if she took this chance, maybe her death could be.

Gold eyes flashed in her mind, their gaze soft and gentle. Alfie. If she gave in, what would happen to Alfie?

Finn looked up at the creature who still wore Ignacio's face. She met its blackened gaze. "No."

It cocked its head. "No?"

"I have reasons to stay here."

"Him?" it spat. Ignacio's face fell away to reveal the eerie reflection of herself once more. "A prince who will leave you once he sees who you truly are?"

"No, a prince who loves me." As she stood, the realm of magic grew taller, the walls moving apart to give her space. "He's shown me too many times for me to believe your *lie*."

The creature laughed, throwing its head back. "And why would he love you?"

"I have no idea!" Finn shouted. It was freeing to say it. She didn't need to have some perfect list of all the ways she was good. She saw it in Alfie's face every moment that they were together. "I don't know and I don't care. You keep telling me I don't like myself. You're right, I don't," she admitted, another weight dropping from her shoulders. "Maybe I never will, but he doesn't care. *He doesn't care!*" she shouted into the eternity of the realm of magic.

"Do you know how pathetic you sound?" it sputtered, trying to keep up, to poke holes in her newfound resolve. "How can you two be together when you hate yourself?"

Finn stared the creature down. In children's stories, the hero always learned to love themselves. Only once they accomplished that did they receive their well-earned happy ending. But maybe it didn't have to be that way. Maybe life was messy and love messier still.

Maybe she could still love Alfie while she fought to one day like herself.

"It'll never work," the creature said.

"It *will*. It's simple," Finn said, and it always had been. "I love him more than I hate myself. And that's enough for now."

Fire is hot.

Ice is cold.

Finn loves Alfie.

The two of them had saved the world together. She'd tried to stay away from him, to move on, but fate had brought them back together again to find Los Toros. And now they'd learned they were prophesied to be in each other's lives. There was no force on Mundo, not even Sombra himself, that could make her believe Alfie was better off without her.

Death was easy and living was hard, but only one of those options included Alfie, and that was what she would choose.

Finn could feel the resolve inside her growing stronger, as if she were building it herself, brick by brick. The creature took a step backward. It could feel it too.

Finn glowered at the monster and took a step forward for every step it took back. If the realm of magic still recognized her as an extension of Alfie, she'd use that to her advantage. "I imagine the tiniest box that this realm of magic can muster," she said. She would lock this creature away forever before it could hurt someone else.

"Don't." The creature's eyes widened. "No—"

"*Wait, Finn!*" Dezmin shouted. Finn startled at his voice. She thought he'd left. "Use it to make a weapon. Only a god can kill a god! Sombra said it himsel—"

Dezmin's voice cut off, as if a hand had been slapped over his mouth. Had Sombra heard him? Had he been caught? She couldn't be certain, but a surge of purpose filled her. The prophecy had spoken of facing what she feared, and she had—she had faced herself. Maybe her reward was a weapon to kill Sombra—and thanks to Dezmin, she knew just how to make it. He was right. What could kill a god if not a god?

"I imagine all the darkness I drained from Alfie becoming part of this dagger," she said to the monster, holding out the dagger she'd used to cut Alfie and drain the poison. "I imagine you making this simple dagger a blade that could kill a god."

The creature shrieked as its form began to rip apart into strings of black. The threads of goo laced themselves over the length of Finn's dagger. She fought the urge to throw the thing—she never wanted to be this close to Sombra's essence. Finn felt an itch in her throat, persistent and strange. For a moment, she thought she needed to cough, but no. Something was crawling up her throat. She gagged and drops of darkness flew past her lips to the dagger. She stared at it in shock. She'd accidentally swallowed some when she'd drained Alfie! If she hadn't commanded the darkness to fortify the dagger the black goo would've stayed in her stomach, infecting her from the inside out. The dagger blackened and stretched until it was a full sword.

She'd done it!

Finn felt a lightness in her body and she knew that her *propio* was back, that her magic was no longer a flat scarlet but a tapestry of reds. Finn reached for her face and imagined her nose longer. It lengthened at her touch, but she returned it to normal.

She could change her face now, but she didn't want to, didn't have to.

"Finn?" Alfie murmured, finally waking up.

"Alfie." She rushed to his side, dropping the sword.

"What happened?" Alfie slowly sat up. The darkness around them began to clarify into the endless web of strings that Alfie had designed.

Finn gave a wan smile and pulled him into a hug, burying her face in his neck.

"Wait, where did that sword come from?"

THE GIANT

When Dezmin shouted for Finn to make a blade that could kill Sombra, he knew he would be caught. He *knew*.

Sombra had already stopped feeding, but Dezmin had stayed with Alfie and Finn anyway. He'd been so afraid the poison Finn had drained from Alfie would hurt them both. He should have retreated and let her handle it, but he couldn't. Not when his little brother lay so vulnerable, and not when the solution to stopping Sombra was right in front of them.

Sombra had said it himself.

Only a god can kill a god, and your brother is no god.

It struck Dezmin in that moment that a blade infused with Sombra's residual power could be enough to kill him.

But as soon as he'd shouted, Sombra had seen him.

It was as if Dezmin's body was a house and he was trapped in its attic, and a giant had squatted before the window, its gargantuan eye staring in.

"Well, now," Sombra said. "What exactly are you up to?"

Dezmin was pulled out of the toy dragon with such force that he feared pieces of him had been left behind. His consciousness slammed back into the attic.

"Who were you speaking to?" Sombra asked him.

"No one," Dezmin managed. Sombra's presence bore down on him, the pressure excruciating. He couldn't breathe.

"Come now, Dezmin," Sombra tutted. "Don't make me take the information from you the hard way. You were doing so well. You'd already started giving yourself to me of your own will. You were nice and quiet."

"I wasn't doing anything!" Dezmin shouted. There was no point in lying. He knew Sombra had seen him, but there was a strength in knowing that he would not give up the information willingly. Sombra would have to take it from him.

"Very well," Sombra said, sounding exasperated.

Dezmin felt Sombra's fingers crack his mind open, just as he had done to Svana. He screamed, the pain of it tearing out of him. Sombra gave a cursory glance at Dezmin's memories, not caring as much for the details as he had with Svana.

"Oh, I see what you did." Sombra laughed, but there was no mirth in it. "You began to meld with me just so you could use my power. Very clever." He sounded almost impressed. "You found a way to sneak past the protective magic around the palace by cloaking my power with your essence." Sombra squeezed Dezmin tighter still, talking over his screams. "I wish you'd shared that strategy with me. But now that I know it, how about we try it again?"

Dezmin's blood ran cold. He could see what Sombra intended to do. "Don't be so shy now," Sombra said mockingly. "Let's pay your family a visit."

"Please don't," Dezmin begged. Would he find out about Alfie and Finn's plans to restore balance and end Nocturna, whatever they were? "Please—"

Sombra laughed, reading his mind. "You think I care about whatever childish plans your brother has made to stop me?"

The god was still too vain to believe that mortals could best him.

"I'm going for another reason entirely. You will learn your insignificance," Sombra said, his voice low and cold. "And the lesson will be written in your family's blood."

THE WOMAN IN RED

Amada sat on the ground of her cell, her scarlet gown covered in grime.

The floor was littered with trays of food she'd refused to eat and cups of water she'd refused to drink. It was of no importance to her. She lived in a place beyond thirst and hunger now, a place that echoed endlessly with the sound of her fears.

Where were Alfie and Luka? Were they lying dead next to her husband's cold corpse?

She dug her fingertips into the wall, another nail snapping backward at the pressure. She was the only one who understood that they needed to stay here in the palace, safe and sound.

Ah, but you're wrong, my dear, came a low voice.

"Who are you?" Amada lurched upright, scanning the darkness. "Show yourself!"

I am simply a friend, the stranger said. *A friend who understands your plight. You are right to want to protect your children, but this palace cannot save them from everything.*

Amada shook her head of matted curls. "What do you mean?"

This palace may protect them from an enemy's attack, but can it protect them from illness? From old age? From heartbreak?

Amada's blackened eyes filled with tears.

Don't fret, the voice said, warm with comfort. *There is a way to save them from this world, and save yourself too.*

As the voice described the solution, Amada was surprised that she hadn't thought of it before. This would save them all, and they would always be together, safe and sound.

Go, the voice said, and the door of her cell swung open. *Go save them all.*

The queen stood, her purpose finally clear.

Amada walked out of the cold dungeons, up the stairs, and into the light.

THE SLEEPLESS NIGHT

Luka snapped upright in his bed and shoved his comforter off.

Ever since they'd left the palace to speak with the dueños of the past, Luka had been dreaming of returning to his plush bed, but now the luxurious pillows and sheets smothered him.

It was just before six in the morning on the fifth day. Even on a good day, Luka never got up this early, but he couldn't sleep. He was exhausted from his journey but couldn't stop his restless legs from twitching beneath the sheets. He massaged his temples, sighing.

Alfie and Finn still hadn't returned. He and Paloma had discussed what he'd learned from the dueños. Paloma had tried to hide it, but Luka could tell she was disappointed that the only thing they knew for certain was that Sombra needed to don all his relics to be defeated. But she and the other dueños didn't wallow for long. They retreated to strategize among themselves, leaving Luka and James to their own devices. James fell asleep as soon as he sat, but Luka was full of nervous energy. For once, he hadn't the patience for a long bath. He washed as quickly as possible and tried to force himself to rest.

That hadn't worked.

Luka didn't know if it was his anxiety over waiting for Alfie and Finn to return, his fear of what would happen when they gave Sombra his relics back, or his guilt at the thought of Amada trapped in a dank dungeon that kept him awake. Likely a combination of the three.

Frustrated, Luka got out of bed. He roamed the palace, sleep-walking while awake. He sped past Alfie's room, a lump in his throat. Then he tried to doze in one of the many sunrooms, with no luck. Finally, he made his rounds on the ground floor. As he turned a corner, he spotted something that made his stomach drop.

A body.

Luka ran, slamming to his knees next to the man. The stranger lay on his stomach, his brown eyes unmoving. His back and sides were soaked with blood from more stab wounds than Luka could count. He stared at the trail of blood the man had left in his wake. The poor man had dragged himself down the hall to get away from whoever had done this to him.

Luka did not know the man's name, but he remembered his face. He was one of the people Luka had saved from the poachers. His hands shook. Who would do this?

Then came the screams from the banquet hall.

Fighting against the fear pitted in his stomach, Luka ran toward the sound and burst through the doors.

Nothing could have prepared him for the sight before him.

The floor of the banquet hall was covered in cots for the people they'd saved from the poachers, but they were no longer asleep. Their throats had been slashed one by one. And at the center of it all stood Amada, her hand on the slim shoulder of a little boy—Jorge. He shook in her grip, his eyes wet with tears. The sharp edge of a dagger was pressed against his soft neck. When he saw Luka, his mouth opened to cry out, but he looked too afraid to make a sound. Luka wanted to tell him that everything would be all right, but he knew better than to waste time lying.

"Mother!" Luka shouted. He knew the being before him was not his mother, not in that moment, but he didn't know what else to call her. The hands she killed with were the very same ones she'd used to raise him. "Stop!"

"Luka," she said, her face softening. Her dress was splattered with blood. "You're home."

A handful of survivors cowered in the corners, but Amada didn't seem to notice them any longer. Her eyes were for Luka and Luka alone. She must have killed most of them quietly by cutting their throats in their sleep, but someone had shouted and woken the others.

"Let the boy go," Luka said, his voice quaking.

"Why are you upset?" She walked toward him, pulling Jorge along. "I'm helping him, and the rest." She gestured at the corpses as if she'd tucked them into bed instead of killing them.

"Helping them?" Luka asked. "You've *murdered* them."

"Mi amor," Amada said, her expression one of motherly concern. "You're confused."

"Don't come any closer," Luka said. "Not until you promise not to hurt him."

Amada stopped and touched Jorge's face gently, the way she would when Luka was a little boy, crying after scraping his knee. Jorge closed his eyes, trembling.

"You're confused," she repeated. "I was too. I was so upset when King Bolivar was taken from us." Her fingers curled into shaking fists. "But now I know he's the only one of us who is truly safe." She smiled down at Jorge. "This little boy can be just as lucky. We can send him to the spirit realm, where he'll be safe and loved. He'll never get old or sick; he'll never have his heart broken. He'll be free."

"You think cutting his throat will free him?" Luka shouted. "*He'll be dead!*"

Amada didn't seem to hear him. She was still looking at Jorge, caressing his dark curls. "He doesn't have to go alone. We'll go with him. We can leave this world that took my husband and my baby girl."

Luka's heart clenched as he remembered the silent baby Queen Amada had birthed when he and Alfie were just boys.

"We can join them and your family too. No sickness, no pain. Just peace," she said.

"Please don't talk about them," Luka whispered, tears running down his face. He'd seen them too recently. The wound was still raw.

"You know loss, Luka," she said. "But we can go to them. We can end this and go see my sister, your dear mother. She's missed you, I know she has."

She was right. His family was free from loss and pain, he'd seen it himself.

"I'll send you first." She stepped closer, and Luka didn't have the strength to tell her to stop. Jorge was sobbing now, beads of blood rolling down his neck from where Amada pressed the blade. "Then I'll wait for Alfie to come home, and he and I will go together. We'll all be a family again. Wouldn't you like that?" She kissed his cheek, and Luka buried his head in her shoulder, sobbing. He could smell the spiced perfume she loved, a scent that would always remind him of home. He could feel Jorge shaking between them.

"Don't cry," she cooed.

Luka looked at the corpses strewn on the floor. Men and women. Children.

"It'll be quick," Amada said. "I promise. Just like falling asleep."

Luka pulled away slightly and looked in her eyes, searching their black depths for any hint of the mother he knew. The woman who had raised him to step over flowers instead of trampling them, who had laughed at his jokes. The woman who looked at him softly and cupped his chin before saying, "Oh, but there is so much of your mother in your face."

Amada stepped back, her grip on Jorge's shoulders still tight. "Him first, then you." Her hold on the dagger tightened. "Close your eyes."

Luka's body moved before he could stop it. He pulled Jorge from her grasp, shoving him out of harm's way. With the boy gone, Luka could stop her from hurting anyone else, and when everything returned to normal, he'd never tell her what she'd done. She'd never have to know.

Amada's gaze hardened and she raised the dagger high. "I won't go back to the dungeons!" She swung the blade down, and Luka grabbed her by the slim wrist, his strength stopping its descent. It'd be easy to break her arm, but he couldn't. He couldn't bear it.

"Leave him alone!" Jorge was running back into the fray. He didn't understand that Luka was holding back his strength. The boy thought Luka needed his help.

"Stay back!" Luka shouted, but it was too late. Amada had wrenched her hand free.

"He wants to go!" she said. "Don't you see?"

Her arms were outstretched, her dagger poised. Luka grabbed her from behind by the waist, pulling her to his chest. She bucked against him and tried to stab at him over her own shoulder. She sliced through his cheek, missing his eye by mere inches. Luka gripped her by the wrist and pulled her arm downward.

He only realized what he'd done when the blood gushed over his hand. He'd only meant to get her to stop, but he'd pushed her hand downward, right into her chest. The dagger sank through her flesh and she went limp in his arms, the fight draining from her as quickly as the blood.

"No," Luka gasped, the gravity of it falling upon him. "No, no, no."

Luka didn't realize he was falling until his knees hit the floor. He laid her on her back.

"I didn't mean to," he sobbed. He didn't know who he was telling—little Jorge, who stood aghast, a line of red still dripping from his neck, the remaining survivors who stared at him in silence, or himself. It didn't matter. He needed to say it before it destroyed him from the inside. "I didn't want—I didn't mean to."

Amada stared up at him, her anger gone. "You'll come with me, won't you?" she asked. "You'll use the dagger and come with me?"

Then she went still, her black eyes stagnant.

Luka sobbed. "Please," he begged. "Please."

Amada's body twitched. For a moment, he thought his prayers had been answered. "Mother?"

Amada's mouth widened as a tendril of ebony smoke emerged from her lips.

Take this as a warning of all you will lose if my relics are not returned to me.

Luka's spine turned to ice. Sombra had done this. Sombra had destroyed the balance of the world and forced Luka to look his birth mother in the eyes and walk away. And now he'd forced Luka to kill the mother who'd raised him.

By the time the dueños found him, Luka wasn't uttering words, only sobs.

Dezmin watched it all unfold.

It was impossible to look away. Sombra's control over him was like fingers forcing his eyelids open. He watched his mother slaughter innocent souls who begged for mercy. Watched all hope drain from Luka's body as he wept, holding Amada's corpse.

The pain of it left him silent. There were no words to express what he felt. So why try?

Sombra was speaking to him now, berating him for reaching out to Alfie behind his back, but Dezmin could barely hear him. He was too tired.

There was so little of him left. He'd sacrificed pieces of himself to Sombra to be able to wield his power, and for what? For this? In that moment, Dezmin wondered why he'd ever swum against the riptide of the god's power, when he could just disappear into it, cease to be. Cease to hurt.

Dezmin stopped swimming and let the current pull him under. When his lungs begged him to emerge, to gasp for breath, he ignored them. He gave himself to Sombra fully.

He did not resurface.

THE LAST RELICS

"Okay," Alfie said from where he still sat in the realm of magic. Now that he was awake, the strings had returned, crisscrossing into the distance in every direction. "You sucked Sombra's poison out of me like snake venom. Then it turned into your mirror image and tried to convince you to let it kill you, and Dezmin told you to funnel it into your dagger to kill Sombra, which led to . . ." He gestured at the black blade.

"Pretty much," Finn said.

Alfie engaged his *propio* to confirm it again. Finn's magic was colored in shifting shades of red. "And your *propio* came back."

Finn nodded, looking triumphant. "So I'll be able to help you handle Sombra's shifty magic. When it's time to use the sword on him, we'll match our magic to his and the sword'll go right through him."

Alfie nodded. It made sense. He'd spent his life matching his magic to others' and breaking through their defenses. With Finn's shifting magic returned, and the sword, they finally had the perfect strategy to defeat Sombra. The dueños would find a way to separate the god and Dezmin, then he and Finn would finish Sombra with the blade. Simple. It was a relief to have a plan in place, but Alfie also felt embarrassed by all that had happened. He'd felt so ill since Sombra's monsters had touched him; it made sense that he'd been somehow infected. Maybe that was why he'd been able to transport them directly to the relics this time—maybe being marked by Sombra's horrible creations made it easier to land right on top of them. He was ashamed that he hadn't thought to examine his wounds and get rid of the poison himself. But then, maybe the dregs of the darkness inside him had stopped him from thinking clearly. He was even more disappointed for getting so sick that he missed a chance to speak to his brother.

"Did Dezmin have any news to impart?"

"Not really," Finn said, uneasy. "But after he told me to use Sombra's poison to make a blade, he disappeared mid-sentence."

Alfie's eyes widened. Dezmin had said he had to be careful so that Sombra couldn't tell he was siphoning his magic and using it to reach out to Alfie. "Do you think . . ." Alfie couldn't even finish the sentence.

"I don't know, Prince," Finn admitted.

Alfie cradled his head in his hands, his heart beating a merciless rhythm against his ribs. What would Sombra do to Dezmin if he caught him? He still needed Dezmin's body as a vessel. But surely the god could get creative with his punishments.

Alfie swallowed thickly. "What if he's dead?" The words slipped past his lips so quietly, as if he was afraid saying it aloud would make it true.

"He isn't," Finn insisted. "And I never would've thought of using Sombra's poison to make a weapon without him. He knew it was worth the risk to say it, and I'm grateful for that."

She was right. Dezmin would risk anything to make sure the world could be saved. Whatever punishment he received had to be worth it, but it still hurt to think of his brother in more pain.

"The sooner we get the last relic, the sooner we can go home and save him," Finn said.

She was right again. Sitting here thinking about it wasn't going to save Dezmin from that pain, but moving forward would. It had to.

"About the last relic . . . ," Alfie said.

She stared at him.

"The last relic is already gone."

Finn's eyes widened. "How?"

"When the creature touched me in Weilai, I saw into its memories just like last time." Alfie shivered at the cold feeling that burrowed into his bones when he'd touched it. "There were only two creatures present in Weilai because the other two were retrieving the relic in Ygosi. The other monsters already had it and were on their way to return it to Sombra."

Finn stared at him. "That's what you were trying to say when I woke you up, wasn't it?"

Alfie nodded, remembering how he'd groggily tried to tell her.

I touched it . . . I saw . . . They already have the other one . . .

"Coño." Finn screwed her eyes shut and massaged her temples. "Could we hunt the things down before they get to Sombra?"

Alfie sighed through his nose. "By the time we track them down—"

"—they'd already be back at Sombra's," Finn finished. "Damn it. But we still have the majority of the pieces. That has to count for something, right?"

Alfie wished he had the answer. "I hope it does."

"So there's nothing left to do but go home and find out what's next," Finn said, weighing the black sword in her hand.

Alfie nodded as he stood. "Then let's go." He was anxious to get back, but he was afraid too. For now, in the realm of magic, he could live in hopeful possibilities. He could convince himself that they'd done enough by collecting most of Sombra's relics. He could tell himself that Dezmin was just fine. But the answers to those questions were waiting for him in Castallan, and who knew what they'd be.

Alfie tried to think of something—anything—else.

Together they walked into the webs of magic, and Alfie shuddered as he felt the person attached to each string before moving on to the next. He'd left his pocket watch in his satchel, so now there was no way to know how much time was left. What if they were too late? He couldn't take the silence any longer. It only gave way to his most anxious thoughts. He needed a distraction.

"Did you and Dezmin talk about anything else while I was asleep?" Alfie asked. He had missed out on time with his brother and hungered to know every detail.

Finn looked away from him. He could've sworn she looked a little embarrassed.

"I'll never know everything that happened back when I turned into a baby and you'll never know everything that went on while you were asleep," she said. "You snooze, you lose."

Alfie let it be. After all, when Finn had turned into a child in the Englassen forest, Alfie had found the time and space to figure out not that he loved her—this he already knew—but how to love her in a way that would make her feel the safest. That moment had been private. Alfie had a feeling something similar had happened to her.

He supposed he'd never know until she was ready to tell him, and he was fine with that.

Alfie unfurled his shared parchment. He was lucky that the Weilainese guards had taken his satchel and not his cloak too. But there was still no message from Luka. He sighed.

"We'll be able to talk to Bathtub Boy in person soon enough," Finn said as he tucked the parchment away.

Alfie shot her a grateful smile. "When did you become the optimistic one?"

Finn shrugged a shoulder. "It seems we have to take turns."

When Alfie finally found the string that would take them home, he paused, afraid to touch it.

"What is it?" Finn asked.

He couldn't hide in hypotheticals anymore. They were knocking on the door of reality now, and touching the string would force it open. "Sombra has two of the relics."

"The arms and the feet," Finn agreed somberly.

Alfie's jaw worked, every muscle in his body tense. "What if that's enough for him to win? What if we've already lost?"

Finn shook her head. "We still have most of them. That has to count for something."

"Maybe it doesn't," Alfie said, panic surging through him. "What if Sombra's twisted game is all or nothing?"

"Then we'll find a way to cheat," Finn insisted. "Listen, I don't know if we have enough pieces or not, but we'll find out when we get back to Castallan. So let's go."

Alfie knew she was right. Maybe having more relics than Sombra would mean something. They wouldn't know until they consulted the dueños.

"I hope you're right," Alfie said, shifting the relics in his arms.

"I'm always right." She squeezed his shoulder.

Together, they gripped the string and let the magic carry them home.

THE TRUTH

Alfie, Finn, and Sombra's legs landed on the ground just before the palace stairs.

"*Ow*," Finn deadpanned as she pulled herself off the floor and picked up the relics.

"Sorry," Alfie said, grimacing. "It's harder to control how we land when we're traveling across oceans."

"It's all right," Finn said. "Just glad to be back in one very tired, very smelly piece."

It had been days since they'd bathed or properly rested, but Alfie couldn't give in to his fatigue. Not when the dueños and Luka might already know the solution to defeating Sombra and freeing Dezmin. Not when the fear of not having enough of the relics was burning him from the inside out. They didn't even know how many days they had left, or if there *were* any left. Alfie had to assume six days hadn't passed yet because the world hadn't ceased to exist.

"Take a breath, Prince," Finn said, exhaustion etched into her face. "We made it back; that should be enough for the moment."

"I know," Alfie said as they approached the palace doors. "But I fear the real work begins now." Who knew what the dueños had discovered in the spirit realm? The way to defeat Sombra could involve them sprinting all over the world again. (He fervently hoped it didn't.)

The doors swung open at their approach, revealing Paloma waiting for them in the entrance hall. As soon as Alfie saw her face, he knew things were worse than he'd feared.

"What happened? Did the relics make it to the palace?" What if the magicked satchels hadn't worked and their journey had been in vain? He hadn't even thought to be afraid of that.

Paloma nodded, her face drawn. "They did, but we have much to discuss."

Alfie's stomach tightened. "Is Luka all right?" Alfie hadn't heard from him on the parchment in days.

"Master Luka is fine," she said, but from the way she spoke that final word Alfie knew he wasn't. "Please, come with me. We have no time to waste."

Alfie and Finn looked at each other uneasily before following the dueña.

"How much time do we have left?" Finn asked, and Alfie braced for the answer.

"It's two o'clock in the afternoon on the sixth day."

Alfie swallowed. Only ten hours left. The amount of time it took to travel seemed to get longer with every attempt.

She led them down the hall to an open banquet room where the dueños were gathered. The relics were on the floor at the center of the room, surrounded by intricate written magic. The diviner surveyed them, her strange eyes assessing. Skimming the chalk symbols, Alfie could see that the magic was suppressing the power emanating from the pieces. A pair of dueños took the relics from Finn and got to work.

"Alfie," Finn said, her voice low with worry.

Alfie followed her gaze. In the crowd of dueños he hadn't noticed Luka sitting on the ground in the far corner. He looked like a marionette whose strings had been cut, his face distressingly blank. James was crouched in front of him, trying to get him to talk, but Luka was unresponsive.

A dueño stepped in front of him. "Prince Alfehr, we now have a plan to—"

"What's happened to Luka?" Alfie asked, ignoring him. "You said he was fine."

"We don't have time for such concerns," the nameless dueño said. "The boy served his purpose by learning how we can stop Sombra."

"He is my family," Alfie insisted. "He is more than just someone carrying out a mission. What happened to him?"

The look on Paloma's face said that even she was afraid to tell him—she who always insisted on the truth.

"Paloma," Alfie said, his eyes burning. "Please."

"Your mother," she finally said. "We kept any civilians who still had their shadows in the palace for safety. Sombra found a way to slip past our defenses and possess her in some way. She escaped and . . ." Paloma shook her head, as if she couldn't bear to say it. "She escaped the dungeons and slaughtered them."

Alfie's body went cold, his only anchor to the world Finn's hand in his.

"Master Luka tried to stop her from stabbing a child, and in the process she was killed," Paloma finally said, her voice growing more hushed the longer she spoke.

Alfie didn't know he was crying until he tasted the salt of a tear as it passed over his lip.

"We too grieve the queen," the impatient dueño said. "But we don't have time—"

Alfie ignored the man and walked across the room. James startled, looking unsure whether he should hold his ground or step back, but Alfie simply moved around him. There was no room inside him to hate James, not in the face of all that had happened. Alfie got on his knees and pulled Luka into a fierce hug. He wept into Luka's shoulder, and Luka thawed under his touch.

"I'm sorry," Luka whispered, his voice thick. "I'm so sorry. Your mother is gone."

Alfie gripped Luka's shoulders and looked him in the eye. "*Our* mother is gone."

That simple sentence seemed to crack the shell of numbness Luka had built for himself. Together they sobbed while Finn and James hovered nearby, close enough to show support but with enough distance to respect a grief that was not theirs.

"I'm sorry," Paloma said. "But that is not the only difficult news. And we don't have much time."

Luka's face crumpled.

"What more could there be?" Alfie said, wiping his nose. "What could be worse than what has already happened?"

"Luka learned how to defeat Sombra," Paloma said. "We cannot defeat him until we first give him all the pieces of his body. He must assume his full form."

Alfie blinked. "But that'll only make him stronger." They'd traveled around the world to gather these pieces only to deliver them to Sombra himself?

Paloma nodded gravely. "Yes, but it is what needs to be done."

Alfie watched her face. That was bad news, but still not the worst. "What else?" he forced himself to ask. "What about Dezmin?" The dueños of the past had to know how to save him. After all, they were the people who'd defeated Sombra before.

The next sentence would obliterate the last grain of hope Alfie had been holding on to. He knew before Paloma even spoke it, yet the pain was as fresh as if it were a surprise.

"The dueños do not know if Prince Dezmin can be saved," Paloma said. "We're on our own. We'll have to try to kill Sombra and just hope that Prince Dezmin can survive it."

For a moment he could hear nothing but his own shallow breathing.

He and Finn had risked their lives to procure Sombra's relics for nothing.

His mother was dead.

The dueños did not know how to save Dezmin, which meant they might have to kill him to save the world.

Alfie ran out of the meeting chamber, away from the hopelessness of what he'd just heard.

THE CABINET

Alfie's ears were still ringing as his feet carried him through the halls and up the stairs, straight into Dezmin's room.

He slammed the door shut behind him, then sagged against it. The room was untouched, as it had been for months. The red comforter was perfectly placed, unwrinkled. The dark wood desk and night table were spotless, dusted daily by servants. Alfie waited to hear someone knock, to demand that he accept the truth, but no one came.

His mother was dead, lost forever, but his brother was still here.

Alfie had *spoken* to him. He'd heard his brother's voice. There was supposed to be a way to save him. There had to be. How could anyone expect him to run into battle and kill Sombra if they didn't know what it would do to Dezmin? There couldn't be a world in which he got to speak to his brother again only to learn that they couldn't save him.

The glass cabinet holding Dezmin's carved figurines stood

against the far wall. Alfie stepped over to it, close enough for his nose to bump against the glass. What he saw stole the breath from his lungs.

Last time he'd seen them, the figurines' faces had been twisted with pain. Alfie knew now that was because Dezmin had been trying to communicate that Sombra's possession of his body was destroying him.

Now the figurines had no faces, no shape at all—they had become mere piles of dust, wood, and paint.

"No." Alfie wrenched the cabinet open. "No, no, no."

What did this mean for Dezmin? Alfie touched the dust, willing it to take shape once again. Finn had said that Dezmin had disappeared mid-sentence the last time he'd spoken to her, while Alfie was passed out. Had Sombra caught Dezmin communicating with Finn? Had the god torn him to shreds out of spite?

"No," Alfie said through gritted teeth. He slammed both fists against the cabinet again and again until it shattered, shards tearing at his skin. With an angry shout he gripped it and threw it onto its side, breaking the last of the glass.

Alfie stared at the carnage, his breaths ragged. He couldn't understand how he could possibly feel everything and nothing at the same time. The searing flame of anger and the chill of numbness. His shoes still on, Alfie crawled onto Dezmin's bed. He pulled the comforter aside and burrowed under the sheets.

This was the bed that Alfie had come to when he had a nightmare, when there was a thunderstorm—or when he just needed to see his brother. He would fall asleep here and wake up in his own bed, as if carried there by the currents of magic.

Now Alfie wished he could close his eyes and not wake up at all. He wanted to crumble to dust like the figurines. That would be better than learning his brother was alive only for Alfie to possibly lose him in this final battle.

He didn't know how long he'd been lying in the dark when the doors eased open. Alfie's gaze clung to the ceiling as he heard someone stepping through the shards. Then the bed shifted and creaked, someone's weight pressing it down.

He didn't care if Finn or Luka begged him to come down and strategize, he wouldn't do it. He couldn't.

"I think the love of my life is dead," Paloma said.

Alfie startled. He hadn't expected her to be the one to follow him, and even with all the impossible things that had happened over the last five days, Alfie would never have expected to hear her say something like this.

She didn't meet his gaze; she just stared at the shards of glass littering the floor. "Svana was on a ship, on her way here, when Sombra returned. I haven't heard from her since."

Alfie blinked. "Why are you telling me this?"

She finally looked at him then, a tear rolling down her cheek. Alfie had known Paloma since he was born, since he was too young to know anyone, and he'd never seen her cry.

"Because I don't want to fight anymore either," she admitted.

Alfie swallowed the lump in his throat. His mother and father had been taken from him, and now his brother's life hung in the balance. These last days had been spent gambling and losing, over and over. Not only when Sombra came; before then too, when Alfie had decided to marry Vesper to save his people but ended up losing his father instead.

He didn't want to gamble anymore, didn't want to feel Sombra take any more from him. He wanted to give up. Let the god have what he wanted. At least then there would be some control over the outcome. No more hope bubbling up only to be destroyed. Choosing destruction was so much simpler than fighting for good and losing.

"Too much has been taken from me. Yet there's still so much more to lose," Paloma said.

She was right. Finn and Luka were still alive, and each breath they took was a weapon that Sombra could use against him.

An idea flickered to life in Alfie's mind. "You said that since people with *propios* carry their own source of magic, they can be sacrificed to perform powerful spellwork. So sacrifice me," Alfie begged. "Use me to kill Sombra and save Dezmin." He would do anything, give anything, to end this. Anything.

Paloma shook her head. "Even if I would consider such a thing, your sacrifice alone wouldn't be enough to kill a god. It would take many more. Too many more. If it's even possible to begin with."

"Then can we stop?" he asked, his voice thick with emotion. He hated how he sounded, like a child who needed to be rocked to sleep. But he was too tired to be brave anymore. He could spend his last day here in the palace he grew up in with the people he loved. Let the dueños give his parents their final rites. Hold their hands one last time. Then they all could watch the world unravel into whatever came after. They didn't need to fight. They didn't need to lose. They could just *be*, until there was no world left to be in. "Can we please just stop and let this end?"

"No." Paloma shook her head, looking pained. "We can't."

The tears came faster now, pulling broken sobs from his throat. "Why?"

"Because we're not the only ones here," she said. "Countless souls live in this world, and we don't get to lie down and decide their fate because we're too tired. We don't make that choice for others; we're not Sombra."

Alfie buried his face in his hands. He was too tired, and she was right.

Paloma gripped his hand. "We aren't like him. We won't choose who lives or dies," she said. "We will roll the dice, and we will fight one last time."

THE WRITTEN MAGIC

With eight and a half hours until the end of the world, Alfie and Paloma returned to the meeting chamber.

Alfie felt embarrassed to have run away, but while he saw impatience in most of the dueños' eyes, there was only sympathy in Finn's and Luka's. He looked at them and nodded.

"Pardon me for leaving." He still wanted to bite his tongue and swallow it whole before admitting that Dezmin might die when they tried to kill Sombra, but he had to do what was right, even when that wasn't easy. "I had much to consider and process. I am now ready to proceed."

The dueños stared at him in silence, looking far from confident in him.

"None of us know what it means to carry the weight of a prophecy," the diviner said, her unwavering gaze on him. "There is no need to apologize."

Alfie stared at her. For once, had the diviner made him feel . . . comfortable? It truly was the end of the world.

LUCERO

"Well!" Finn clapped her hands. "What's the plan then? You pendejos have had a while to sit and think now. So speak up!"

Even though his eyes were still red from weeping, Luka snorted. Alfie was grateful for Finn's ability to make even the smartest and most respected people feel like children.

Dueño Bruno stepped forward. "First we must return the pieces to Sombra so that he can assume his immortal form. Once that is done, Your Majesty, you and Finn are the only two who can end it. Together you must kill him, as the diviner said."

Alfie scrubbed at his eyes with the back of his hand.

Finn brandished the black blade. "We've got something to help us on that front."

"What is that?" Paloma asked, reaching hesitantly toward the blade before stopping.

"It's a sword infused with Sombra's own essence," Finn said.

"Dezmin helped her make it," Alfie said, his voice breaking around his brother's name. "He told us that only the strength of a god can kill a god—even Sombra has admitted that is true. This blade is the closest we will get to wielding a god's power. Finn and I will match our magic to it and defeat Sombra by his own power."

The dueños whispered among themselves, their eyes on the blade.

"Okay, so we have most of the relics, we know we have to give them back to Sombra first, and we have the blade, but what's the plan beyond that?" Luka asked. "How are we going to defeat him? We can't just walk in there, give him his relics, and hope it all goes well."

Finn crossed her arms. "The prophecy doesn't say much about

what to expect when we try to kill him. We don't have a plan aside from trying."

"There has to be a plan!" A dueño gawked at Finn. "You expect us to walk completely blind into a battle with a god?"

"Well, if you're so damn smart," Finn sniped, "you can tell me what the plan should be."

Chastened, the dueño fell silent.

"Maybe we can't have a perfect plan in place," James said at Luka's side. "But we can still have something. You two are supposed to kill Sombra. The rest of us must do whatever it takes to make that as easy for you as possible."

Finn cocked her head. "That's a good start."

"Maybe after Sombra assumes his final form, we could try to hold him in place for you, the same way the ancient dueños did before turning his body to stone," Luka offered.

Alfie wondered if Luka's strength would matter against a god.

"Holding him in place took very intricate written magic," Dueño Bruno said. "It's not something we can do at the drop of a hat. Sombra isn't going to stay put long enough for us to write it."

Paloma's brow furrowed. "But maybe we can do it ahead of time."

Finn squinted at her. "You wanna sneak into Sombra's house early, write a desk magic trap on the floor, and lure him into it?"

"No," Paloma said. "But we have something those dueños didn't have. We have several pieces of his body right now. Pieces that we *know* he'll put on. We could write the magic on the relics to keep him frozen in place. We don't have all the relics to enchant, but we'll have to hope that what we have is enough to weaken him. We could magic the ink to become invisible so he wouldn't see it coming."

The dueños murmured in agreement, and Alfie felt a spark of hope ignite in his chest, tender and fragile. He was almost afraid to speak it aloud. "If you can apply magic to weaken Sombra, can you apply some to try to protect Dezmin from harm? We could make sure he's protected when we use the black blade."

"That's brilliant," Luka said, his eyes wide with excitement.

Paloma nodded. "The magic would be complex, and we don't know if it would work, but we will attempt it."

The dueños and Diviner Lucila nodded.

Though Alfie did not want to risk hoping anymore, he allowed himself this moment. Maybe it would work, maybe it wouldn't, but that small, infinitesimal possibility of success would be enough to give Alfie the will to try.

"So the plan is that you librarians"—Finn motioned at the dueños, who stared at her in annoyance—"will use desk magic on Sombra's relics. Then we find a way to give them to him so he can assume his immortal form. Once he does, the magic keeps him trapped in place and protects Dezmin, and Alfie and I will kill him with this." She raised the black blade above her head and scanned the room. "We don't need any cowards turning tail at the last minute. So if that plan's too scary for anyone, they can back out now."

Silence swept the room. Alfie waited to hear the retreating footsteps of those who refused to follow him and Finn into the jaws of an angry god. But the silence stretched on, the dueños' loyalty unwavering even in the face of death.

Finn took his hand and squeezed.

"That sounds promising," Paloma said. "But we still need to

find a way to get the relics to Sombra in a way that will work to our advantage."

"The pieces could be delivered via magic," Dueño Bruno said. "As a show of goodwill. After he has assumed his final form, he might grant us an audience."

Paloma shook her head. "No, we need to be there with the pieces when they're delivered. The last thing we want is for Sombra to return to his immortal body and attack us unawares."

James moved to stand beside Luka. "Then perhaps we go to his sky palace and present the relics ourselves," he suggested.

"We can't just knock on his door like we're looking for a cup of azúcar," Finn said. "We need a reason for him to let us in and let us witness his transformation. We need him to be comfortable with us being there. All of us."

She was right. Going in alone would be a suicide mission. If they wanted to stand a chance, they needed the dueños to be present, as well as Luka and James.

Chastened, James cleared his throat. "Right, of course."

Luka bumped him in the shoulder, and Alfie wondered once again what had happened on their journey to build this sudden camaraderie—but then again, plenty had happened to him and Finn in the same span.

"Then what options are left?" Dueño Bruno asked.

Alfie closed his eyes, the answer sprouting painfully in his mind. "We give ourselves up."

Finn crossed her arms, grimacing as if she tasted something sour. "Qué?"

"Sombra is vain. So vain that he found a way to sneak past our magical defenses but didn't kill us. He could've, but he didn't. He doesn't see us as a threat—he wants us alive to witness him win, to humiliate us," Alfie said. He'd seen it when he'd touched Sombra's monsters. "That much has always been clear. If we approach him begging for forgiveness, telling him we surrender, he'll invite us straight into his palace."

"So we declare our surrender and ask to deliver the relics to him . . ." Luka cocked his head. "It could work."

"Preying on a deity's hubris would seem a sound strategy," the diviner added.

"Perhaps, but he could also kill you before he even assumes his final form," Paloma said.

"He won't." Alfie shook his head. "He'll want us to see him in all his glory before he kills us. He would never give up the chance to watch us cower before him."

"But will he believe that we just want to deliver the relics?" Luka asked. "Surely he can't be that gullible, even if he is vain."

"I can make him believe," Alfie said, his voice rough. He knew what would whet Sombra's appetite, what would send the god running to throw open his palace doors. "I'll announce it publicly, humiliate myself. I'll say that I just want to see my brother one last time, that I don't want to fight anymore, that I'm ready to die, to be reunited with my family. I'll give him the relics in exchange for one last moment with my brother and a quick death." Alfie scrubbed at his eyes with the back of his hand. "He won't be able to resist. He's too vain to think we'd actually try to fight against him and too vain to think we could win even if we did try."

Silence swept the room as Alfie sank into the indignity of what he had to do.

Luka's hand found Alfie's shoulder. "Alfie, are you—"

"I'm sure. There isn't any other option. I'll do what has to be done," Alfie said, the sense of finality in his voice bringing everyone in the room to a hushed silence. He stood, swaddled in the tense quiet, until Finn stepped up.

"All right!" She clapped her hands. "You dueños do your desk magic thing. Once that's done, Alfie will reach out to Sombra."

Her command spurred the room back to life, and Alfie was thankful for how quickly she took control when he couldn't bring himself to.

As the dueños discussed the magic they'd need to perform on the relics, and Finn showed Luka and James the black blade, Alfie took comfort in the knowledge that if this plan failed—if they died and the world died with them—then at least they would perish knowing that they'd given their all.

LUKA'S LAST DAY

Luka sat on his bed, his eyes sore and red.

After the plan had been finalized, he'd sobbed in his rooms over all that had happened. He was thankful when Alfie asked for some time to himself so that Luka could guiltlessly do the same. He had wanted to sink into his sadness and let it eclipse him. Now it seemed that it had. He had no more tears. Nothing left to give.

These last five days had broken his spirit in every way possible. He'd been the first to learn that Dezmin might not be saved, and then he'd had to carry that knowledge home to his family—a fragile bomb that would destroy the only shred of hope they'd had left. As if that wasn't enough, he'd killed his own mother and lost King Bolivar too.

Part of him wished he'd stayed in the spirit realm with his family. Amada's voice ricocheted in his head.

We can join them and your family too . . . no sickness, no pain . . . just peace . . .

Luka let the memory burn him from the inside out, leaning into the pain. Maybe he should've let Amada kill him. Maybe she was right. Maybe that was the only way to end the suffering.

Luka gazed out the windows. The moon was still shattered. There were seven hours left before the end of the world. He should have felt afraid, but he felt nothing. Numbness had burrowed into his body, a hard callus covering a wound. He had felt so much over these past days that now he could feel nothing at all. He was grateful for the respite.

A knock sounded at his door, soft and hesitant.

"Come in." Luka didn't turn but felt the weight shift on the bed as James sat down.

When he opened his mouth to speak, Luka beat him to the punch.

"If you're going to ask me how I am, the answer is not great." His lifeless voice sounded foreign to his own ears. "But the show must go on."

"I wasn't going to ask you that," James said quietly.

"Bueno." Luka met his gaze, and it was so soft with sympathy that Luka wanted to scream. "Then, by all means, say what you came here to say."

"What do you need?"

The question was so simple, yet Luka felt it pierce through the numbness like an arrow, his grief bleeding from the wound. He swallowed it back down—he had to or he'd fall apart. Luka collected himself before he spoke again, closing the door on his grief and bracing his back against it.

"What I need right now is to be distracted." His eyes lowered to James's lips before meeting his gaze again, his intentions clear.

"Until it's time for all of us to die. Can you do that for me?"

A flush spread up James's neck and into his cheeks, but he didn't look away. "I can."

"Good." Luka pressed a searing kiss to his lips, his fingers shaking as he undid the buttons of James's shirt. And when James leaned forward, pressing his weight against him, Luka let the Englassen carry him down into the softness of the bed.

PALOMA'S LAST DAY

Paloma had always been a woman of few words.

When she was born, she was uncharacteristically quiet. Her mother would have thought she was dead if not for Paloma's small fist curling around her finger. As the youngest of three sisters and two brothers, by the time she was born there didn't seem to be any words left for her to use. They'd all been spoken and screamed and whispered and cried well before she entered the world.

Paloma had grown from a girl of few words to a woman of even fewer, but today, for the first time in a long time, all she wanted to do was scream. Maybe this was why she had always been so quiet. She had been squirreling away her words for today, a day so full of pain that she'd need a lifetime's worth of words to exorcise it from her body.

For the last two hours Paloma had watched the other dueños paint their magic onto Sombra's relics. Their strokes were exact, their faces tense. They had only five hours left to defeat Sombra and no one wanted to be the reason why this plan failed. She imagined how they would react if she screamed so loud and so long that the effort took her to her knees, coughing and gasping for breath.

But Paloma did not let the howl burst out of her. She stifled it, as she always did.

That had been one of her favorite things about Svana. She'd told the Uppskalan dueña that people had a hard time reading her because she said so little.

"What do you mean?" Svana had asked. "You speak volumes."

Paloma stared at her. "On most occasions I barely say a word."

Svana graced her with a small smile. "You don't need words to speak volumes."

Paloma buried the memory before it could destroy her. She had no way of confirming that Svana was dead, but she felt it in her bones. Still, she wished to know, to extinguish that last flame of hope and fall into the numb cold.

When Sombra had returned, Paloma had been with Diviner Lucila to ask for a divining. With Alfie marrying Princess Vesper, she'd felt it might be the right time to step away, perhaps retire. Svana was ready too. Paloma hadn't even had a chance to receive an answer from the diviner before the light was snuffed out and Nocturna began.

Later, after they'd left Luka and James to find the oasis, Paloma had swallowed her pride and returned to the diviner's rooms, asking for help in figuring out Svana's whereabouts. The diviner had no answers yet, but the pragmatism that had always driven Paloma told her that she already knew the answer, though she refused to consider it.

Not fully.

No one noticed when Paloma drifted out of the meeting chamber, letting her feet carry her through the palace that she'd lived in for decades. The halls that had once been bustling with servants and guards, royals and diplomats, were silent now.

She'd known that she herself would never have children, but she'd watched a trio of boys grow up here. She could see the ghosts of them at different ages—Dezmin and Alfie hosting their great sword fights in the library. Paloma would always wait a few minutes before she came in to chastise them.

She walked past the open doors to one of the palace's many parlors, remembering how gently Dezmin and Alfie had spoken to Luka when he'd bawled on the sofa over his first heartbreak. Paloma had reported that she was too ill to teach them, letting the boys comfort him instead of having class.

Paloma had spent years watching her pupils grow up and then, in a matter of days, she'd watched them die. Not physically, of course, Alfie and Luka were still breathing—Dezmin too, albeit in the worst of circumstances—but they were no longer alive. Not in the same way they had been as children taking root and growing in these halls.

She'd been tasked with teaching them, guiding them as young scholars and into mature bruxos, but she'd also been tasked with keeping them safe. At that, she'd failed spectacularly.

She remembered the days after Dezmin had disappeared into the dark, when it was clear they were not going to be able to get him back. King Bolivar had sobbed with abandon, while Amada had been unsettlingly silent. Paloma had brought Queen Amada soup, trying to coax her into eating.

Amada had pushed the bowl of sancocho away, her face blank. "No parent should have to bury their child. We're supposed to die first."

Now Paloma envied Bolivar and Amada. They would not have to watch what was to come.

Paloma's feet carried her through a maze of hallways to her rooms. She wanted to sit there among her books and memories one last time, and open the hidden compartment in her desk where she kept letters from Svana.

As she approached her door, she saw that it was already cracked open. Paloma pushed it open to see the diviner standing beside her desk.

"Diviner Lucila," Paloma said, her heart thrumming in her chest. "What brings you here?"

On any other day she'd be upset that the woman had just walked into her private room, but not today. She'd wanted so badly for the diviner to give her an answer, to end the agony, but now she wished she'd never asked.

"I fear I must ask you to grieve her now, while there's still time," the diviner said, her light eyes solemn. "Take these last hours to mourn so that you are ready for battle."

Then and only then did Paloma release the sounds she'd been holding back since birth.

Still, it was not enough.

FINN AND ALFIE'S LAST DAY

Finn looked everywhere for Alfie.

She'd checked his rooms. Then she'd checked Luka's, where she'd seen more of Bathtub Boy and the Englassen than she cared to.

"One place left, then," she murmured to herself after dodging the pillow that Luka had thrown at her head. She didn't know why she hadn't just started in the library to begin with.

Finn walked through the halls, remembering the first time she'd been in the palace, when she had snuck in through a roast pig and scurried through hidden passageways like a mouse. Now she walked freely, looking to comfort the same prince she'd almost poisoned that first fateful night.

Finn only started to worry when she thrust open the library doors and found it completely empty. A surge of panic flowed through her, paralyzing her where she stood. Where could the prince be? Had Sombra taken him? Or worse, had he left to fight Sombra without them? He wouldn't do that, would he? Finn forced the storm of anxiety inside her to calm. She just needed to look harder.

"If I were a somber, sensitive prince, where would I go?"

Finn thought for a long moment, then she set off toward a wing of the palace that was neglected, dusty—and familiar—with no paintings or enchanted candles to light the way.

At the end of the hall, a set of doors was cracked open and Finn knew her instinct was right.

Of course he'd come here.

Finn stepped into the Blue Room. It looked the same as it had the day she and Alfie had met for the second time. This was where Alfie had discovered Finn wearing the vanishing cloak and threatened to report her to the guards—and where he'd begged her to stay with him while he tried to save Luka's life.

Where they'd first released Sombra.

Alfie stood at the center of the room, his back to her. The furniture was still draped in white sheets, making the prince look like he was standing in a room of ghosts. Perhaps, in a way, he was. He didn't startle at her entry, and she wondered if he'd known that she'd find him. That she would always find him.

"I've been looking for you," she said.

When he finally turned, his golden eyes were so lost that Finn couldn't have stopped herself from embracing him even if she wanted to. "I don't know why I'm here."

She closed the distance between them and pulled him to her. "When something is about to end, you always think about how it began."

Alfie nodded, slowly stepping back from the embrace. His eyes were bloodshot and tired. "I don't want to talk about my parents."

"Then we won't." She had complicated feelings about the deaths of her own parents and knew better than to pry. "What do you want to talk about?"

"I don't know," he admitted as he lowered himself to the floor, sitting cross-legged on the dusty blue carpet, leaning back against a covered chaise longue. "Just not that."

Finn sat beside him, drumming her fingers on her thigh. She wanted to say the right thing, the thing he needed to hear, but she'd never been very good at that. So she said what was on her mind instead. "The last time you and I were in here I elbowed you in the face."

"I remember well." Alfie smiled at her. "When I asked you what you were doing here you didn't even try to lie. You just admitted to your thieving and crossed your arms as if daring me to challenge you."

"Well, if you'd snuck into the palace in a pig you'd be too tired to lie too." She shrugged.

"Wait." Alfie cocked his head. "You told me you came in through a pig when I caught you here. You meant that *literally*? You snuck into the palace by hiding in the roast pig? I thought you were using weird slang or something."

"Yeah, I came in through a pig. Almost got cooked too." Finn laughed. "And of course I meant it literally. What would that even mean metaphorically?"

"I don't know," Alfie admitted. "But now I know why I found hair in my pernil at the banquet."

Finn snorted.

"And there wasn't much time for me to ask you for clarification. Things happened so fast after that." The laughter drained from his face then, his eyes darting to the floor where Luka had once fallen, blood pouring from his nose and eyes.

"Yeah," Finn said. "Things did."

Mid-conversation, Luka had burst through the doors, sick from a poisoned sleeping tonic that had been intended for Alfie. And then there was only adrenaline as they'd raced to stop the evil they'd released.

"You know, Dezmin and I used to play here a lot as children. Hide-and-seek. Tag." He gave a broken laugh, his face drawn. "Nothing makes sense. Nothing's right. I've already lost everyone else—why should I have to lose him too? How do I go into this battle not knowing if he'll come out of it alive?"

Losing his brother wasn't set in stone. After all, the dueños were going to try to use protective magic to keep Dezmin alive, but Finn couldn't blame Alfie's mind from going there. No one knew if it would work.

Once again, she grappled with what to say and settled on the truth.

"It's not fair." Finn leaned her head against his shoulder. "I'm sorry, Alfie."

"I know. Everyone is."

Silence settled over them like dust.

Every second that ticked by was a second closer to their last stand, to probable death. There were things that Finn wanted to tell Alfie while there was still time. But was now—in the midst of all this pain—the right moment? Back in Weilai she'd thought they were going to be executed and she still hadn't been able to tell him how she felt. The threat of death didn't seem to be the best motivator for her. She wondered if she was too used to that feeling thanks to Ignacio. Fear of death couldn't force her to surrender the way it could someone else.

Alfie hunched over and buried his head in his hands, the bend of his body as broken as his spirit. Finn found that more motivating than death ever could be.

"When you were asleep, after we got the relics from Weilai," she said quietly, "your brother asked me if I loved you."

Alfie raised his head. "He did?"

Finn nodded. "I never answered him." She forced herself to meet his gaze, and the hope blooming on his face was something she wanted to remember long after she'd grown old. If they even were allowed to grow old. "But he already knew."

"Knew what?" Alfie asked gently. Finn picked at a loose thread on her trousers. When she didn't respond, he spoke again. "Finn, please."

Finn had hoped she wouldn't have to say it aloud, that she could imply it and move on, but the look in his eyes told her that wasn't an option. The love on his face was so bright, so fierce that she felt the urge to raise her hand to shield her eyes from the brilliance of it. But at the same time it was vulnerable, delicate, the lit wick of a candle that she curled her hand around to protect it from being blown out by the wind.

She swallowed thickly. "Yes." That one small word had held on to her tongue for dear life. She'd had to drag it out and into the open air. "I do love you."

She watched as tender relief spread through Alfie, relaxing the stiffness of his shoulders and unclenching the fists in his lap.

He'd been laced tight with grief and pain and fear, but with just four words from her he'd come undone. It wouldn't last forever, she knew. A moment like this was born and died in the same breath, and eventually they'd have to exhale. For now, though, she held her breath.

"You don't have to say it back," Finn said hurriedly, embarrassment washing over her. She couldn't bear to look at him, not when the look on his face was proof of the power of her words. No one should have so much power. "I know this is a weird time to say it. I just needed to tell you before . . . everything."

"Finn," he said, and she loved the softness he brought to her name. He spoke it as if he were saying a prayer. "I already told you I love you."

Finn blinked at him. "What? When?" She knew she was easily distracted, but she was pretty sure she would've noticed that.

"In the Englassen forest. You were a baby in the crook of my arm. It was the only way I had the courage to say it to you out loud," he admitted, his soft palm cupping her cheek.

He touched her as if she were made of glass. From anyone else she would see such gentleness as proof of her own weakness, proof that she was something fragile to be handled carefully, but from him it was different. She didn't feel weak. She felt beloved, precious. She'd spent her life being tossed about, her resilience tested at every turn, but he held her as if he would never let her touch the ground, as if she'd never have to prove how much she could endure ever again.

"I watched time tug you into the past, back to before you knew me or Ignacio," Alfie said, his thumb rubbing slow circles on her jaw. "Your younger selves told me the truth of where your pain comes from. And it only made me love you more."

Finn felt an overwhelming need to run from the room. Would she ever stop feeling this desire to flee from whatever wanted to hold her close? Would she be at constant war with herself for as long as she and Alfie were in each other's lives?

"Why?" She knew it was the wrong thing to say, but it was what she felt and what she likely would feel for a long time.

"I cannot undo the hurt you've endured." Alfie pressed his forehead to hers, his warm breath ghosting over her lips. "I cannot make you see yourself through my eyes. But I will be right here beside you while you fight that battle."

When he leaned forward and kissed her, on his lips was a promise.

A promise she hoped he would live long enough to keep.

THE PERFORMANCE

The dueños finished their work on the relics with three hours to spare.

Three hours until midnight, until Alfie and Finn's birthday, until the end of the world.

The palace roof had once been a quiet place for Alfie and Luka to stargaze and think, but it had been transformed into a shrine to Sombra.

His relics stood surrounded by a legion of candles, as if for worship. The stage was set. Now Alfie and Finn need only play their parts.

Luka gave him an encouraging nod. "Ready when you are."

Alfie didn't want to tell them that he would never be ready for this farce and what would follow it. His shadow curled tightly around his feet. There was danger in every outcome. If Sombra acquiesced, they'd be facing a god in a battle to the death. If Sombra ignored them, they'd have to come up with another plan, and fast. If they didn't, they had a few hours left to say their goodbyes.

Finn stood beside him, her gaze protective, her fingers twitching for a dagger. He looked at her face—her true face. Even in this unnatural world, in the midst of Nocturna, she was still lovely. He gave her a wisp of a smile.

"I'll be fine," he promised. Alfie walked to the center of the arrangement of candles and relics. Paloma, a small group of dueños, and the diviner were on the roof too. Paloma had insisted on being there, which made Alfie want to laugh. Her endless desire to protect him was comforting, yet at the same time sad.

"Sombra, god of darkness, king of our world," Alfie forced himself to shout. "I call upon you tonight with a request. Though I have obtained three of your relics, we have failed to find a way to defeat you. The prophecy was wrong. We are no match for your power."

Finn crossed her arms, her jaw working.

"I know that soon our world will end, and I cannot let that happen without speaking to my brother one last time." Alfie hated how much emotion seeped through the words. Finn was right. The best lies had a bit of truth in them. "In exchange for delivering the relics to you, all I ask is that you let me say goodbye to Prince Dezmin. After that, I am yours to kill. Let me surrender to your will and be reunited with my family in death."

The possibility of death was outrageously high. Even if Sombra granted them an audience and assumed his true form before them, they still didn't know if the magic the dueños had written on the relics would be enough to stop him. There were no guarantees.

The thought alone was enough to bring Alfie to his knees. "Please hear my call for your mercy. Let me revise my role in your legend, so that I am no longer your enemy but rather a part of your legacy." Alfie bent forward, pressing his forehead to the ground.

Alfie waited for a sign that Sombra had heard him. A sign that he hadn't humiliated himself for no reason. He rose, his forehead marked with dirt.

He looked to Finn, Luka, and Paloma, unsure of what to say. Maybe it hadn't worked. Maybe he was wrong and Sombra wouldn't care about this display of weakness.

A cold breeze swept over the rooftop, extinguishing the candles.

"Hello," Sombra's voice came, carried on the wind like dried, dead leaves. "How lovely to be addressed with the reverence befitting a god."

Alfie scanned the rooftop, but the god did not materialize. Finn's hand had settled on a dagger strapped to her hip. Luka stood completely still, but his hands were shaking—in fear or rage, Alfie couldn't be sure.

Paloma met Alfie's gaze and nodded.

His heart pounding in his throat, Alfie asked, "Do you accept our request, Lord Sombra?" He didn't want to say more. He was afraid that if he did, his anger would reveal itself in his voice.

"I do," Sombra said, magnanimous. "You are cordially invited to a reception in my palace tonight. Arrive at your leisure. I'm in no hurry." Alfie could hear the laughter in the god's voice. His amusement at the fact that the world was ending yet he was in no rush. Then there was a pause, and Alfie felt the god's warm breath on the shell of his ear, as if he were standing just beside him. "Do not make me or your dear brother wait too long."

THE TREK TO THE
PALACE IN THE SKY

With Finn and Luka at his side, Alfie watched the dueños check the written magic on Sombra's relics a final time.

"What enchantment did you put on the pieces?" Luka asked Bruno, who was reapplying ink to the sternum of the torso relic.

"*Enchantments*," the dueño corrected him. "We're doing everything we can to give the prince and his companion the best chance—"

"Companion." Finn rolled her eyes.

"—to protect and heal Prince Dezmin and enchantments to paralyze, confuse, and weaken Sombra," he said, talking over Finn. "We can only hope that at least one will hobble him long enough for you two to strike."

The horses had already been prepared for their ride through the city to Sombra's palace.

The armory had been raided for all they could carry—daggers concealed under clothes, swords strapped on backs, long blades tucked into scabbards, throwing knives hitched to their waists. After all, they did not know what they would face on their journey, let alone once they got to the palace.

The diviner had prayed for the gods' favor. The dueños had brewed and packed as many healing draughts as they could carry, and Alfie wondered how many it would take to reverse the damage done by an angry god.

When Sombra had first returned, there were just under thirty dueños aiding them. Now there were only eight. Including Luka, Alfie, Finn, James, and the Diviner, their final stand was only thirteen strong.

"It's time," Paloma said. "All preparations have been completed."

Silence swept over the room, and they all looked at one another, mirroring the uncertainty in each other's eyes. How many of them would survive this? Was it naive to think any of them would?

"Very well," Alfie said, trying to drown out that thought. Beyond the windows, the world still lay suspended in the strange glow of a shattered moon. One wouldn't think the clock would soon strike midnight, maybe for the last time. "Then let's go."

When their small caravan approached the stables, Alfie found a chestnut-brown horse, nearly the exact shade of Dezmin's eyes.

He wasn't ready, and how could he be? Nothing could have prepared him for this.

At that thought, his father's voice bloomed in his ears.

Being ready for the next step in life is a luxury few can afford.

They mounted their horses.

"If any shadowless attempt to harm us," Paloma said, "incapacitate or kill them as swiftly as you can manage. Tonight is our last chance to stop Sombra. We cannot tarry."

Alfie flinched. Dueños abhorred violence. It was as much a part of their image as the telltale robes they wore. There was something so unsettling, so unnatural about hearing her speak so flippantly about killing, but Luka hadn't even reacted. Alfie wondered what horrors he and Paloma had faced together, what they'd been forced to do.

"Understood," the dueños intoned in unison, and Alfie couldn't help but notice how soft their voices were with age.

Remembering the frailty of his older body in the Englassen forest only made him more grateful for their service and their bravery.

"Before we leave," Alfie said, knowing that if he didn't say it now, it might never be said, "you have my sincerest thanks for going on this journey with me, for risking your lives for this kingdom and the world. I am honored to know that I will have you as advisors when we return."

The dueños and Diviner Lucila bowed their heads in acceptance of his praise.

"Thank you, King Alfehr," Bruno said, with genuine respect in his voice.

Alfie blinked. No one had ever called him king before. Now it felt real.

"We are honored to serve," Paloma said, her hand finding his shoulder and squeezing it tenderly.

Alfie put his hand over hers and met her gaze, his eyes burning. He knew she wouldn't want him to say such things aloud, so he could only hope that she could read his face—*I'm sorry that we have both lost so much and yet still more loss is on the horizon.*

Paloma nodded, then let him go. "We ride in formation,

surrounding Prince Alfehr and Finn!" the dueña shouted.

With no further preamble, their caravan began to move, Alfie and Finn surrounded by a triangle of allies. Paloma led the charge while Luka and James protected the rear, leaving the flanks to the other dueños and the diviner. Their horses crunched through the dead grass and dry earth of the palace grounds. Alfie held his breath as they proceeded past the barrier that the dueños had placed to keep the shadowless away from the castle.

But his worry was misplaced.

As their caravan passed groups roaming the countryside between the palace grounds and the first rings of the city, the shadowless stared at the caravan but did not approach. It struck Alfie then that Sombra had done this—he'd cleared their path so that they could arrive at his palace alive and well.

Sombra wasn't worried; he was *excited*.

Alfie's stomach tightened into a tense knot.

They rode through each ring of the city, the population of shadowless growing denser as they moved from the Crown to the poorer rings.

Somehow their blank, silent stares were worse than the attacks that Alfie had anticipated. Throughout the city there were cracks and holes in the fabric of the world. Finn had warned everyone of this since she'd seen it herself in Weilai, but it still was a sight to see. Chunks of haciendas were missing, transformed into windows to the void. One of the dueños' horses nearly fell through the ground.

Alfie rode numbly until they reached the port where Sombra's palace floated over the Suave. The air was thick with the smell of dead fish and boiled seaweed. And there, at the very end of a wooden dock, a stairway of clouds had extended down.

"Dioses," Luka gasped. Even parts of the ocean were gone. The boiling seawater was draining through the cracks, disappearing into the abyss. Alfie wondered if the water would fall forever in an endless loop, but there was no time now to focus on those questions.

When they approached the stairs, the horses nickered, rearing back on their hind legs. Alfie tried to calm his mount, but the poor creature wouldn't stop shaking.

"We might as well let them go now," Finn said, rubbing her quivering horse's ear. "It's a big palace, but I doubt Sombra has a stable up there."

No one laughed at her joke, but it seemed that everyone agreed because they all silently dismounted. The animals galloped away at full speed, and Alfie wondered if they could feel Sombra's horrible miasma. It was the same feeling he and Finn had experienced while tracking down the relics, but exponentially stronger now. Before he had simply felt unsettled, gooseflesh bursting over his body, but now he felt Sombra's dark presence pouring into him, just as he'd felt after touching the monsters Sombra had sent. The scent of rot was overwhelming. Luka clapped his hand over his mouth, and Alfie knew it wasn't just he and Finn who sensed it anymore.

Sombra had attacked the very soul of their world. Was this the scent of that soul rotting under their very feet?

Paloma looked at the sight, her face tight with fear. "Let us go."

The stairs looked to be made of gray clouds, thunder rumbling through them. Alfie gingerly put his foot on the first, expecting it to sink through, but it was solid. Sombra might be a monster, but his magic was a sight to behold. He could see the lightning and feel the rumbling of thunder, his hair standing on end from the static pull.

Finn gripped his hand as they led the group up the stairs. Her face was nonchalant, but he could feel the fear in her.

The towering obsidian front doors of the palace swung open, silently welcoming them.

Alfie had never seen anything so terrifying yet beautiful. They stood in a vast foyer, the ceilings impossibly high. The walls were made of the same strangely solid storm clouds, but they were dotted with blue gems. Many as small as a fingernail, a few as big as a fist. It took Alfie a moment before he realized it was larimar.

Luka wrinkled his nose at the display. "Gaudy."

Finn snorted.

"He wants the gods to witness it all," Paloma said, eyeing the walls.

It made sense. Sombra was obsessed with getting revenge on the gods who'd kicked him out of the heavens. It was the reason why he wanted to destroy this world in the first place—to spite them. Larimar was how they'd had an audience with the gods. Perhaps he thought lacquering the walls with it would force the gods to watch.

"Well," Finn said, leading the way. "I hope the gods are ready for a show."

Before them was a long corridor with a towering doorway at the end. Alfie glanced behind him, and his stomach dropped. The door they'd entered through was gone, dissolved, a wall of cloud and larimar in its place. Though the palace was gargantuan, Alfie felt a sudden wave of claustrophobia. They were animals being funneled forward, herded to slaughter.

He could feel waves of panic emanating from his comrades, and he wondered if Sombra could feel it too—if the god was smiling as he lay in wait.

"Chin up," Finn murmured. "One way or another, this'll all be over soon."

She was right. After all, there was only an hour left until midnight.

Alfie was surprised by how something could at once be so morbid yet so comforting.

THE CHOICE IS YOURS

The doors opened slowly.

The world was ending tonight, yet the palace moved as if it had all the time in the world. All the time the world had left anyway.

Alfie wasn't sure what to expect, but he certainly hadn't been expecting an immaculately decorated banquet hall, its walls glimmering with yet more larimar. The center of the room was bisected by a table of shining black stone.

"Welcome!" Sombra crowed from the head of the table.

Alfie's stomach turned. While Sombra pulled Dezmin's lips into a gleeful grin, his brother's body looked worse for wear. He looked nothing like he had when Sombra first returned—glowing with vengeful purpose. His complexion had shifted from a rich brown to an ashen gray, and his cheekbones looked far too sharp, as if his skin were pulled tight over his face.

Dezmin was dying, along with the world.

His brother was suffering, and Alfie had no plan to make it stop aside from plunging a blade into his chest and hoping that the due-ños' magic would save him.

"So glad you could make it to your own untimely end." Sombra surveyed them from his high-backed chair at the head of the table.

Alfie wanted to scream at him, tell him that he was a grotesque monster who deserved nothing but pain for what he'd done to this world. But Alfie had a part to play to ensure that they got their chance to kill him.

Alfie bowed low. The others—even Finn, begrudgingly—joined him.

"King Sombra," Alfie said, keeping his gaze on the ground. "We've come to beg your forgiveness for our audacity. And we offer you our lives as payment. In exchange I ask only for a final moment with my brother."

Summoning every bit of restraint he could muster, Alfie let the heat of his glare bore into the cloud floor.

Dezmin slept, the darkness cocooning him in an eternal slumber. When he'd given himself to Sombra, he'd been afraid that it would be painful, but that wasn't the case.

He had fallen into a soft nest of black. He was naked, but felt neither cold nor hot. Tendrils of shadow swaddled him tight, safe and sound, growing thicker and thicker. Only his head and face remained uncovered.

He wondered if this was what it was like before one was born.

This was better than the void he'd been banished to—that had been a prison. But this—this was a sanctuary. The longer he lay in the dark of Sombra's will, the less he remembered of his past life, of what he'd lost, what he'd had to fight for.

He was dissolving, just one piece of many in the god's patchwork. He could slumber for the rest of his days, peaceful and pliant.

He hadn't opened his eyes since he'd seen . . . someone die? He hardly remembered anymore. A woman in a red dress. He knew it had upset him, but that was neither here nor there, not when dreamless sleep rocked him in its embrace.

A voice spoke, and he stirred. He had heard the echo of many voices as he slept, but this one was different. It was too familiar.

King Sombra . . . We've come to . . . offer you our lives as payment. In exchange I ask only for a final moment with my brother.

Dezmin's brow furrowed. Who was that?

He shook himself free of that thought. Whoever it was had nothing to do with him. He nestled into the dark, turning away from the noise of a life he no longer recognized.

Sombra didn't seem to hear Alfie's request. He only frowned, giving each of them a once-over. "This attire simply won't do."

With a flick of Sombra's wrists, Alfie felt a cold, wet sensation ghost over him, as if the clammy hands of a hundred corpses were touching his body.

In an instant, their clothes transformed. Alfie's armor, scratched and worn from their adventures, changed to a black ensemble, perfectly fitted down to each shining button. Finn's trousers bloomed into an obsidian ball gown that left her shoulders and collarbone exposed. He only realized that his hair had been fixed as well when he saw that Finn's curls had become perfect, glossy ringlets.

"Of course," she said. "Of course this is what I wear when I die."

Even the diviner's and the dueños' clothing had changed. Alfie had never seen Paloma in a gown; it looked strangely wrong. Alfie was relieved to feel that his weapons were still in place under his clothes. Had Sombra not noticed them? Or did he see them as so little threat that he didn't bother to remove them?

"Much better!" Sombra said with a clap of his hands.

"We have what you have been seeking," Alfie said, before the god could speak another word. "Let us present your gifts to you."

There was no point in putting it off. After all, they could not kill Sombra until he assumed his true form with the stone pieces. And Sombra looked so terribly pleased with himself; Alfie had no desire to keep up a charade that entertained the god so much.

"Nonsense," Sombra said. "Take a seat. Let us, as you humans do on special occasions, break bread."

A row of chairs appeared on either side of the table.

Alfie's palms grew slick with sweat. "We couldn't possibly—"

"*Sit*." Sombra's gaze hardened.

Alfie swallowed thickly. "Very well."

"Wonderful! The pair *allegedly* prophesied to kill me may sit in the seats closest to me," he said with a laugh. "The rest may sit wherever you please."

Alfie and Finn met eyes before walking down opposite sides of the table and sitting on either side of Sombra. He watched them, his fingernails tapping idly on the table. It was absurd that he'd let them get this close when the prophecy said they'd been born to defeat him, but then again, it made sense—Sombra wanted to make sure the gods knew he wasn't afraid of them. Alfie could see him constantly glancing at the glimmering, larimar-inlaid walls. It was pathetic how much he worked to impress them. To think that he would destroy a whole world just to prove a point, a toddler throwing a tantrum.

"After consuming so many of your people, and combing through their mundane memories, I've learned what Castallan's most cherished dishes are," Sombra said.

Alfie's spine straightened.

"What do you mean by consuming?" Finn asked. Alfie was impressed that she could demand an answer from Sombra as if he wasn't a god.

"An interesting question that we can discuss over supper." Sombra snapped his fingers and mounds of shadow appeared on the table. They bulged and contracted before settling into shape.

Alfie nearly gagged.

The long table was covered in Castallano delicacies, the centerpiece a full pig roast, but the food was covered in rot. The smell of decaying meat filled his nostrils.

Luka pushed his chair back from the table with a gasp.

"No, no, no," Sombra tutted, and Luka's chair snapped forward. "This is what you enjoy, is it not? This is what your people ate during the holidays, what they begged their mothers to cook for them when they were children."

Once again, Alfie wondered what Sombra meant by consuming, but part of him didn't want to know.

"We only wish to return your relics," Dueño Bruno said, and Alfie could see his eyes watering from the smell. "Please, allow us that honor."

Sombra cocked his head at the dueño before releasing a bark of laughter. "You truly think I believe you're here to praise me and return my relics? You think I didn't feel all the weapons you have hidden on your frail bodies? You think I'm a fool?"

Bruno didn't get a chance to answer. Sombra stretched his hand toward him and the bones of the dueño's face caved in. His cheekbones snapped inward, his nose following suit as if he'd been viciously punched. His neck cracked downward, pulled deeper into his body like a turtle. In the space of a breath his head had collapsed in on itself, sinking and twisting into a gnarl of blood and flesh.

Paloma sat beside him, spattered in his blood, her eyes wide.

Alfie wanted to scream, the fear inside him begging to break free, but he was too shocked to utter a sound.

Sombra's laughter filled the silence as he looked at their horrified faces. The god's nose began to bleed—more strain on Dezmin's body from using magic.

"You used the relics as an excuse to get close to me. To try to make your little prophecy true. And I let you keep your little weapons, because you are *nothing*." He looked about the room, the larimar glinting like a sea of eyes. He was performing for his audience. "I do not fear you.

"And to answer your question," he said to Finn. "To keep this mortal body alive, I needed to eat. You humans consume that which you feel is beneath you," Sombra said, gesturing at the rotting pig. "None of you question whether the pig should live. You simply open your mouth and gorge upon it." Sombra waved a hand, and the cloud walls of the ballroom grew transparent. Alfie gasped at the sight of the world stretched out beneath his feet. "This world, the very souls of your people, are my feast. I cannot help but consume." With a look from Sombra, the walls of cloud returned.

Alfie looked away from him in disgust, but it only delighted Sombra more.

"Your brother felt similarly about my eating habits, but, alas, he was not allowed to look away," Sombra said, and Alfie felt ill at the thought of Dezmin begging to be spared from such horror. "We all have our place in the natural order and yours is *beneath me*. I will consume each of you, one by one. Then I will assume my true form and swallow this world whole."

Alfie's stomach dropped, panic surging through him. Sombra was going to kill them now, before he even donned the relics.

They were going to fail.

With a shout, Finn rose from her chair, a small dagger in her hand. Alfie's heart stopped as she swung it down toward Sombra's chest, but the god only had to look at her to make her freeze.

Sombra smiled. "A very nice try."

"Finn!" Alfie stared at her in fear. "What are you doing?" Why would she do that knowing full well that harming him before he assumed his true form was useless? But Finn ignored him, her eyes locked on Sombra.

"Back to your seat now." Sombra's teeth were splashed red with the blood dripping from his nose.

Finn's body folded back into her chair. She struggled against Sombra's grip, shaking with the effort, but it was no use. With another look from Sombra, her free hand slammed against the table, palm down. The dagger flew out of her fingers, and with a simple nod from Sombra it descended slowly until the tip pierced the back of her hand, sinking into her flesh torturously slowly.

"Stop!" Alfie shouted, but he found that he couldn't move either. By the looks on Paloma's and Luka's faces, neither could anyone else. "Just stop! Please don't hurt her—"

Finn mashed her lips together, her throat working as she tried not to scream, but she could only hold out for so long before cries of pain tore out of her throat. But Sombra was too cruel to stop there. Once the blade's tip hit the stone of the table, it began to slowly spin, the knife carving a circle into the back of her hand.

Finn! What are you doing?

Dezmin screwed his eyes shut. There it was again. That same voice shouting in fear followed by the sound of a girl screaming. It sounded . . . familiar.

Just stop! Please don't hurt her—

Dezmin didn't look. Whatever was beyond his closed eyes would only harm him. He was better off here, in the quiet of Sombra's darkness.

He burrowed deeper still, letting the bands of shadow constrict around him. Threads of black began to crawl up his head and face, thin as a spider's web.

Dezmin welcomed it.

Finn screamed as the blade spun through her hand, pressing herself against the back of her chair as if trying to get away. Rivulets of blood poured over the edge of the table.

"Stop it!" Luka shouted.

"Leave her alone!" Alfie said from where he was frozen in his chair, but he knew it was no use. Their cries only made Sombra's smile widen.

"Just kill us," Finn ground out from behind clenched teeth. "Kill us before you put on your stupid relics. I'd rather die than see you in your disgusting final form."

The knife stopped its torturous spin.

Sombra stared at her, first in cold anger, but then a smile stretched across his face.

Alfie's eyes widened in understanding. Sombra had been planning to kill them before he even donned the relics, but Finn attacking him and insulting his immortal form had made him change his mind. They still had a chance.

"Kill us," Paloma said, steel in her voice. "You have taken everything from me. I have no desire to live a moment longer, to see your power grow, to watch this world end. Kill us and be done with it." She'd clearly caught on to Finn's caper, but Alfie knew there was truth in her words too.

"You know, I didn't think any of you heathens deserved to see me in all my glory, and that is still true, but today I will make an exception. Think of it as my parting gift."

Sombra stood from the table, taking long strides backward, as if he needed space to perform. Or perhaps he wanted to take center stage to make sure everyone had a good view. Curling a finger, Sombra beckoned at the satchel hanging from Paloma's shoulder. The bag floated to him, and he reached in, pulling each relic out. There was a giddy excitement in his face, like a child opening a present. As each piece floated before him, Alfie could feel the relics seem to buzz with anticipation. The remaining pieces materialized before

Sombra—the arms he'd stolen from the vault and the feet that his creatures had brought him from Ygosi.

Still unable to move from the table, Alfie and Finn stared at each other. It was time.

Sombra opened his arms wide. "Come to me, old friends."

Alfie held his breath as the relics snapped toward the god like a magnet. They encased Sombra's body, and the god gave a contented sigh as they sank beneath his skin. A dark glow emitted from him, as if he were lit from within by a black flame. It was still Dezmin's face and body, but the jaw was stronger and wider. His skin no longer looked sallow; it glowed with power, darkening into a rich brown. His features grew sharper, more pronounced. He didn't look human anymore; he looked like a statue come to life—something so startlingly beautiful that it was unsettling.

This was the form of a god.

In his ecstasy at being reunited with his pieces, he seemed to have forgotten about Alfie and the others. The magic holding them still began to fade, and they could move once more.

"*Now!*" Finn shouted as she pulled the dagger out of the back of her bloodied hand.

The dueños and the diviner began shouting the enchantments they'd written on Sombra's relics, the ones to weaken Sombra and the ones to save Dezmin.

"*Paralizar!*"

"*Proteger!*"

"*Confundir!*"

"*Debilitar!*"

Alfie could see the written magic glowing under Sombra's skin, a bright light shining through the dark.

Sombra looked down at himself. He swayed on his feet, startled and sluggish.

The magic was working! And if the magic to paralyze and weaken him was working, then the magic to protect Dezmin had to be working too!

Just as they'd planned, James grabbed Luka and sped over to Sombra. Luka held the god in place with his strength as the dueños kept chanting spells, making even more written magic glow beneath Sombra's skin. Just like the Tattooed King, there was scarcely a patch of skin that hadn't been written on.

Finn rushed to Alfie's side, pulled the black blade from beneath her dress, and held it out. Alfie covered her hand with his and let his magic pour into hers until it matched the shifting darkness of Sombra's essence that was trapped in the blade. He felt it snap into place. They were ready.

She looked at him for confirmation, and he could only nod. Everything was happening so quickly there didn't seem to be time to speak. Together Alfie and Finn ran toward Sombra, the blade shared in their hands.

This was it.

His and Finn's lives had built up to this. He would kill Sombra and save Dezmin. He would return their world to its former balance. He only needed to do this one thing.

They were only a breath away from Sombra when the god thrust out a hand, a sudden alertness in his features. Finn and Alfie froze where they stood, his magic holding them in place. "Perhaps run a little faster next time."

With a laugh, Sombra shrugged Luka and James off. They flew back, slamming into the cloud wall. Alfie's stomach sank. Sombra had been faking, pretending to be affected by the written magic, which meant the enchantments to save Dezmin weren't working either.

"Mierda," Finn said through her teeth. They stood frozen in front of Sombra, the blade so close to the god's chest that it grazed his shirt.

"You thought you could trap me and protect your brother with your sad magic," he said, entertained. "You thought you could defeat me with your little sword? *Me?*"

With a swipe of his hands the dueños and the diviner were thrown back too, crashing onto the ground. By the force of the fall, Alfie knew that some of them would never stand again.

"And now you're making me ruin your clothes," Sombra tutted. He gripped Finn by the arm and tossed her down the length of the dining table, rotten food splattering her.

Then Sombra turned his black eyes on Alfie.

"You truly thought you could win." He looked amused by their boldness, as though he were watching a dog attempting to learn a difficult trick. "Your antics have been entertaining, but it ends here."

Gripping Alfie by the neck, Sombra raised him high off the ground. As he did, Alfie found that he could move again. Sombra could've kept him frozen, but he preferred to see him suffer. He choked and gasped, kicking at Sombra. He stared at the god's blackened eyes, trying to find Dezmin's brown somewhere in their depths, but it was gone. Would the protective enchantments have helped at all? Or was there no Dezmin left to protect?

Sombra squeezed tighter until Alfie felt as if the pressure would make his eyes burst from his skull. Then the god slammed Alfie onto the ground, his back meeting the floor with a terrible *crack*. Pinpricks of light crowded his vision, his ears filled with a loud, droning hum. The pain was so intense that, for a moment, he couldn't even feel it, his body incapable of processing so much trauma all at once. Then it swallowed him whole. A broken sob burst past his lips.

"*Are these your prophesied saviors?*" Sombra shouted at the larimar-covered walls. "The ones you said would defeat me?

"These weak." Sombra gripped Alfie's torso and squeezed. Alfie's rib splintered beneath the pressure, and he cried out. "Fragile." Another rib broken. Alfie screamed and tried uselessly to push Sombra's hands away, but the god wasn't even looking at him; his eyes were still on the larimar-covered walls. "Children."

Sombra gripped Alfie by the ankle and threw him across the banquet hall, sending him skidding across the floor like a stone over a pond.

As he rolled to a stop, Alfie couldn't think. He was nothing but a mass of pain. Pieces of him had shattered beneath his skin, and every breath seemed to jostle them, bringing another wave of agony.

"Alfie!" Finn was standing over him, still covered in rotting food. She knelt over him, and by the way she hobbled he knew she'd hurt her ankle when Sombra threw her. She still had the black blade in her hand. "We have to try again!"

Over her shoulder, Alfie watched the dueños try to use the written magic again, but Sombra only laughed. The diviner lay on the floor unmoving, her neck bent at an odd angle.

"I can't do it," Alfie admitted, his eyes burning. "If the protective magic isn't working, then killing Sombra will kill Dezmin. I can't—I won't do it."

Finn stared at him, wide-eyed. The blade slipped from her grip and clattered on the floor. "Alfie—"

"There are my two favorites!" Sombra was so fast that he materialized behind Finn in the space of a breath, a mad grin on his face.

Finn reached for the black blade but he kicked it away, letting it bounce against the wall a few paces behind them. With each hand, he grabbed Alfie and Finn by the necks again.

"Dezmin!" Alfie cried out in gasping breaths. He didn't know what else to do, what else to try. "If you can hear me, please . . ." There wasn't enough air to continue. His pulse pounded around Sombra's vise grip. "Dezmin . . ."

"The gods were wrong." Sombra tightened his hold. Alfie could hear Finn struggling to breathe. He clawed at Sombra's wrist, trying to pry the god's fingers from his neck, but it was no use. "I will end this world and there will be no one left to remember you. No one left to repeat your sad tale. You were not destined to defeat me. You were destined to die by my hand—"

Sombra froze.

Dezmin! If you can hear me, please . . .

But wasn't that his name? Dezmin?

No. He wasn't anyone anymore. He was a fragment of Sombra, no more, no less. Whoever was speaking was of no concern to him.

Dezmin trembled fitfully. He could not fall back asleep, could not descend back into the numbing dark. The once soft and protective blanket of shadow felt suffocating, a restraint rather than a comfort. His legs twitched, fingers spasmed, something inside him screaming to wake. His nose and eyes were still uncovered. If he just waited a moment, he would be fully cocooned and there would be no going back, no more pain. He would be *free*.

But he couldn't let go.

In the end, Dezmin did not know if it was fate or coincidence that made him finally open his eyes.

In truth, it was neither.

It was simply love.

Dezmin opened his eyes and saw through Sombra's once more, his vision blurred and patchy. It hurt to look, but he forced his tearing eyes to gaze at the face of the boy Sombra was choking.

He cocked his head.

The boy was looking at Sombra with so much fear and resignation, yet there was also hope, desperate hope.

The memories snapped into place with a dizzying quickness.

It was his little brother. The baby boy he'd held in his arms and marveled at, so wonderstruck that it caused his *propio* of bringing objects to life to flicker into existence. The boy he'd watched grow up. The boy he'd shielded from the responsibilities of the crown. This boy was the last thing he'd seen before he was left trapped in the abyss.

Alfie. It was Alfie.

"Stop!" The black threads netted over his eyes as Dezmin fought against the strands holding him in place. "Let go of me!" He could barely hear himself, his voice muffled by the cocoon.

With a shout of anger, Dezmin's arm broke through the casing, and then another. The black threads tried to pull him back, criss-crossing over him every time he tried to break free, but Dezmin wouldn't stop. He tore through over and over again.

He struggled onto his feet. And with every ounce of energy he had left, Dezmin shouted, "*Stop!*"

Sombra froze.

For a moment Alfie thought he was hovering so close to death that he simply couldn't hear anymore, but no—Sombra had stopped speaking, stopped moving. Then his grip began to loosen, until Alfie fell from his hand like a forgotten toy tossed by a child. Finn plopped to the floor next to him.

Alfie coughed and gasped. He watched as Sombra's black eyes shifted into a rich brown.

Dezmin's brown.

"Dezmin," Alfie gasped, overwhelmingly grateful that he hadn't killed Sombra. Dezmin was still here, and even if all he got was this last moment with him, that was worth it. "Is that you?" When he turned to Finn for confirmation, the thief was frozen in place. Alfie looked about the room; everyone was still, unmoving.

Time had stopped.

Dezmin gave a grimace, as if he was straining to hold Sombra back. "Alfie, we don't have much time." He crouched down beside Alfie. "He's going to kill you."

"Dezmin." Tears slipped down Alfie's nose. "I can't do this. I can't—it could hurt you. I can't lose you."

"Alfie, look at me," Dezmin pleaded.

"I can't," Alfie sobbed. "I won't." Now that the adrenaline had ebbed, he couldn't stand the thought of trying again.

"Look at me," Dezmin said.

After years of wishing for nothing more than to see Dez's face, Alfie couldn't bear to look at him. Because he knew exactly what Dez was going to ask.

"I can't," he gasped, his hands gripping Dez's shoulders. "I can't."

"Hermanito," Dez said again. "Look at me."

Alfie finally looked up, and there was his brother. The one he'd searched for, only to find him in a moment like this.

"I cannot be separated from Sombra," Dezmin said, and Alfie shook his head in protest, willing his brother to stop. "I can't. I gave pieces of myself to him so that I could use his magic to find you. We're intertwined. If there was a way to save me, I would tell you. If love were enough, you would have set me free long ago."

Alfie sobbed. "Please don't ask me to do this, Dez. Please, I can't. I—"

"Alfie," Dez said. "I need you to know something." He held Alfie's gaze. "You can choose to kill me and save the world. Or you can choose to spare me and let the world fall to ash. No matter what you choose, no matter what you do, I will always love you. Always, from wherever I am. Do you understand?"

Alfie was shaking, his face wet with tears. He looked into his brother's eyes and knew what had to be done.

"One way or another, it's almost over." Dez nodded at him with a tired smile. He pulled Alfie into a gentle embrace, and even as his splintered ribs protested, Alfie leaned into it, gripping his brother tight. "And this is a great place for it all to end."

After a moment that was far too short, Dezmin pulled free of the hug and looked at Alfie. In his brother's tired, worn face, Alfie saw the boy he'd been before. The one waging sword fights with Alfie in the library.

In the books you always have to have a sword fight in a big, dramatic place. And when you shout the whole room echoes.

A broken laugh stumbled through Alfie's lips. "Because it's got a great echo."

"Exactly." Dezmin cupped the back of Alfie's head and pulled him closer again until their foreheads leaned against one another's.

"Te amo, Dez," Alfie said.

"I love you," Dezmin said back, his voice straining as Sombra began to overpower him once more. "And I'll always be with you, little brother." The blackness began to fill Dez's eyes once more, creeping in from the corners like ink spilled on a sheet of parchment. With a pained look, he stumbled back, and Alfie knew this truly was the last time they would speak. "Para siempre."

Time snapped into motion once more. Sombra reared back, fighting for control of Dezmin's body.

Finn gripped Alfie and skittered backward to where the black blade had clattered against the wall.

"Alfie," she said. "We've got to—"

"I know," Alfie said, trying to stop the sobs from crawling out of his throat. "I know."

Sombra twisted Dezmin's kind face into a sneer of fury. "How dare your pest of a brother try to overpower me."

Alfie paid the god no mind. The weight of what he had to do made him oddly calm. He took Finn's hand, wrapping his fingers around hers where she held the blade, letting his magic pour into her.

Finn's face tightened with concentration. At first Alfie felt nothing, but then there it was, her spirit in the magic, not obeying his but contributing, making the shade match Sombra's shifting black patchwork of magic.

"We end this *now*," Sombra spat.

"Are you ready?" she asked.

"No." Alfie swallowed. "I'm not."

She nodded.

There wasn't an ounce of fear in the god's eyes, only excitement. He was done playing with his food; he was going to kill them. Alfie could feel it in his gaze.

Sombra surged forward, his hands reaching for Alfie's neck.

Just in time, they hefted the sword into place, the hilt pressing against Finn's stomach. Sombra ran into the blade with such force that Alfie felt it fly through the god's chest and burst out of his back.

Sombra froze, silent. For a long moment, Alfie couldn't tell if it'd worked or if this was another trick, but then Sombra spoke.

"No," the god said. There was no pain in his voice, only confusion. The look of surprise on his face would be satisfying, if only it wasn't Dezmin's face he was wearing.

Blood gushed over their hands as Sombra stared down at the wound.

"No. I am a god," he stammered, stumbling back, taking the blade with him. "I cannot die. . . ." For a moment he swayed, unsteady on his feet. Then he fell to the ground, a turtle trapped on its back. "I can't. My destiny . . ."

Alfie wanted to look away from Sombra's slow death, to stop seeing it play out on his brother's face, but he needed to watch the monster take its final breath. To know that it was over.

With a shuddering sigh, Sombra fell still.

"Dezmin?" Alfie murmured as he crawled to the body, his ribs jostling painfully. "Please," he begged. He touched Dezmin's cheek, but the body was still, indifferent to his pleading. "Please, Dezmin."

He heard footsteps closing in around him. He knew he was among friends now, that they were safe from Sombra, but he felt an odd protectiveness. He pulled his brother's body close, away from prying eyes.

"Alfie," Luka said, James standing close behind him. Luka's bloodied face was wet with tears. He crouched next to him. "We have to let go."

"No," Alfie said, his hand cradling the back of Dezmin's head. "No."

"He's free now," Paloma said. Her nose was bleeding. A gash on her forehead poured over her left eye. "Free from Sombra."

"No, he's dead!" Alfie roared. "*Dead!*"

He was tired of platitudes. He couldn't bear to hear them.

Finn's hand found his shoulder. "It isn't fair."

Those words were just as true now as they'd been when she'd said them in the Blue Room, so terribly true and terribly unchangeable. Alfie sobbed, burying his face in the soft juncture of Dezmin's neck and shoulder.

Finn sat beside him on the ground, not speaking another word, letting him fill the silence with his endless grief.

Alfie didn't know how long he held Dezmin before a voice echoed around them. "No, it is not fair."

Alfie scanned the room but could find no one but the corpses of the dueños they'd lost.

Finn stiffened, her eyes searching too. "Who was that?"

Paloma moved forward, shielding Alfie as she looked around. "I don't know."

"We're in no shape for a fight," Luka said, casting a look at James's blanched face.

"The fighting is over," the disembodied voice replied, and once again Alfie couldn't pinpoint where it was coming from.

The shards of larimar began to glow so brilliantly that Alfie had to close his eyes. They detached from the cloud walls and collected in the center of the room, melding into a new shape. When the brightness finally lessened, Alfie saw that the larimar had formed the shape of a body. It had no face, no defining features, just a three-dimensional silhouette.

"Fine," Finn growled, gripping a dagger in her hand. "I'll—" But Paloma raised a silencing hand.

"It's the gods," Paloma breathed before carefully falling forward into a bow. There were legends that claimed the gods were made of larimar, but Alfie had never fully believed them.

"You come *now*?" Alfie seethed, still holding Dezmin close. "After all this death and pain? Where were you when my brother needed your help? When he was trapped alone in the dark? When he was *dying*?" Paloma shot him a look of caution, but Alfie could not bring himself to care. "I will *never* bow to you again."

"We do not ask for such things." The voice was strange, as if not one single person spoke but several. The voices were braided into one, some soft and high, some low and baritone. It was a cacophony that somehow found a way to harmonize.

"I thought you didn't interfere with human affairs, that you'd turned your back on this world," Alfie spat, bitter. "Why are you here now?"

"The destruction of an immortal is no longer a simple human affair." Alfie wanted to scream at how calm the voice was, how detached. "We are here to tell you of your final sacrifice."

A terrible laugh burst from Alfie's lips. "More sacrifice? You want *more*?"

Finn rose to her feet and stood in front of him, leaning off her broken ankle. "You've asked enough of him. Of us."

"Yes," the voice agreed. "And yet there is more. Your brother will fulfill his great destiny."

"His destiny is gone," Alfie shouted. "Gone because you didn't help. Because you just watched—"

"Alfie."

Alfie froze, the hairs on the nape of his neck prickling at the sound of his brother's voice. And there he was, standing beside him, just above his own corpse. It was Dezmin, but it wasn't. He was silhouetted in light, as if the sun had returned for the sole purpose of rising behind him. While Sombra's eyes had been black to the very edges, Dezmin's were luminous, so bright that Alfie could barely stand to meet his gaze.

Alfie carefully set Dezmin's body down. "I don't understand."

"Sombra slaughtered the light," the voices intoned. "And for that he has been punished, but this world can only exist with the balance of light and dark intact. Someone else must take the place of the light. Dezmin was born for this purpose."

Alfie could only stare. The story of the balance was that a

woman of light stood tall while a man of dark fell before her, becoming her shadow. Dezmin would take her place to restore the balance.

"When I held you as a baby for the first time," this new Dezmin said, "I gained my *propio* of bringing objects to life. Now I will become the light and resurrect this dying world. It was always my destiny, Alfie. There was nothing you could've done to alter it."

"His legacy would be eternal." Paloma raised a shaking hand to her mouth, repeating the words of Dezmin's divining. All this pain and grief, it had all been decided long before they were born.

"Yes." Dezmin walked to the side of the larimar avatar. "And I must fulfill that now." Alfie wanted to reach out and stop him, but he couldn't move. He stared at Dezmin's body. The embrace they'd shared when he'd saved him from Sombra—that had been their goodbye. This Dezmin wasn't his.

The larimar being raised a hand, and the fabric of the universe parted to reveal a world of darkness—this was the heart of the world, the place where the balance of light and dark lived, though thanks to Sombra it was bathed in only darkness now. Alfie assumed this new Dezmin would simply walk through and say nothing more, but he was wrong.

Dezmin looked over his shoulder, and Alfie's mind scrambled to remember this moment, to hold on to it for as long as he could. "I will make this world whole again, and in doing so I will become a part of the very fabric of magic. When you use it, know that I am with you."

And for the second time, Alfie watched his brother disappear into the void, the universe closing behind him. Alfie's jaw worked in an effort to stop himself from shouting, from demanding a different fate from the gods.

"There is one final step before Sombra is vanquished for good," the gods said.

Panic thrummed through Alfie.

"Are you kidding?" Finn asked.

The gods ignored her. "This world was built upon balance. You have vanquished Sombra by using his own power against him, but he is still an immortal. He will re-form slowly over time and reclaim his place unless one last sacrifice is made. Then and only then can a new god of darkness be born to take his place. The dark must have a deity. We will make sure the next one respects the sacred balance."

"Just tell me," Alfie said, numb. "Tell me what you want from me."

"In the name of balance, for a god to die, a mortal must become immortal."

Alfie couldn't imagine a worse fate. Who would want to live forever, to watch everyone they loved die around them, to never find eternal peace?

Finn brightened. "I'll do it!"

Alfie stared at her.

"It must be one of the prophesied pair," the gods said. "But it cannot be one who desires such a fate."

Alfie's heart froze in his chest. His only consolation in all this had been that one day he'd be reunited with those he'd lost. Immortality would mean never seeing his family again.

"What?" Finn asked, seeing the look of horror on Alfie's face. "Why?"

"Balance," the gods repeated. "Sombra did not wish to lose his immortality, and so we can only grant it to one who does not wish to live forever. The pain of one side must match that of the other."

Luka gripped Alfie by the shoulder, looking forlorn. Luka had seen what waited in the realm beyond—his family. He knew better than anyone what Alfie would lose. "I'm so sorry."

"Do it," Alfie said, his voice a rasp of pain. "Just do it."

The larimar being walked forward, its steps slow and measured. It placed a warm hand on the crown of Alfie's head. He wanted to pull away, to shout at the gods for what they'd done, but he couldn't. Not because he wasn't angry, but because he was too tired to fight anymore. A strange heat spread through Alfie, starting in his forehead and flowing down to his toes. His shadow rippled at his feet, like a stagnant pond disturbed by a thrown pebble.

"It is done," the gods said, but Alfie would not look at them.

"Leave me," he said through gritted teeth. "Leave us all be."

The gods spoke no more, but granted them the last favor of carrying Sombra's cloud fortress back down to earth. The larimar disappeared into nothing, winking out of existence. When the walls and floors of Sombra's palace faded, dissipating without the hands of a god to keep them up, Alfie saw that they were on the palace grounds.

Fresh grass sprouted from the dirt. The branches of the gnarled, naked trees began to flex and soften. The skies cast away Sombra's strange nightfall, and the moon, whole and full, hung over their heads for the first time in six days.

Where Dezmin's body lay beside Alfie, flowers sprouted, stenciling him in bright hues of red and orange, yellow, magenta. These were flowers of summer; they shouldn't be growing now, but there they were, cradling Dezmin's body in their soft embrace. Braided into the flora were Dezmin's carved figurines, his creations made anew.

The two-faced clock gave a long, intricate chime—the special chime for the birthday of a royal. And now the birthday of a thief too.

"Happy birthday, Prince," Finn said to him.

Alfie could not stop himself from collapsing into her arms. His tears rolled over her collarbone, soaking her black gown. "Feliz cumpleaños, thief."

ALFIE AND FINN'S NEXT DAYS

And so, just as quickly as the world had been thrown off its axis, it righted itself.

The first months after they had defeated Sombra were the most painful.

Millions of souls awoke from Sombra's control, their shadows returned, only to realize that their loved ones hadn't survived. Or worse, that they themselves had killed them.

Communities worked together to repair their cities and neighborhoods. Whole kingdoms relied on one another, each facing the same uphill battle. Slowly but surely things began to *look* normal, but there was a quiet understanding that nothing would ever *be* normal again, not fully. The memory of Sombra's return hung over the world like a veil over a grieving widow's face.

In accordance with tradition, Dezmin, King Bolivar, and Queen Amada were cremated. Alfie told the story of how his brother's sacrifices had righted the balance of magic and saved the world. Thousands from all over the world had attended the ceremony, and Alfie was comforted by the fact that his brother and his legacy would never be forgotten. How could it be? For as long as Alfie lived he would tell the story—and, thanks to the gods, Alfie would live forever.

Soon after, Alfie held his coronation and was officially crowned king of Castallan.

Whenever he was overwhelmed by the magnitude of his role, Paloma took him aside and, as always, gave sage advice.

"There are endless tasks that you will have to oversee, but choose one project to pursue tirelessly and passionately, just for yourself. It will make everything else easier."

Alfie raised a brow. "And if it is something that my advisors would disagree with?"

Paloma gave a smirk that would make Finn proud. "Do it anyway."

So Alfie did.

And nearly a year after the world had almost ended, he took Finn to see it.

"Where are we going?" she asked as the carriage rolled down the dirt road. They were far from the city, riding into open land.

"You'll know soon enough," he said.

She rolled her eyes. "I hate surprises."

"You do," Alfie agreed.

"Where's Bathtub Boy?" Finn asked. "If he were here, I could get it out of him."

Alfie smiled. She was right. Luka was the worst at keeping secrets.

"He and James are preparing for their next trip," Alfie said.

After recovering from the battle, Alfie had pardoned James for his crimes, and James committed himself to rebuilding Englass. The kingdom would have the hardest time since Sombra killed the entire royal family. On top of everything else, there would be the issue of succession.

Only a handful of the late Englassen king's advisors had survived, and Alfie made sure to pull them aside just after the funeral.

"You will return to Englass and facilitate the selection of the next ruler. Castallan will financially support the rebuilding of your nation as was discussed before Sombra's return, but know this," Alfie said, his voice low. "The magical caste system will be destroyed. Today. Is that clear?"

The advisors swallowed thickly, nodding.

"I'll hold them to it," a voice called. Alfie turned to see James standing behind him. "If that's all right with you, of course."

Alfie granted him a nod. Their relationship would always have a slight tension to it, but Alfie had seen the lengths to which James was willing to go to save their world. "Of course."

So James had become a go-between of sorts, serving as a dignitary who crossed the bridge of their two countries. Luka had joined him as an ambassador representing Alfie's interests in Englass. After Sombra was defeated, the extra *propios* that had been forced upon James disappeared, his own magical balance restored along with the world's. Once they disappeared, his health returned.

"I hope he packs some seasoning," Finn quipped, tapping her foot impatiently. She really did hate surprises.

The carriage finally slowed to a stop.

"We're here." Alfie couldn't wait for the footmen. He clambered out the door, holding out a hand for Finn. She swatted it away and climbed out herself.

Before them stood a sprawling edifice with tall spires and countless stained glass windows. The surrounding land was lush and green. The gardeners had only just started planting, but Alfie already imagined a grove of mango trees and a reading garden.

Finn squinted up at it. "Is this your mini vacation palace?"

Alfie shook his head. "Come on, I'll show you."

"Very well," Finn said in her practiced impression of Alfie.

Together they climbed the stairs to the tall double doors.

When they walked into the vestibule and around the indoor fountain, their voices echoing against its towering ceilings, Finn still wasn't quite sure what the place was.

It was only when he took her to a classroom that it became clear.

She turned to him. "Is this some kind of school?"

Alfie nodded. "The first of many. A school where we'll teach the children of Castallan all forms of magic. There are even kitchens and dormitories, so that every child has somewhere to sleep and a desk to learn at, if they want. No child will be left to fend for themselves. They will always have a home here. For as long as I live," he said softly.

Finn stilled and looked away from him. Her fingers ran over the surface of a polished desk. "Magia para todos, then." Her voice was hushed.

"Magic for all," Alfie agreed. "I'm going to spend my reign making those words mean something."

He thought of what she'd said to him long ago when they'd faced Sombra for the first time. Words he'd never forgotten.

People like me, we're ants, and rulers are just a big foot looming over us ready to squish us into the dirt. Doesn't matter whose body the foot is attached to, the purpose is still the same.

He would never let himself become that. He would be a hand extended to help his people up.

Finn turned in a slow circle, taking in the rows of desks and bookshelves. "When did you even start building this?"

"A year ago."

She stared at him, impressed. "You managed to keep this from me for a year?"

"Somehow I did." He watched her drift around the room, testing out the chalkboard, opening drawers. "You know, I got the idea from a little girl I met in a forest," Alfie said, and when Finn finally looked at him, her eyes were shining. "She needed a place where she could feel safe, so I decided to build one."

A tender silence swept the room.

When Finn's lips quirked up, they weren't in her signature smirk, but a soft smile, one that he would hold in his mind forever.

She cleared her throat and walked back to him. "Well, are you going to give me the full tour?"

"Of course, but I didn't just bring you here for that. We've got some important matters to discuss too."

Finn raised an eyebrow. "Oh?"

"I have a job for you. That is, if you're up to it."

Finn squinted at him, taking the bait. "Of course I'm up to it."

"You should listen to the offer before you say that." He couldn't help riling her up.

She crossed her arms and looked at him as if he'd just uttered the most foolish sentence known to man. "Just spit it out."

His lips quirked at the edges. "I need someone to work in recovery for the kingdom."

She tilted her head. "Recovery?"

"Many of our ancient artifacts were destroyed during enslavement, but others were sold or traded, scattered across the globe. Some were even hidden in other kingdoms by our ancestors who fled—pieces of our history that are now considered the property of other nations. I built this school to give every Castallano child a future. I also want to educate them and myself about the past. About who we were, and who we can become. I want our artifacts here to be studied, cherished. It's time we brought them home."

Finn's smile was sharp as a dagger. "You want me to steal them."

"You can't steal what is already ours by birthright. I'm asking you to *recover* them."

Finn nodded, playing along. "Right, of course, *recover*. And these artifacts, where would I start?"

Alfie rubbed the back of his neck, considering. "I'd give you a ship and a crew and you'd start wherever you wanted. There are countless leads on where to explore. Underwater temples our ancestors built off the coast of Weilai. Hidden troves deep in the northern mountains of Uppskala." Finn's eyes were lighting up. He could see the compass inside her swiveling toward another adventure. "Of course, if this doesn't interest you, feel free to decline."

Finn smoothed her expression into one of nonchalance and held out her hand for him to shake, suddenly all business. "I suppose I could do it until I get bored. I think I could handle the job quite well, Your Highness."

"Then we're finally agreeing on something." Alfie smiled and moved to take her hand, but she jerked her palm away at the last moment.

"First, I have some conditions."

"I am a king," he said, raising his chin in a pantomime of arrogance. "I'm afraid I'm not one for conditions."

Finn raised her chin to match his. "You're also not usually trying to secure the help of a world-famous thief with many job prospects."

Alfie shook his head with a laugh. "Fine. Name your price, thief."

She held up a finger. "One, I want to select my own crew. Women only."

"Fair enough."

"Two, I want a very expensive captain's hat." She waved her hand around her head in a sweeping arc as Alfie tried and failed to hold back his laughter. "With a big feather in it."

He nodded, his expression that of a man in the midst of a serious negotiation. "Consider it done."

"And, finally, on these adventures, I might need some . . . assistance from time to time. That magic paint thing you do could come in handy every now and again. You know, when racing through secret passageways—"

"—and breaking into hidden vaults," Alfie added.

She nodded up at him, her eyes alight. "Scouring black markets, dodging booby traps, scaling mountainsides. I'm just saying that you could be useful. Maybe."

"Very well," he said. "I think I could make the time to provide the occasional assistance. These are missions of royal importance, after all."

"Extreme importance. Some might say monumental," Finn played along. But then she was staring up at him, holding his gaze like a child cradling a lightning bug between their palms. "You'll come when I call for you?"

"Always." Alfie marveled at the flush of excitement blooming on her face. He raised his hand for her to shake. "Just say when."

Her smile was brilliant as she took his hand. "When."

EPILOGUE

The prince and the thief never married.

After all, she wasn't one for responsibilities or crowns.

"Pointy knives make sense. Pointy hats?" Finn made a face. "Not so much."

In normal times, this would have been unacceptable, but after the kingdom had witnessed the world nearly ending, the marital status of the king was hardly of any concern.

Between her many adventures, they lived together in the palace. Their children's very first toys were the lovingly carved figurines of the fox and the dragon.

Finn fought against her unofficial title, showing little respect for tradition. She showed up to balls with daggers strapped to her ankles and up her sleeves. She attended Alfie's meetings seemingly with the sole purpose of interrupting his advisors and poking holes in their suggestions. She walked among the people wearing different faces and entertained herself by surprising them with her identity.

She thought this would make the people reject her as their

unofficial queen, but it did the opposite. She was lovingly dubbed the Thief Queen and the People's Queen. After all they'd been through, the people valued a survivor over a noble. They saw her presence at Alfie's side as an asset—a real Castallano in the palace who could represent their interests instead of a bunch of nobles making decisions for them. She didn't love either of her nicknames, but a thief through and through, she took the former over the latter.

Time passed, days folding into months and years.

Alfie found that as soon as he knew he would live forever, the topic of death became strangely commonplace.

Long after they'd thwarted Sombra, Finn and Alfie sat in the palace gardens, lounging in the grass. Alfie had a rare break from his royal duties and Finn had dropped in for an extended visit, a breather between adventures for the Thief Queen of Castallan.

Alfie had continued to age until he looked to be somewhere around thirty and then hovered there. Finn was jokingly searching his curls for any white hairs.

"And you'll stay with me when you're the one with white hair and I still look like this?" he asked.

"As if I'll ever get old enough to get white hairs," she snorted, tugging absentmindedly on a stray curl.

Alfie stiffened. "Don't say that."

"Only the boring live long enough to get old. That's not my style, thank you very much." When he still looked down at her, frowning, she went on. "And what does dying matter anyway, when I'll be back for another round?"

"Is that so?" Alfie asked with a grin. "You expect to reincarnate?"

"Obviously."

"Are you saying you'll be leaving this earth with some unfinished business to attend to? Adventures uncompleted? Innocent bystanders un-swindled?"

Finn didn't laugh. She only looked at him, her gaze uncharacteristically earnest. "As long as you're here, I will always have unfinished business."

Before Alfie could speak, she kissed him until he forgot to worry about what would happen when she kept aging as he stayed the same. When she walked steadily toward death as he jogged in place.

In the end she'd been wrong.

She had lived long enough to see her fair share of white hairs, to become a queen who was not to be trifled with, and to watch their children grow. She'd lived a good life. But, still, for Alfie, it would never be enough. And when she took her last breath, Alfie's world seemed to tilt and never right itself again. He'd simply had to learn to live at a sloped angle, constantly trudging uphill as he looked for the memory of her in his endless days.

Those he loved disappeared into the next life, Luka last of all— the dark magic had strengthened him in a way that let him live well past one hundred.

Their final conversation had been brief. After all, they were brothers. There was nothing they hadn't already said.

"I'll tell them you say hello, sourpuss," Luka had said, and in his weathered voice Alfie could still hear the laughter of a young man who never had to look for trouble.

Alfie's throat burned as he cradled Luka's frail hand. "Tell them not to wait for me."

"Since when have I ever done as you asked?" Luka's words were hushed, as if he were falling asleep. "We will always wait for you."

Then there was only Alfie.

Alfie stepped away from the crown, letting his and Finn's children and then grandchildren and then great-grandchildren take over. Soon the memory of an immortal, un-aging king became nothing but a myth, though the dueños knew the truth and that, should they need him, they could call on him for help.

He traveled the world, watched kingdoms rise and fall, watched the feud between Castallan and Englass peter out to give way to others, watched the world become so different and yet stay exactly the same.

Time flowed around him like water around stone.

Eventually, after nearly nine lifetimes away, Alfie found himself back in Castallan. He walked through the Brim, a fresh maze of shops replacing the ones he remembered from his childhood.

In every corner of the city were memories of Luka, of Finn and their children, but enough time had passed that such thoughts didn't pain him anymore. Now he felt only the throb of nostalgia and a sense of gratitude for the time he'd had with them.

As Alfie moved from stall to stall, a small hooded figure rushed out of the crowd, a stack of books in their arms. Before Alfie could step out of the way, they collided with him. The stranger was barely tall enough to reach his chest—a child. Their books fell to the ground with a loud *thud*.

"Are you all right?" Alfie asked as they crouched to collect the books.

"I'd be more than all right if you watched where you're going."

At the sound of her voice, Alfie tilted his head, like a dog pick-ing up on a familiar sound—the warm call of home after spending ages away.

This was not the first time in his long life that he thought he'd heard Finn's voice only to wake and find nothing but disappoint-ment, and this certainly wouldn't be the last time either. He should just walk away, accepting that she was lost to him forever.

And yet Alfie did not move.

The logical part of his mind, the part that had lived far too long to believe that destiny could be kind, would say that he chose to engage his *propio* at that moment simply out of habit. But the part of him that would forever be the boy Finn had shown her true face to, the boy she'd returned to with the scent of the sea on her as she'd climbed up his balcony and into his arms, said it was fate.

Alfie looked down at the girl shoving books angrily into her satchel, her face still obscured by her hood. He let his eyes attune to the hues of magic that swirled in the world. He felt his heart stumble in his chest.

Her magic was a red that shifted shades as freely as the breeze changed direction.

Finn's magic.

The girl rose from the ground, pushed the hood back, and looked up at him, a scowl curling her mouth.

It really was Finn, but younger than when he'd met her. Per-haps twelve years old. It was the face that she'd been born with. The very same thicket of curly hair. The same stubborn swagger that had lived in every pane of her face when he'd known her. And yet she was different. He could see it in her eyes.

When he'd watched her age backward in the Englassen forest, he'd seen who she was before Ignacio had hurt her—a child who was unguarded and hopeful. How he'd wished he could turn back the clock and give her that fresh start, a life where she wasn't hunched beneath the weight of what Ignacio and the world had done to her. A life where she could grow up free of fear, just as she'd made sure their children had.

And here she was doing just that.

"What are you looking at?" She squinted up at him. "Are you lost?"

Alfie marveled at the familiar snap of her wit. "I'm sorry, just startled."

He spotted the telltale red-and-gold uniform under her cloak, his breath catching in his throat. She was a student at the school that he'd built for Finn.

Something within him healed so quickly that it felt exactly like breaking.

"Hey! We're gonna be late!" A boy in a matching uniform appeared behind her, red-faced and sweaty. He paid Alfie no mind.

"Let's go, then," she said.

Alfie wanted to tell her that she was precious, that every loss, every ounce of pain he'd endured was worth it because it led to this second chance for her.

But those were words from another lifetime, another world. He could not speak them now.

So as she moved past him, Alfie said the next best thing. "Be careful!" And again, because once was not enough. "Cuídate."

She turned, walking backward as she rolled her eyes at him the way only a twelve-year-old can.

Then the thief pulled the hood of her cloak over her head and disappeared into the crowd.

Alfie watched her go, a warmth spreading through him, filling him with light. He'd thought that after living so long there would be no surprises left.

He was thrilled to learn he'd been wrong.

Perhaps living forever wouldn't be so bad after all.

Finn had been granted a new life, a new story. A story that he could not be a part of this time—but perhaps, somewhere in the years that stood before him, there was a new story for him too.

Perhaps there was another adventure waiting just around the bend.

Maybe it had already begun.

ACKNOWLEDGMENTS

I started writing the Nocturna trilogy when I was twenty-three years old, and as I write the acknowledgments for the final book of the series, I'm thirty-one. Nearly a decade of my life is tenderly housed in these books. When I reread each of them, I can hear a different Maya in the pages.

Nocturna has all the hope and promise of twenty-three-year-old Maya, who had just moved to New York City to chase her dreams. Somehow, she succeeded.

In *Oculta*, I can hear the struggle of the Maya trying to get through the sophomore slump, the thick of the pandemic, and the political upheavals that followed. Somehow, she got through it all.

But in this book, in *Lucero*, I read a sense of peace and understanding, which, funnily enough, is what I'd been told I'd find in my thirties.

When I started writing *Nocturna*, I always knew that this would be the ending. Upon getting my book deal in 2017, I sent my editor a version of the epilogue, which has, for the most part, stayed the same. It is strange and comforting to see that connective thread between the twenty-three-year-old Maya drafting *Nocturna* in cafes after work and me today. She knew I'd get through to the end of this story, but she had no idea what an adventure it would be getting from A to Z.

I'm so thankful I got to write the book series I always looked for in my local libraries.

To my editor, Kristin Rens, thank you for guiding me through my very first book and my very first series. I am lucky to have had someone so kind at my side throughout this process.

To the editorial assistants who worked on this series—Kelsey Murphy, Caitlin Johnson, and Christian Vega—thank you for all your hard work! It does not go unnoticed.

To the cover artist—Mark van Leeuwen—and the cover designers—Chris Kwon, Aurora Parlagreco, and Jenna Stempel-Lobell—thank you for creating such an iconic look for my series. I always get compliments on how gorgeous and unique the covers are.

To managing editor Mark Rifkin, production editor Erin DeSalvatore, production lead Vanessa Nuttry, publicity lead Anna Ravenelle, and marketing leads Audrey Diestelkamp and Michael D'Angelo, thank you for your tireless work bringing this series to life and getting it on the shelves.

To my amazing agent, Thao Le, thank you for helping me pick myself up and dust myself off. I can't wait to work on a project with you from scratch!

To Hannah Milton, thank you for supporting me since not day one, but day zero. It all started that summer at Columbia.

To my family, thank you for the love and support.

To Kristina Forest, Charlotte Davis, and Alison Doherty, thank you for holding me together since the day I got this book deal. I couldn't have handled even half of it without you all.

And, finally, I'd like to acknowledge you. Giving a debut author a chance is a gamble in and of itself, but sticking around for the whole series is nothing short of a small miracle. Thank you for waiting so patiently to hear the end of Alfie and Finn's story. I hope I get to thank you again at the end of my next book.